D0892708

I would like to dedicate this book to my children - Ruth, Joe, Emma and Ryan - my joy, my inspiration, my life...

ACKNOWLEDGEMENTS

Special thanks must go to all the children, bookshop owners, schools and libraries that embraced 'The Magic Scales' and made this sequel possible. To my long-suffering friends; John and Ellen, Jim and Isobel, and Greg - who nurtured my creativity way-back and gave me the grounding in all things musical. To my childhood friends who unwittingly helped form my imagination and sense of adventure – Gary, Charles, Ian and Craig. To my current stalwarts; Scobie and Allan, who still help me on my way. Most of all, I would like to thank my wife Katrina, for her fire, her passion, her strength and her endless endurance.

CHAPTER ONE

THE CARETAKER

It was an unusually clammy September evening in Drumfintley. Loch Echty was as still as a millpond, and Craig Harrison thought that Ben Larvach looked bigger than it had the day before. It towered over the smaller hills to the north and cast a gloomy shadow over the ribbon of dark water below. The reflection of the mountain shimmered on the perfect surface and looked like a giant, black dragon from where he was standing. *A trick of the light*, he supposed.

Tall for his age and covered in a generous supply of freckles, which he hated, Craig was busy being dragged along by his best friend, a young Golden Retriever called Bero. This was his fifth night of caretaking, and he was beginning to enjoy his long chats with the one who now lived at Forty-Five Willow Terrace.

There should, though, by now, have been a voice in his head: a deep, gnarly sounding voice with more than a hint of smugness. As yet, however, there was nothing; only the distant screech of a buzzard and the occasional zoom of traffic on the bypass.

Number Forty-Five would seem normal enough to most people. A small, detached, kit-house skinned with red brick and finished with leaded windows, it nestled amongst a further eleven exactly the same. Inside, however, someone very special needed feeding and, while James Peck and his family were on holiday, it was Craig's job to look after him.

He pulled Bero in closer as he edged round the road-works on Main Street. Glancing down into a long hole guarded loosely by a row of red and white traffic cones, he noticed the old cobbles, kept hidden for so long by the recently ruptured skin of tarmac. He strained in further, using Bero's tight lead for balance, and saw the old tram tracks. "Cool," he muttered. Bero cocked his head and moved closer, causing him to slip and reach for a wobbly cone. "Stay boy." Scrambling up a pile of earth, he brushed himself down and continued up past the village hall.

Slightly confused by the lack of any welcome, he scanned the upstairs window nearest to the Peck's beech tree. Craig looked round for any sign of the neighbours before whispering, as loud as he could, *"Mendel?"*

He listened for a reply, but there was nothing.

Mendel could always reach his thoughts as close to the house as this.

He fumbled with Bero's lead and undid the latch on the Peck's front gate. Stepping into the garden, he shivered as a cold finger of fear traced down his spine. Bero's hackles were up and a deep growl was beginning to build in the young dog's chest.

He gave Bero's lead a gentle yank. "Stop it. I can't hear anything if you do that." He listened as hard as he could and then called up again –"Mendel!"

Barely a whisper, a distant trail of words traced his thoughts, *"Can't have… Stop it… More of them… You stupid old fool… Artilis?"*

Bero tugged away from the front door and whined. "Mendel, is that you? It's me, Craig. Is everything okay?"

It had definitely been Mendel's voice, Craig decided. The wizard, however, sounded as if he was somewhere else other than in the tin bath. He should be there, next to his pretend plastic castle, flicking his fins and blub, blub, blubbing in that silly way that he always did, but Craig just knew that something bad had happened.

He heard the voice again, *"I can't explain it but… Best not… Can't reverse it!"*

The faint fishy voice wavered for a moment in his mind, then fell silent.

Craig broke into a sweat as he knelt down on the garden path and craned up at the window. Distractedly, he twisted Bero's soft fur round his freckled fingers. His mind raced. Every other night there had been nothing to it. Simply plop the fish-food into the tin bath and then have a chat with Mendel, a ten thousand year old goldfish, about the mysteries of the universe. After about twenty minutes he would simply return home to his mental brother and sister and his mum's attempt at dinner.

Nothing too strenuous. But now… Now he was in a sweat, completely frozen to the spot and clueless as to what to do next.

Craig winced as a bright blue, luminescent flash lit the trees in the Peck's garden. It had come from James's bedroom window. *Should I go and get help?* he wondered. In Drumfintley, there were two other people who knew of Mendel's existence, but there was no time to spare. The wizard, for all his powers, was just a small, helpless goldfish and Craig knew that he had to go into the Peck's house and see what was wrong. He had to try and help. He owed Mendel that, at least.

Carefully, Craig made his way towards the front door. "I'm coming in," he mumbled, unconvincingly. He'd meant to sound like some avenging cowboy but instead his voice was more like the pleading, namby-pamby moan of someone who'd just been marched into the headmaster's office. He walked up to James's front door and pinched the scratchy corner of the doormat. He edged it up a few inches and flicked the key from underneath. It felt cold and sticky in his hands as he clunked it into the lock. The front door swung open. He wavered. "Mendel?" A rush of dank air caught him by surprise. Bero's ears flattened, his doggy eyes blinking shut as dust and debris whisked out of the front door. Craig took several steps back and gazed up at James's bedroom window with renewed horror. He looked down at Bero who had begun to whine. "What is it, Bero?" There was another distinct blue flash and Bero barked up at the window.

"Quiet boy. You might draw attention to us." He knelt down and gave the dog a hug, never once taking his eyes off the window above. Again, another blue flash of iridescent light arced across the ceiling of James's bedroom and flashed over the garden. Craig glanced down the street at number fifty-nine. That had been Ephie Blake's house before she had married Father Michael, and moved into St. Donan's Rectory. Father Michael and Ephie were the only two other people in Drumfintley who still remembered everything about their adventure in Denthan. Perhaps he should go down to the Rectory and ask them to come with him. They were used to the magic and mayhem that surrounded Mendel, but something niggled at him. He felt sure that the wizard would protect him if any evil were truly brewing, but James used to tell him about the *knock, knock, knocking* sensation that preceded Mendel's spells. Mendel had some kind of link with James that was unique, and it was very probable that Mendel's magical powers would be rendered useless without Craig's spotty pal doing his bit. Craig had never felt the knocking sensation, never performed Mendel's magic.

Inexplicably, the front door swung open another four or five inches.

The house seemed to be urging them inside.

Against his better judgement, Craig pushed the door open. His breathing was laboured and beads of sweat trickled into his eyes.

"Are you alright, Craig?"

"Mend... What?" In an instant Craig snapped out of his hypnotic state and turned to face Kwedgin Blake, Ephie's brother from number fifty-nine.

A slight, balding man, in his fifties, Kwedgin Blake had a kind demeanour and a reassuring smile. "Alright, are we?" he pressed.

"I... Yes," Craig lied, turning away from Kwedgin to look back at the door. "What the...?" It was shut tight.

"You look very pale, Craig. Are you sure...?"

"Yes, yes I'm okay. I just thought I saw something, that's all." Craig glanced up at the bedroom window.

Kwedgin picked up a garden hoe and continued, "Maybe I should come with you tonight. You never know..."

"No, no, I don't think that's necessary. I mean, there was a bit of a funny breeze. It freaked Bero, that's all." Craig could feel his face flushing. Mendel wouldn't take kindly to anyone *not in the know* interfering, if magic was afoot. The wizard had always tried to keep his presence in Drumfintley limited to as few people as possible. Ever since Craig and his family had arrived in Drumfintley, however, people had a habit of poking their noses in. The place was too small. There was nowhere to hide.

"I'm just going to feed James's fish. No big deal. I'm sure Bero would let me know if there was any real danger."

Kwedgin raised his bushy eyebrows and stared down at the growling dog.

Craig forced a smile and turned the key. He pushed the door, expecting it to open.

"Ahh!" The door hadn't budged and now his wrist was throbbing.

"Here, let me." Kwedgin shook his head, turning the key as he twisted the door handle. The door swung open and they stumbled inside. Bero shot past them and clattered up the wooden steps ahead.

"Bero!" Craig tried to push past but Kwedgin held him back by the shoulder. "Let me go first. Just in case." Hoe raised high, Kwedgin looked slightly out of place, if not comical, as he moved up the stairs.

Craig couldn't take his eyes off Kwedgin's chequered, tartan trousers. *How could someone think they looked good in those things?*

Bero's growling came to a sudden stop.

"Bero?" Craig's trainers squeaked on the pine as, impatiently, he tried to push past Kwedgin.

"Steady," protested Kwedgin.

Upstairs, James's bedroom door lay open. They peered over the top step.

Craig dashed into the room and yanked on Bero's lead. "Bero, stop that." The stupid dog had stopped growling because he was busy lapping water out of an old tin bath that sat in the middle of the floor. Craig checked himself and peered through the ripples. "Mendel?" he whispered. Small wisps of blue smoke still whisked over the surface of the water. Craig waved them away as quickly as he could before Kwedgin caught him up. The tartan-clad Kwedgin, however, was too busy opening cupboards and prodding the garden hoe under the bed to notice.

At first, there was no sign of Mendel, and then Craig glimpsed the corner of an orange fin. It pulsed at the edge of the pretend plastic castle. He sighed with relief but he couldn't relax. Kwedgin, having ceased his prodding and slashing, stood beside the bath and smiled as he rearranged the wisps of hair that dangled limply from his temples. He licked his fingers and plastered the strands back into place. "Nothing to report, young Craig, just a young boy's imagination. Mind you, nothing wrong with a good imagination." Kwedgin gave him a knowing wink. "Still got one myself, you know. Ephie says men never grow up." He tittered then stared down into the bath. "There he is. Coochie, coochie coo..." Kwedgin peered down at Mendel and wiggled his finger.

Craig screwed up his face in disbelief. *What an idiot*, he thought. *He's not a bloomin' furry kitten, you stup—* Craig instantly stifled a yell. "Mmm Ah..."

"You okay?" asked Kwedgin, his baggy tartan suit catching on the bath.

Eyes wide and his fingers still covering his mouth, Craig nodded, unconvincingly.

Craig forced a tight-lipped smile and looked straight at Kwedgin.

Kwedgin struggled to free the tartan material from the metal rim of the bath.

He had to keep Kwedgin looking down. He couldn't let him see the things that hung down from the ceiling inches above his balding head.

Craig's pulse raced as he forced himself to look down into the bath. "Let me untangle you there." He had to get the old boy out of the bedroom before he chanced a look above him.

Craig yanked at the cloth. "That's done it!" He saw Kwedgin's face drop in disappointment.

"Just a small tear," he reassured. *Had Mendel seen those pod things? What were they?*

"Mend-able," he blurted, emphasising the 'Mend' part and scanning the water for a sign, a warning, some kind of spell brewing...

Kwedgin was beginning to look around him.

"No, no down there," said Craig, panicking, as he pulled down on Kwedgin's baggy tartan sleeve. "Look, it's moving. Look!"

"I am looking," said Kwedgin, his brow furrowing.

"Well, I have to go. You see, my mum..." Struggling to complete the lie, Craig gripped Kwedgin's sleeve a little tighter and physically led him from the room. "My mum's expecting me back."

"But you haven't fed the wee thing yet," he protested.

"No," replied Craig. "He's fat enough. Never good to overfeed a goldfish, you know."

Kwedgin formed a vacant expression on his puffy face. "Ah..."

Approximately twelve inches above the spot where Kwedgin hesitated, four small transparent sacks began to vibrate. Bero's hackles rose along his back. He almost gave the whole thing away until Craig said his very own magic word: "WALKIES!"

That instant, all hell broke loose as the crazy dog jumped up and yelped in complete ecstasy.

"Hold this for me." said Craig, wrapping the leather strap of the choke chain round Kwedgin's hand.

"But—" Kwedgin screamed as he was dragged from the bedroom. The hoe fell to the floor with a clatter as he disappeared out of the door. Still moving fast at the top of the stairs, he lifted and missed the bottom eight steps completely.

"Ooff!" Kwedgin thudded onto his back and let out a small wheeze, "Eeee..."

Craig grimaced as he slid down behind him, holding both banisters. He thumped down beside Kwedgin. "Why did you let go? Bero could get knocked down out on the street. C'mon!"

Kwedgin, winded, was still unable to move and only managed to raise a limp forefinger. Craig decided that he looked a bit like a burst bagpipe. Already on the front step, Craig reached back and grabbed Kwedgin's raised finger.

"Aghh! Ow!" Kwedgin yelped.

With a vice-like grip, Craig hauled him out of the house and slammed the Peck's front door shut.

Kwedgin coughed, tucked his sore finger under his arm and struggled to his knees. "Wait... I... I can't breathe."

"Sorry. Nasty fall, that. Have to get after Bero!" Looking down towards the path that led to the village hall, Craig caught a glimpse of a blond, wind-milling tail and broke into a run. He shouted back over his shoulder. "Thanks!"

Craig caught a glance of Kwedgin waving him onward with a wobbly, swollen finger.

Luckily, Bero had stopped. He'd met someone he knew very well.

"Helen, what are you doing here?" Craig looked at his young sister's normally brown hair and continued. "What a numpty. Why is your hair bright red?"

"Shut up. It washes out." Helen rebuffed. "You forgot the fish-food. Here."

Helen handed Craig a small, crumpled plastic bag with a few fragments of fish flake protruding from a sizeable rip.

"And Mum says you've to buy me and Wee Joe some tablet from Galdinie's shop." Helen shoved Bero's lead into her big brother's hand. Craig, however, was busy peering behind his little sister at the trail of fish food that stretched all the way back to the village hall. A noisy flock of starlings had begun to feast on the easy meal.

"Our tablet?" Helen prompted.

"Whatever, numpty girl." Craig turned to leave, but Helen jabbed him in the side.

"What's the church warden doing?" Helen pointed up at Kwedgin. Bent double, he managed a small wave.

Craig, pointing down at Bero with one hand, gave the puce-faced warden the thumbs up with the other.

"He was... He tripped up... Never mind, numpty g—"

"Stop calling me that or I'll get you back," Helen interrupted.

Craig knew what 'get you back' meant in Helen-speak. It meant wrecking his room. *The little...* He wondered if he should go back to James's house straight away.

"Duuuh! Galdinie's. Tablet. Remember?" Annoyingly, Helen pointed at her open mouth as if talking to a complete imbecile. She produced two fifty pence pieces from a little pocket on her dress and slapped them down into his hand. "MUM SAID!"

"Awch! Fine, fine," snapped Craig. He'd decided to get some help, but first he had to get rid of his pesky sister. "C'mon then."

Galdinie's shop was like a little piece of history frozen in time. Inside, the old fashioned woodwork was painted a deep maroon colour. There were smoky glass panels, decorated with flowers, separating the dining cubicles and the whole place was dimly lit by a single strip-light suspended from the nicotine stained ceiling.

The people of Drumfintley had long neglected the dining area and the only functioning part of the shop was a narrow counter piled high with magazines and sweets. Galdinie's ice-cream was probably the best Craig had ever tasted in his life and the home-made tablet was simply wonderful but Mrs. Galdinie was a force to be reckoned with. The tiny, olive-skinned terror became instantly aggressive when any customer dared to disturb her from the TV that flickered in the corner.

"Whaat do you wanta dis time, eh! I'm a watching you, eh. Don't you dare steal anyting noo, eh!"

"Charming. I'm just here to buy some of your tablet. Don't panic." Craig never failed to be amazed by the nasty tone of her voice. He nipped himself, stifling a chuckle as he thought of all the tricks his school mates had played on the old dear. Helen reached up towards a tall pile of freshly made tablet. Still warm and aromatic, the heady flavour of melted butter and sugar wafted over him. He had never smelt or tasted anything so good when he'd lived in England and now his family were completely hooked on the sugary solidified fudge.

"Eets a made way real butter, you know, and eets no for touching unless you gotta di money to pay for it. Okay!"

Craig thought her accent was funny. He called it Scotaliano.

"An getta dat dug oota here, eh!" Mrs. Galdinie jerked her thumb behind her at the sign on the wall that read: NO PETS.

"Ah, okay. Sorry. I'll take these two bars of tablet, please." Craig slid the two fifty pence pieces towards the old metal till and was just about to jerk Bero and Helen from the dingy place when he happened to glance up at an orange box of chicken-flavoured crisps. Just above the box, hanging down from the yellow ceiling, there were three small pods, see-through and about four inches long. They were exactly the same as the four he'd just seen in James's room, not ten minutes before. These particular pods were, as yet, hanging perfectly still but they definitely did not belong in Drumfintley, nor, Craig suspected, in this world. Craig forced a smile as he backed out of the shop with Helen and Bero, but his heart skipped a beat when he saw Mrs. Galdinie follow his gaze and look behind her. Luckily, she was so close to the pile of crisp boxes and so small that she saw nothing. "You trying to play tricks on me, eh? Ama no daft, sonny!"

Craig stepped out into the sunshine and handed the tablet over to Helen. "Look, why don't you get yourself home. Tell Mum I'll be back about five." Craig pointed down the hill towards the Beeches Council Estate where they lived.

"Why? Its boring inside, and Mum said I could play with you." Helen began to unwrap the shiny, greaseproof paper from her tablet.

"Go and play with Wee Joe. He'll be waiting on his tablet, and if it's not back soon he might get bored too and start playing with all your stuff." Craig saw his sister mull this over.

"He better not steal my money," said Helen.

"There you go, you see. He might." Craig raised an eyebrow. "I would."

Helen gave him a withering stare. "You would, wouldn't you?"

"Definitely!" said Craig, a mischievous grin forming on his freckled face.

With a petulant stamp, Helen snorted then turned away. He watched her for a few seconds, skipping back down the path towards the Village Hall and the Beeches Estate. *Another few yards and...* "Right." Craig screwed up his eyes in the direction of Loch Echty and St. Donan's Rectory.

His mind was still racing with thoughts of big maggoty pods when he reached the Rectory gate. As it squeaked open, he heard a familiar voice call out his name.

"Craig?"

He glanced across at Father Michael and his little dog, Patch, sitting on the bench that looked out across the Loch. Ephie, his wife, was struggling out of the front door with a pile of old books. Neither of *them* had spoken, though. Their eyes were fixed on a spot behind him.

"Craig!"

He turned round, his eyes widening. "James! Ye numpty! What are you doing back? You're supposed to be in Majorca, or wherever it was." He waited for his friend to catch his breath.

James was bent double, his hands on his knees. Still looking at the ground he muttered: "They... They fell out again." James coughed and produced his blue puffer.

Father Michael squeaked open the rusty Rectory gate, pausing politely for a moment until James had used his inhaler. "Are you okay? Come in and sit down."

"I thought you were in Spain," said Ephie, her cheeks glowing bright red.

"Got back early," said James, beginning to straighten up.

"Yeah, his mum and dad fell out again," blurted Craig.

James shook his head and shut his eyes. "Thanks, pal."

"Oh well, these things happen," said Michael. As he ushered them into the Rectory garden, he gave Ephie a little nod. "The boys look as if they could do with some cake."

Craig shook his head. "There's no time for that, Ephie. I think something is happening again."

"Now, now. Why would you say that?" said Michael, in an over sympathetic, vicar-type tone.

Craig caught James's arm. "You haven't been into your house yet, have you?"

"No. Why?" James pulled away.

"Didn't think so," said Craig.

James turned to look up the hill towards Willow Terrace. "What's going on?"

"Well, I went up to your house to feed Mendel, you know, as usual. But today, I noticed a flash of blue light coming from your bedroom window." Craig mimed a flash by thrusting his hands forward while fluttering his fingers.

"And?" Ephie moved closer.

"And after your brother, Kwedgin, noticed I was a bit..."

"Scared?" enquired James.

"No," snapped Craig. "Concerned."

"Same thing," muttered James.

"It was when we were in your room that I saw them."

Father Michael edged closer. "Saw what, Craig?"

"They looked like some kind of pods." Craig indicated their size by holding his two forefingers about four inches apart.

James reached for his inhaler again. "What do you mean by pods? You mean this isn't one of your wind ups?"

"And Kwedgin...?" Ephie lowered Craig's fingers. "Did Kwedgin see them too?"

"Eh, no. Bero saw to that."

Bero and Patch were running about in circles round a cherry tree in the Rectory garden.

"And what did Mendel do?" pressed James.

"Not a lot, apart from mutter some stuff that didn't make any sense. I reckon he's lost the plot."

"Lost the plot?" The look of terror in James's eyes was soon reflected on all their faces. "My Mum and Dad are up there right now."

Michael straightened. "Good grief, we better get up to your house right away."

"And there's one more thing," said Craig.

James was beginning to wheeze again.

"I've just seen some more of the self-same pods in Galdinie's Shop."

CHAPTER TWO

MENDEL'S VISITORS

It was two o'clock in the afternoon when Cathy Peck stormed into Forty-Five Willow Terrace. Her son, James, had made himself scarce after spotting his best friend Craig while her husband, David, busied himself with the elastic ropes that held the luggage to the roof rack of their Volkswagen Polo. He muttered to himself as he struggled with the heaviest case, cursing when one of the plastic wheels scratched the car's black paintwork.

Cathy shook her head in dismay and dumped a small green rucksack on the kitchen floor. She extracted her purse and the passports before popping into the downstairs toilet to wash her face. The flight had been delayed due to bad weather and they'd spent eight hours in Palma airport trying to avoid each other. She'd declared the holiday null and void after seeing David flirt with one of the blonde hotel reps and had demanded to go home at once. David had pathetically protested his innocence and she, knowing well enough that her husband was just being friendly, had used the situation to get back home. The hotel was full of pitiful, complaining Brits, who constantly harped on about the bacon not being the same or the fact that they couldn't watch their favourite T.V. program. Cathy had also had enough of her family. Life was much easier when David was away working and when James was safely in school. Seven days was too long to bear. She should never have agreed to go in the first place.

In the house for just a few minutes, she was already becoming restless, so she picked up the car keys and decided to go for a drive. Out in the forecourt, David was still hauling at a red hook that had lodged itself in the rubber seal of rear window.

"You are truly pathetic!" she scolded, before opening the car door and turning on the ignition.

"Wait! I've not finished yet!" David protested.

Her anger building, she revved the little car twice and, wheels spinning, raced out of the drive in reverse. The tyres screeched as the car spun onto Willow Terrace then, with a lurch and a horrible grinding of the gears, it bolted forward. The last of the cases toppled off the back of the car, spilling its contents over the road. *Not my problem*, she thought.

* * *

David watched in disbelief, his mouth half open, as the black Polo zoomed out of the street, with the remaining red strap, like a party streamer, dangling from the rear window.

David sighed. "We must be home." He began to mutter a string of little regrets as he gathered up the clothes from the middle of the road.

There were, of course, the usual onlookers. Some flicked their curtains others, feigning indifference, continued pruning their roses or cutting their grass.

"A complete twenty-two carat nutter..." he declared, in-between pants and little curses. He plucked a red bra off the gatepost and shoved it, briskly, into the case.

* * *

They'd just stepped onto the pavement outside the Rectory when James saw the familiar black Volkswagen Polo skidding round the corner ahead of them. It narrowly missed the kerb as it zoomed past, dust and litter slamming into them. James coughed and rubbed his eyes.

"Well, either your mum has just seen one of those pod things or she's had another row with your Dad," said Craig, removing an orange crisp poke from his hair.

Father Michael patted James on the back. "Now James, she's probably just late for some appointment or..." but Michael stopped when he realised that his 'always see the good in people' sermon was falling on deaf ears.

"Now might be a good time to have a look at those pods," said James, desperate to guide the conversation away from his crazy mum.

"Yes. Well, I'll take a walk up to Galdinie's shop then," said Ephie. "I mean, now that your mum's otherwise engaged, the situation might not need all of us to go up to your house."

James remembered how the once portly Ephie used to be Galdinie's number one customer. This was before she fell for Father Michael during their adventure in Denthan the year before. He wondered if she'd really volunteered to check out Galdinie's for old time's sake. Still, everyone had been amazed by her transformation. She'd lost over four stone.

"Remember Ephie; don't get distracted. The pods are just above the chicken crisps," said Craig.

"Thank you for your advice," she snapped.

Father Michael was becoming tangled in Patch's lead. "Could you take Patch, dear?" He handed Ephie the tiny black and white Jack Russell's lead.

"Yes, yes. C'mon Patch."

So, slightly disgruntled, Ephie carried on past James's house towards Galdinie's shop while Michael and the boys strolled up James's drive, following Bero to the front door.

"*James…*"

James suddenly stopped. "Did you hear that?"

Craig widened his eyes and nodded his head. "Nope."

"Shut up, Craig. This is serious. I'm sure it was Mendel, and he doesn't sound too good. Quick upstairs!"

They all followed him up the wooden steps. Bero's hackles rose as he sniffed at the bottom of James's bedroom door. Michael looked back downstairs. "Your Dad. Where is he?"

"He's probably gone for a walk to calm down," said James, placing his hand on the door handle.

"I hope not," whispered Craig. "Look what happened the last time he did that. Zapped into a…"

"For goodness sake, button it." James edged up towards his bedroom door and gave it a push.

"Good God in heaven!" Michael gripped onto the doorframe.

There, above the old tin bath James counted four huge white pods. They looked like giant cocoons and there were things, strange wormlike things, slithering about inside them.

"I thought you said they were tiny?" said James, punching Craig in the shoulder without once taking his eyes off of the gruesome sight.

"Please! None of you move," said Mendel.

James spotted a splash of gold in the tin bath. He spoke like a ventriloquist, trying not to move his lips. "Endel, hut are dose hings?"

"They are *Lintoptera vagidelin*," said Mendel.

"Mendel!" Craig chastised. "Just tell us in plain English."

"Shhh!" hissed James.

"They are not dissimilar to the Centides you encountered in Denthan. These, however, are the winged variety from a place called Artilis."

Bero growled then began to bark up at the twitching pods.

"NO!" They all shouted at once watching in horror as Bero jumped into the tin bath and stood up on his back legs. He bit into the nearest pod and began to shake it, snarling and spilling water everywhere.

James dashed forward in an effort to restrain him, but Craig had already caught hold of his collar. "No, boy!"

"Do something, Mendel!" James waited for the *knock, knock, knock* in his head that always preceded magic, but he felt nothing.

"I can't do anything just now, James. Get me out of here. I'll explain later if..." Mendel's words were cut short when the half-gnawed pod splashed down into the tin bath.

A large, wet, insect leg punched out of the leathery white membrane.

"Arrghhh!" Craig heaved Bero back and screamed, "Mendel's on the floor!"

James looked about him in panic, then seeing a bronze coloured jar on his bedside table, grabbed it, and dived forward just as another hairy insect leg burst out of the pod. Michael tugged James back and scrambled about on the slippery, water-covered pine floor, desperately trying to get hold of the even more slippery goldfish that lay, gasping, inches away from Craig's feet and Bero's sharp, skidding paws. "There!" He popped Mendel into James's jar and backed out of the room just as Craig and Bero broke free from the bath. A set of red pincers snapped above their heads as one of the other pods tore open.

They all rushed out onto the landing and slammed James's bedroom door shut behind them.

As Craig and Michael looked at each other in disbelief, James dashed into the upstairs bathroom and filled the leafy jar that held Mendel with tap water. "Mendel? Are you alright?"

"Yes, yes… Just a little short of oxygen." Mendel's voice sounded thin.

"You were right, Mendel," gasped Craig, peering into the jar. "They were just like the Centides in Denthan. Did you see the one that almost got Bero? It had red wings and…"

"Craig…" James could feel his chest tightening. He needed Craig to shut up.

"Just take big, slow breaths," said Craig.

"I'm bloomin' trying… to," gasped James.

"Come on, James, lets get out into the garden," said Michael.

James took another blast of his inhaler and followed them out of the house.

Mendel splashed in his jar as he moved. "James; say this carefully:"

"Say what? Hurry!" snapped James holding onto a cherry tree for support. Through his bedroom window, he saw the blurred flapping of giant insect wings and the twitching of long antennae. A deep drone sounded for a second before there was a sound like stones clacking together.

"What on Earth is that?" said Michael, pulling the boys further back from the house. They all knelt down behind a clump of red-hot poker plants.

"*Lanternbrek.* Say it, James." Mendel's voice was very faint and James's head began to thump. The wizard's magic was building inside him. He could barely push the word from his lips. "Wwwlan-wwterww…"

"Wrong. That's not it. Say the whole thing! It's…"

Bang!

The window disintegrated. A giant insect burst through the glass and hovered about ten feet from the side of the house. Its hideous mandibles clacked together as it veered left and then right like an enormous dragonfly.

With a high-pitched scream, two more of the giant creatures joined the first. The deadly drone of their wings intensified.

"Wwwlanwwterwwbwwrekww!" This time James managed to push the second part of the word from his mouth and a bright blue light began to fill his room behind the hovering creatures. The last insect to emerge from his window looked as if it had either been attacked by the first three monsters or perhaps had failed to develop properly in its cocoon. Its wings were crumpled and it was missing an antenna.

The light grew brighter and a large bolt of forked lightning stabbed at the sprawling creature that teetered on his windowsill. James winced as it broke in two, the front half spilling onto his mum's azaleas. It oozed black liquid over the manicured lawn. The other three flying Centides split up and made off in different directions. One that headed out over Loch Echty got as far as St. Donan's spire before the blue lightning flashed again and frazzled its crimson wings. Another, still hovering above them, flicked its long antennae before whooshing down onto Bero.

Bero jumped up to meet the creature and bit hard into one of its dangling legs.

"Bero. No!" Craig rushed forward before Michael could stop him and was instantly gathered up by the remaining five legs. The leg Bero was holding onto had simply snapped off and the giant flying Centide continued to rise into the air.

Michael ran underneath Craig and waved his arms. "Jump down. I'll catch you."

Almost ten feet above the lawn, James saw Craig duck as another fork of blue lightning screamed out of his broken window. It separated the Centide's clacking head from its horrible body and sent it spiralling down onto the lawn.

As it bounced onto the grass, Craig issued a stifled grunt and then a long drawn out moan.

They all ran forward and pulled at the insect's jagged legs until Craig managed to wriggle himself free. "There's one more," said Craig, feebly, pointing over to the road where the Fyffe's new Mondeo car was parked.

The forth Centide had lighted on its metallic blue roof and now appeared to be vibrating. As its movements intensified they edged closer. The whole car shook violently as the creature folded its wings behind its back and began to circle. James looked up at his smashed bedroom window and realised that the magical blue light had faded. He took another puff of his inhaler and tugged on Craig's sleeve. "Keep back. We're getting too close."

There was a ripping sound at first, like stitching being pulled apart, and then a screaming sound like a siren. James screwed up his eyes and ventured a little closer. He watched as a large tear appeared along the first of the Centide's shiny orange segments. As each of the ten segments split, the creature's erratic shaking increased until...

Crash!

The front windscreen of the Mondeo blew out and the car began to fall apart.

"The Fyffe's car!" James shrieked.

"Never mind the bloomin' car. What about my back?" snapped Craig. "I fell about fifty feet."

"Ten, actually," murmured Mendel.

"Good Lord. Look at that," breathed Michael, as first the wheels, then the metalwork began to fall off the Mondeo and clatter onto Willow Terrace. As the last body segment of the creature divided, a small white grub emerged from the hole and dropped down onto the road behind what was left of the car. The mother insect fell dead and there was complete silence.

Michael straightened himself and tentatively walked forward. He looked down into the bronze-leafed jar at Mendel. "What should we do now?"

There was no reply.

James knew that Mendel was still weak. He could sense it. "C'mon, let's go back to the house and see what the damage is." Wincing at the devastation that surrounded them, James led Michael and Craig back into the garden. His window lay in pieces on the lawn. Glass, wood, and lead was interspersed with strange looking body-parts. The ugly head of the creature that had lifted Craig off the ground lay on the newly mown grass, its mandibles twitching involuntarily.

James crouched down to get a better look. "The creature's head; it's beginning to disappear!" The body parts of the Centide shimmered then began to fade into the grass. In the street, what had once been a nice family car lay in heap, completely destroyed.

James looked around at the mess. *Where have the remains of those bugs gone? And where is that thing that slithered out of last flying Centide?* he wondered.

"Back to where they came from, I expect," said Mendel, reading his thoughts.

"Mendel!" They all shouted at once. His voice seemed stronger now.

"The thing," Mendel continued, "that slithered out of the Centide's ovipositor."

"It's probably still on the road," said Michael.

"It won't harm you," said Mendel. "The first larval stage is harmless and..."

"Never mind the biology, what's going on?" snapped Craig.

Undaunted, as usual, Mendel finished his lesson: "In threatening situations the winged Centide produces a solitary grub which burrows into the ground and escapes. Fascinating, and one day, Craig, you'll be glad you listened. Knowledge is power."

"Knowledge is boring." Craig dusted himself down. "Now, almost being scrunched by an alien insect ... That *is* something else."

James looked back towards the road. "Look at the state of that car." He made for the remains of the Fyffe's Mondeo. "Mendel, you're saying that thing burrowed through a tarmac road. And how could the mother one have a baby so quickly? The flying Centide only hatched a few minutes ago." Somehow, asking Mendel to elaborate made James feel better; it took his mind off of the nightmare and annoyed Craig at the same time.

"At last, some decent questions." Mendel had regained his usual tone. "Firstly, the grub's mouthparts are capable of dealing with granite rock, never mind tarmac, and secondly this species is proto vivipaurous."

"Proto, vivi, what?" said James.

"Don't encourage him," complained Craig, tugging on Bero's lead.

Mendel splashed excitedly. "It means that they are born with live young in them already. It's a kind of double birth. The offspring are born with their own fully developed larva inside them already."

"Fascinating, indeed," whispered Michael.

Craig shook his head, mournfully. "Never mind that. Why has no-one heard this racket? The Terrace is totally empty."

"Tea time?" suggested Michael.

"Wait a minute. What's that?" said James. In the distance, he could hear an incessant barking.

"Patch!" Craig lifted his gaze from the deep hole in road.

"We forgot about Ephie!" Michael flushed and then bolted off in the direction of Galdinie's shop.

Still half stunned, James noticed his neighbour, Mr. Fyffe, open the front door of number forty-seven. Ducking behind the hedge that divided their gardens, James squinted through the foliage. His neighbour stood open mouthed as Craig, Bero and Father Michael ran off in the direction of the underpass. Mr. Fyffe scratched his head then wandered out of his front gate. At his front gate, he came to an abrupt halt. "What the...?"

James hunkered down, trying to make himself as invisible as possible.

"My car," squeaked Mr. Fyffe.

The devastation was total. No windows, no wheels, no lights, a crushed roof and a torn bonnet. He ran out onto Willow Terrace just in time to see the little band, led by Father Michael, disappear round the corner. "Surely things haven't sunk this low?" he babbled. "Surely not..."

James stifled a giggle at the thought of Father Michael and Craig being blamed for mindless vandalism. He picked up Mendel's jar from the lawn and snuck round the back of his house, lest he would be tarred with the same brush.

CHAPTER THREE

CUSTARD AND METEORS

Still traumatised by the ruction back at the house, James eventually caught up with Craig, Father Michael and Bero. They had almost reached Galdinie's shop. It stood at the base of a small incline that led up to the underpass, the only safe way to access the Tank Woods and Bruce Moor without being squashed flat on the bypass. Galdinie's had remained in the same decrepit condition for as long as James could remember. A frosted window with a bold, black and yellow sign read: GALDINIE'S SWEETS AND ICE-CREAMS stood proud of the frontage. The words formed an arch over some roughly painted roses and a badly drawn heap of tablet that looked more like a steaming pile of off-brown dog poop. The double doors had been painted maroon, about fifty years ago, by the state of them, and they leaned precariously on their rusty hinges. It was from behind this, partially opened, flaking façade that the incessant barking emanated.

"It's definitely Patch," said Michael, cautiously.

James nodded but he was still short of breath. He paused to hold onto the black metal fence that lined the gardens behind Willow Terrace. Something caught his attention in the corrugated underpass ahead, something big. "Did you see that?"

Craig and Father Michael tensed.

"Another flying bug?" enquired Michael.

A small man, wearing a blue fleecy jacket and a pair of olive-coloured shorts, appeared from the entrance of the tunnel. Struggling to untangle his binoculars from the zipper of his coat, a blast of air, displaced by an articulated lorry on the by-pass above his head, showered him with dust and ruffled his dark hair.

"Dad?"

David Peck opened his eyes and took a deep breath. He beamed at the little crowd of onlookers. "Hi there boys, and Michael too. Out for a spot of bird watching?"

"Not exactly," replied Michael. "I just need to check on Ephie and Patch."

"There's Patch," said James, spying the black and white terror dart out of Galdinie's shop door.

"Patch!" Michael stepped forward to greet her, but the sight of Michael simply seemed to intensify Patch's yapping. She jumped up and caught hold of his sleeve, trying to pull him into the shop.

James could tell that his dad was suspicious.

"What's going on, Son?"

Craig and Bero bolted into the shop after Michael.

"It's Patch; she ran off. I think she's been playing up in Galdinie's." James replied.

"Sounds like she still is. She's tearing the place apart. I better go and see if I can help."

"Dad, it's okay. Father Michael is in there already." James was in no mood to begin explanations about giant bugs from another world.

His dad moved forward.

"Why don't you go home and make up with Mum?"

"What?"

He could tell his dad instantly smelt a rat. "What have you been up to? Have you been teasing Mrs. Galdinie again? Is Father Michael trying to mediate?"

"No. No, of course not. I just wondered if you'd both calmed down and…"

"And why have you got your goldfish with you? You've been up to no good."

James noticed Mendel squint up at his dad from the jar. "He… I…"

"You're digging yourself a very deep hole, Son. You'd better spit it out."

A horrific scream resonated from the shop.

David Peck stiffened with fright. "What, in God's name, have you done?"

He broke into a run while James followed, sheepishly, a few feet behind. The water sloshed about dangerously in Mendel's jar.

"Brilliant. This is just brilliant," muttered James, making his way towards the front door of the shop. "Why is it, Mendel, that you always go completely dumb whenever I really need you?"

Again, another high-pitched wail echoed out onto the street.

With a crash, Craig and Bero were first to leap out of the maroon shop door followed by the white-coated Mrs. Galdinie, Patch, Father Michael and, last of all, Ephie. Michael dashed back and pulled the doors shut just as something slammed into them on the other side.

"The keys!" yelled Michael, holding the double doors shut while twisting round to shout at Mrs. Galdinie. "Do you have the keys?"

"I no gotta mi keys way meh, eh! Der in di shop, estupido!"

Mrs. Galdinie was in the middle of crossing herself when his dad dashed past her and began wrapping his binocular straps round the door handles. "There! That should hold it."

Tentatively, David and Michael took several paces back, wincing as something tested the door yet again.

Crash!

"What on Earth is that?" said David, pulling James across to the other side of the street to join the others.

"A dog. A mad dog," Michael lied, his fingers crossed behind his back.

"Dat wisa no dug!" screamed Mrs. Galdinie before babbling in Italian and crossing herself yet again.

"Oh, I think it was," said Ephie, unconvincingly. She'd begun to dig her nails into Michael's arm.

"Whit? Are ju all mad, eh?" Mrs. Galdinie was just about to set off on a rant again when they all heard a deep, menacing drone.

"Eh, I must say, that doesn't sound like a dog," David Peck declared. He gripped the black mesh fence that lined the pavement as, for the third time, the doors strained. "James! What the heck…"

James had just seen something long and orange whip past the small window at the top of the shop doors.

"James?" Mendel's voice filled his thoughts.

"Oh, you've decided to speak then?" said James, between clenched teeth.

"Just say the same spell as you said back in your garden," instructed Mendel.

"What one was that again?" said James, his head too full of flying Centides and the strangled expression on his dad's face to concentrate.

"Lanternbrek," Mendel reminded.

The annoying thumping sensation that always preceded Mendel's magic began to cloud James's thoughts.

"Wwwlanwwterwwbwwrukww!" said James. He didn't like the look on his dad's face.

There was a sound like a curtain ripping in two, followed by a loud slosh then silence. Even Patch had stopped barking.

"Did it work?" said Craig.

"After a fashion," interrupted Mendel. "What James actually said was: '*Lanterbruk*', so things are going to be rather messy in there."

Despite mucking up the spell James thought that Mendel sounded content enough so he sighed and handed the wizard's leafy jar to Craig. A yellow liquid was oozing out from under the maroon shop doors.

Unable to hear Mendel, James's dad looked very suspicious. "What's going on? Father? Ephie? Craig?"

Thankfully not one of them seemed willing to offer any decent suggestions at that precise point. James waved them back from the shop. "Let's go down to the Rectory and phone the police. Constable Watt should be informed about this dog. It's obviously calmed down now, but I wouldn't risk annoying it again."

David Peck shook his head. "Dog? What's that stuff on the pavement? It's coming out from underneath—"

"Custard," snapped Craig.

Nice one, thought James.

David Peck screwed up his eyes. "Cus..."

"...stard," finished Michael, trying his best to ignore Mrs. Galdinie's gasps of exasperation. "And there's no point in risking a fight with a rabid dog, David."

"Rabid... No, I suppose not..."

James noticed his dad focusing in on his binoculars.

"Dad," barked James. "I would leave them there for the time being. The dog..."

"Dat wis no dug, a tell you. Eet juusta burst oota the counter way eets big legs an..."

"And I think you've had quite a shock, Mrs. Galdinie." Ephie put her arm round the smaller woman, ushering her down Willow Terrace. "A nice cup of tea will calm us all down."

"But a tell you..." Mrs. Galdinie whimpered.

"On you go dad. Make sure she's alright. I'll pop my goldfish back into his tank."

"A goldfish shouldn't be out of the house in the first place. What were you thinking?"

"I know, Dad, but I had to keep him safe."

"From what?"

James saw his dad being accosted by Ephie and Father Michael. "If I see Mum I'll tell her where you are." He watched as his dad wandered down the hill towards St. Donan's Rectory. Ephie and Michael had to keep prompting him on with little pats and tugs.

"Poor sod," Craig piped up. "He never really gets to see the whole picture, does he? It's as if the whole world just drags him along. Helpless, like a puppet or..."

"Yes, well thank you very much, Mr. Psychologist, or whatever you think you are. Just leave my dad out of your stupid theories."

"Alright, alright. I was only saying..."

"Well bloomin' don't!" James snapped, cradling the leafy jar that contained Mendel.

Craig shrugged his shoulders and pointed down the road towards the rest of the party, who were edging round the road-works. "I'll..."

"...nick off with them in case there's any chance of meeting my mum," James finished.

"Something like that," Craig mumbled.

* * *

Back along Willow Terrace James saw, to his utter despair, that John Fyffe had dragged his wife out onto the street to examine what was left of their car. He crouched behind a lamp-post and listened in to their conversation.

"Would you believe it? A man of the cloth resorting to mindless acts of vandalism. Is no-one safe these days? I mean, a man of the cloth!" Mr. Fyffe ranted.

"Well, how often have I told you to park it in the drive?" reminded Mrs. Fyffe. "And as for blaming it on Father Michael... Well, honestly dear, I think you're stretching it a bit far there." Joan Fyffe spoke in a very droll, condescending tone.

"Stretching it a bit far! Look at my car. My pride and joy that was! Godzilla couldn't have done a better job!"

"Yes dear. Well, I think Godzilla is probably a more likely suspect; don't you?" With this, she turned and walked, briskly, back towards their house.

James had to bite his lip to stop himself from laughing.

Her parting jibe was, "You'd better call the RAC or something."

"The RAC? The bloody RAC?" The last 'C' was very high-pitched. John Fyffe looked completely exasperated. He stepped back and almost fell into the hole in the road caused by the Centide larva.

"And what's that all about?" he blustered to himself, eyeing the hole suspiciously.

James realised that he wasn't going to get into his house without being seen so he decided to head back down the hill after the rest of them. St. Donan's Rectory seemed a safer option right now.

* * *

Cathy Peck had almost finished her usual circuit: once round the five mile stretch of the by-pass, down to the old road next to Loch Echty, where she stopped to skiff stones, and then back up to the house via the wine section of the village shop. It had been a twenty-two-skiffer session, which was about average for the mood she was in. Back in her car, she put her foot down and muttered the usual regrets. "If I'd only married the rich oilman's son, Barry, or whatever he was called. He might have been home a bit more, kept his eyes on me instead of some blonde-rinsed holiday rep."

As she turned into Willow Terrace, she stretched across with her left hand to prevent the bottle of white wine from rolling off the passenger seat. This balancing act, combined with a sudden craving for some homemade tablet, meant she missed the devastation outside her house. She came to a sudden stop at Galdinie's, failing to catch the wine this time before it thumped onto the foot well of her car. She looked up to find that the shop was closed.

"For goodness sake," she moaned, wrenching the handbrake on with enough force to snap a fully-grown man's neck.

Still muttering as she stepped outside the car, she soon noticed a pair of very familiar binoculars wrapped round the door handles. She tested the doors and began to unwrap the straps. "These are definitely David's," she whispered. "The idiot's left them behind. A pair of five hundred pound binoculars just abandoned. Idiot!" The rage boiled up inside her as she tested the doors. *They're not locked.*

"Yuck; some fool's left ice-cream to melt at the door." She flicked the gunk from her left shoe. "Mrs. Galdinie? Mrs. Galdinie, are you in there?" She stepped inside and immediately slipped. "Uh!" Landing on her backside with a gooey thud, she studied the yellow liquid that covered her hands and began flicking it off her fingers. "Mrs. Galdinie?" She picked herself up and wandered a bit further into the shop. *Custard?* she mused. *What a mess.*

The ice-cream churns lay open, and there were shreds of cardboard and broken sweet jars everywhere. She backed out of the shop, her backside soaking wet and her feet covered in custard. It didn't smell like custard, though. *That was it.* "It's like…" She peered back into the shop and there, lying smashed on the floor, she spied a large jar of the red and yellow pear drops. "Pear drops." *This place definitely reeks of pear drops and now my clothes stink of it too.*

She lifted a pack of seemingly untarnished tablet, before untangling David's binoculars and heading for home.

* * *

Down in the Rectory kitchen, Mendel had suddenly come to life again. He was swimming round in little circles inside the amber-coloured jar. He did this when he was annoyed or deep in thought. "This is all very strange, you know," he said.

"You think?" interjected Craig, his mouth dropping open in mock amazement.

"And now that Mrs. Galdinie is involved, the whole village is going to know about it," said James. He pointed out of the kitchen window into the Rectory garden. "Look at that. My dad and her are nattering right now." Michael and Ephie were too busy making tea to respond, it seemed. He turned his attention on Mendel.

"I mean, why did those things come here in the first place? Did you summon them or something?"

"No, I did not," Mendel expurgated. "At least, not intentionally."

"Did you hear that, Craig?" whispered James.

"Yes, I did. Radio Mendel is loud and clear."

Mendel popped a googly eye above the surface of the sloshing water in the amber jar.

James and Craig's angry faces were reflected in the surface of the water.

"I was just trying to do a simple spell by myself. I was bored and I wondered if it was possible to do a rudimentary piece of magic without your help, James."

"Rudi-what?" whispered Craig.

"Simple," explained James, staring straight into Craig's eyes.

Mendel sounded ashamed. "I may have triggered something, by mistake."

"What do you mean when you say 'triggered something?'" James asked.

"And how many more of those pod things do you think you might have brought to Drumfintley?" added Craig.

"That should be it," Mendel splashed an orange fin, "for now."

James cupped the jar and whispered down, "What, exactly, did you do, Mendel?"

Mendel's rich tones sounded wearisome as he tried to explain. "I wanted to see if I could do some simple kinetics." Mendel mouthed the surface of the water. James eased back.

"Kinwhatics?" moaned Craig.

James hated it when Mendel assumed they knew all those big words. He hated it even more when Craig prolonged it all by asking the wizard to explain.

Mendel ducked under. "I simply tried to move James's lamp from one end of his room to the other, but something else happened instead."

"I'll say," retorted Craig, a cheeky grin forming on his freckled face.

James bristled. "You think this is just one big laugh, don't you, Craig. You see, it's not your house that's wrecked and it's not your dad who's about ten yards away, and…"

"Boys. That's enough. I will just have to accept the fact that I need James to perform any spells, safely, while I am in my present form."

"The pods?" James reminded. "Why did the pods come here?"

"Now, I'm not too sure why they would have come all the way from Artilis. It's possible that my spell could have generated them, but unlikely," said Mendel.

"So?" James pressed.

"So, that leaves two other possibilities. Possibilities that, I think, we need to discuss with everyone."

"Everyone?" blurted James.

"Obviously, once your father and Mrs. Galdinie have left." Mendel assured.

Ephie handed the boys a mug of tea and a coconut-covered snow-ball biscuit each. "Mendel's talking to you and Craig, isn't he?"

"Yeah," confessed James, feeling a little ashamed. "But we don't want to get Mrs. Galdinie and Dad involved."

"Quite," agreed Ephie.

Once they'd drank their tea and convinced Mrs. Galdinie that it *had* been a dog in her shop after all, Michael suggested that David might take Mrs Galdinie up to the police station. His dad and Mrs. Galdinie were soon ushered out of the Rectory and they resumed their seats on the sofa.

"Right, they've gone. Mendel wants to tell us something," said James.

"I should think he does," broached Michael.

Almost immediately, Mendel began to enter all their thoughts. "Eh-hum!" He cleared his throat and proceeded. "I am, of course, very sorry for the trouble I may have caused today."

Ephie and Michael began chattering.

"None-the-less," the wizard interrupted, "I would like you all to consider the more important consequences."

"There'll be lots of those when his mum gets started," gibed Craig. He patted Bero and noted the time on Father Michael's grandfather clock. It was 4 P.M., exactly.

"Shut up, Craig."

"Eh-hum!" Mendel seemed annoyed by the distraction. "It was not my intention to unleash the Flying Centides of Artilis on Drumfintley. None the less, they may have come here because I was trying to practice magic in James's absence. If nothing else has been established to-day, at least I know now that I cannot do my magic without James."

"Please hurry up, Mendel. We've got about ten minutes before dad gets back to Willow Terrace," James interjected.

"There are, however, two other possibilities. The first, is that the Jesus Rocks have been reactivated by someone else using another crystal."

Ephie butted in. "I've never quite understood the whole Jesus Rocks thing."

Mendel began in a placatory tone, "The Jesus Rocks on Bruce Moor are the gateway we used to get to and from Denthan."

"Yes but..." Ephie still looked confused.

"The other possibility is that there is another gateway here in Drumfintley."

"A second gateway?" asked James.

"Quite so." Mendel answered.

James saw that Ephie was struggling with the concept of the gateways. He tried to make things a little clearer for her. "The crystals are needed to activate the standing stones. They act like keys that unlock their magical powers. And since we used the last fragment of crystal to fix Dad's..." James searched for an appropriate word, "...predicament, we haven't any way of making the ones up on the moor work any more."

Ephie's puzzled expression didn't change in the slightest.

"Yes, well, as I recall," said Craig, "we don't just need a blue crystal; we also need this other set of stones to be built in exactly the same pattern as the Jesus Rocks. And they should have an inscription on them too. They won't work without all that. Right Mendel?"

"Precisely!" said Mendel, sounding quite impressed.

Ephie and Michael still looked more than a little bemused.

The doorbell buzzed.

"I'll get it," said Michael, fastening his dog collar and flattening a few hairs on his head with a lick of his fingers and a quick press down.

"Father Michael Parr?" said the voice.

"You know I am, Constable Watt," replied Michael. "Why all the formalities?"

"I have to ask you some questions, Sir. If you don't mind?" Constable Watt was ushered in. "Ah, the other suspects," he added, on seeing the boys.

"Suspects?" Michael and Ephie said at the same time.

"Father Michael, can you tell me your whereabouts at precisely 2:30 P.M. this afternoon?" Constable Watt licked his thumb before flicking through his little black book.

"My whereabouts?" said Michael, in a highly disgruntled fashion.

"Yes."

"Up by Willow Terrace, I should think," said Michael, reluctantly. He sat down beside Ephie and put his arm round her.

"Ah! Well, you were all seen, excepting yourself madam," Watt nodded toward Ephie, "running away from the scene of a crime."

James could tell that the young constable was embarrassed. His hand was shaking over his notepad. James could also feel a familiar sensation building in his head. The horrible knocking sound he hated so much, like stones clacking together. Then he said it.

"Wwfotrwwgotwwenww bwwut wwrememwwberwwed!"

Constable Watt's face went completely blank. The young policeman seemed to freeze on the spot.

Quickly, Mendel whispered the exact words that James should say.

James began, "Today, at 2:30 P.M., a meteorite glanced off of number Forty-Five Willow Terrace, ricocheting off of a green car before burying itself in the road. Also," James paused as he listened to Mendel, "a stray dog managed to get into Galdinie's shop and spilled ice-cream and custard everywhere. The dog has since escaped and is no longer in the area." James clapped his hands together, as instructed. The young policeman blinked, stepped back and then sat down hard on the sofa behind him. A puff of dust rose up into the air.

Craig, Ephie, and Michael all stared in amazement at James then turned to see the constable's reaction.

Watt stared, blankly, at James and then said, in a weak voice, "Today, at 2:30 P.M., a meteorite glanced off of number Forty-Five Willow Terrace, ricocheting off of a green car before burying itself in the road. Also, a stray dog managed to get into Galdinie's shop and spilled ice-cream and custard everywhere. The dog has since escaped and is no longer in the area." He rubbed his head. "There has been no trace of the dog or the meteor since," he added, unscripted.

With a stifled titter, Ephie proceeded to offer him a fairy cake and a cup of cold tea.

"Eh, thanks Ephie, but I better get back to the station. I think." He stood up and, rather distractedly, closed his black notebook. "I hope that..." He seemed to drift off again, "...puts your minds at rest."

Craig winked at James. "Bye then, Constable Watt."

"Yes..." Watt doffed his hat then made his exit.

As soon as the door closed, they all began to laugh.

"Brilliant!" said Craig. "An absolute classic. I love it when you do that *Bedknobs and Broomsticks* bubbly voice-thing."

"Very ingenious. Although I'm not all that comfortable with telling lies." Michael directed his comment at the little goldfish that circled inside the amber flask.

"Custard and meteors indeed," said Ephie, with a little giggle.

CHAPTER FOUR

THE SILVER FISH

Constable Watt had only walked as far as the village hall when he received a call from the station. He had to make his way to Willow Terrace. This time it had been the Fyffe's next-door neighbour, Cathy Peck, who'd phoned. "What's that, Sarge?"

Constable Watt heard the old sergeant take a slurp of his tea. "Her window's fallen out. And now Mrs. Galdinie and David Peck have just bundled into the station babbling on about some rabid hound running amuck in her shop. What's going on?"

On hearing this new snippet of information, young Watt glazed over again and put the sergeant right by informing him that, "it was just a stray dog that had since escaped and was no longer in the area."

"Oh. But how do—?"

"And," Constable Watt interrupted. "I think you'll find that any damage reported in Willow Terrace will probably have been caused by the meteor that struck around 2.30 P.M.," Constable Watt checked his watch, "precisely two hours ago."

There was a pause at the other end of the phone before Sergeant Carr cleared his throat and continued. "A meteorite, eh? And I suppose you've got witnesses then?"

"Yes, Sergeant; several. Father Michael was running away from the thing. He didn't cause the damage. You didn't think, for one minute that he...?"

"No. Of course I didn't. Now if Archie MacNulty had been there, that would have been another matter. Father Michael gives him far too much leeway. MacNulty's nothing but a low down, nasty croo—"

"Yes, Sarge; you've said before. I'm here now." Clicking off his receiver, Watt stopped and took in the devastation in Willow Terrace. "Whaaw!" he sighed.

"I'll 'whaaw' you," said Cathy Peck, storming out of her front gate to meet him. "Never mind about that heap." She pointed at the Fyffe's' squished Mondeo. "Who's going to fix that!" She grabbed his sleeve and pulled him into her garden. There on the grass were the remains of her window frame, and above it, the gaping hole that led into James's room.

"It's all perfectly simple, Mrs. Peck," said Constable Watt, carefully pulling himself free of her vice-like grip.

"It was Father Michael!" said John Fyffe, his head appearing above the lattice fence between their gardens.

"I don't think so, dear." Mrs. Fyffe's little voice wafted up behind her husband.

"Now, everybody calm down." Constable Watt walked over to the fence and explained. "Today at 2:30 P.M., a meteorite glanced off of number Forty-Five Willow Terrace." He pointed at the hole that had once been James's window. "Then it ricocheted off of your car before burying itself in the road."

They were all stunned into silence except for Mrs. Fyffe who said, from somewhere behind the fence, "I told you it wasn't the vicar."

Watt heard the sound of a bucket being kicked against the side of the fence before John Fyffe's bright red face popped back into view.

"So why was the vicar... I mean Father Michael, running away then?" He looked back down at his wife. "Will you stop digging me in the ribs or…" But he never finished the sentence. Momentarily losing his concentration, he slipped off the upturned bucket he was standing on and cracked his chin on the fence.

Constable Watt and Cathy Peck wandered onto the street followed by the bickering Fyffes.

"There it is." Constable Watt pointed to the hole in the road. "The meteor must have buried itself in there."

"Deep, isn't it?" said Mrs. Fyffe. "The vicar probably got the fright of his life. Poor man." She continued as if her husband wasn't even there. "He'll probably blame the vicar anyway when the insurance company tells him it was an 'act of God'." She smirked.

Watt caught Mr. Fyffe's manic expression. It looked as though Mr. Fyffe was seriously considering testing the depth of the hole with his wife.

"See, that's better. You're beginning to see the funny side of things now," said Mrs. Fyffe, totally misreading her husband's intent.

John Fyffe's devilish smile fell as he narrowed his eyes and gave her a withering look.

"Oh, suit yourself then." Joan Fyffe shrugged her shoulders, shook her head at Cathy Peck and Watt, and then disappeared back into her garden again.

They all stared back down at the hole.

"What's that yellow sticky stuff then?" asked Cathy. "It's just like the gunge in Galdinie's shop." She reached down and picked up a gloopy lump with her fingers. She sniffed it and pinged it away, several blobs spattering Mr. Fyffe and the constable. "Pear drops. You know something, Constable Watt?"

"Yes?"

"I think your whole theory about meteors and dogs is the biggest load of junk I've heard in ages." She sniffed the warm summer air then screamed up the street, causing Watt to jump back. "DAVID!"

David Peck had just appeared at the end of Willow Terrace.

Watt saw her husband's face turn puce. Everyone in Drumfintley was terrified of Cathy Peck. Most would make any excuse to avoid her, people had enough hassle in their own lives without listening to Cathy Peck berate her family or anyone else, for that matter. She normally hovered somewhere between total rage and spitting mad.

"Idiot! Where did you disappear to this time? You're never here when I need you. And where is James?"

David Peck almost got his mouth open before she started up again. "Where's the number of the insurance company? You had it last so you can deal with this. I've always got to sort this kind of thing out. I mean, you're either away, gallivanting or out at your precious Scouts." She spun round, whipping the constable and Mr. Fyffe with her long, black hair, as she marched back towards the house. "And why did you leave your binoculars dangling from the handle of Galdinie's shop door? They cost over five-hundred pounds! Don't think your going to get another pair if they go missing." Without waiting for David to offer any kind of response, she disappeared back into number Forty-Five, leaving the three men standing beside the Mondeo."

David Peck mouthed the word: *sorry.*

"You know, the good thing about living next to you, David," whispered Mr. Fyffe, "is that no matter how bad it gets, I know it could always be a lot worse."

David Peck sighed. "Thanks, John."

Constable Watt helped John Fyffe retrieve his wallet from what was left of his glove compartment before sauntering back to the station.

* * *

Down in the garden of St. Donan's Rectory, James walked across the manicured lawn to join Craig, Ephie and Michael. They were standing round the old sundial discussing what they should do next.

James looked out over the dark Loch before peering down into the strange jar formed from a tangle of weird, amber-coloured leaves. "Mendel, where did those flying Centides come from? Did you say Artiles?"

"Artil*is*," corrected Mendel.

James eyed a particularly thick piece of chocolate cake that Ephie had just produced from a red biscuit tin.

"I explained that already," said Mendel.

"You probably did, but where have they come through? Where's the second gateway?"

"I was hoping Ephie could help answer that one. You've lived here longer than any of us." Mendel pushed his golden lips above the surface. "We're looking for nine pillars of stone, arranged in a circle, with one bigger than the rest, like a citadel pointing to the heavens."

The great, alabaster citadel of Gwendral that dominated the Denthan capital city flashed through James's mind as Mendel continued.

"Are there any other standing stones in the area that are arranged in the same pattern?"

"No," said Ephie. "There is nothing even remotely like those stones up on Bruce Moor. Not for miles."

James thought he heard a splash out on the Loch. He glanced across the murky water.

"Did you see that?" said Craig, pulling his foot free from under Bero.

"Yes," said Michael. "A flash of silver, out there. Was it a fish or...?"

"There it is again," said James.

"There's what again?" said Ephie, becoming frustrated by them all.

Mendel splashed loudly in his flask. "Everyone, get down. We are being watched."

James held the flask against his chest and slouched down, his back against the sundial. "Watched by what?"

"Something that, as yet, I cannot identify." Mendel flicked his orange tail. "Put me in the Loch."

"Loch Echty? Are you mad?" James didn't want to lose the wizard. Not like the last time in Denthan. "It's maybe not a good time to go exploring, Mendel. Just tell us what's going on. It wasn't a fish, was it?"

"I just want to rule something out. If you don't mind."

"We do mind," Craig interrupted. "I mean, we both remember the nightmare last time you disappeared." Craig pulled Bero in closer. "You're about three inches long, tops, and if that's not your normal, every-day Loch Echty brown trout, you could end up as..."

"Fish food," finished James.

Father Michael was just about to reason with the wizard too but choked on his first word. "I...ahhh!" He pointed out to the bay, his finger wavering.

A tall, silvery fin, at least six feet high stood proud of the water. Membranous, like a bat's wing, it was supported by a set of cartilage rods, each tipped with an iridescent purple hook.

"Wh... What in God's name is that?" Michael made to move forward but Mendel splashed in frustration, soaking them all. "She's seen us."

"She?" broached Michael.

Ephie yanked on Michael's sleeve but Patch and Bero were already off at full tilt toward the Loch. "Come back here. Patch!" hissed Michael.

The fin slid back beneath the surface.

"James, there's no time to waste. Take me down to the Loch and put me in." Mendel's voice thumped louder in his head.

"But..." James protested.

"I insist!"

"Okay. Okay." Reluctantly, James took hold of the amber jar and made his way down to the shore. He had to be careful not to spill Mendel as he tried his best to navigate through high tufts of reeds and slime-covered boulders.

Unnerved, Patch and Bero were already growling and barking out over the Loch.

Craig, Ephie and Michael followed. James heard Craig struggling behind him.

"I really need you to come with me, James." Mendel sounded concerned.

"What?" James looked down in utter disbelief at the leafy flask.

Mendel explained. "Although, in my present state, I can see in colour and even make out rough shapes, I can't see sufficiently well to find what I am looking for. Besides, I may need your help to perform the odd spell or two."

"It's freezing in there and I won't see any better than you." James began to panic.

"Trust me." Mendel's voice sounded incredibly reassuring.

"Plus," James pleaded, "I'd be lying if I said I wasn't worried about that thing we've just seen. It was huge. I mean, what was it? It's not from here, is it?"

"Stop panicking, James. You will be safe with me. I think I know this creature." As Mendel's shadow raced round the flask, James felt the knock, knock, knocking sensation intensify in his head. He grimaced then uttered the words, "Wwwaterw wrightww."

As asthma gripped him and his chest tightened, he noticed that the Loch had become very choppy. Then, inexplicably, he found himself below the surface of the water. The Loch didn't seem cold at all, and he could see Mendel's tail ahead of him flashing orange and gold as they swam further out from the shore. James glanced down at his body and saw the same clothes he had worn all day but his skin was covered in silver scales. He stared at his hands as they shimmered in the darkness.

"James. Follow me. You can breathe as I can now, but you have the eyes of a Water Wright. Can you see Ethrita?"

"Wwhwoo?" James felt the bubbles brush against his face as he forced out the word.

"Do not try to speak. Think your words and I will hear them just as you hear mine. Ethrita is the creature we saw from the shore. She is a very ancient animal."

James raced up through the water like a bullet and pushed his head above the surface. On the shore, Craig, Michael and Ephie stood like statues, their mouths hanging open. The flask that had contained Mendel ebbed and rolled at the edge of the water, abandoned, while Bero and Patch continued to bark and whine at the water's edge. James jumped free of the waves and splashed down into the depths back after Mendel. He was getting used to his new state. The tightness in his chest had lifted and he was beginning to enjoy the way he could move, so easily, through the water. He wasn't even cold and he had incredible vision. It was amazing. The murky gloom was transformed into a crystal clear expanse peppered with weeds and rocks while, just beyond his grasp, fishes and eels darted, this way and that. They left little trails of yellow light behind them that glowed brightly before melting into the sway of the currents.

"Those are heat traces." Mendel's voice played on his senses. "You can now see in full Artilian colour which includes the infrared spectrum. Amazing, isn't it?"

"It's fantastic. I can see for miles. Look at all these colours. I can see every fish, worm, eel and…" James paused. "What is that?"

Ahead of them a huge shape twisted down from the surface. It raced towards them. The size of a small boat, it looked hideous as it sped down to the bottom of the Loch. Its head was grotesque. Like a snake's only with eyes that were disproportionately big and fins that ended in razor sharp hooks.

"Ethrita!" Mendel's voice was like a hammer in James's head.

The creature's fins filled to their full size. Like shimmering dragon wings, they flapped gracefully in the ice-cold water. Ethrita's body was fishlike with the most beautiful scales that shone with burning points of green and blue. The way the colours moved round her fin membranes reminded James of oil spilled in a puddle.

"Mendelshhhsss…?" The word Ethrita issued tailed off with the sound of falling coins.

Mendel swam closer to the creature. "Yes, Ethrita, it's me. I am under a spell which I cannot reverse at the moment." Mendel flicked his golden gills and came to a halt.

"I like itsshhhsss…"

"Well, I'm not so keen on it, my old friend."

"Whosss the changeling, shhhss?"

The strange sound of Ethrita's voice made James shiver.

"This is James. He helps me perform my magic while…" Mendel circled. "While I am trapped in my current incarnation."

Ethrita moved closer to James. Her giant fishy iris narrowed as she examined him.

"He is a boy from the village above," continued Mendel. "*Homo sapiens* find things difficult beneath the waves so I have assisted him by changing him into a Water Wright"

"He certainly seems at ease in my domain, ssshhhhss…" Ethrita flicked her enormous wing-like fins and glided further away. "As you know, you have nothing to fear from me, but other creaturesss will come through the gateway soon, ssshhsss. I have eaten as many as I can but a few have escaped me, ssshhsss…"

"Which gateway do you speak of, Ethrita?" asked Mendel.

A deep clanging sound began to resonate through the water.

* * *

On the shore Craig was the first to hear it. The distant peal of a bell sounded from the depths of the Loch.

"It's the Fintley bell," explained Ephie. "You can hear it on still nights when the wind is low."

"Aye an it'chh a bad sign, cho it is."

Craig, Michael and Ephie almost jumped out of their skins when they heard the voice.

"Archie! You're going to give someone a heart attack creeping up on people like that," barked Michael.

Archie MacNulty stepped out from a tangle of gorse and broom carrying a small pair of pruning shears. "Evening Father. I would bring those dogchs back from the shore if a wisch you. They could be in danger." Archie was struggling with a new set of false teeth, which meant his speech was interspersed with little 'chs' and slurping sounds. Unfortunately, it made Archie's strong accent even more difficult to decipher.

Originally from Surrey, Craig couldn't really pronounce the word 'loch' in that Scottish way that sounded as if they were gathering spit in the back of their throats.

Again, the far-off sound of a bell echoed over the shore.

Archie swatted at Patch who growled and snapped at his ankles. "Git, ye wee nyaff!" Bero snuggled into Craig, who was trying to work out what Archie meant. He reckoned it was something close to: *Go away you little pest.*

* * *

Under the still waters James watched as Ethrita turned away from them and swam further down a slope into the darkness.

"Come on James. We need to keep up." Mendel's tail was a blur of gold as he tried his best to catch up with the huge creature.

James found swimming effortless and easily glided past Mendel. He was intrigued by the sound of the bell clanging ahead and, as they banked down deeper beneath the surface, James saw it. There, edged by a forest of swaying weeds, stood the eerie remains of an old village. A cluster of cottages surrounded a simple stone church that sported a modest, open-arched bell tower.

"I've heard of this place from Dad," said James, excited.

Mendel had just managed to catch up.

"Mendel, it's the village of Fintley. It was flooded when they built the dam at the top of the Loch about a hundred years ago."

Mendel's breathing was laboured and his voice was thin. "Look more closely, James. Look at the gravestones behind the church."

In the shadow of the bell tower a little graveyard lay partially covered in weed and brown algae. In the centre, a large obelisk was encircled by a row of smaller gravestones.

"Is it another gateway?"

Ethrita turned and hovered over the obelisk. She eyed James suspiciously. "Clever changeling, sshhsss." Ethrita floated down and lighted on the floor of the Loch sending brown clouds of algae wafting up into the underwater currents. She gathered in her fins and folded them over her back. James looked on as she vibrated one of her huge fins until the hooks took on the form of a clawed hand. She forced this beneath the swirling clouds of dust.

James and Mendel drifted down until they were level with the obelisk.

While Ethrita groped around at the base of the huge stone, James noticed an inscription. He touched the obelisk with his hand. It felt so smooth.

"Look," said Mendel, flicking the swirling detritus away with his tail. "It reads, 'Here lies Robert MacNulty, hero of Culloden, guardian of Fintley. Jesus Saves.'"

"See! Shhssss..."

James switched his attention to Ethrita, who'd just picked out a dazzling blue gem from the grime. She floated up above the murky floor of the Loch.

Mendel began to circle the perfectly cut gem. "It looks completely genuine," he mused, "I don't, however, understand why there should be two gateways so close together. The one on Bruce Moor must predate this one by millennia."

"You mean it was built a long time before this one?" broached James.

"Yes, yes. By thousands of years," said Mendel, impatiently.

James realised that the bell had stopped ringing.

"Listen to messhhsss!" Ethrita glided toward them, enclosing them in her membranous wings. With a mixture of wonder and trepidation, James realised that the hooks at the end of her bat-like wings were razor sharp.

"I have hunted this Loch for ten thousand years. I have seen generations live out their lives above and below the surfacesshhhss..." Ethrita's wide eyes shimmered in the half-light. "This obelisk comes from Artilis. It was brought here through the gateway on the hill by the followers of Isis and Ra."

"Egyptians?" James had been studying the pyramids at school.

"In a way," interrupted Mendel. "I will explain later." The wizard goldfish urged Ethrita to continue. "Please, Ethrita..."

"Sshhhsss... They built it here when this was far above the surface, before any village ever existedsshhss. They obviously had a reason...shssss, for wanting two gateways so close together, but the true motive for building the second gateway was lost when one of their leaders was murderedsshhsss..."

"What was this leader called?" Mendel sounded very worried.

"Beldamsshhss..." Ethrita's huge wings bristled as she spoke the name.

"Beldam?" Mendel flicked his tail and began to make his way to the surface.

"Mendel? Mendel!" James was confused by the wizard's sudden change of mood and embarrassed at his apparent rudeness. "Eh, I'm sorry I'd better go with..." James looked at Ethrita then back at Mendel disappearing up into the light above.

"Go, changeling. Follow your master. Shsssss..."

Still bemused, James began to float up towards the surface.

Ethrita drew in her wings and began to burrow beneath the floor of the Loch. James heard her strange voice in his head. "I knew Mendel from before all this happened...shsss... I have not seen him for an age. Tell him that I will help as much as I can...shsssss... I will hunt down the Artilian monsters that come here, sshhhsss..."

James thought she sounded very sad and forlorn. "Tell him, changeling...shssss..." The currents twisted below him as, with a great push of her wings, Ethrita disappeared beneath the murk and grime.

James looked down again at the obelisk, and felt terribly scared. Something sparkled in the mud below. The blue crystal was still visible, perched on the plinth of the obelisk. He swam back down and hovered inches away from the gem. Feeling its coldness touch his fingertips, he looked round for Ethrita then tried to pick out Mendel above. "Mendel? You forgot..." James wanted to hear Mendel's reassuring voice tell him that it was alright to take the crystal. Why had the wizard swum away without saying goodbye or thank you to his old acquaintance? James was beginning to feel very lonely and vulnerable in the eerie underwater village of Fintley, so he slipped the crystal into his pocket and kicked hard until he broke the surface.

"Where have you been, boy?" said Mendel, in a very waspish tone.

"You just took off. Left me down there with Ethri..."

"Ethrita," reminded Mendel.

"I know her name," protested James. *That was it*, he decided. *He wasn't going to say anything about the crystal now. The grumpy old guppy could just wait.*

They were only yards from the water's edge and, as he felt the slippery stones beneath him, James saw that there were now four people on the shore. He stumbled to his feet, his silver skin shimmering for a second before sloughing off into the water in long, scaly sheets. Dripping wet, he hobbled over the rocks and stones in the shallows until he reached the shoreline. The flask was still lying at the water's edge so he picked it up and held it in the water, begrudgingly, until Mendel swam inside. James walked back up to the bushes that edged the Rectory garden.

Father Michael's balding head was a deep shade of puce. "James. Thank God. What I mean is..." Michael hesitated, unsure what to say in the presence of Archie MacNulty.

"I think it's safe to say whatever you want in front of Archie," said James thinking back to the inscription on the obelisk. "His family seem to have known about the magic of the gateways all along."

"Aye. I schaw you change, chh, and go under after the goldfish, chh. And I still remember seeing you all disappear up on Bruce Moor, before. Don't fink I'll ever forget that, che. But I still kept my mouth shut! Chh." MacNulty's ill-fitting teeth sloshed about recklessly in his mouth.

Craig gripped James's sopping sleeve and whispered: "I wish he would keep his mouth shut all the time. He's going to drown us all in drool."

MacNulty eyed Craig suspiciously.

They bit their lips in an attempt to stifle their sniggers.

"Yes, well…" continued Michael, in a serious tone, "Why don't we get you dried, James? I'm intrigued to find out what you've discovered." Michael tried to peer into the amber flask as they walked on.

"He's fine," said James, suddenly feeling guilty about taking the crystal. "But it's six o'clock and…"

"You'll be expected home," finished Ephie. She gave Michael a knowing glance and took hold of James's hand. She turned it round and examined his palm.

"The scales dropped off," said James. "But it was fantastic under there." He pointed out across the Loch. "There's a whole village and…"

"And that will be enough for now," finished Mendel. "Michael's right; we better get you home and dry."

James gripped his head before saying, "Wwwwbonewwwdrywww!"

His hair thickened, instantly dry, while his clothes became lighter, free of the smelly Loch water.

"Hey, nice one," said Craig, impressed by his friend's impromptu spell.

"That's all very well for you to say." James rubbed his forehead with his fingers. "It bloomin' hurts, you know."

"Not as much as the cuff around the ear your mum would have given you for coming home in that state," reminded Craig.

"True," admitted James.

"Yes, most impressive." Michael shook his head in astonishment. "You'd better get off home then, boys. Ephie and I can sit down with Archie and have a chat."

"Yes, I'm fairly sure all explanations can wait until tomorrow," said Mendel. "I need some time to think. It's always good to have some time to think. And…" Mendel eased a googly eye above the water, "you should all rest. We may have to go on another journey."

MacNulty was busy glancing around him for the source of the voice, but James had focused on the amber flask, all too aware of what *another journey* might entail. Mendel's words hung in the air for a few moments, wavering amongst the ever-increasing clouds of midges. A mixture of anticipation and trepidation gripped him.

"See you all tomorrow," said James, hesitantly. He caught Craig's arm on the way out of the Rectory gate and slipped him the blue crystal. "Shove this in your pocket," he whispered.

Craig was just about to ask what the heck James was doing when James kicked him on the shin.

"Argh!" he yelped.

"Oh, watch that step," said Ephie, grimacing down at the crumbling slab under the Rectory gate.

Craig got the message and reluctantly covered the crystal with his jumper. "See you soon, Numpty." He mouthed the words, unseen by the adults, a streak of annoyance tracing his freckled face.

CHAPTER FIVE

THE STORY OF BELDAM

His mum was still moaning on about the state of the window in James's bedroom while his dad constantly reminded her that he'd already called the glazier and the joiner.

"If you were half the man you should be, you'd be able to fix it yourself!" she ranted.

"Yes Cath; well, I don't think that's very helpful."

"Don't you *Cath* me. If you had been here when you should have been, instead of cavorting with Mrs. Galdinie, it might never have happened."

Behind his mum, James tried to warn his dad by giving him a wide-eyed shake of his head. But his dad was beginning to rise to the bait, as usual.

"Oh, I see. I suppose I could have leapt up and caught the meteor before it smashed the window."

"Don't be facetious!" snapped Cathy.

James stepped out the way of his mum as she launched his dad's striped pyjamas onto the top landing before slamming her bedroom door.

"You're on the couch!" she screamed, still deafeningly loud through her closed bedroom door.

His dad just stood there, completely bewildered.

"Don't worry, Dad, she'll calm down in about two weeks."

"Don't be cheeky about your mum, son. She's…"

His dad seemed to be searching for the right phrase, one that would excuse his mum but explain the whole *barney* at the same time.

"It's okay, Dad. I'll help you move your things into the spare room," he said, patting his dad on the back. "We better see what kind of mess my room is in."

They opened James's bedroom door and peered inside. Devastation was total. His bed lay in two halves and the night air wafted in through the hole in the wall making the curtains swish and flick like a Highlander's kilt. Clothes and broken lumps of plaster lay everywhere and the tin bath had been dented and buckled. James moved into the room and bent down to pick up a small plastic castle. He put it in the pocket of his tracksuit top then proceeded to pick his clothes up off the wooden floor. His dad soon brushed up and managed to pin some tarpaulin over the open window space.

"Right. That'll do for now." His dad sighed.

They cringed as his mum's voice piped up from behind her door. "Have you tidied the lawn yet?"

"It's dark, Cathy and…"

"Lazy git! Pathetic! Wastrel!"

"I'll help, Dad," said James, putting his arm on his dad's shoulder.

"Thanks, Son." James could see a real look of sadness flash across his dad's face. He hated it when she crushed him like that. He really hated it.

After about an hour of struggling in the dark with the rubble on the lawn, they sneaked into the kitchen and made themselves some fried bread dipped in egg. A quick squirt of tomato sauce and they tucked in. James could see that his dad had brightened.

"Some day, Son, eh? Not every day a meteor hits the house?"

"No," said James, dying to tell his dad everything about Mendel, the gateways to other worlds, and his incredible adventure in Denthan the year before. Sometimes he became very sad thinking about Denthan and the creatures that must have died there. Thousands upon thousands of animals and races had all died, the good and the bad, when Denthan's sun had exploded. Instead, he asked his dad about the different birds he'd seen on his travels.

"Next month you can come to Harris if you want," said his dad, finishing his drink.

James yawned. He was certain that the Island of Harris had come up before. He knew there was some connection with Mendel. Or was it Eethan? He couldn't recall, exactly.

Back in the spare room, James put Mendel into a proper goldfish bowl along with his pretend plastic castle and settled down in his sleeping bag. His dad was already snoring. It was then, as he pulled the sleeping bag up to his chin that Mendel decided to invade his thoughts.

"The Fintley gateway is only one way."

"What?" said James, annoyed by Mendel's sudden intrusion. "What do you mean by one…" James gave in to a huge yawn, "…way?" He shook his head in an effort to stay awake.

"Artilians can come through to our world but we cannot use that gateway to get to theirs."

Mendel had obviously been thinking it through. "But why do we have to go to their world? This Arti…"

"Artilis," finished Mendel.

"Whatever. Surely, we could just destroy the obelisk and the circle, and that would be that," said James, wondering to himself how a twelve-year-old boy could destroy an underwater graveyard.

"It's not as simple as that, James. We could, however, use the new crystal to travel to Artilis via the Jesus Rocks on Bruce Moor," said Mendel.

I should tell him that I took the crystal and gave it to Craig now, thought James. *Then again…* "Why do we have to go at all?" James was very tired and the thought of going anywhere or explaining about the crystal was just too much like hard work.

"I will explain." Mendel paused. "After Beldam was murdered…"

James edged up onto his elbows, now resigned to the fact that Mendel was going to tell him a story whether he liked it or not.

"Beldam, the one from ten thousand years ago?" asked James, sluggishly.

"Yes! Just listen. After Beldam was murdered, the gateway could not work in reverse. Only Beldam knew the correct enchantment to return to Artilis. It was then, I suspect, that the person that murdered her…"

"Beldam was a woman?" James interrupted.

Mendel spat grit against the fish bowl.

James drew back.

"The person who murdered her," Mendel continued, "decided that the only way to return was to go back through the Jesus Rocks. Now, as chance would have it, I suspect they had two crystals with them when they came through; one assigned to the obelisk and one as yet unassigned. The murderer must have assigned the remaining crystal to the Jesus Rocks on Bruce Moor and travelled back. He knew a Denthan enchantment already – *sevaasuusej!*"

James felt his eyes grow heavy. "Jesus saves, backwards, right?"

"Yes, with the vowels extended in the Denthan fashion. Are you sleeping or listening?"

"Yes, yes. You're saying that the murderer of Beldam assigned the unused crystal to the Jesus Rocks and returned to Artilis. And you are saying that the crystal we saw today..." James felt his face flush. "You're saying that *that* crystal is useless."

"No, not useless. It's already assigned to the obelisk but it may also be acting as a remote key."

James felt his head ache, not with magic but with the complexity of the whole explanation.

"My stupid attempt at magic must have signalled something in Artilis. Triggered the crystal in the Fintley graveyard to begin working again."

"And we have to go to Artilis? Why?" James yawned, punching his legs as they jumped involuntary. "Why do we have to get involved at all?"

"There are things coming through the gateway under Loch Echty already, and you haven't seen the worst of it yet. The creatures on Artilis are... Let's say *different*."

James didn't want to think how different, just at that precise moment.

Mendel continued in his usual deep drone, "These creatures are either slipping through the gateway by chance. That is, the flying Centides just happened to be in the right place at the right time, in Artilis. Or, as Ethrita suspects, there is some greater malice at work. Someone is actually testing the Fintley gateway below Loch Echty first before using it properly. Either way, we can only safeguard this world if we go to Artilis and destroy the gateway there." Mendel flicked his tail and darted into his castle.

James stretched out under his duvet and wondered, for the second time in so many minutes, whether now was a good time to tell Mendel that he already had the crystal. A cold shiver of regret traced his spine and again he decided to postpone his inevitable roasting. "Could you tell me more about Beldam?" It was only when Ethrita had mentioned this person earlier that Mendel had begun to act very strangely.

"Beldam was an Artilian queen who was directly descended from the 'original race'. These were the people who seeded all the worlds."

"You mean like gods?" James thought he believed in God, the one they talked about in church, but didn't know quite how to describe him. He felt embarrassed by his question already.

"Gods; God; evolution; both... Whatever you believe in is your own particular truth. I am merely talking about history."

"Ah," sighed James, none the wiser.

"Beldam was not only beautiful, she was also a gifted architect. Her skills in building and construction were unsurpassed. She knew the secret incantations and she possessed the 'stylus'. The styli were, and probably still are, devices that can cut and move huge blocks of stone with a precision that is quite staggering. She built many gateways and had access to many of the powers of the original race. As her powers grew, so too did the jealousy of other ambitious people. In particular, one called Dra. He knew he could use her powers to better himself. He had also been her partner once but had been shunned by her for another. This more than anything burned inside him and blackened his heart. He too, was a talented builder but he knew he could never take true power in Artilis for himself until Beldam was gone and he alone possessed the stylus. He suggested charting a gateway to your planet, as it was known that the vast ice expanses had receded and it would be fertile and rich in minerals. So they came here, to the newly formed Loch Echty, and found it was indeed a wonderful place."

"What happened then?" James yawned so widely that he cricked his neck. "Ah!"

Mendel continued regardless. "Well, they found it to be already seeded with intelligent peoples and still far too cold for their liking. It had only been the two of them, Beldam and Dra, who had come through to scout the area so Dra seized his chance. It is said that he killed Beldam using the stylus and that she still lies beneath the 'largest stone'."

"The Jesus Rock on Bruce Moor?" asked James.

"One and the same." Mendel sounded very sad.

"How old are you, Mendel? And how do you know about all this stuff?" James was desperately tired but he wanted Mendel to finish the story.

"I am very old, James, and I know of this tale from the world of Artilis itself. The Artilians eventually came through other gateways to Earth, mostly in the area known as the Green Crescent. The countries of Iraq and Iran now encompass this region. The Artilians mixed with the races of your world and passed on some of their sciences, eventually blending with a people known as the Sumerians and then, as you rightly said, the Egyptians. Their pyramids and obelisks sprung up all over your world but one true Artilian group kept themselves to themselves. They were great seafarers and they inhabited an island called..."

James thought he knew and put his hand up as if he was at school. He lowered it, suddenly feeling stupid and whispered, "*Atlantis?*"

"Well done, my boy. The Artilians, through time, became known as the Atlantians but when their lands sunk beneath the southern seas they eventually faded into myth and legend."

"What happened to them?" James sat up in his bed.

"They returned to Artilis," said Mendel.

"What happened to Dra?" James pulled his duvet over himself again. He couldn't wait to tell Craig all about Atlantis and the Artilians.

"He was accused of Beldam's murder on his return to Artilis and eventually banished to a dying world, far from Artilis."

"What world?" James pressed.

"You've already been there and, as a matter of fact, you've also met Dra, albeit in Hedra form.

"It was Denthan, wasn't it? And Dra is..." James felt a shiver ripple down his spine. "*Dendralon.*"

"Precisely!" Mendel sank down and settled on the blue and red grit at the bottom of his bowl. "Tomorrow I will go back to the village of Fintley and retrieve the other crystal."

James felt a pang of guilt but decided, for the third time, that explaining about the crystal could wait until tomorrow. James reached over and switched off his bedside lamp. He snuggled deep into his duvet and wondered what Beldam had looked like and how Dendralon and Mendel had managed to stay alive for so long and in so many different forms. He also felt a sense of relief that Dendralon had perished on Denthan. James could still see the black haired wizard falling down into the flames of the dying sun, Tealfirth. The wizard's tortured screams still plagued his dreams. So, that night, just in case, he said his special, anti-nightmare prayer before going to sleep. "I bet I have a really bad dream tonight." Long ago, he found out that by saying this one phrase out loud that it somehow tricked whatever it was that gave him nightmares in the first place. Just as he closed his eyes, Mendel's voice floated round in his head one last time.

"James, we will travel to Artilis tomorrow."

CHAPTER SIX

THE FINTLEY CRYSTAL

A pile of greaseproof papers lay scattered on the floor next to a half assembled robot. It teetered on three plastic legs beside Wee Joe's bed. The papers, all stamped with the words *Galdinie's Handmade Tablet*, littered the rust coloured carpet like crumpled confetti. They'd been allowed to gather there, undisturbed, as firstly; Jean Harrison, Wee Joe's mum, had no interest in tidying them up, and secondly; no-one would dare touch them anyway as they were in the area of the bedroom clearly marked as Wee Joe's territory. Anyone passing through his handmade, red string force field, would receive rough justice. He gave no quarter. Only four years of age, Wee Joe already had a bad reputation in Drumfintley for hitting first and then, more likely than not, hitting some more.

Helen watched as her brother lay fast asleep looking every bit the little angel. Stretched out along the length of his pillow, his head was scrunched against the wall while a single bare leg dangled in mid-air. Several inches above his head, pinned to the wall, an empty loo roll had been painted with various signs and mystic squiggles, known only to four-year-olds. Helen had told him it was a dream sucker and that he needed to paint it himself before it would do its magic. Wee Joe believed her. Why shouldn't he? Since she'd pinned it above his pillow there had been no nightmares about giant Tree Trolls or the grey skinned snake-men, the ones that had long black tongues that flicked in and out of their scaly lips before crunching on little boys' bones.

"Joe. Wake up." Helen spoke quietly. She'd been standing over him for several minutes now wondering if she should tell her mum about the cupboard or wake Wee Joe. She had eventually decided to wake her little brother and show him the funny blue light first.

"Joe?" she whispered.

"W… What is it? Go way!" Wee Joe pulled his duvet tighter round his neck, but in his efforts to get further away from his sister, he'd banged his head off the wall. "Awch!"

"You need to look at this." Helen tugged the duvet down from his throat and pointed at the cupboard again. "Look!"

"I don't eed to wook!" He snapped. "It's a blue goblin."

"A what?" Helen had seen no sign of any blue goblin. She gripped onto his bare leg as the light from the cupboard intensified.

"Get off!" he snapped.

The white prefabricated cupboard door was silhouetted by a bright blue glow that flashed crimson, and then vanished.

"De cupboard did dat already. Mmh!" Wee Joe yawned and stretched before kicking the yellow duvet off his bed. "It made me remember de blue goblin thing."

His words sent a chill across Helen's heart as she too began to remember the little blue creature. "What was his name? E… Ee…" She struggled to remember. "Eethan!"

"Di blue goblin, Duh! Dat's wot I said." Wee Joe gave her a look of complete contempt but his expression began to soften.

Helen plumped down on the bed and began to sob uncontrollably.

"Don't cwy Helen. It's just membering it all dats making you all sad."

Flashes of Denthan and their adventure began to spark in her mind. Eethan was the one who had taken them through the Jesus Rocks to Denthan to look for her big brother, Craig. A crimson sky with two suns and great armies of monsters filled her thoughts. It was all too much for her. "Mum! Mum!" Helen cuddled her little brother and wiped her eyes.

"Joe? Helen?"

Helen heard her mum thumping down off her bed.

"I'm coming… Aw!" Her mum lay sprawled on the top landing. She'd tripped over an abandoned robot leg and was now trying to tie her bathrobe. Helen noticed that she was covered in sweat. "It's 6 A.M., Helen. What's going on?"

* * *

Craig heard the commotion outside his room and slipped free of his duvet. He hoped beyond hope that the racket wasn't something to do with the blue crystal that James had given him the night before. His heart sank as he heard the sobs coming from Wee Joe and Helen's room.

Downstairs, Bero began to stir. His wispy blond tail was beginning to thump on the floor as he came to.

Craig saw his mum stagger forward and let out a small gasp.

"You're remembering it too, Mum, aren't you?" asked Helen, wiping her eyes. "I can tell. So are we. The dragon and Denthan and Mendel…"

"What? No, no. Of course not…"

Craig could tell his mum was lying. *Had the crystal somehow allowed the rest of his family to remember their adventures in Denthan?*

"Eethan and the Yeltans and the snake men," Helen continued.

Wee Joe nodded.

"Mum?" Craig gulped as her eyes filled with tears.

"Craig, what…?"

He felt a sensation of relief. It was as if a huge weight had been lifted off his shoulders. "You do remember, Mum, don't you?"

His mum hugged Helen and Wee Joe as she looked up at him and then down at Bero. "Bero…?" She pointed at the young dog as if she had seen a ghost. "Bero…our Bero fell into the…"

"Yeah, he did. But then Mendel or Eethan or…" It was going to be too difficult to explain. "It's just him, Mum." Unable to remember a thing about Bero's fall in Denthan before this moment, his family had taken in the Golden Retriever pup, thinking their own, much older dog, Bero, had run away. They'd called the new dog Bero too, to save any upset for the little ones and to keep some continuity. Only James, Father Michael, Ephie, and himself had known that they were one in the same dog. Despite being able to share some of the most incredible adventures with his family for the first time, part of him became very annoyed at James for entrusting him with the crystal from the underwater village. He just knew that this mass revelation had been caused, in some way, by the crystal he'd hidden in the kids' cupboard. "I don't think Mendel knows that I have the crystal," he blurted.

"The wizard. The goldfish…" his mum mouthed, before screaming, "WHAT CRYSTAL?" She scanned the room then turned to face him. "Please tell me I'm still sleeping." She stood up and whisked the curtains open.

"It's morning, Mum," said Craig, sheepishly.

She opened the window and let the cold morning breeze waft into the room. Specks of rain floated over their faces.

Craig could see the still waters of Loch Echty in the distance. Apart from a few clouds, it looked as if it was going to be another beautiful summer's day.

His mum clipped the window shut again. She turned to face Craig. "You've always known, haven't you? Why didn't...? You kept it secret for a year?"

"Mendel thought it would be less complicated if you didn't remember about Denthan." Craig watched as Bero sniffed at the bottom of the cupboard door. He yelped and wagged his tail.

"I think Bero remembers too," said Helen. Bero turned and licked the dried-in tearstains from her cheeks.

Jean straightened. "Let's get round to the Pecks' house right now. I need to tell Cathy and David before anything else happens."

"NO!" Craig's eyes widened. "Don't you remember how Mrs. Peck was in Denthan?"

"Yes. But I also remember that every one of us played our part, including her," said Jean.

"Incwuding me too, Mum!" added Wee Joe.

"Especially you, Joe," said Jean, pulling him closer.

There was another blast of light from under the cupboard door.

"Mum, James asked me to look after one of those blue crystals. It's in the cupboard. I didn't know where else to put it." Craig pointed to the cupboard door just as it sprung open.

They all winced.

Inside, the translucent shard of blue rock lay on the floor beside Bero's lead. The strange light faded.

"We're going up to the Pecks' right now, like it or not." As she walked out of the room, she yelled over her shoulder. "Get that thing wrapped up and get dressed. All of you!"

Craig's heart sank at the thought of the inevitable meeting with the Pecks. He wished Mendel could do another spell. Perhaps he could. That was his only chance. He had to get to Mendel and James before his mum could spill the beans to the Pecks.

As they left the house, The Beeches housing estate was totally deserted. Bero walked ahead, seemingly uninterested in making a bid for freedom. In fact, he was much more like the old dog that Craig had known and loved so much.

"Why did the crystal glow all blue like that?" Helen asked Craig.

"I don't know, but I shouldn't think it was a very good sign," Craig replied.

"Which is why I'm very annoyed with you, Craig." Jean was struggling to get Wee Joe to keep up. "Oh, come on Joe. Please?"

Craig didn't know whether to tell her about the giant flying Centides or the pods. *No point if Mendel clears their memories,* he decided.

Skirting the road-works, they walked past the old, green-painted village hall and up the lane towards Willow Crescent. Just as they caught sight of the Peck's house, however, Wee Joe stopped dead and waved his finger at the sky. "Wook!"

In the distance, Craig saw what looked like a flock of geese coming down the Loch but they all knew, even Wee Joe, that something wasn't right. The distant cries, which were fairly un-goose-like, echoed over the village.

Jean picked up Wee Joe and ran. "All of you! Hurry!"

They were only yards from the Fyffe's battered Mondeo when the strange flock of creatures veered towards them. Their eerie cries grew louder.

To his horror, Craig saw that they looked like the insects they'd seen the day before. "Faster!" he shouted.

They crossed the garden and his mum battered on the Pecks' front door as loud as she could. Craig wasn't sure which would be more scary, the giant bugs, or Cathy Peck being wakened at ten past six in the morning. With every knock the racket in the skies over Drumfintley grew louder and louder. The constant humming sound was mixed with a clacking and rasping noise that grated on Craig's brain. It had completely shattered the peace of the early morning. There weren't even any cars on the bypass to mask the din.

The Pecks' door creaked open. "Jean?"

It was David Peck. His mum pushed past and dragged her children inside the house.

Cathy Peck's voice sounded down the stairs: "David? David? What idiot's knocking the door at this time of the bloody night?"

James's dad had already stepped outside to see what was causing the racket.

His eyes widened when he saw the Harrisons. One second later, his mum pulled on Mr. Peck's pyjama sleeve, tugging him back into his own house.

Craig slammed the door shut.

"But…" James's dad was utterly confounded.

* * *

A thumping on the stairs caused James to rub his eyes and look at his alarm clock. His bedroom door burst open.

"Catch, numpty!" Craig threw a heavy object onto his sleeping bag. "Where's that fish?"

James tried to focus. "What the heck are you doing!"

"Boys, what's going on?" As Mendel's voice filled their heads, Jean, Helen, Wee Joe and his dad all bundled into the small box-room behind Bero and Craig. Everyone, apart from his dad, had fixed his or her eyes upon the glass goldfish bowl.

"James! What have you done?" Full volume was instant as Cathy Peck, wrapped in a pink bath towel, stormed into the crammed box room.

James was already convinced that this was going to be the worst day of his life.

"Where is it? Who has the crystal?" said Mendel, in an accusatory tone.

Everyone stopped what they were thinking or doing and turned to face the goldfish bowl.

Mendel squashed himself against the glass and made sure that they could all hear his words, even David and Cathy Peck. "I said…"

Meekly, James pointed to the package that lay on top of his sleeping bag. He glanced at Craig. "It's in there, isn't it?"

Craig stepped forward and swished open the curtains. "Yes, but look outside!" He pointed out of the window.

"James, for the sake of all our survival, I'm going to let your mum and dad remember exactly what happened last summer," said Mendel.

James shut his eyes. "Wwdewwmemwwrabalww!"

His mum glanced about the spare room in an effort to see where the voice was coming from. "Who is that talking and…oh…" Cathy Peck's words were cut short by an audible gasp as Mendel tapped on the glass of his bowl. "Explanations can wait. James, give me the crystal you stole from Ethrita."

James began to wheeze. He reached for his inhaler then emptied the blue shard from its wrapping.

"What is that doing here?" The tone of his mum's voice softened.

"Again, explanations can wait," said Mendel. "Please put the crystal on the floor and point the narrow end towards Ben Larvach!"

His dad gripped his shoulder. "Son, don't touch that thing!"

"It's okay, Dad." James knelt down and turned the blue crystal until it pointed north by northeast. James's head pounded and then, with a final piercing jab, he said, "Wwwstowwnriwwghtww!" James blurted out the words in his characteristic fishy way that sounded as if he were talking while pinging his lips with a forefinger.

His dad emitted a nervous chuckle.

Craig grabbed James's arm and hauled him over to the window. "Look what your crystal's done now."

At least a hundred creatures, not unlike the flying Centides they'd seen the day before, stopped in mid flight. They went into spasms, their huge wings twitching uselessly, as they fell from the sky into Loch Echty.

Open-mouthed, James watched them splash into the Loch one by one. The leading creature, however, plummeted down in the region of St. Donan's Rectory.

"Did you see that?" said Craig. "It fell onto the Rectory."

"Yeah…" James screwed his eyes up in an effort to home in on the Rectory.

"James, I will not ask why you took the crystal from Fintley, needless to say; it was not a clever thing to do." Mendel's voice sounded a little weaker.

"Em, I… I'm sorry," said James, flushing crimson. He reached over for his green rucksack and pulled out the brandy barrel that had once carried Mendel through the chaotic world of Denthan.

"Put me back in," said Mendel. "We need to go on another journey right now."

"And who exactly do you mean by we?" snapped Cathy.

"Well, obviously I need James, Craig and…"

"Just stop right there!" Cathy moved over to James who was busy tipping Mendel back into his barrel. She gripped his elbow. "There's no way you are going anywhere this time." She turned to her husband for reassurance. "Tell him, David!"

David Peck, however, was completely at a loss for words. He didn't seem really sure who Cathy was talking to, nor certain, for that matter, of what he'd just seen. He poked a finger into his mouth. "I can taste sunflower seeds."

Cathy Peck looked disdainfully at her husband and mouthed the word: *pathetic.*

Helen tugged on her mother's dress.

Jean Harrison cuddled her in and sighed.

"See, Mendel! No-one wants to go. So why don't you just swim away, or should I just flush you down the toilet?" Cathy's lips twisted into a wicked smile.

"What about de big flappy bug fing dat dropped down out de sky den?" interrupted Wee Joe.

"At last, someone with a little sense," said Mendel.

James saw that his mum was now glowering at Wee Joe.

Mendel flicked his tail and plopped into the brandy barrel. "Whether you all like it or not," he continued, "you have a situation here in Drumfintley which can only be resolved by travelling through the gateway on Bruce Moor."

"What gateway on Bruce Moor?" David Peck stared round the room, waiting for a reply.

James screwed the lid tight on the brandy barrel. "The Jesus Rocks, Dad. We went through the last time to look for you."

"Not all of us went through that stone circle voluntarily," snapped Cathy.

His dad began to stammer. "I'm s-s-sorry. I don't follow. Where's that voice coming from?"

"Did you all see the creatures over Loch Echty just a few seconds ago?" Mendel eyed them through the little window in the barrel. "Well?"

"Yes, but..." said Jean, desperate to break the silence.

"Well, those creatures and much worse, I can assure you, will continue to appear in Drumfintley unless we act now. They come from a world called Artilis"

Some looked more confused than others, but James knew everyone had seen the flying creatures over Loch Echty, and none of them could disagree with the wizard-fish as they didn't have all the facts at hand. They were, it seemed, yet again, dependent upon Mendel's superior knowledge.

His dad suddenly pointed down at Mendel whose big, orange eyes were clearly visible through the window of the barrel.

His mum caught his dad's arm. "Yes, that's right, dummy. The fish is actually a wizard and he's talking to us."

"She's right, Mr. Peck," said Craig. "Not about the 'dummy' bit," he added, flushing scarlet.

Mendel squinted up at James. "James, I'd like to go down to the Rectory. I want to see what we are dealing with."

Jean stood up and gathered in her children. "And we need to check that no-one was hurt."

"That too," said Mendel.

"Are you all completely off your heads? I take it we all remember what happened the last time we went through that…" Cathy struggled.

"Gateway?" said Craig.

"Stone circle." Cathy corrected. "We were nearly all killed." She rounded on Jean. "Are you seriously considering taking your young kids through that stone circle again to face God knows what?"

"I'm not sure Cathy, but I don't think flushing Mendel down the toilet will exactly solve much either." Nervously, Jean checked the sky-line again.

"Quite!" agreed Mendel, sounding relieved to be safely back in his barrel.

James couldn't believe how stupid he had been for not telling Mendel about the Fintley crystal. Why had he picked it up from the floor of Loch Echty?

Craig proceeded to fasten the tatty Swiss brandy barrel round Bero's neck.

Mendel circled his familiar home. "If we all just try to calm down, we can go down to St. Donan's Rectory and sort things out there. We can decide who needs to come and who doesn't, etcetera…"

James looked on as his best friend, Craig, received a long, loving hug from Mrs. Harrison. Craig's mum seemed to be the complete opposite of his own. His own mum usually pushed him away if he tried to hug her. So, with a sigh and a slight pang of jealousy, he picked the green rucksack off his bed and moved across to the door. He saw his dad place a hand on his mum's shoulder, gently, as if trying to cajole her in some way. Typically, she flicked it off. James wavered at the bedroom door, expectant. "Mum?"

"Let's go and see what the damage is then," she mumbled, reluctantly.

"Okay Mum," he said, still feeling sorry for his dad. He hated it when his mum embarrassed his dad in front of people. He tried to sound cheery. He was determined to seem unaffected by the strange situation or the fear rising in his chest.

CHAPTER SEVEN

ETHRITA'S DEMISE

Having chatted with MacNulty well into the early hours, Father Michael and Ephie were in a deep sleep when their roof collapsed. Timber, plaster and broken slates showered down into their bedroom causing them to sit bolt upright, their backs squished against the headboard. Still unsure whether he was really awake, Michael reached over and found the bedside light. As he switched it on, however, something heavy and hairy smashed down into their wardrobe.

"For the love of …" he whimpered. "Ephie! Ephie, are you okay?"

Whatever it was that had crashed into their room had left a hole in their roof. A beam of sunlight cut across the end of their bed, making it difficult to see. Dust hung in the air like a curtain.

Ephie gripped his arm. "I'm fine. Are you okay?"

"Yes…" Michael flexed his arms free of her painful grip and wiggled his toes just to make sure, "I think."

Amazingly, their bed stood in the middle of the carnage, relatively undamaged. Michael looked over the edge of the mattress and shrieked. Their floor was pitted with holes that revealed the living room below.

Ephie shifted away from a slate that had pierced the mattress, inches from her head.

Still fighting the notion that this was some kind of dreadful dream, Michael heard something flap and shift inside what remained of his wardrobe. He found Ephie's hand and gave it a little squeeze.

"Father Michael, Ephie. Keep quite still." Mendel's voice filled their heads.

"Mendel?" shrieked Ephie.

The wardrobe moved again before a buzzing sound interspersed with a series of clicks and knocks filled what was left of the room.

Mendel continued, "Tell me what you can see."

Ephie spoke first. "Something big has fallen inside our wardrobe. It sounds like a bee or..."

The wardrobe door toppled off its hinges and crashed onto the floor.

Michael pulled the duvet tight round his throat. "I can see it. It looks like a giant fly, or wasp."

"It has wing covers. Bits that hang down over its shoulders," added Ephie.

Michael could see what Ephie meant. The creature had the appearance of an insect, but it stood up on two legs like a human. Its mandibles clicked together as a hairy front leg combed its antennae. Every few seconds a pair of gossamer wings vibrated behind its back.

Mendel's voice tailed off to a whisper. "Are its antennae red or black?"

Michael was becoming impatient. "Mendel, what difference does that make? Just get us out of here."

"Red, they're red!" exclaimed Ephie.

The creature turned its huge, brown, bubble eyes on Ephie and began to walk towards her. About three feet high, it had the hunched stance of an old man and the smell... The smell that filled the room was sweet, like nail varnish remover. The creature staggered over the rubble as it advanced.

"The red antennae means that this Artilian wasp is male," said Mendel.

Ephie fingered the piece of slate embedded in her mattress. "Don't tell me. Red antennas mean we're in trouble?"

Mendel tensed. "Not exactly. The males are more aggressive and have enough venom in one sting to kill a blue whale, but they can communicate. They can sometimes be reasoned with."

* * *

Outside, Cathy Peck moved forward, towards the Rectory front door. "I hate the word 'sometimes'. Too wishy-washy. Just kill it."

"Mum?" James protested. He watched as she ran towards the Rectory. His head began to pound.

"Wwwrainwwwfastwww," he blurted.

With a long peal of thunder, the clear morning-blue sky flipped to an ominous muddy brown. A gust of cold wind made the crowd on the lawn wince, but his mum was already inside.

James ran in after her.

Through a frenzied buzzing sound, James heard Ephie scream. He clattered onto the top landing and skidded to a halt. His mum had edged round the back of a large insect that stood on two legs, like a man. It hadn't noticed her as it was too busy snapping, viciously, at Michael and Ephie. He waved to his mum and tried to mouth the word: *stop*, but it was too late. His mum had pounced on the creature from behind and, with a sharp twist of its head, she detached it from the hideous body. Its wing covers stopped twitching and, with a final buzz, it fell, clumsily, over the rubble that covered Father Michael's bedroom floor.

Holding the dripping insect head by a red antenna, Cathy assumed a self-satisfied look that gave him a chill.

Heavy droplets of rain pattered down through the gaps in the roof as Father Michael and Ephie scrambled free of their bed covers and followed Cathy down the stairs.

"Well done, Mum," said James.

"Hmm."

She'd never been good at receiving compliments and, once back outside, James flinched when his mum threw the gory head at his dad's feet.

"If you were half a man you would have sorted this out instead of leaving it to me. But then, it's always me who's left to sort out any kind of mess; isn't that right, David?"

"Well, I don't..."

"Exactly," blazed Cathy. "You don't. You're just flat line twenty-four-seven."

James sighed again and tried his best to avoid everyone's pitying gaze.

Mendel's voice cut through the tension. "Cathy; I wish you would consult me a little more before performing your heroics!"

"Shouldn't that be heroine-oics?" said Craig, annoyingly.

If a fish could have given a dirty look, it would be the look Mendel would have thrown Craig at that very moment. Instead, Mendel pressed on. "I set the rainstorm in motion for a reason, Cathy."

Nonplussed, Cathy sniffed.

"The male Artilian wasp is rendered harmless by water as they never leave the desert regions. They become confused and unable to sting if wet."

James heard Mendel splashing about.

"Artilian wasps can communicate. They are very intelligent."

They all stared down at the dismembered head. Rain was splashing off of its big, shiny compound eyes.

Jean huddled into the children. "Mendel, can't we finish this conversation inside? We're all getting soaked through."

"Wwwstormwwwstopwww!"

The instant the words left James's mouth, the rain stopped, the clouds parted, and the morning sun cut through. Loch Echty was transformed into a million golden highlights as a breeze played with its surface.

For the second time that day, Mendel's magic had been so quickly performed that James had no time to prepare himself for the sensation.

"I need to see if there's still time," said Mendel. "Bero, walk over to the wasp's head."

Obligingly, Bero strolled over to the gruesome lump on the grass, his panting interspersed with deep-set growls. James could actually feel Mendel delving deep into the thoughts of the wasp. There was still a glimmer of memory left. "Ahh... It's gone."

"What's gone?" enquired James.

"The last thoughts of this poor wretch," replied Mendel. "But I think I retrieved enough to put us on the right track. As I suspected," he continued, "the wasp had a memory trace of a place I've visited before. It came through a gateway, in Artilis, near the city of Martilia. *Hymenoptera envigouralis* are mainly a desert dwelling species, as are the flying Centides you met earlier."

"Excuse me, have we missed something?" interrupted Cathy.

"Mum, let Mendel explain."

Cathy gave him a particularly nasty death-stare.

"There seems to be someone in Martilia who has connected with the Fintley crystal and, as I suspected, they're testing our resolve. I suppose my solo attempt at magic may have caused the gateway in Loch Echty to become functional again. I suppose..."

"Numpty," whispered Craig, under his breath. He glanced down at the brandy barrel that contained Mendel and shook his head disparagingly.

Mendel bristled. "Yes, well unfortunately for us I couldn't identify the person on Artilis who sent these creatures here. The wasp's memory traces only last a few minutes after its head becomes separated from its body."

Everyone now turned to Cathy and frowned.

"Oh, get lost!" She rounded on Ephie. "I just saved your life, despite what the smelly, old kipper says."

"Mum, please!"

Craig tapped him on the shoulder. "Tell the kipper that someone's coming."

James was thankful for the distraction. "It's MacNulty."

Mendel cut in so everyone could hear him, "Cathy, don't worry about MacNulty, his family has a connection with the gateways in Drumfintley. Also, I have already decided that we should split into two groups. One party needs to remain here and help deal with any uninvited visitors while the other group goes through the Jesus Rocks Gateway in order to destroy the Artilian portal once and for all."

Cathy Peck shook the rain out of her long, black hair and moved forward. "And when this Artilian portal is destroyed, how exactly does the away team get home again?"

Mendel spoke softy, "I will think on that matter soon."

"Not good enough!" Cathy barked.

James had a count up. There was Jean, Helen, Wee Joe, Craig, and a confused looking MacNulty; all standing next to Bero. Then there was his dad, his mum, Ephie and Father Michael. Twelve, if he included himself, Bero, and Mendel. Someone was missing... "Patch?"

"Oh my God; where's Patch?" said Ephie, staring at Michael.

"Patch! Patch!" Michael shouted back into the Rectory.

A whimpering sound, very close by, echoed out over the lawn. "She's here. I found her up in the woodschh. Terrified out of her mindschh." The toothless MacNulty produced the little Jack Russell pup from his manky overcoat, her needle-sharp teeth nipped at his fingers as he placed her on the grass. "I put er in mi ferret pocket, chh.."

"Oh, thank you, Archie. We've had a bit of trouble with the Rectory roof," said Michael.

"Schho I Scchhee!" said Archie, his gaze firmly fixed on the giant wasp head.

His dad moved closer to Archie MacNulty. "Yes, I seem to have missed quite a lot here myself. I mean, what is that, exactly?" He pointed down at the Artilian Wasp. But, just as he did, it shimmered silver then blue and disappeared.

They all stepped back.

"See, that's exactly the kind of thing I'm talking about," said David.

His mum poked his dad in the arm. "Don't worry, whatever goes on from this point will be a lot more interesting than Mallorca."

"I'm sure," replied David.

James saw his mum's face lighten. It was then that he tried to convince himself that she loved his dad, deep down, in her own funny way.

"Listen." Mendel's dismembered voice filled their heads. "Cathy, James, Craig, Bero, and myself will go through the Jesus Rocks Gateway. While David…"

His dad let his eyes wander for a moment before they settled on the Swiss brandy barrel he'd brought back from a training course in Zurich.

"David, I know this is all very strange for you just now but I need you, Michael, Ephie, and MacNulty to stand guard here. Craig, James? One of you has the Fintley crystal."

"I had the sense to bring it." Craig slipped the shard of crystal from his jacket pocket.

James spoke up, "I should have told you, Mendel but…"

"But you didn't," Mendel scolded. "And it's too late now. The crystal is the reason that everyone who went to Denthan now remembers their adventure, and the crystal, now removed from its resting place, may have disturbed other checks and balances in the area."

James whispered, "Sorry, but…"

"Never follow the word 'sorry' with the word 'but'. What have I told you?" spat his mum.

"They cancel each other out, Mum. I know."

"Very true, Cathy," said Mendel.

His dad gave him a consolatory pat on the shoulder. "What did the goldfish mean when he said that the crystal *may have disturbed other checks and balances in the area*?" Just as his dad's question drifted across the soaking wet lawn, however, a thrashing sound echoed up from the Loch. The Rectory lawn was only separated from the shore by a small, rusting fence covered in chicken wire, so they all clambered out of the Rectory garden onto the damp sand.

James recognized the huge, sail-like fin as it burst through the surface of the Loch. It was Ethrita, and she was in trouble. Her monstrous form flapped and writhed as she tried to pull herself free of the water. He edged back from the beach when she leapt right out of the Loch, her huge, iridescent wings flaying desperately. Something big had a hold of her. It pulled her down every time she broke free of the surface.

Ethrita screamed. It was an unearthly scream that froze everyone to the spot. The note she produced in her agony resonated off the brass bell in St. Donan's church tower. It hummed and vibrated in sympathy, causing the whole area to shake, blasted by a drone that seemed to sound the end of the world.

"Ethrita!" shouted Mendel.

James could tell that Mendel was at a loss. The knocking sensation built then died again. Mendel didn't know what to do. Ethrita lashed this way and that on the surface of the Loch. Then, with a deafening roar and a brief glimpse of some kind of claw or pincer, Ethrita, the wonderful creature he'd marveled at the day before, stopped thrashing. She lay completely still. Spread over the water like an outstretched angel there was a moment of stillness before she was roughly tugged down from below. Ethrita disappeared beneath the cold, black water.

As the commotion came to an end on the Loch, the great drone of the church bell was gradually replaced by Craig's scream. The crystal he held in his hands glowed white-hot. In panic, he struggled to throw it away. James saw the pain register on Craig's face then watched in disbelief as his best friend disappeared. Before James could say a thing, there was rush of bubbles and splash only yards away from the water's edge. Ethrita's mangled body bobbed up to the surface again. Motionless on the Loch, her beautiful wings were ripped to shreds. A thousand floating coloured scales began to lap against the shore.

His dad had dug his nails into James's arm. "What the...?"

But before he could finish, there was another growl from beneath the waves and Ethrita's immense carcass was sucked down into the blackness for the last time.

James had sensed the presence of something very evil. He felt helpless as he looked at the spot where Craig had stood a few seconds before. The crystal had taken his best friend.

Amongst the onlookers, Bero's fur stood on end as he sniffed the spot where Craig had disappeared. Tears streamed down Ephie's face.

James remembered MacNulty disappearing during the disturbance. He was now racing back across the Rectory lawn with his shotgun.

It won't be long before the rest of the village arrives, thought James. *No-one could have slept through the screams of Ethrita or the deafening peal of the church bell.*

"James, only you can hear me. We're in serious trouble." It was Mendel.

"Tell me that Craig's okay." He said it into himself but knew Mendel would hear him.

"Craig has been taken," said Mendel, somewhat hesitantly.

"Taken where?" This time the words slipped out. The trouble with talking to Mendel when no-one else could hear the wizard apart from him was that his answers were usually audible to everyone else around him and were often taken for crazy babblings.

Michael viewed him with suspicion. *Had anyone else realised Craig was gone?*

James bit his lip and turned away, still scanning the garden for any sign of his best friend.

Mendel's words continued in James's head, "There is only one creature I know of that is capable of using a crystal from another world in such a way but..."

James knelt down and stroked Bero's fur. "But he died on Denthan, didn't he?" said James, his heart as heavy as a lump of lead.

* * *

Far away in the Artilian city of Martilia, a tall figure clutched a gnarled staff with a badly burned, reptilian hand.

CHAPTER EIGHT

THE GATE TO ARTILIS

Completely distraught about the disappearance of her son, and failing to get any real reassurance from Mendel or James, Jean announced that she was going to the police.

Ephie tried to reason with her. "But what good will that do, Jean? You can't exactly tell them what happened and—"

"And I have to do something!" she snapped, trailing her two remaining children in the direction of the Drumfintley police station.

* * *

Sergeant Carr was in his usual position, slouched behind the front desk flicking through the Drumfintley Herald using a tea-stained biro. He mumbled to himself as various articles and snippets of gossip came into view, eventually settling on an article by David Peck. Jean saw David's picture. She'd already read his article, *Keeping your Hamster Happy.*

"Eh hum!"

"Ah, Mrs. Harrison." The sergeant's voice was deep and gravelly.

Jean held onto Wee Joe's hand as she ushered Helen into the station.

"Mum," Wee Joe complained. "De policeman's not going to find Craig anywhere. He's gone. Magicked away by the crystal thing."

Sergeant Carr stared down suspiciously at Wee Joe. Jean knew that Carr had shouldered some of the blame for failing to get to the bottom of the disappearances on Bruce moor the year before. The whole village, however, knew that Carr was still convinced that Archie MacNulty had something to do with it. There was a lot of bad blood there.

"Magicked away, sonny? What do you mean, exactly?" He looked to Jean for some kind of explanation and gave a yellow-toothed grin.

Wee Joe continued, "There were flying buggy things and monsters in di Loch and..."

"And that's enough, Joe." Jean tried to compose herself. "I think my son, Craig, may have wandered off." Tears welled up in her eyes.

"Now, now..." Sergeant Carr opened the hatch in the front desk and patted Jean on the arm. He drew a chair from the poster-clad wall. "Sit down. Just start from the beginning, Mrs. Harrison."

"Craig didn't wander off, Mum; Wee Joe's right, he just disappeared. I saw it too," said Helen.

Carr screwed up his big face in disbelief and reached back for his tea. "When did you last see your son, Mrs. Harrison?"

"About thirty minutes ago. At St. Donan's. Next to the lake."

"You mean the Loch." Carr adopted a patronizing tone.

"Yes, of course..." said Jean, already realising she'd made a mistake in coming here.

"Well, for goodness sake. Thirty minutes is nothing. Admittedly, it's early in the day," Carr glanced at the station clock, which read: 7.45., "but I'm sure he'll turn up later this morning."

"No he won't," interrupted Helen.

Carr glanced down at her, his big, rubbery lips hovering over his mug of tea. "So who was all there beside the Loch?"

"Well, there was Father Michael, of course, Ephie, David Peck..."

Carr raised an eyebrow.

Jean continued, "Cathy Peck, James, Archie MacNulty..."

Sergeant Carr burnt his lip and spilled a portion of the tea down his uniform. "There's your man!" Carr wiped himself down with a Missing Dog poster and then ushered them out of the station. "I'll have to lock up. Constable Watt won't be in until nine." He pulled on his coat. "I'll go and see what MacNulty's got to say for himself. You, Mrs. Harrison, would be better off waiting at your house."

Jean felt really stupid now and she wished she'd taken Ephie's advice. She would go back and find Mendel. She realised now that the wizard-goldfish was her only hope.

* * *

Back at number Forty-Five Willow Terrace, James felt uneasy. They'd doubled back to the house for provisions, though James couldn't see what they could do now. Mendel came into view as he floated nearer to his plastic window. "Craig has been taken through the gateway. We have no crystal and…"

"And there's something very big and nasty in Loch Echty," finished James.

"That too." Mendel sounded worried. "We will have to contact Eethan."

"Eethan?"

"Yes; and I've changed my mind about a mass entourage."

His mum banged about in the kitchen drawers. "James, have you seen the torch?"

"No, Mum."

Mendel's voice cut through the din. "I think we should go alone."

James liked the idea of escaping the chaos of Forty-Five Willow Terrace, but had some reservations. "Yes, but I'm scared."

"About Artilis?" asked Mendel.

"No, about coming back and explaining to Mum."

"Ah… Quite." Mendel nibbled on a flake of red fish food.

As quietly as he could, James slung the green rucksack over his shoulder, lifted Bero's lead from the banister, and edged towards the front door. They stepped out into the morning sunshine and made for the underpass. The rest of the band were to meet at James's house in less than ten minutes and he'd just seen Craig's mum in the distance, coming towards Willow Terrace with Wee Joe and Helen. *Probably got short shrift at the police station,* he thought.

Geeing Bero on a bit faster, they soon passed through the corrugated tunnel and up onto the farm track that led to Tank Woods. James looked down at the Loch. He picked out the spot where Ethrita had fought her last battle and imagined he could hear the Fintley Bell. In his mind's eye, he could still see her huge multi-coloured wings as she moved gracefully through the depths towards Fintley and its eerie graveyard. James looked up. A few clouds dusted the peak of Ben Larvach, to the north. *It's going to rain.*

* * *

Having seen the spot where the Harrison boy allegedly disappeared, Sergeant Carr quickened his pace. He'd just caught sight of his main suspect and arch-enemy, Archie MacNulty, making for the old poacher's path that led up to Tank Woods. It eventually petered out at the edge of the Jesus Rocks on Bruce Moor. He would follow him all the way up the hill if he had to.

Unfit from years perched behind the station desk, he struggled on-wards uttering an indiscernible mixture of pants and rants. *Even if he doesn't lead me to the Harrison boy, he might reveal one of his poaching stores,* he thought. Carr cracked his shin on an old, discarded paint tin and tumbled into the long grass.

"Bloody fly tipping," seethed Carr, brushing mud from his trousers.

* * *

At the entrance to the underpass, Cathy Peck spied Mrs. Galdinie outside her sweet shop. She shook her head in disgust as she watched Ephie, Galdinie's one-time best customer break off from the group and make for the flaking shop door. Still mopping up the mess from the day before, Mrs. Galdinie sniffed when Ephie Blake approached. It was still only just after eight in the morning.

"For goodness sakes," she hissed, backing into the half-opened shop door. "Well, whata do *you* waant?"

Ephie hesitated. "Eh, I know it's early…"

"So do I. Very early, eh?" snapped Mrs. Galdinie. "I'ma no even dressed."

"I've got ten pounds," whispered Ephie.

Cathy let the rest of the group wander on so she could listen.

"So?" snapped Mrs. Galdinie.

"Can I buy some tablet?"

"At eight in de morning? Are you crazy?"

The word 'crazy' ricocheted up the underpass.

Everyone skidded to a halt.

A scraggy-looking cat stretched, jumped down from a windowsill and purred.

"Just getting some snacks for the kids." Ephie's face shone pink.

"Yeah, right," interrupted Cathy.

Mrs. Galdinie skulked off into her shop before re-emerging with a box of carefully wrapped tablet. She snaffled Ephie's money.

Already slavering, Helen and Wee Joe moved in on Ephie as she re-joined the group.

"What happened to your diet then, Ephie?" gibed Cathy.

David Peck fidgeted. "Shh, dear. You don't have to—"

"Don't you shush me! We wouldn't be climbing up here in the first place if you'd kept a proper eye on James. He's your son too, you know." Cathy gave her husband a dig in the ribs before rounding on Ephie once more. "I thought you'd found the cure?" She nodded in the direction of Father Michael, who'd become tangled in Patch's lead. "You know…to your sugar addiction."

"Get lost, Cathy." Ephie fumed as she pushed past.

The noise of cars, zooming above their heads, followed them all the way through the underpass and up the hill a little until it was eventually replaced by the calls of curlews and skylarks. There was some warmth in the air now and the kids were busy munching on Galdinie's tablet.

"First Craig, now James and Bero," said Father Michael. "I only hope they're safe."

"Are you kidding," snapped Cathy. "They've got the kipper taking them to God knows where chasing God knows what."

"Cathy," replied Michael, calmly. "God will certainly know where and what. There's no need to…"

"Oh, I know." Deep inside Cathy's soul, there was still the slightest smidgen of respect for a man of the cloth, not much, but enough to cause her to pause every now and then. "We just don't need all *this* again, though, do we?"

"Awch!" Father Michael yelled out as Patch yanked free of his grip. She'd spotted a brown hare and was already a good hundred yards away. "Patch! Come."

"Patch!" Ephie called down the hill after her too, but she was almost at the underpass. "We'd better go back and get her."

Jean shielded her eyes form the sun and tried to pick out the little dog in the distance. "I'm sure she'll go back to the Rectory. Bero always gets himself home eventually."

"Well, I think I should go back after her," said Ephie.

Cathy bristled. "Oh, so you think your dog's more important than our children?"

Jean gave Cathy an anguished stare that said: 'don't start.'

"No, I never said that. I simply said…" Ephie stumbled over her words.

"You may as well have," said Cathy, slyly.

"Now, Patch will be fine, Ephie," said Father Michael. "Let's push on."

"But…" objected Ephie.

Cathy's lips twisted into a triumphant sneer. "That's decided then."

* * *

A molehill had distracted Bero as James stepped out onto the springy heather. He felt relieved to be out of the closely packed Larch trees that formed Tank Woods. Mainly because he could still recall the bites and nips of the vicious Denthan Zental Moths that had attacked him and Craig the last time they'd come this way. James saw the brandy barrel swinging beneath Bero's neck as the dog snuffled round the loose soil. He was just about to ask Mendel where he thought Craig might be when there was a shout.

"James!"

He spun round and noticed Archie MacNulty, about a hundred yards behind him, striding through the heather. There was a patch of high bracken behind MacNulty and James couldn't see if there was anyone else with him.

"We've got company, Mendel."

James guessed that Mendel already knew it was MacNulty and he wondered if the wizard would invite the old gardener along with them rather than becoming delayed in argument.

"Good idea," whispered Mendel, obviously reading his thoughts. "MacNulty and his family have a long standing connection with Bruce Moor. We'll wait for him in the middle of the stone circle."

"Are you sure MacNulty knows as much about all this as you think?" asked James.

Mendel, however, was already deep in thought, preparing his spell.

Someone else appeared from the tall bracken next to Tank Woods. "Mendel…"

"Shhh! I need to think, James."

"But…" James wondered what Mendel was up to. He knew they didn't have another crystal to operate the gateway. "It's Sergeant Carr," he murmured.

"Where?" said MacNulty, a worried look spreading over his ruddy face.

"Behind you," said James, glancing between the policeman and the brandy barrel. His head was pounding.

Mendel's magic spilled from James's lips and echoed out over the twisted stones. "Wwwsummonwwweethwwanwww!"

A blue glow emanated from the largest stone and soon spread round the whole circle until Bero, MacNulty and James became completely enveloped by the light.

James could just make out the figure of Sergeant Carr, covering his eyes as he edged closer. He felt the air grow heavy, a bit like it does before a thunderstorm. There was also a sweet scent that he knew but couldn't place.

MacNulty steadied himself on one of the stones as a warm wind hit their faces. Bero flattened his mismatched ears.

Sergeant Carr braced himself against the gust and tried his best to get nearer but, by now, it was as if a tornado had begun to spin around the circle. White sparks and yellow cinders circled MacNulty, James, and Bero.

A small, leathery hand touched James's arm.

"Ahh!" James screamed out.

"Eee my friendee, James. Eets just mee," said the voice.

The diminutive figure of Eethan Magichand stood amongst the magic that spun round the ancient stones. James beamed down at him.

Eethan's thick shock of white hair fluttered in the gale. He blinked his tiny black eyes and tittered. "Tee hee. Good to see you all. I seee Beero is all better and theet Mendel ees steel a little fishee."

The gale subsided.

It took James a few moments to get used to Eethan's strange, high-pitched voice.

Ignoring MacNulty and the mesmerized Sergeant Carr, Eethan continued, "What ees your problem theees time, my old friend?"

No more than three feet high, Eethan knelt down beside Bero and stretched a grey-blue hand towards the barrel. He tapped Mendel's window with his middle finger.

"I fear Dendralon is still alive," said Mendel.

"No ees dead. Wees saw heem fall." Eethan sounded worried.

The stones continued to shine brightly and James felt their heat on his face.

Sergeant Carr had wandered into the circle, behind MacNulty, in a kind of trance.

Mendel continued: "Take us to Artilis, Eethan. I'm sure he's there. And," Mendel paused. "He has young Craig."

"Hold tightee," said Eethan, touching the Jesus Rock with a slender blue finger while chanting the words, *"Ah Chee tee leet Artilis!"*

The circle hummed as the sparks spun faster; then, as before, the turf peeled back from the surface of the moor and they all stood, momentarily, on an oily sheet of glass. Suspended above a pitch-black void that seemed bottomless, James felt his chest tighten.

Sergeant Carr shook with fright, his fingers digging into the nearest lump of stone.

Eethan stamped his foot twice, tittering as a million cracks spiderwebbed across the surface. With a deafening bang, the glass film shattered and they all tumbled into the abyss. James, Bero, MacNulty, and Sergeant Carr toppled and turned over and over as the air rushed past their faces. Slowly, their senses closed down.

* * *

Cathy and David Peck had seen everything. "I remember this," said David. "This, that hole... Last year, the ground rolling back but then..."

"Never mind that now." Cathy Peck pulled him forward and shouted, "Run. Everyone run. Get into the circle!"

The rest of the group raced towards the stone circle on Bruce Moor.

They had emerged from Tank Woods just as Eethan appeared in the circle, and now they all bolted towards the black abyss where they'd seen James and Bero fall moments before. Cathy had seen two other figures, silhouetted by the blinding glow of the magic light, but she hadn't been able to tell who these other two were.

Ice gripped her heart, as she ran forward. Something drew her closer, lifted her from her feet, and sucked her into the abyss. She fell, along with everyone else who had been near to the edge, into the darkness. The dot of light above her disappeared as the turf raced back over the surface of the moor to replace itself.

CHAPTER NINE

THE SHADOW IN ARTILIS

Craig opened his eyes and instantly struggled for breath. He was soaked in sweat and his throat was completely parched. "Water. I need water," he gasped, kicking back from the warm rock, but he soon yelped and jerked to a halt. His leg was chained to the wall. As his eyes adjusted to the gloom, he focused on a rough hole that had been cut into the stone ceiling. Through this skylight an eerie pink light streamed in and covered a patch of ground in front of his feet. The rocks around him assumed a rosy hue and were studded with, what looked like, smooth, polished coal.

"It's jet, my friend. Jet," said a voice.

Craig sucked in a mouthful of foul air. "What...?"

A figure crouched in the shadows behind him. He couldn't make it out. Trying to steady himself, he broached, "Jet?"

"It's a mineral, found here, in Artilis. We use it for fuel in our combustion cells."

This was all gobbledygook to Craig, but he sensed that the creature talking to him was pleasant enough. As his eyes adjusted further and his breathing steadied, he realised that he was in some kind of prison cell. The last thing he remembered was being on the beach beside Loch Echty.

"They brought you here last night," said the voice.

"I..."

"And..." the creature moved out of the shadows. "You've been talking in your sleep."

Craig shrank back as he viewed the creature's unusual eyes. They sat on either side of its green-skinned face, which resembled a bald dog, or perhaps a turtle. Craig's main concern, however, were the long, curved, black teeth, that sparkled as the thing spoke.

"I need something to drink," said Craig. He couldn't bear the heat.

"You need to get back home, don't you?" the creature continued, winking a wrinkled purple eye.

"That would be very nice," said Craig, "if you could arrange it." He was beginning to become irritated by the ugly creature.

"Mendel and James will come for you and take you back to Drumfinti," said the creature.

"Drumfintley, actually," corrected Craig.

"Here." The creature offered Craig a cupped hand, of sorts, filled with water. He eyed the creature with mild suspicion before pulling its hand to his mouth. He drank deeply. The liquid was warm but still amazingly refreshing.

His eyes widened as he saw what the creature was doing. It offered him another cupped handful but it had taken the liquid from a downy slit on the side of its body.

Craig spat on the ground. "What have you given me?" He stared at the creature's second offering in disgust.

"We are ninety percent water. I store ten percent of my share in here." With that, the creature lifted up a flap of skin in its side to reveal an orifice that contained four hair-covered sacks.

"Yuck!" Craig spat again.

"It will sustain you for more than twelve hours; and it has many vitamins and minerals which will help you deal with the heat here." The creature laughed.

"Who are you, and where am I?" said Craig, already feeling a little more able to deal with the heat.

"I am Princess Elandria and this place... This is a holding area."

"Holding area...?" Craig noticed that Princess Elandria was now free of her chains. "How did you...?"

Elandria laughed again. "Escape? It was always an option. Recently, however, I've preferred the thought of death to living with my kind anymore."

With a pang of dread, Craig tugged on his chain. "Death?"

"Yes." She sighed. "We will be fed to the sandworms in about three hours."

"What the heck are sandworms?" Startled, Craig tried to wriggle his hand free of his manacle.

"About the length of your arm, Artilian Sandworms can devour a whole Artilian in about five minutes. It should take them less than that for a boy of your size. We shall only feel excruciating pain for about a minute, but it will be an honourable death."

Craig tugged on his chain once more. "Are you mad? Why do you want to die?"

Elandria moved closer. "My kind have sided with the wizard lord. I would rather die than side with that evil creature. Already, the whole world is flocking to his side like moths to the flame. He talks of conquering the Artilians and then of taking his followers back to the Earth world. He has tempted many races with stories of fresh air and endless wealth." Elandria swept her hairy arm over her head. "He has already used his dark magic to slaughter those who would oppose him."

Craig's mind was elsewhere. "I do *not* want to be eaten by sandworms!"

"You don't?" Elandria sounded surprised.

"No, I don't, funnily enough."

"I suppose we could escape."

"That's more like it." Craig jumped up. "What about the hole in the ceiling? Can we go that way?" He pointed up at the roof of the cell.

Elandria crept over to Craig and exposed her razor-sharp teeth.

"Wait!"

"Hold still, boy," she whispered.

"Don't kill me. I..." He braced as Elandria's teeth snapped shut. She jerked her strange head twice and Craig's chain fell, with a clatter, onto the stone floor.

He scampered back. Elandria was much bigger than he'd first imagined and, to his utter horror, he noticed another six legs. "You're... You're a..."

"A beautiful specimen. Don't you think?" She laughed and shot a line of silk up to the ceiling. With a swift leap, Elandria left the floor of the cell. She spun round above Craig's head. "Jump up and I will catch you."

Craig remembered being lifted off the ground by a similar set of legs in James's front garden. But those had belonged to a flying Centide. Elandria looked very similar from this angle. Thinking, once more, of the Artilian sandworms, Craig leapt up. He was immediately grasped by her legs and raised up from the floor of the dim cell.

Elandria rustled out of the skylight and then jerked Craig through behind her.

He landed, with a thud, onto hot, stinging sand. Once his eyes adjusted to the pink light, he saw an endless, rolling desert under a deep pastel-pink sky. There was no sign of any sun or moon. No clouds. In fact, it was a very even kind of light. From time to time, there was a distant crackling sound, like bacon sizzling in a pan.

"Well, Craig from Drumfintley; what do you want to do next?" said Elandria. "It's evident that you don't want to die an honourable death."

It was then that Craig chose to look behind him. Huge, smooth walls rose more than a hundred feet towards the strange sky. Darting over the parapets, he recognized the flying Centides, Artilian wasps, and a few other things he didn't like the look of. "You've still not told me where we are."

"Ah... We are on the outskirts of Martilia." She rose up high on her six legs and waved her arms towards the shining silver gates of the city. "Yes, that is Martilia and, no thanks to you, I've just missed a rendezvous with death."

Craig thought Elandria had a very strange outlook on life, but he couldn't help admire her beauty; not in a human sense, of course. Her bulbous body was covered in fine, green, velvety hairs that hinted purple in the cooling breeze. She definitely had the head of a reptile but the body of a spider, of sorts.

"Racnids. We are called Racnids, Craig of Drumfintley. Unfortunately, my kind have decided to side with the Inubians and the wizard Dra, against the Artilians. A race..." Elandria circled him. "...that is very similar to yours in appearance." She pointed a long, hairy leg at Craig's face and formed something that resembled a smile.

"Wait. Wait." Craig's head was spinning. "Who are the Artilians and..."

Suddenly uneasy, Elandria shuffled round a large dune, pulling Craig with her. "Out of sight; out of mind," she whispered.

"My mum says that," said Craig.

"Your mother? Does she now? Well, the saying is over one million years old."

"It is?"

"At least. So your mother; Jean, is very wise."

"How...?" Craig screwed his face up until his freckles formed a thick orange line on his forehead.

"Oh, you told me her name in your sleep."

"What else did I say?"

Elandria lowered her body down onto the sand and adopted a less threatening stance. She answered in a coy tone, "You said lots."

He gulped.

"The Artilians have been here almost as long as us. It is said that they arrived over thirty million years ago. They lived on the surface at first."

He looked around him in surprise. "Is this not the surface?"

"No. We are one thousand feet below, what is left of, the surface."

Craig stared up at the rose-coloured sky. "So what's that, then?"

"That is the firmament. The light emanates from a trillion billion luminescent bacteria set into the roof of a vast cavern. The races that remain on Artilis survive in a bubble, of sorts, beneath the surface. The crackling sound you hear, from time to time, is static electricity. We have spectacular static storms in the back season that recharge the bacteria and perpetuate our atmosphere. It's fascinating."

"You know, you sound just like someone else I know." He stared hard at the firmament. "I wonder where he is…"

Elandria interrupted Craig's thoughts. "Look, we better move now if you really want to avoid an honourable death. The sandworms are waiting."

She was beginning to sound like a sweet old lady.

"Jump on my back and tell me where you want to go. I can run fast on the dunes."

Excited, Craig leapt up onto her back. He loved riding horses and thought back to Denthan and his attempt at riding the Yukplugs, the hairy, two-legged yak-like creatures that belonged to the Yeltan root dwellers.

"Ah, well…" Craig scanned the horizon. "I don't really know." He gripped Elandria's downy body with his knees. "Where would be a safe place; away from… What did you call him?"

"I called him Dra, actually," said Elandria in a thin, wispy voice.

"Dra…" mused Craig, "it kind of rings a bell." He dug in his heels and spun Elandria round to a halt. "It reminds me of a wizard's name. Someone who nearly killed me once."

"And what was his name, child?"

"Dendralon." Craig felt silly. "I saw him die on… On another world."

"Really. So you think that Dra and this Dendralon are one and the same person?"

"I don't know."

"Mmm…" Elandria removed another of her water sacks and drank deeply. "If we go to Artilia your kind will try to kill me, so you will have to protect me."

"My kind?" said Craig.

"They look just like you." She began to move over the sand. "Then again, we could simply submit and receive an honourable death at their hands."

Craig shook his head. "What is it with you and this 'honourable death' thing?"

Elandria wheezed, and then hissed a little laugh. "Let's go."

Craig gripped Elandria's soft green hair as she gathered speed. Racing over the dunes, his blond hair swept back from his freckled face. He felt his exhilaration build as they gained speed and he smiled.

* * *

Mendel had remained conscious through the transference and had already stirred Bero to get a better idea of where they were.

Eethan too had remained conscious during the fall. "Wees ees definitely en de cite of Martilia. Look theer are ee twin statues of theere Ibis god."

They had appeared in an alleyway in the huge city of Martilia, but Mendel knew something wasn't right.

"Lookee Mendel," said Eethan. "No Artilians; only insectees and dog-men."

From the darkness of their vantage point they peered up at the seamless sky. Giant flying Centides and Artilian wasps buzzed overhead. Racnid guards patrolled the city walls and the jackal-headed Inubians snapped and snarled at each other in the busy streets. "No Artilians." Eethan placed his thumb in his left nostril and began to probe.

"Mmm," mused Mendel. "The Artilians would never back Dendralon, but the underlings and insects of Artilia are another matter."

Thumb still firmly planted in his nose, Eethan nodded.

"I fear Dendralon has somehow survived his fall in Denthan and come back to Artilis?"

"Ees not impossible," whispered Eethan. "But where are thee Artilians?"

* * *

James noticed the two men lying beside him. Sergeant Carr drooled and gibbered in his sleep, while MacNulty twitched and smiled. Still sleeping, MacNulty began to say something: "This is a bad place."

"Where is?" whispered James.

"Here," replied MacNulty.

"And where is here?" said James, his eyes gradually becoming accustomed to the strange pink light. He was in some kind of alley and it was roasting hot. "Are you awake, Mr. MacNulty?"

"James?" It was Mendel this time. He could just make out Bero at the end of the alley. "James, come here."

James glanced between MacNulty and Bero before pulling himself to his feet. He crept over to the entrance of the alley. "Wow. Flying Centides and…"

Eethan caught his arm before he stepped out into the pink light. "Careful, my friendee."

James tensed.

Mendel sloshed round in his barrel to face James. "The last time we were here, in Martilia, the humanoid Artilians held this city. Now the giant insects of Artilia, the jackal-faced Inubians and the Racnids, once the spider slaves of the Artilians, are in control. I'm sure now that Dendralon has survived. I can feel his presence. "

James's skin tingled. "But he died on… Okay, let's just say he is alive. Why then is he sending those things through to Drumfintley and why has he taken Craig?"

"I'm not certain. Perhaps…"

"It's you he's after, Mendel," said James. "It was always you. You are the only one who threatens him." James sounded weary. The process of travelling through gateways was draining. His anger subsided.

"You are probably right. I'm sorry," sighed Mendel.

James felt terrible. "No, I'm sorry."

There was an uncomfortable pause before Mendel spoke. "You know, the exact exit point, after transference, is extremely unpredictable. We've been fortunate to appear in a deserted alleyway and not a busy street."

"Yeah." James's mind drifted back to MacNulty. The old man had spooked him.

Sergeant Carr stirred behind him and immediately pounced on Archie MacNulty. "Got you this time, you old thief."

MacNulty spluttered as he woke and took a swing at Sergeant Carr.

"MacNulty, stop it!" James was well aware of the deep-rooted hatred that existed between the two men. "You'll get us all killed!"

Sergeant Carr and MacNulty loosened their grips. Their eyes darted between James and the end of the alleyway. Carr blinked sweat from his eyes. "What...? W-W-Where...?"

When the tiny three-foot, goblin-like figure of Eethan edged in beside James, Carr bolted.

"Wwwstandwwwstillwww..." said James.

Carr froze to the spot, unable to move.

"Awch!" James gripped his temples.

Mendel began, "I'm sorry, Sir. But had I not stopped you running out of this alley you would most certainly be dead."

Carr could move his eyes, nothing more.

Mendel continued, "You were uninvited, Sir; but as you are here, you should know that you've been transported through a gateway by Eethan and myself to a world called Artilis."

Eethan gave a small bow.

Carr's eyes widened.

"Do as I say," said Mendel, "and you may survive. Run into the street, in blind panic, and you will be eaten by sandworms in the arena, or worse." Mendel forced his eye against the window of the plastic barrel and splashed loudly until Sergeant Carr squinted down. "Yes; that's me. I'm, at present, a small goldfish in the care of young James Peck. The blue man who addressed you is one Eethan Magichand, a dear and trusted friend. And, of course, you know MacNulty."

As the paralysis spell wore off, Sergeant Carr fell to his knees and nodded, dolefully. He unbuttoned his collar and tried to stand. His legs shook.

Eethan turned to face James. "Wee'll have to go down thees alley and sees where eet goes. Theeres no point een going that way." He pointed towards the bustling street that buzzed and hummed with a hundred different drones.

"I agree," said Mendel. "I can only presume that Dendralon has enticed us here on purpose. Craig will probably be in one of the Martilian dungeons."

Bero cocked his brown ear and whined.

"Don't worry, boy," said James. "We'll find him. We'll find Craig."

The young version of Bero didn't look so young anymore. In fact, he seemed more like his old self, heavier and not so steady on his feet. He panted, letting his tongue loll out of the side of his mouth.

Carr and MacNulty eyed each other suspiciously before following Bero, Eethan, and James up the alley.

As they walked further into the darkness, James caught up with Eethan and asked, "How are the Yeltans, Eethan? What about Jal and Whindril?" These were all creatures James had met the year before in Denthan. They'd all fought Dendralon before.

"Theey're all well for thee time being," said Eethan.

James wondered what Eethan meant by "for the time being".

"Theeey often ask about you eend Craig eend your family. Not so much about your motheer," Eethan tittered to himself.

James knew his mum had proved challenging in Denthan.

Eethan continued, "Whindril, being ee dragon, ees exploring thee Halsian Desert and Dee Grey Mountains to thee north. Jal ees helping thee Yeltans build a new home near to Gwendral."

"What world did you go to, Eethan?" asked James. "Mendel never said."

"Ebos," said Eethan. "Half good and half nastee. Very nastee," he added. "Full of Stone Larths een Martinelles."

"Yuck," said James, none the wiser.

Following Eethan further into the darkness, James had a funny feeling that his mum was nearby. "Mendel, could my mum…?" *Nah. I'd just sound like a numpty if I asked that*, he decided.

* * *

Sitting deep the in bowels of the temple of Ibis, he tapped his gnarled staff on the stone floor.

Almost at once, a red-haired Racnid, with a triangular black patch on its back scampered up to the ornate throne. It moved tentatively, edging forward a little at a time before speaking. "Sire, I am sorry to tell you that Elandria and the boy have escaped."

"What?" He stood up. "Why were they not fed to the sandworms, as I instructed?"

"The spider-like creature took several steps back. "Sire, we would have but, the sandworms had just been fed and…"

Dendralon waved a withered hand and the Racnid stopped in his tracks. He stepped down from the throne and began to circle the terrified creature. Dendralon had grown himself some long, black hair with the help of his magic. He'd become accustomed to it in Denthan. It flicked in silky folds as he shook his head. He lowered his reptilian face down to the level of the Racnid's purple, bulging eyes and opened his mouth. Dendralon's forked tongue darted between his serrated teeth. It traced across the Racnid's wrinkled, red face. "Why did I come here?" He spun round and shouted. "Why?" The Racnid stood motionless.

Two Inubian guards flattened their dog-ears and began to pant.

"Send an assassin after the boy and the princess. An Ibissynian," snapped Dendralon.

Ibissynians were never evaded. They possessed the body of a man and the head of an Ibis. Their long, curved bill sensed prey from great distances and they never stopped until their victim was caught and killed. Immortals, their dark magic was even feared by the humanoid Artilians. He tapped his staff on the stone floor.

The red-haired Racnid, suddenly able to move, shuffled out of the chamber. "Yes, Sire. I will arrange this straightaway."

Dendralon beckoned the jackal-headed Inubians. "The sandworms will still be hungry. Make sure they are fed properly this time." With a nod in the direction of the departing Racnid, Dendralon turned, once more, to his books.

He was trying to establish where the last remaining red crystal of Artilis was hidden. He already had the Racnid crystal, which he'd found in a labyrinth below Martilia and his plan was well underway to take the second. He knew it was set inside the great pyramid of Ra, in the city of Artilia. It was the third and final crystal that frustrated him. It was reputed to lie deep in the caves beneath the Stygian desert, guarded by a powerful demon called Belloc. The ancient texts did not say where this demon was or what kind of magic it possessed. Only that *'the child of a great queen will dig the crystal from the sand....'* There was also a text from the book of Ra that said: *'They who see Belloc may command her in the confines of her lair...'* He sometimes wondered if the crystal had been found already. If so, he would have to find another way to send a whole city between the gateways. He needed three crystals to move his army to Earth. The scouts he'd sent so far had performed their task. Mendel's attempts at magic and his over-inquisitive nature had secured the bait in the form of the boy named Craig. Mendel must also have found a way to survive the destruction of Denthan. Still, his new army was poised to take the city of Artilia. He would claim the crystal and then let old wizard Mendel find the one in the desert. The old fool would need it to get his earthlings back home. Let him face the demon, Belloc. Mendel would either die or retrieve the crystal for him. Either way, it was a good result.

As the Inubians marched off to feed the worms, he paced the floor of the temple and muttered to himself. "Who is the child? Where is Belloc's lair?" He thumped his blackened fist on the pile of books in frustration. He'd sent the Racnids to search the tunnels below the desert too. As yet, however, they'd uncovered nothing. He pulled out a map of Artilia and drew several arrows towards the heavily defended city. He summoned an Inubian captain called Orsa and spoke. "This map shows you how we will take Artilia and the crystal of Ra therein."

Orsa bowed and flared his nostrils. "Yes, Sire."

"You will take the Inubian army and form a pincer round the city of Artilia while the Racnids attack from below, via the tunnels. I will then take our armies to Earth where, along with the creature I've awakened there, we will take back what is rightly ours."

He would never have known that Mendel was still alive if the old fool hadn't tried to perform his magic. He'd thought Mendel and the rest of his followers destroyed on Denthan. His tough reptilian Hedra scales had given him the time he'd needed to perform his own magic, escape the fire, but he still hadn't worked out how Mendel and the rest of the humans from Drumfintley had escaped the destruction of Denthan. If Mendel failed to find Belloc and the third crystal, there was a chance that the old wizard would reveal another way to move between dimensions other than with the help of crystals. He had read Mendel's theory about the Eden Tree on Denthan, about its power of regeneration and transference. But it was gone forever now. There was no way to use its power now that Denthan was destroyed.

Dendralon sent the Inubian captain off to prepare his forces and then turned to face a recess in the corner of the chamber. A single red-flamed candle flickered beside a gold-rimmed mirror set into the wall. He moved closer. He'd managed to heal most of the scars he'd endured on Denthan but a single deep furrow on his scaled cheek proved impossible to mend. That, and the fact that his bait, the boy Craig, had escaped, annoyed him greatly.

* * *

Behind Sergeant Carr, Archie MacNulty checked his poacher's pocket. It was still there. Not his favourite pet ferret, Sarg, but something else; something he wanted to keep to himself for the time being…

* * *

Her mind racing, Cathy Peck sat with her back against a large rock that protruded from a seemingly endless desert. "If I've told you once, I've told you ten times. I don't know where we are."

Helen let go of Cathy Peck's sleeve and snuggled back into her mother. "Horrible woman."

"I heard that," snarled Cathy.

The sky was a deep pink colour and a light breeze flicked sand in their faces as they boiled in the unbearable heat.

Michael stood up and wiped his balding head. He was already drenched in sweat and looked very uncomfortable. Ephie began to cry. She sat next to David who was shielding his eyes from the glare of the sand. "There's no sign of James or Craig. I thought you said…"

Cathy bristled. "We're alive, aren't we? Which means that there's a good chance James is too."

"Of course. I know. I was just saying."

"Well don't. You would just have given up and let him disappear beneath the moor."

David Peck looked round at the other's pitying stares and felt his cheeks flush. "I'm sure I would have jumped in if I'd known what the heck was happening."

Cathy Peck stood up and dusted the sand off her white shirt. "Don't lie."

Michael tried to placate her. "Now Cathy, David has never—"

"Never done a decent thing in his whole life," Cathy finished.

"For goodness sake," said Jean, placing Wee Joe down on the sand. "That's just ridiculous. David runs the Scouts and—"

"And you can keep out of my affairs."

"I might, if you could keep them to yourself."

"Mum!" Wee Joe tugged at his mum's skirt. "Wook!"

Cathy looked down to see what the youngest member of the Harrison clan was talking about. He was clawing at an inky black piece of stone.

"Wits got words on it wike a book."

Michael peered over Wee Joe's shoulder. "He's right. There's a name engraved on the stone. Oh dear, it's upside down."

David Peck bent down and turned his head to read it. "W. MacNulty."

They all squinted down at the stone in disbelief, except Wee Joe who continued to scrape more sand away from the base.

"Who is W. MacNulty?" asked Jean.

"Well," said Michael, "there's only one MacNulty in Drumfintley, and that's Archie."

"We're not in Drumfintley, Michael," reminded Ephie.

"I know, dear but..."

"Although Archie's father was called Willie," she surmised.

David Peck waved his forefinger. "He was the one that went missing in the war, wasn't he?"

Ephie nodded. "Yes. But why would someone write his name on a piece of stone here? Wherever *here* is," she mused.

David clawed at the sand with Wee Joe.

Crash!

"Get back!" shouted Cathy.

A set of stairs appeared before them as the sand fell away into a deep pit below.

"Be careful, Joe," said Jean. But Cathy Peck had already caught Wee Joe's arm.

"Thank you," Jean offered Cathy in a begrudging tone.

Cathy smirked and began to tug at the black stone. It came loose and fell away, clattering down the stairwell into the darkness below.

Poised at the top of the stairs, Ephie asked, "What was Archie's dad doing here?"

"I'm not sure, but it's more than a bit of a coincidence, if you ask me," said Michael.

Cathy stepped down into the darkness. "James?"

The rest of the party looked on in trepidation.

She could hear David wittering on behind her. "Cathy, you don't like tunnels. Are you sure you'll be okay down there?"

Cathy felt the rage build in her chest. She gave him a look of complete loathing and continued downwards.

"Well, it's better than roasting to death up here," said Michael.

"Yes, yes. Of course it is," said David. "We'll need some form of light. It's so dark."

As they moved down the stairwell, however, they noticed that the same pink glow, though much weaker, persisted in the tunnel below.

Cathy waited for them in the tunnel. "Come and see this." Her eyes had adjusted to the light and she was pointing down at the fallen black stone.

David produced a tiny torch and shone it on the stone. "*To those who pass below; good luck. Proceed north for two miles and then turn left, through the maze. Beware of the Dust...* The next bit is worn away, but it was clearly signed by *W. MacNulty.*"

Cathy straightened. "Right. What way is north?"

"But it says that we should beware of something," said Jean.

"The Dust," added Helen.

"The Dust..." mused Ephie. "It's spelt with a capital letter."

Cathy's pulse quickened. She turned to face David. "Did you remind James to take his inhaler?"

"Eh..."

She felt an uncontrollable rage surge through her. "Useless."

"I've got a compass," David pleaded.

"See. He's got a compass," said Helen. Her face brightened.

Cathy eyed the small, cheeky girl suspiciously. "Really."

"It's just not making much sense but the needle hovered in that direction for a bit." David pointed down the tunnel.

"Mmm... Let's get a move on, then." Cathy pushed ahead of the pack and shouted out: " James!"

Michael moved forward. "Do you think it's wise to shout out like that, Cathy? I mean, we don't know what's down here," he whispered.

"And what exactly is the point of being here in the first place, Michael?" she muttered.

"I know, but we..."

"JAMES!" Cathy Peck's unrepentant shout echoed along the tunnel.

"Jesus," said Ephie, tugging on Michael's sleeve. "She's going to get us all killed."

"My eyes are getting used to this light now," said David. "There, on the walls... They look like diamonds." David Peck ran his fingers over them but soon pulled his hand back with a yell. "Awch!"

Cathy stopped and glared back at her husband. "Idiot."

She marched on while Ephie and Jean examined David's hand.

"I'm okay," he said. "It was like static, or something. Gave me a kick, that's all."

The strange crackling sound persisted as they walked on.

Cathy had to pause every few minutes while the kids caught up and she wished, more than once, that Jean and her brood had stayed home.

The tunnel narrowed. It seemed to be completely straight, cut by some unknown hand, rather than forged by nature. Always dimly lit, it had an eerie feel and a cheerless atmosphere.

As the roof of the tunnel grew steadily lower, Wee Joe climbed off of Michael's shoulders and began to walk. Cathy waited on them behind a large stalagmite. She'd heard something ahead. She pressed her finger to her lips to signal silence.

"You sure you don't want to scream out your son's name, like a maniac, again?" whispered Jean, tugging Wee Joe away from Cathy.

Cathy formed a fist with her right hand and took a deep breath.

A scuttling noise echoed down the tunnel followed by a louder clicking sound.

Cathy grabbed hold of a smooth black stalactite and snapped it free of the roof.

The clicking sound stopped.

"Each of you, break one off," whispered Cathy. "Just in case." She waved the stalactite like a sword at the group that now backed up behind her.

The scampering of many feet grew nearer and she heard a hissing sound. Someone was whispering ahead of them.

For a moment, she wondered if it might be James. David must have been thinking the same thing and she saw he was about to shout out. Cathy covered his mouth with her hand and whispered, an inch from his face, *"No!"*

Ephie pointed out a ridge of rock to their left. They all edged back behind it and lay flat. Wee Joe began to giggle but Cathy heard Helen sniff back a tear.

"Mum, will there be monsters again?" she asked.

Jean held her children close and gave them both a non-committal tight-lipped smile.

The whispering sound seemed to be right beside them. They could hear the strange voices behind the ridge.

"I'll never take orders from Orsa again. Never," said a high-pitched voice.

"We'll chew on his doggy bones. Crunch them up," a lower voice replied. "Imagine, sending us off again down these stinking tunnels.

There's no red crystal here. Never was. Let's sting him next time and wrap him up for our children."

The voices suddenly broke off.

Behind the ridge the Drumfintley party shut their eyes and held their breath. Even Wee Joe was shaking with fright now.

"What's that?" said the high-pitched voice. "Look. Sticking out from behind the rock."

The lower voice, somehow more sinister and threatening, replied, "Yes. Let's take a closer look."

Cathy was just about to jump up and fight for it, when Michael caught her foot and shook his head.

"I'll get it!" hissed the lower pitched voice.

A long, hairy spider-like leg stretched over their heads and gripped onto a glittering stone, half-buried in the wall of the cave above their heads. It tugged at the gem.

Dirt and small stones showered down on top of them.

"Is it the red crystal?" hissed the high-pitched voice.

"Of course not. It's only rubbish. I'm going back to kill him." The low-pitched voice became more distant: "Let's get back to Martilia. We should not be taking orders from Inubians anyway. The Artilians would never have sent us into the tunnels, to hunt for stupid rocks that don't exist." The scampering became fainter and eventually disappeared.

David Peck peered over the ridge that had kept them hidden. "What was that thing that pulled the stone from the wall?"

Michael sat up. "I'm not sure, but they were looking for a crystal."

Ephie dusted herself down and tried her best to help Jean with the kids. "Whatever they were, they weren't too happy about being here in the first place."

"No," said Jean.

"Wook." Wee Joe kicked at something on the ground.

Two silver trails glistened on the floor of the tunnel. Like squiggles on the floor, they were thicker where the creatures had stopped to examine the rock. Before Cathy could stop him, Wee Joe pinched a silvery strand with his hand and pulled it free from the ground.

It pinged back, with a snap.

"Joe!" Jean hugged him close. "Never touch things when you don't know what they are."

* * *

Half a mile ahead of them, Elhada, the female, stopped and bared her curved, black teeth. "Something tripped over us." Her low-pitched voice echoed down the tunnel. She opened her reptilian nostrils and shut her eyes tight. "An Artilian child, I think."

"Nonsense, more like a Cave Rat or a stinking Dust Goblin."

"Not!" Elhada scampered round to face her mate. Torsus was much smaller and coloured quite differently. He had crimson down all over and possessed no sting.

Elhada continued, "I can tell whatever walks over my trail. No matter what it is."

"Of course." Nervously, Torsus edged back. Elhada's sting glinted in the pink light. "Fine, if you say so, my dear. But..."

The slight hint of disagreement pushed Elhada's patience too far. Her sting lunged forward, through her six legs, and pierced Torsus's neck.

He fell dead on the cave floor, his six legs twitching in spasm, his two arms limp and lifeless.

Elhada had now killed seven partners, but this was nothing out of the ordinary for a Racnid of royal blood. She examined her fur and licked a deep red patch of down that marked her oviduct. Two moist eggs had begun to move and twist in her belly. Torsus had finished his work in this world. She thought about turning back to hunt the Artilian child but instead decided to feast on Torsus. He deserved this last honour, and his offspring would then benefit directly from his demise. She removed the precious water sacs from a slit in his side and began to feast.

* * *

After waiting for five minutes or so, Cathy suggested that they move on. The rest of the party, though still uneasy, grumbled for a few minutes and then followed her, picking their way through the dusky pink shadows of the tunnel.

After Jean complained of feeling sick, Cathy took a turn of carrying Wee Joe. She soon found out that the little tike had resorted to kicking his mum like a horse every time she fell behind. He only tried it once with her, though. Cathy waited until Jean had moved on a little before twirling Wee Joe round to face her. She looked him in the eye and shook her head. "Look son, I'm not your mummy and I'll smack you if you kick me one more time. Understand?"

Wee Joe gave her a reluctant nod.

After another three hundred yards, they all came to a stop. Something was making the most horrendous din round the next corner.

Helen looked up at her mum and whispered, "It sounds like a monkey trying to eat a jellyfish with a straw."

"Yes dear," she whispered back. "I know what you mean. I think…"

The horrible sucking sound continued.

Cathy signalled to Michael and Ephie to take Wee Joe before creeping up to the bend ahead. She was careful not to step on the silver strands that lay on the floor of the tunnel. Cathy's eyes watered as a wave of ammonia hit her. She winced as the strange spider-like creature came into view. Its bald, turtle-like face was totally drenched in black blood as, like some African vulture, it plunged its head into the carcass and fed. It bounced, excitedly, on six hairy legs and gripped the remains of its prey with two other arms covered in long hairs. She also saw the needle-sharp point of a sting, glinting in the pink glow. It slipped in and out of the creature's abdomen every time it bit deeper.

Cathy looked back to see David edging forward, so she motioned him to stop.

Obviously desperate to see what was going on, David and the rest of the party continued to move towards her.

She was just about to wave them back, more vigourously this time, when she saw the look of fear on their faces. Then she heard it. There was a loud rustling sound coming from behind them. This time it sounded as if a whole swarm of the spider creatures was on its way. They all crushed up against Cathy and almost knocked her out of her hiding place. Straining against the group from Drumfintley it occurred to her that this din was different. Like children chattering in a playground it filled the tunnel behind them.

David gripped Cathy's arm. "Now what?"

Agitated, Cathy was pushed into view. She braced, but the spider-like creature was gone. A half-eaten carcass lay on the floor. "This way," she urged. "We can go forward now." She ushered them round the stinking corpse. The smell was overpowering.

Helen screamed. "Ahh!"

"I'm gonna puke!" exclaimed Wee Joe.

The murmuring behind them stopped for a moment then resumed with renewed vigour.

"Run!" shouted Cathy. She waited until the last of the group had passed her before sprinting.

"Uh!"

The pain...dizzy...darkness closing in...

CHAPTER TEN

MACNULTY'S TALE

After walking for more than two hours through the dark, but deserted alleyways that meandered behind the main city streets of Martilia, James came to a halt behind Bero.

"We need to rest," said Carr.

He looks awful, totally unfit, thought James.

MacNulty seemed to read his thoughts and nodded in approval.

The heat is sapping my energy too, James decided.

They stopped and Carr slumped down against a red-stoned wall, as far away from MacNulty as possible.

James, thankful for the break, began to rummage about in his rucksack. He found his blue inhaler and placed it against his lips. "It's not like it was in Denthan, Mendel. I still get breathless here. It's probably all the sand and dust." He forced a cough and gulped.

"There's nowhere near the same oxygen content in the atmosphere here," said Mendel.

As MacNulty and Carr drifted off to sleep, James noticed that Eethan had disappeared. He gave Bero a pat and, gently, twisted his soft, brown ear round his fingers. Mendel's voice drifted into his head. "James?"

James sighed and slumped down until his eyes were level with the barrel.

Mendel swam over to the plastic window. "James, this is the first time I've been able to read MacNulty's thoughts."

"What do you mean?"

"MacNulty has always had a connection with the stone circle on Bruce Moor." Mendel blew a stream of bubbles. "But there's more to it than I thought."

"What?"

"Well," continued Mendel, "MacNulty lost his father during the war."

"That's a shame."

"Yes. You see that's why MacNulty felt particularly sorry for you last year when you lost your father. It was more than a mere coincidence."

"What do you mean, Mendel? I'm really tired."

"His father disappeared beside the Jesus Rocks too."

"You mean he…"

"Just listen," interrupted Mendel. "His father was called Willie MacNulty. From what I can gather, he'd been a bit of a poacher just like Archie is now."

"Archie's a poacher?" asked James.

"It would appear so. In fact Archie's dad, Willie, fed most of the village during the war and became a bit of a local hero with everyone apart from the local constabulary. It's all very strange," said Mendel.

James moved closer to the barrel.

"You see, Archie was also ten when his father disappeared on Bruce Moor. He actually saw him fall. All that was left was a brush and a tin of paint sitting at the edge of the circle. James, MacNulty and his family are the guardians of the circle. By some instruction issued long ago, they'd been told to renew the words 'Jesus Saves' on the main rock."

"By whom?" asked James.

"I'm not sure, as yet. But anyone from Denthan, with a little thought, would be able to translate the words into the necessary phrase to operate the circle," said Mendel. "And there's one more thing."

"What's that?" said James.

"Archie still holds out some hope that he'll find his father. Here on Artilis."

"What? How many years ago did his dad pass through the Jesus Rocks?"

Mendel became distracted. "Wait, there's something else."

Archie began to snort and snore in an irregular fashion. His eyes flickered open.

"James, my boy chhh!"

James forced a smile. He would have to wait for Mendel's further explanations.

"You hungry chh…son?" asked MacNulty.

James was reminded of Archie's badly fitting teeth, as the old gardener slid them back into place with a dirty finger. He stuck a chubby fist into his overcoat and offered a piece of something James hoped was carrot cake.

"Eh, no thanks," said James, the bile rising in his throat. He shuffled into the shadows and watched as Carr stirred and eyed MacNulty.

The old church gardener slurped a strand of drool back into the side of his mouth and shrugged.

To James's amazement Carr piped up, "I'm hungry, MacNulty."

Carr moped over and took a piece of the cake. It was obvious that they despised each other but they were both in a very strange situation, James supposed.

"Why don't you take that ruddy coat off? You must be boiling," grumbled Carr.

MacNulty viewed Carr with renewed suspicion. "Never!"

What was all that about? James thought.

The two older men jumped when something crawled on the wall above them. It was just Eethan, however, clinging to the stone in his usual spider-like fashion.

"For goodness sake!" said Carr, spitting out a large chunk of cake.

James looked up. "What did you find out, Eethan?"

Eethan issued a needle-toothed smile. "Theere's a wagon ahead. Eet looks as though eets ready to leeeve the citeee. Wee can probably get inside eet," he said. "Eet's part of beeg convoy. Veree beeg."

"Well, better there than here," said Mendel. "Let's press on."

"I thought you said that Craig might be in the city," said James.

"I don't sense that now," replied the wizard.

James slipped on his rucksack. "I hope you're right."

"Ee come now. While wees have theee chance."

Still tired and dripping with sweat, they made their way to the edge of the alley and clambered into a stationary wagon. They clipped down the canvas to conceal themselves and shuffled along the floor, leaning back against, what looked like, sacks of grain.

James cuddled into Bero and was just about to ask Eethan what they were going to do next when he heard the crack of a whip and felt the wagon lurch forward.

"Shhh!" Eethan pressed a scrawny, blue finger against James's lips.

As the wagon pulled away Bero began to sniff at something behind the sacks of grain. He became agitated.

Mendel spoke, " We are in an Inubian cargo wagon."

Carr squinted down at the barrel. "Inubian? What does that mean?"

"The reason Bero is agitated is because the Inubians are part canine," explained Mendel.

"Which part?" pressed Carr.

"Theere heads," said Eethan, with a titter. He turned his back on Carr and began cutting a small hole in the fabric that covered the wagon. Like lightning, he caught the collar of Carr's police uniform and drew him close to the hole. "Lookee!"

Carr peered through then sat back with a gasp. "Mary mother of mercy…" His little prayer faded into a garbled mutter.

Mendel caught James's eye. "If we all remain calm and stay very still we may yet escape this city alive."

Peeking through the hole he'd just made, Eethan gave a running commentary on their progress. "Wees are near to thee gates, Mendel."

James pushed in beside Eethan to look. There were no chains or cogs needed to open these great gates. With a bark-like shout from the Inubian driver, the gates swung silently open to reveal the desert beyond. James saw a long unbroken line of the jackal-headed Inubians stretching over the sand until they disappeared into the horizon. Kneeling down in front of the plastic barrel, he dropped some fish food inside. "Mendel, why is it always light here? I've not seen any sun or moon or clouds."

Mendel's rich tones filled James's head. "That's because we're below the surface of the planet. We're underground, James."

Carr and MacNulty screwed up their eyes in an effort to see the little goldfish inside the barrel.

"We're inside a massive cavern," explained Mendel. "Created when the planet was hit by an enormous meteor. The impact was so devastating that it blasted a third of the planet's surface into space. The remainder of the surface was forced up in such a manner that the crust split, trapping a huge amount of oxygen and bacteria. The roof of the cave, or as it is known here, the firmament, is one thousand feet above us and is actually the underside of the upper crust of the planet. Through time and through the ingenuity of the surviving Artilians, the photo-luminescent bacteria settled on the cooling stone and began to produce the pink light that bathes us and, more importantly…"

"Let me guess," pressed James, "the oxygen that we're breathing now."

"Exemplary thinking, young James." Mendel issued a deep chortle and another stream of bubbles. "They use a type of iridium which they convert to a pink light then, in a most unique way, they use their own light to convert carbon dioxide into oxygen using photosynthesis."

"Photo what?" said James, cautiously.

"The process by which plants, algae, and bacteria produce oxygen," explained Mendel.

"Oh," said James, pretending to fully understand.

"Well I didn't understand a ruddy word you said, whoever *you* are," said Sergeant Carr, scathingly. "But one thing's for sure..."

"Whach's that then, Carr?" sprayed MacNulty.

"I was right. I knew you were involved in all of this. The disappearances and..."

"No. You're quite wrong there, Sergeant Carr," interrupted Mendel. "The disappearances last June were my doing, one way or another. However..."

"You knew about the circle, Mr. MacNulty?" interrupted James.

MacNulty shrugged.

"So if you suspected that my dad went through the Jesus Rocks to... Well, wherever, why didn't you tell me?"

MacNulty shook his head dolefully. "I couldn't. You were too young."

"But Mr. MacNulty, I was the same age that you were when your dad went through."

MacNulty looked genuinely shocked. "Aye, boy chh. But my dad never chhame back."

Carr seemed to be struggling with it all. "So you did know about the disappearances?"

"Wait a minutecch, Carr. Let me ecchhxplain to the boy." MacNulty shifted his weight. "I didn't want chho tell you that chhour dad might never come back, chhson."

James could see his point.

"I just thought I'd watchhh che stone chircle in case anything turned up."

"Likely story," spat Carr.

MacNulty stiffened. "But when I chaw you, the Harrichson boy and the dog fall through, just like my dad had done all chhose years ago, I..."

"You withheld information and lied," announced Carr.

"And you would have believed him?" pressed Mendel.

Carr fidgeted with his intercom. It crackled, uselessly, as they bounced across the sands in the searing heat. "I suppose not," he muttered. "But you're still a ruddy poacher!"

James shook his head in despair at Carr's bitterness. "I get enough of this at home. Please!"

They mumbled their apologies.

"Let's address the problem at hand," said Mendel, impatiently. "Let me summarize."

Eethan chuckled and patted Bero's head. The old dog was panting with thirst.

Mendel splashed impatiently. "The whole Inubian army is on the march."

Carr and MacNulty jostled edgily.

"The Inubians are the half-man, half-dog creatures who were left to evolve, here on Artilis, after the Artilians dabbled in dark magic. They kept them as slaves and then honed their fighting skills to protect their cities against enemies here in Artilis."

"The giant insects?" asked James.

"In part," said Mendel.

James stole another glance through the hole in the canvas. "The Inubians. They're like those Egyptian things; the ones you see on the pharaohs' tombs and stuff."

"Well spotted, James," said Mendel, a hint of pride in his voice. "Eethan and myself had dealings with the Inubians, on Earth, about nine thousand years ago."

"Naughtee dogees thee are. Not like you, Bero." Eethan patted Bero's head and whispered a small charm that produced a bowl of cool water.

Bero lapped it up, gratefully, while James and the older men licked their dry lips.

Eethan tittered and used his magic to produce another three cups.

Soon, they were all drinking deeply while Mendel continued to expound his theories. "It's my guess that Dendralon, having somehow survived his fall in Denthan, returned here to raise a new army. During the last year he's obviously convinced the Inubians to follow him. What's worse, he's managed to convince the Racnids. They lived with the Artilians. He will try and find all three of the Artilian crystals and then take the whole city of Artilis back to Earth."

"What?" spat Carr, a bemused look spreading across his big pomegranate of a face.

"You mean," enquired MacNulty, "that thichh Dendralon creaturecchh will take those thinchhs to Drumfintley?"

"Oh yes," said Mendel. "To begin with."

James opened the canvas, very slightly, at the back of the wagon and stared back at the city of Martilia. "Mendel?"

"Ah, you've noticed."

"The city has the same outline as the Denthan city of Gwendral," said James.

MacNulty looked over James's shoulder and muttered, as best he could, "Itch juchh like the Jesus Rocks."

"Exactly," said Mendel. "One large citadel, the same as the one in the Denthan city of Gwendral, with eight other towers set in the optimum position. Artilia, however, is far better designed to transport a whole army."

"So that's why," pressed James, "the Inubian army is marching away from Martilia and towards Artilia? So why," continued James, his thoughts tumbling free, "did Dendralon take Craig?"

"It could just as easily have been you, James. Dendralon can see through the eyes of anyone holding a gateway crystal. If I'd known he was still alive, I would never have let any of you touch it! I suspect he was trying to draw me here, either to kill me or..."

"Will he need three crystals to activate Artilia?" asked James.

"You really *are* getting better by the day, my boy." Mendel floated closer to the window of his barrel. "I can only guess that he has the Racnid crystal by now. He must be using that to send the creatures to Loch Echty. The second crystal of Ra will still be in the city of Artilia and the third... The third was lost many years ago. He needs all three to operate the giant ark."

"Mendel, perhaps we can find the third crystal before he does," said James.

"Perhaps. Before he turns Artilia into a giant battle-ark."

"Ark?" enquired Carr.

"The whole city and everything inside can be transported," said James.

"Oh," said Carr, matter-of-factly.

MacNulty sneered at the policeman, behind his back.

"No, Dendralon definitely has the Racnid crystal, otherwise they would not be running round, like rats, after him," mused Mendel. "The

Inubian army is obviously set on taking the one that lies in Artilia, the crystal of Ra. It's set on a plinth in the stone ring of Artilia. You will see, if we get that far, that the city of Artilia is in fact a giant pyramid. The Artilian ring of stones is set inside the apex of the structure. The tip of the pyramid pierces the firmament. It remains above the surface of the planet."

"But surely the Artilians will fight to defend it?" asked James.

"I'm sure they will," said Mendel.

"Dependees," said Eethan. "Dendralon might use ees speceeal beastie."

"And what's that then?" asked Carr.

"Ee thinks that Mendel and James ave seen eet alreadee," said Eethan.

Mendel went very quiet. He circled his barrel.

"Dee krakeen," squeaked Eethan, covering his eyes in mock fright. "Eet cannot be killed. Eet has two giantee pincers and two unstoppable hearts. Eeee…"

"Quite," said Mendel.

James nodded slowly. "You're saying that this Kraken creature is what killed Ethrita in Loch Echty? But it lives underwater."

"For the moment, but it's equally deadly on land or in fire," said Mendel, mournfully. And now that Dendralon has the blue crystal from Craig, he can, in theory, not only send creatures through to Earth, but also take them back again."

"Wait a minute. If he has three crystals already…"

"The one you borrowed from the Fintley graveyard?" enquired Mendel.

"Eh… Okay."

"They must all be red Artilian crystals. The red crystals need to work as one. They are assigned to this planet." Mendel paused. "The blue crystal you found could not work for the Artilian ark. We need to find the third red crystal. We need to find Belloc."

The wagon jolted to a halt.

A series of barking sounds and snarls erupted all around their wagon.

"Don't move," urged Mendel. "Not a sound."

The noise grew steadily louder outside the wagon.

"What should we do?" whispered James.

A bulging fish eye floated up to the window of the barrel. "Say your magic word, James."

James thought back to Denthan and his magic sword, Firetongue; the red bladed sword that had given him such great strength and agility. "But the markings on my arm have gone and…"

"Just say it!"

"WwwFirewwwtongueww?" he blurted.

A fog began to whisk round James's arm, sparkling and crackling like hot fat just before the pain gripped him. "Arghh!"

Something heavy dropped to the floor of the wagon.

Carr and MacNulty jumped back.

"Look out the hole in the canvas. I need to see what's happening," snapped Mendel.

"My bloomin' arm is still sore," James protested. His breathing became laboured.

The commotion outside intensified as he peered out of the hole cut by Eethan. The Inubian soldiers gathered round their wagon were looking at a strange chariot racing across a red dune. It veered towards them, its tall charioteer pulling hard on the golden reins until he came to a halt beside the wagon. A red hood covered the charioteer's face but his bronzed muscles glistened in the dimming light. His steeds, a pair of Racnids tethered to the main shaft, had green down that rippled in the growing breeze. He raised his hand and signalled the nearest Inubian captain to step forward. The Inubian captain looked terrified.

"Yes, my Lord?" The Inubian bowed his head and began to shake.

The charioteer removed his red hood to reveal a long, slender bill that curved down from his gray face. The loose skin on his wrinkled, bald head shuddered as he stepped off of the chariot. His voice was extremely deep, his tones so low that the jackal-headed Inubians tilted their heads to pick out the meaning. "I have the scent of a boy. It blows in the breeze, through your camp. He is mine."

The Inubians looked at each other in wonderment. The Inubian captain spoke, "We have no boy here, my Lord. Only weapons and grain."

The Inubian fixed his black-eyed gaze on their wagon. "You lie." He drew a long, curved sword and moved forward.

James's mouth dried up.

The Inubians parted to let the creature through.

"I can assure you," protested the captain.

James braced himself. He picked up the crimson-bladed sword that had served him so well in Denthan, unsure of what to expect.

Mendel could see everything through James. "James, this creature is very fast. There can be no dialogue, only action."

Carr and MacNulty looked in trepidation between the barrel that swung round Bero's neck and the sword in James's hand.

"Now young Mr. Peck, don't be thinking of doing anything silly. You could get two years just for having that thing," stated Sergeant Carr.

MacNulty screwed up his eyes in disbelief. "Are you off chewer rocker, Carr?"

James tried not to become distracted.

Eethan was nowhere to be seen. *Typical*, thought James.

The Ibissynian knocked the jackal-faced captain aside and raised his bronze sword.

As the Ibissynian sword cut through the canvas, James leapt upward and cut through the roof of the wagon. He somersaulted through the air and landed behind the tall assassin.

Poised behind the Ibissynian, James saw Eethan's scrawny arm shoot out of the tear in the canvas. He gripped the Ibissynian sword between his fingers and a blue light shot up the blade.

The Ibissynian yelled out in rage as he tugged in vain at his trapped sword. He cried out again as James's crimson sword plunged into his broad back. Looking down at his chest and the protruding point in disbelief, he screamed out a hideous curse and fell to his knees.

The Inubians were completely disorientated. They scattered as James retrieved his sword and then lobbed the curved-billed creature's head off. Howling and barking, they shrunk back further.

The Ibissynian crashed forward into the sand and lay still.

James, unsure of what to do next, turned on the Inubians and cut his sword through the air in a semicircle.

"N-n-no Ibissynian has ever been defeated in battle," stuttered the Inubian captain.

"He has now," said James, the power of the sword rushing through his veins. "Stand back."

The Inubians drew back in fear.

It was then that Eethan stepped out from the wagon with Bero, raised his left hand and uttered, *"Seth na chen ta lee!"* There was a blinding blue flash.

The Inubians, about thirty in all, froze where they stood.

The breeze continued to ruffle the green down on the Ibisyynian's spider-like steeds. They too had been frozen to the spot.

James saw that his sword had disappeared. On his palm there was a red, bird-like creature with a lion's head, every feather and claw wonderfully etched onto his skin. He smiled as he remembered his mum's reaction to the tattoo the year before. He knew all he had to do now was say the magic word, Firetongue, and the sword would reappear in his hand any time he needed it.

Mendel spoke in their heads, "We need to leave this place. The creature James has wounded would have killed us all."

"Wounded? Wounded?" Carr rubbed his eyes and removed a black notepad from his jacket. "He's just cut its ruddy head off!"

"Yes, well—" muttered James.

"Yes, well?" Carr looked close to exploding. "James Peck, I'm sorry to say that I'm going to have to take some notes. You have the right to remain silent..."

"Don't be shho bloody stupid," snapped MacNulty. "That thing would have killed usshh. Besides, we're in another dimension or on another planet or..."

"Never mind where we are. I will continue to do my duty. That boy is a murderer!" Carr's pencil wavered over the blank page in his notebook.

"Sorreee to interpuptee," interrupted Eethan, "but my spell weell only hold theeese doggies for a few more momeeents."

"There!" said Mendel, pointing a fin towards an outcrop of rock.

They all turned and gazed at the outcrop.

"I can sense someone," said Mendel.

"Who?" asked James. "Craig?"

"The Ibissynian was clearly sent to find someone. They have unrivalled senses and are usually hired to track bounty."

"Had," added Carr, slamming his notebook shut. "This one 'had' unrivalled senses."

They all ran across the sand, unseen by the other phalanxes of Inubian soldiers who were far too busy erecting their tents.

The light had dimmed considerably, and what had been a gentle breeze was now a sand storm. The fine grains whipped against their faces as they ran towards the rocks.

"Look!" exclaimed James. "There's a set of stairs leading down below the desert. I bet Craig's down there. Mendel, what do you think?"

Mendel swam over to the window of the swaying barrel and squinted down at the steps. "Better to be down there than up here. It's a miracle that we've not been seen yet."

They all dashed down the steps behind a black rock, but as they reached the base of the stairs, James skidded to a halt. "What the...?" He picked up a greaseproof wrapper from the floor of the tunnel. It read: *Galdinie's homemade tablet.* "Look at this."

Sergeant Carr took it from him, folding it carefully before slipping it into his top pocket. "Evidence," he muttered.

Archie MacNulty, however, was preoccupied with something else. He had found a smooth piece of black granite. He held it up to the pink light that emanated from the roof of the tunnel and read: *"To those who pass below; good luck. Proceed north for two miles and then turn left, through the maze. Beware of the Dust..."* He mopped his brow and choked back a tear. "Part of it is worn away, but it's signed *W. MacNulty.*"

"Your dad?" said James.

MacNulty nodded, blankly.

* * *

Eethan made sure they had all descended before taking one last look round. Next to the wagon, the giant, bird-headed Ibissynian twitched. Black tendrils wiggled free of his neck and gripped his severed head, pulling it back into place. His withered fingers formed a claw as he shifted his massive frame and sat up. Eethan hissed before ducking down the stairs. A wave of dread washed over him.

CHAPTER ELEVEN

THE DUST GOBLINS

They'd travelled over the Stygian desert for more than three hours before Elandria scuttled to a halt. Still charged with adrenalin, Craig involuntarily dug his heels into her sides.

"Awch! Be careful where you're jabbing," hissed Elandria.

"Oops. Sorry. I got a bit carried away."

"You held on well, youngling."

"Ta. I'm getting better." Craig's gaze shifted to a city built round, what looked like, the base of a huge pyramid constructed from gigantic blocks of crimson stone. Red birds sailed between russet-tiled rooftops while bronze-skinned people milled around the city walls trading and haggling with each other between an assortment of tents and stands pitched on the battlements. *They don't look under threat*, thought Craig. They seemed content and peaceful.

The light was fading. The firmament had assumed a purple hue, and the desert that surrounded them had grown noisier. There were grunts and yelps that Craig hadn't noticed before.

"Dust Goblins, and Gringles," explained Elandria, in a strangely upbeat tone.

"And I suppose they'd all give us an honourable death too," gibed Craig.

"Very honourable," said Elandria.

"I thought so. Let's see if these people will let us into the city."

Elandria began to scuttle forward again, her green and purple down brushing against Craig's bare knees. His football shorts and his orange and green rugby top were looking decidedly filthy. As they approached the main gates, Craig reckoned he heard a trumpet or some kind of bugle.

"Who dares to enter the city on the back of a Racnid traitor?" said a voice.

It seemed to be coming from a woman, who sat at the base of the opened gate. She'd been sewing but now stood up to address Craig.

"Em, my name is Craig Harrison."

"Ah, well that's alright then. Just come in and take what you like." The woman smiled.

"Okay," replied Craig, coyly. "Elandria," he whispered. "What should I do?"

Elandria turned her turtle-like head round and said, "I think she's being sarcastic."

"I knew that. I'm not a complete numpty," he whispered.

"Numpty?" asked Elandria.

"Never mind." He decided to dismount Elandria and try a different tack. He moved a little closer to the woman. "Look, this Racnid saved my life and I need to find a way home."

"And where's home? Dendralon's citadel?" the woman asked, her sword now drawn.

"I wish I still had Greenworm," Craig whispered.

It was at this point that something completely unexpected and very painful happened. With a searing jab of agony, Craig fell to his knees and yelled out. A cloud of steam rose up from his arm, as if he'd just been branded by a hot iron. He'd felt this pain before. "Greenworm?" he muttered.

The woman stepped back. "Impressive." She waved more Artilians forward. "And I suppose you intend to kill us all now with your magic spear?"

"This is the work of Dendralon," someone shouted.

"What? How?" Craig looked at Elandria.

"They know him as Dendralon," whispered Elandria.

"But he's dead!" Craig whispered back.

He saw Greenworm, the magic spear he'd used in Denthan, lying on the sand at his feet. On his palm, the tattoo of a green serpent coiled between his fingers. He opened his hand, and the spear jumped up from the sand. He looked round, searching for some sign of Mendel.

The woman screwed up her eyes and walked forward. "What do you want, magician?"

"Shelter," said Craig, somewhat hesitantly. "Somewhere I can be safe from... Dendralon."

"We were both about to be fed to Dendralon's sandworms, until I helped the boy," said Elandria.

As soon as Elandria spoke there was a murmur from the crowd assembled at the city gates.

"It's princess Elandria!" someone shouted.

Elandria bowed in the direction of the crowd.

Craig's mouth had gone completely dry.

"Kill them!" someone else shouted.

But the woman who'd first spoken to them shushed the crowd and walked right up to Craig. She had an olive complexion and long, black hair that tumbled over her elegant shoulders. Her eyes were the colour of beaten bronze and her mouth was fixed in a mischievous smile. She exuded confidence and the crowd behind her quieted as she approached them.

Craig couldn't take his eyes off her.

"Why does princess Elandria return to Artilia with a wizard boy?"

Elandria seemed to recognize the woman as she came closer. "Junera?"

The woman bowed.

Elandria bowed back. "I was imprisoned by my own kind, and sentenced to death for refusing to follow the necromancer. This boy, although I know not why, was to die with me. He is also an enemy of Dra, or as you call him, Dendralon. I knew it was a mistake to leave Artilia."

"But your kin did not," snapped Junera.

"They are my kin no longer," replied Elandria, forlornly.

Just as Craig was about to speak, a man ran in from the direction of the desert, a band of three horned, goat-like creatures scattering behind him. "There's a great army of Inubians camped in the desert. There must be thirty thousand or more and..." He adjusted his robes and pulled a bow from his back. "And there's an Ibissynian coming this way too."

They all looked up at the ridge of sand behind the herdsman.

A cloaked figure with a red hood whipped his Racnid steeds and urged his chariot down the tall dune.

"If you've escaped Dendralon's prison, I can only assume that the Ibissynian assassin is after you two," said Junera. She pointed to Craig and Elandria, then turned to the assembled crowd and laughed. "We shall see some sport today, after all."

"Thanks a lot, numpty," said Craig, his words drowned out by the wailing of the crowd. He turned to look at the red-hooded pursuer. "Elandria, what is that thing?"

Elandria sighed. "That, my boy, is an Ibissynian assassin. They can never be killed and they always find their prey."

"Cheery, cheery," said Craig with disdain. "Any more good news?"

"Well, there is one way to kill it."

"And what's that then?"

"If you kill the Kraken," explained Elandria, "a two-headed monster which itself is immortal, then all Ibissynians will die. They are linked by an invisible heart string."

"And how does that help us now?" whimpered Craig. The Ibissynian charioteer was only two hundred yards away, and closing fast.

"It doesn't really, does it?" hissed Elandria.

The Artilians had drawn back and the city gates were already closing. Junera was nowhere to be seen.

The Ibissynian spun his chariot round, throwing a large curve of sand into the air, which landed at Craig and Elandria's feet.

Craig saw the charioteer remove his hood. He gasped when he spied the creature's long curved bill. His palm began to itch.

Elandria rounded on the Ibissynian. "Wait! You have been misled."

The Artilians mumbled and tittered above on the battlements.

The weird looking Ibissynian drew his bronze sword and assumed a strange stance. He bounced on his knees, and cut the air with his sword. He blinked his black, bird-like eyes and flicked his sword. It was as if he was summoning Craig.

Elandria pushed Craig forward with one of her legs.

"Steady! I thought you were on my side?" whimpered Craig.

"You have made a mistake, my friend, but if you take one more step the boy will cut you down."

"Elandria!" Craig snapped. He was amazed at the height of the creature. At almost seven feet tall, the Ibissynian was like a hewn statue of grey marble. He took a step forward and picked up the green spear..

"Great." Craig tightened his grip on Greenworm and closed his eyes in anticipation. He'd forgotten the rush of adrenalin that preceded the wielding of the magic spear.

Unexpectedly, the Ibissynian lunged forward and cut down with his sword at Craig's neck.

Craig sidestepped the giant and threw his spear up into the purple sky. It sailed high then dipped, arcing back on itself. Surprisingly, it veered to the right and seared through grey flesh and brittle bone, exiting the Ibissynian's left shoulder.

"Ahhhh!" The Ibissynian clutched his shoulder, which oozed black blood, and staggered back.

The crowd on the battlements 'oohed' and 'aahed'.

Elandria sneaked behind the Ibissynian and edged towards the Racnid steeds.

Greenworm came to rest, gently, in Craig's right hand. "Please, I don't want to hurt you. Go away!"

The creature moved forward at such speed that Craig was caught off balance. He fell over his own feet, throwing the spear aimlessly as he tumbled. Greenworm sliced down, of its own accord, cutting through the Ibissynian's sword. The shaft of the spear then flicked Craig to his feet before thrusting upward through the creature's throat. A torrent of black blood spilled out onto the sand as Craig rolled away from the flaying figure. The creature thumped down onto its knees, desperately clawing at the wound.

A ripple of applause echoed down from the battlements.

Craig glanced up and found Junera. He mopped his brow and bowed, cheekily.

Elandria scuttled across to the chariot and spoke to her kin. "Do not get involved in the fight; I order you."

The Racnids bowed in agreement. "Yes, my princess." Both green furred females, like Elandria, they withdrew their stings and shuffled back from the fray.

Craig snapped his fingers and felt Greenworm's cool shaft in his hands. The Racnid steeds that had pulled the creature's chariot moved back. The Ibissynian looked to be dead and Elandria was back at his side.

"I'll bind him fast," said Elandria.

"But he's dead," said Craig.

"He is not," replied Elandria, busy pulling silver strands from her abdomen. "They never die unless…"

"Unless we kill the Kraken thingy."

"Correct. Good boy," hissed Elandria. The Ibissynian was already an indiscernible lump beneath a thick layer of webbing.

Craig scanned the battlements and found the figure of Junera. He shouted up at her. "Are you going to help us or are you just going to let us be slaughtered by the Inubians?"

Junera smiled. "You fought well, boy." She turned to her guards. "Let them in!"

The huge gates swung open just as the first unending line of Inubians appeared on the dunes behind them. Their skin was as black as jet, their jackal-faced heads as smooth as silk. Craig had never seen them before but he found them just as repulsive as the Ibis-headed assassin. Half man, half beast, they howled up at the darkening sky.

Elandria tensed.

"What is it?" whispered Craig. He didn't want to appear frightened.

"My kin are on the move. A whole army."

"Where?" asked Craig.

"Beneath your feet, my boy. Beneath your feet."

* * *

They had run for a good ten minutes before David Peck stopped for breath. He peered back into the gloom, down into the tunnel where the light had become even weaker and assumed a purple hue. He screwed up his eyes and whispered, as loud as he dared, "Cathy?"

"De nastee lady's gone," said Wee Joe.

"Wait." David hauled on Michael's sleeve. "Wee Joe's right. Where's Cathy?"

Jean Harrison, Ephie, Michael, and Helen all stopped scrambling forward and peered back into the darkness. Through their panting, David heard the scampering of feet and the ceaseless high-pitched chattering that had caused them to run in the first place. It was all around them now. Things scrambled round them. He could see their eyes. Hundreds of them, blinking red in the half-light.

"Cathy!" shouted David. "Are you there?" His voice shook.

"The spiders have her," said a thin voice, ghost-like and broken up, like a radio not properly tuned in to the station. "You are in our domain now. You are lost…"

Helen began to cry. Her big, wet tears traced down her mother's cheeks as she snuggled in to her face.

They all huddled together.

"Spiders? What spiders?" whispered Michael. He'd grabbed hold of David Peck's arm.

David lowered Wee Joe and nervously licked his lips. "I've no idea." He tried to focus on the figures in the gloom, but they flickered in and out of his vision like ghosts.

The grey, ethereal figures closed in on them. Only two feet high, they had long pointed noses and oversized ears that looked as though they'd been chewed. The nearest figure exposed a set of broken, yellow teeth and traced Helen's dark hair with a long, hoary finger.

Helen screamed, "Mum!"

"Leave her alone," shouted David. "Who are you? What do you want with us?"

The one who'd touched Helen's hair jabbed at David with a metal hook. "Artilians know what we are, and Artilians know what we want." The creature's voice crackled.

"I have no idea what an Artilian is," said David, his arm still smarting from the jab.

The creature turned to the rest of his kind. "He has no idea what we do to Artilians."

There was a roar of laughter and taunts.

The creature licked his black lips. "We eat Artilians. Especially the childlings."

"Be quiet. You'll frighten them," spat Jean.

"Look," said Ephie, trying to gain the creature's attention. "Why don't we trade?"

The Drumfintley group stared at Ephie in utter disbelief.

"You see," continued Ephie, "I have something here that will make your taste buds sear with delight."

The diminutive grey creature nearest to Ephie hushed his companions and grinned up at her. "We like to trade, but how can you trade when we could just take anything we want from what's left of your clothes and bones?" He raised his hook as if to strike her, but she held her ground.

"Do you want to see the secret substance, or not?" she pressed.

"Show me," snapped the creature.

Ephie rummaged in her jacket pocket until she found an intact bar of Galdinie's tablet. She waved it under the grey creature's long nose.

He sniffed and thinned his lips. "Give!" he demanded.

"Oh, I can give, but wouldn't it be better if I could tell you where there is much more?" Ephie snapped a piece of the buttery tablet off and placed it in the creature's outstretched, wrinkly hand.

The creature extended his black tongue and probed the sugary morsel. "Mmm, very, very tasty." He turned and nodded to his kin. "We must have more." He gripped Ephie's wrist. "Give me that!" He snatched the rest of the bar from her hand and fought his kin off in an effort to eat it all himself. Still chewing, he smiled and pushed his crooked nose an inch away from Wee Joe's face. "Is this as tasty as you, childling?"

Wee Joe spat on his knuckles and then caught the creature in the eye with a well-aimed fist.

"ARGH!" The creature's scream turned into a splutter and then a gagging cough. The flaking tablet had gone down the wrong way and now the creature was fighting for breath.

"Kill them now; they've poisoned Terth," said an old, crooked female.

To David's horror, the one named Terth fell to the floor of the cave and lay quite still, his gaping mouth stretched wide in a last, futile gasp for air.

"Wee Joe's killed him," whispered Michael. "Lord in heaven."

The dusty looking creatures closed round the Drumfintley party and raised their hooked maces.

"Close your eyes," said Jean, tears already rolling down her cheeks.

But before they could strike, one of them, a creature with particularly tattered ears and a pronounced hunch shouted out, "The leader, Terth is dead. We cannot do anything until we elect a successor."

"But they must die," said the female, her face contorted in sheer hatred. "They tricked us. They must die in the fire and be eaten." She rounded on Wee Joe. "This one is mine."

"No, the old one is right, we must elect a new leader first. It is written," said one of the taller creatures.

"You can't even read; kill them!" screamed the old female.

"No!" The older creature with the hunch held his left fist as high as he could. "Wait!"

Their screams of hate tuned into discourse and argument. They drew back from the Drumfintley party and began to build a fire.

"What's going on?" Jean wiped her eyes.

David had Helen between himself and Michael. "I think Ephie and Wee Joe might have bought us some time. It seems that they have to elect a new leader."

"Let's hope it takes a good few weeks." Michael forced a smile. "Where do you think Cathy is?"

"I don't know; but I can't believe that she would just sneak off," said David. "Something bad has happened to her."

Ephie shook her head in disbelief. "Something bad is happening to us."

"Cathy might be a bit challenging at times but she wouldn't desert us." David stole a glance at the creatures. The mêlée of shouts and incoherent mutterings died down. All that was left now was the crackling of a great fire. Pops and roars ricocheted off the cave walls. "They're having some kind of vote. Look, I wouldn't be surprised if Cathy comes back with help, any minute now. Trust me."

Chapter Twelve

The Golden Key

James read Willie MacNulty's message one more time before leaning back against the wall of the tunnel. To his relief, it was becoming cooler but the light that emanated from the rock was dimming. Mendel's voice filled their heads. "Before we move on, Sergeant Carr, look at the floor of the tunnel. Tell me what you see."

Carr squinted down at the sandy loam. "Sand?"

"As I thought," said Mendel. "What about you, Archie?"

Archie MacNulty was still in a state of shock at finding some tangible evidence of his dad's existence. He gently placed the polished stone slab against the cave wall and scanned the ground. "Seven sets," he muttered.

James moved closer to MacNulty. "What do you mean?"

"Judging by chhat piece of Galdinie's tablet wrapping you found and the footprintschh, I would schhay: five adults and two children, all from Drumfintley." A self-satisfied expression spread across the old poacher's weathered face. "Imagine a great detectivechh like yourchelf missing that, Carr?"

"Right. That's it. I'll have you right here and now, MacNulty." Sergeant Carr rolled up his sleeves and assumed a boxing stance.

James took a few steps back.

"Enough!" said Mendel.

The two men lowered their fists.

"I'm not sure how, but it would seem that your mother and father are here, James."

"They are?" He saw the goldfish sail past the window in the barrel.

"Along with Father Michael, Ephie, Mrs. Harrison, and the children."

Sergeant Carr dusted himself down. "They were behind us at the edge of the stones on Bruce Moor."

"They're in great danger down here. Eethan, James, run ahead quickly!"

"They ees gone north," said Eethan. James watched as Eethan licked the wall of the tunnel with his long, black tongue. "Theeys sweat is steel fresh on thee stone. Mmm…"

"That's minging, Eethan. Can we just go?" urged James.

"Ee can taste Dust Goblins too. Not so nice eee." He spat a yellow jelly-like blob onto the sand. "Yuckeee."

"Very," agreed James. He fumbled about in his rucksack for his blue inhaler as he began to run. He took a quick puff and called on his magic sword. Once Firetongue rested in his hand he felt a renewed surge of energy race through his veins. In fact, he nearly crashed right into Eethan who had stopped, suddenly, beside something on the floor of the tunnel. James held his nose. The smell was overpowering. "What is it?" James suspected the worst.

"Eet's not your speecies, James. Eeee!" Eethan kicked at the remains of the corpse. Six crumpled legs stood proud of the sand.

They look like an assortment of abandoned drinking straws, thought James. "It's one of those spider things we saw in Martilia, isn't it?"

"Eet's a Racnid. Male, ee thinks. Come!" Eethan began to run again, faster this time, into the tunnel ahead. The light had dimmed further and James had to be very careful not to trip.

Ahead, Eethan skidded to a halt and then scampered up onto the ceiling of the tunnel. "Eee'l approach them thees way. If you attack feerst eend destract them ee will try to find thee cheeldren. They eer most at risk."

James thought he understood and braced himself for the next turn in the tunnel. He'd heard chattering and the crackling sound of a fire, but it had all gone quiet. He looked down at the crimson sword and felt it twitch, eager for the fight. It was the sword that fought, not him. He reminded himself of this as the guilt gripped him. He merely gave it some direction and intent. He stepped out from behind the rock. There, in front of him, a huge fire blazed behind a gathering of the strangest looking group he'd seen since his time in Denthan. An assortment of ragged-looking creatures, no more than two feet high, huddled in conversation. Scrawny, with long noses and ears like tattered dishcloths, they turned round one by one until all hundred or so stared across the cave at him.

"James!"

The voice had come from behind the creatures. His pulse raced as he peered over the dusty looking crowd. There, in a small alcove behind the fire, James saw his dad, Michael, Ephie, Jean, and the kids. They looked terrified. He forced back the urge to look up at the roof of the cave for Eethan in case he gave him away. Instead, he fixed his gaze on the Dust Goblins and moved forward.

"Another Artilian has joined us for our celebration dinner." An old hunched creature bared its teeth and pointed at him. He held a bronze-coloured mace with a single hook protruding from the top. "Although," the creature continued, "he looks too pale to be a true Artilian." He turned to his kin and shouted, "Kill him!"

With a roar that shook the walls of the cave and reverberated down the tunnel behind him they ran straight at him, their maces held high.

"Run James. Run!" his dad shrieked over the din.

And James did run. Not out of the cave in a state of terror, but full pelt into the thick of the Dust Goblins, his crimson sword slashing and arcing through the dank air. The only thing he cut into, however, was the air itself and the occasional mace, which splintered as soon as the sword made contact. He jumped high and cut down at the leader's misshapen skull with a blow that should have finished him, but his sword simply sliced through the goblin's skull as if it wasn't even there. Like ghosts, the Dust Goblins' bodies seemed to be no more than grey mist.

A goblin mace suddenly found its mark and James felt pain sear up his shin. Luckily, his crimson sword had partially blocked the blow. He somersaulted backwards out of the thick of them and surveyed the scene. Where were Eethan and Mendel now?

"James, I meant to tell you," Mendel said, "the only thing your sword will touch is their weapons; their bodies are no more than dust and smoke."

He could still see his dad and the others cowering against the far wall.

Four hooked maces flew through the air toward his face but his sword sliced two in half while he dodged two more. He couldn't remember being able to move as fast as this in Denthan. *Was his power increasing?*

At least ten of the Dust Goblins had rounded on the Drumfintley group. They dragged them towards the fire in the middle of the room. Jean Harrison screamed. He ran round the main group, beside the wall and then bounced to a halt in-between the Drumfintley group and the roaring fire. "Stop! Leave them alone, and I will spare you." Inside, terror riddled him.

The Dust Goblins lifted their clubs and made to advance, but as they did, a great curtain of blue drifted down on them from the ceiling. It covered everything in a cold, damp fog, chilling him to his very bones. It doused the fire with a loud hiss and caused the Dust Goblins' skin to glisten like wet, dewy leaves. James struck out at the nearest creature and saw its head roll back off its shoulders. The Dust Goblins began to scream in fear now as they tested their own skin with their long, wet fingers. With a shout, James advanced and cut a devastating path through the confused goblins until he reached his dad. "Everyone, move towards the far wall."

Bero appeared in the cave with Carr and MacNulty. The Golden Retriever barked and bit hard on any goblin unfortunate enough to get too close to the exit of the cave, while the older men, having retrieved some fallen maces, used the hooks on the goblins, cutting the wretches down as they advanced.

There was an agonized command from the hunched leader of the Dust Goblins, "Leave this cursed place; leave now!"

Almost at once, the Dust Goblins fell back and seemed to disappear into the very rock of the cave. The clatter of discarded maces was soon replaced by an eerie silence.

"Son?" David Peck's voice echoed out across the vast cave. Even in the purple gloom James could see the whites of his dad's eyes. "What did you just do?"

"I saved your life, Dad. Although it wasn't just me." He looked down at his right hand, but the magic sword had disappeared. "Eethan made them killable."

His dad stared up in trepidation at the little, blue man who, James realised, did not look that dissimilar to the Dust Goblins.

Eethan dropped down from the ceiling, cat-style, and landed on all fours. "Pleeesed to meet thee; fatheer of James."

To James's embarrassment, Eethan performed a theatrical bow.

"Pardon?" said David.

"He said that he is pleased to meet you," said Helen. "He talks a bit funny," she added, wiping her tearstained face with the edge of her jumper.

"You know this... This *man?*" broached David.

James saw the hurt in his dad's face.

"We all do," said Michael. Ephie, Jean, and the kids all nodded in agreement.

"For goodness sake, and I suppose MacNulty and Sergeant Carr are in on this as well?" said David.

"I didn't know about any of this before today," wheezed Sergeant Carr, apologetically.

His dad's attention drifted to the plastic barrel swinging beneath Bero's chin. "James's goldfish?"

"You may call me Mendel."

David Peck stared down in astonishment.

"And it looks as though we got here just in time," Mendel added.

James watched as his dad looked across at the doused fire and sighed with relief. "You can say that again."

"Dad, where's Mum?" His chest tightened.

"I was hoping you could tell us that," said David.

James wondered if the old wizard could sense his mum; he sometimes could, if the person was near enough. "Mendel, any ideas? Can you feel anything?"

Mendel blubbed against the plastic window before circling the inside of the barrel. "It's difficult to say. There's still a connection between you and her; so she's not..."

"Dead?" finished James.

"Quite," said Mendel. "Wait!"

"What?" yelped Ephie, still looking very shaken.

"Wisten!" said Wee Joe.

They all looked down at Wee Joe and then around the cave, fearing that the Dust Goblins were about to return.

The low rustling sound became louder. It was coming from the main tunnel.

"It sounds like an army of giant ants," said Helen. "Millions of them."

"She's not far off the mark," said Mendel. "Quick; hide behind the rocks at the back of the cave. With any luck they'll pass us by."

As they took their positions, back in the alcove where the Dust Goblins had held them, the marching sound grew steadily louder until

the whole cave shook. Clouds of fine sand filled the air and loose stalactites crashed down around them. James began to cough. Without
the sword, Firetongue, in his hand, his breathing became more difficult.

The first of the Racnids marched past the entranceway of the cave,
their hairy feet scampering across the bare rock. Row after row moved
across the entrance of the cave. There must have been a thousand
green-furred Racnids followed by even more that seemed to be pure
black. After about an hour the last sounds of the spider army faded
away.

James was really worried about his mum now. "Where were they all
going to, Mendel?"

"To war, I presume. Just like the Inubians above ground, they are
all heading for Artilia. I'm surprised Dendralon isn't with them."

"Is he near?" James whispered.

"This is the first time I've felt his presence. My scales are tingling
with static."

MacNulty was inadvertently fidgeting with something in his
poacher's pocket.

James had seen the old gardener wipe away a tear or two and he
supposed that he must have been thinking about his dad, Willie. James
knew what it was like to continually be wondering; torturing himself,
while everyone else was just trying to survive. He felt sorry for old
Archie. "Your dad was trying to warn us about the Dust Goblins in his
message on the stone: '*beware the Dust…*' There must be a good chance
he survived them. But the message had also mentioned a maze, which,
as yet, they hadn't reached. *Had his mum found the maze and pushed on
without his dad?* "Dad, when did you realise Mum had gone?"

"I… I don't remember. She told us to run on and then…when we
stopped, she wasn't there. She was supposed to be right behind us."

"Didn't you look for her? You didn't retrace your steps?"

"No we didn't," admitted Michael.

What would she do when she found out that his dad hadn't even
missed her in the tunnels, just left her behind? He looked across at his
dad. It looked as though he was thinking the same thought. His dad's
face was fixed in a very serious expression; his mouth shut tight, his
thumb massaging his right temple. "You alright, Dad?" asked James.

His dad forced a smile. "Yes. Yes, I'm just so relieved to see you
again, Son."

"Just a pity you lost Mum, eh?"

"I feel so bad. It's just a pity…"

"It certainly will be when she catches up with you," interrupted Ephie.

"No sign of Craig?" asked Mrs. Harrison, an anxious expression already fixed on her dirty face.

"Nothing yet," replied Mendel. "I didn't feel his presence in Martilia."

She looked confused.

James explained. "We ended up in an alleyway in this city. It was full of all sorts of weird creatures. Mendel didn't think Craig was there. Maybe he's with Mum."

"Maybe," she answered, dolefully.

"James?" Mendel's voice cut through the tension. "Now that the Racnids have passed by, we should go back towards Martilia."

"Why?"

"We should find out what Archie's dad meant when he told us to 'go through the maze'. I have a feeling there's something in there that could help us."

"Help us do what?" objected Ephie. "Why aren't we trying to find Cathy and Craig as quickly as we can and get back home?"

"Ephie's got a point," agreed Michael.

"She has, but there may not be any way to get back, ever, if Dendralon gets his hands on the third crystal he needs."

"We have to find it first," said James.

"Exactly," said Mendel. "We need to try and stop him from coming through to Drumfintley with his army. We must close down his gateway, and…" Mendel splashed in the barrel, "we will still be looking for Cathy and Craig."

Ephie didn't seem particularly satisfied with the explanation.

Eethan managed to produce some food and a little water before they headed north again. There was no chance of picking up any tracks on the tunnel floor after thirty thousand Racnids had scuttled over the sand so they didn't waste time trying. After a mile or so, they found the tunnel to their left that, according to Archie's dad, would lead them to the maze. They listened hard as they walked onward, keeping a close eye on the walls of the cave lest any Dust Goblins might appear from the shadows. There were a few false alarms, mostly due to Sergeant Carr becoming disorientated or the kids seeing things but they carried on, as best as they could, until they reached a strange looking wall.

"Is it a castle?" asked James, trying his best to focus in the purple gloom.

They all squinted up at a structure that could only be described as an underground palisade. Built from the same stone as the tunnel, its high walls were studded with long spikes, each of which sported a bleached human-like skull.

"Nice," said James. He instantly realised that this was just the kind of thing Craig would have said and felt a pang of regret.

Craig's mum put a hand on his shoulder.

"Theeres thee entrance," said Eethan, ducking beneath a rugged archway.

"Wait!"

Mendel's warning, however, came too late. As soon as Eethan pressed his bare blue toe on the ground beyond the archway, the floor of the cave began to move. Bumps appeared under the sand, shifting small boulders around their feet.

"Mum!"

Jean yanked on her daughter's hand. "Stay close Helen. Joe, hold your sister's hand."

As James called on Firetongue, pink, hooked mouths emerged from the sandy loam at their feet.

"*Strongalus arenus!*" warned Mendel.

"What?" wheezed James.

"Sandworms. They're carnivorous," Mendel yelled.

Screams filled the cavern as they all hared after Bero towards the palisade, kicking the maggot-like worms to the side or leaping high to avoid their snapping mouthparts. The archway seemed to be the only spot on the floor of the tunnel free of the snapping worms. James stood outside the arch hacking as many sandworms as he could in an effort to keep them at bay while the rest of the group got inside. Ephie was the last to go through but as James turned, he felt a hooked mouth grab onto his leg. The raw pain of the razor sharp teeth was followed by an incredibly agonizing stinging sensation. He hacked the worm in two and dived through the opening. Its hooked jaws were still attached to his leg.

"Mendel!" He felt his legs wobble before slumping to the ground.

Eethan stood over him and whispered a charm. His mind was becoming muggy. Dark wriggling shadows seemed to be dragging him below the ground. "Get off! Leave me alone!" He kicked out.

"Jameszzz..."

Slowly, he opened his eyes. His face was sticky with tears.

Craig's mum was leaning over him. "Are you okay?"

He looked down at his leg and saw a faint red mark. The pain had gone.

"Eet weel nip for ee few days. Ee got thee bitey teeth out."

"Thanks...I..."

"That was very brave of you, James." Craig's mum squeezed his hand and smiled.

Lying inside the archway he noticed that the pink and purple hue of the cave had changed completely. They were in a narrow tunnel bathed in a yellow light. The archway flickered then disappeared.

"The walls is moving. Mum wook..." Wee Joe's voice was unusually thin. He tugged on the torn, silk hem of her skirt.

James forced himself to his feet. "The walls are closing in on us."

All of them ran further into the arched tunnel and soon had to choose between a turn to their left and a passage on their right. The passage on the right emitted the same yellow light, but the one on the left was full of green light that danced and crackled like a mini lightning storm.

"Left," said Mendel. Be quick before the walls trap us."

"Are you sure?" panted James.

"Of course not. Just run," snapped the wizard.

Bero's tail just slipped into the green tunnel when a huge stone slab slid down with a crash to shut them in. It went completely dark.

"Mum?" It was Helen's voice this time.

"Don't worry Helen; I'm here," said Jean.

Eethan whispered another charm. A blue glow emanated from his fingertips. It was enough to let them see that they were in another long tunnel with a charred wooden door at the far end.

"Now what?" said Ephie, her normally curly hair plastered to her head with sweat.

"Keep us safe, Lord." Michael's eyes were wide with fright.

The tunnel suddenly became very warm.

"It's only an illusion," warned Mendel. "Just think about ice and cool water and..."

"I'm burning up!" screamed Helen.

"Right," said Mendel. "Well, just think of..."

"Get us out of here!" screamed Jean.

Again. James said his magic word and the crimson sword, Firetongue, settled in his hand. But he didn't know how to use it against heat, against this burning sensation that sapped his energy and stole his breath. He ran at the door and slashed at the wooden panels, but nothing happened. Michael and Ephie charged the door with MacNulty and Carr, but still it didn't budge.

"Leth na ta chan!"

Eethan's words had barely left his thin, blue lips when a large, red figure appeared behind them.

The heat intensified.

Jean covered her children's' eyes and crouched against the door.

Eethan's fingers continued to emit a blue haze, which now spread over Jean and the kids, forming a blue bubble round them. It continued to immerse David, MacNulty, Carr, and then Bero, Michael, and Ephie. Only James stood outside the cooling blue mist that swirled round Eethan.

Although panic gripped him, James imagined the cooling waters of Loch Echty and dark underwater graveyard. He could almost see the black obelisk...

"James!" Mendel's voice seemed far away. He screwed up his eyes and tried to pick out Bero behind Eethan's blue magic. "I can't..." His head pounded. He saw the red figure move towards him. "Wwwcoolwwwaterswww!"

As the walls of the tunnel began to char, to his relief, he felt a beautiful wave of iced water creep up his arm from the hilt of the sword. Firetongue was protecting him. He crouched and faced the red figure. Crimson ribbons of flame leapt from the shape that now confronted him. James glanced back, once more, at the Drumfintley group then turned and braced. The creature had changed form. It was now a single burning effigy of flame. It wavered briefly before assuming the outline of an old man. Strangely, James recognized him. At least he thought he did. "Archie?"

The figure tilted its head and stared at him. James glanced back at Eethan's bubble. Archie was still huddled underneath it with Carr and the rest of them.

The creature's voice was ghostly. Distant. "William MacNulty, at your service, sonny."

"You're alive!"

The red figure's face drew in on itself, its eyes sinking deeper into their hollow sockets.

James took a step back. "Maybe not. Are you a ghost?" James felt his heart quicken. Sweat dripped into his eyes.

"Please, have a little tact, sonny."

"I'm sorry." James knew he was on his own. Mendel and Eethan seemed to be busy enough maintaining the cooling bubble round the rest of the group.

"I don't have much time, so listen."

James studied the wraith-like figure of MacNulty Senior. Still dressed in his poaching tweeds his image wavered, shimmering every time he spoke. "I knew Archie would come for me eventually. I take it he has the key?"

The question took James by surprise. "The key?"

"How else could you have come through? If I'd taken it with me I could have returned to Drumfintley all those years ago."

"We came through the Jesus Rocks with the help of a wizard called Mendel. I don't know anything about a key."

"A wizard, eh? Never liked wizards much." Archie's dad took a step forward. "Look, sonny, I played with fire and got burned. I failed. Curiosity got the better of me, and now look at what I've become. The only reason I can speak with you after all this time is because I've done a deal with Belloc."

"Belloc?" enquired James.

"The demon that guards the third crystal of Artilis. When I discovered her lair, tried to take the crystal, she struck me down. I am to guard this maze for eternity unless…"

"Yes," James prompted.

"Unless one of my sons sets me free."

James screwed up his eyes and wiped them with his sleeve.

"Belloc thought it unlikely that both would come through to Artilis at the same time, if ever." The ethereal figure of MacNulty Senior looked over James's shoulder. "They can't see me. But it is enough that I can see them one last time."

"Them? What do you mean?"

"Archie and Albert, of course…" The wraith's eyes sunk in once more. "They are brothers."

"Albert? Who's Albert?"

"Albert Carr. His mum wanted him to keep her name. It's so sad to see them as old men…" The wraith began to cry. It shook and wept in utter despair.

"You mean that Sergeant Carr and Archie are…?"

"It's a long story, sonny. I've seen them now and that's enough. Get them home safely, you and your wizard. Use the key. I can rest now."

MacNulty's image flickered like an old movie caught in the reel, his voice fading in and out. "Use the key…" He vanished.

The red light disappeared.

David Peck pushed his face against Eethan's bubble from the inside. "James, are you still okay?"

Dazed, his leg now aching, James nodded.

With a pop, Eethan's blue bubble burst. James stood in a state of shock, shaking as blue globules of light ebbed away through the cracks in the floor.

The intense heat now gone, the Drumfintley group stepped forward towards him. Their hair, at least those who had hair, was pressed flat against their heads and their clothes were drenched in sweat.

Wee Joe began to shiver. "Dis place is much worse dan the udder place, Mum."

James saw Jean nod her head, quietly. "You're right, Son. Much worse than Denthan." Her eyes were fixed on some indiscernible spot in the distance. "What was that thing? Was it talking to you?"

"Well…" James paused, trying to think of the best way of answering her. He pointed to MacNulty. "It was your dad, Mr. MacNulty." He met MacNulty's stare.

"Ischh he alive? Where…" MacNulty ran over to the spot where his dad's ghost had stood. "I only schhaw a schhape. Couldnae make it out."

"He said to get you both home safe."

"Both?"

"He meant all of us, of course; but he meant you and Sergeant Carr, in particular."

"Me and…" MacNulty drew Carr a scathing look.

Carr shuffled awkwardly, staring down at his feet. "You never knew, did you?"

"Knew whatch?" snapped MacNulty.

James saw Mendel push an orange eye against the window of the barrel.

"Your mum died just after you were born," said Carr.

Archie MacNulty looked close to tears. "Aye, she did. Never knew her. What's that got to do witch you?"

James was trying to work it out.

Carr continued. "You see, my dad was lost in the war. Never came back to Drumfintley." Carr stared down at his feet, mournfully. "I was just fourteen."

"You're four years older than Archie, then?" James pressed.

"Aye, son." Carr loosened his collar.

"Look," continued James, trying to ignore the throbbing pain in his leg, "I've just spoken to a ghost, or something, that told me you were brothers."

"Aye, right! Ch you... Don't you..." Archie MacNulty's teeth became loose as he scrambled for the right words.

"When mum died having you, I was brought up by her sister in Stendleburgh. Dad looked after you. I never saw him again." Carr's face went puce. He looked close to breaking point. When you came along I lost both my parents!"

Father Michael tried to placate Sergeant Carr but Archie lunged out and almost knocked James over. He caught Carr on the chin.

"Steady!" James drew his sword. "No need to get violent. There's enough of that here. Look, I saw something that claimed both his sons were here, okay?"

Helen's muffled voice sounded out from behind her mum's sleeve: "That's why Sergeant Carr is always nasty to Mr. MacNulty, mum. He blames him for something that wasn't even his fault."

"It was his fault," spat Carr, eyeing Archie contemptuously.

James cut in. "Archie, your dad went through the Jesus Rocks and became trapped here. But he said he could have got home if he'd remembered to take some key or other."

Carr nursed his chin. "What key?" He shook his head.

Archie was fixed to the spot, standing, trancelike, with his hand inside his jacket.

"He said you had the key, Archie. The one that he wished he'd taken with him to Artilis. A key that might get us all home."

MacNulty drew his hand away from his poacher's pocket, a guilty expression forming on his wrinkled face. "He did, did he?"

"How do you suppose your dad got through this maze? I mean," James glanced down at the brandy barrel and saw that Eethan was busy patting Bero. "We've got two wizards and a magic sword and we're still not through the first door yet. Your dad must have been looking for the third crystal. He was looking for a way back home because he forgot to take the key with him. He met a demon called Belloc. As far as I can make out, he made a deal with the demon. He agreed to guard these tunnels in the hope that he would see his boys again, one day. Finally, he said that he'd seen you both now and that he could rest."

Carr looked up at MacNulty and shifted sulkily. "I..."

The old gardener, his weathered face flushing, tightened his lips and looked down at James, a mixture of anger and guilt in his eyes.

"There's something in your pocket, isn't there? In your poacher's pocket," urged James.

"It's just Sarg; my ferret," lied MacNulty.

"Oh com'on, Mr. MacNulty, you left Sarg back in Drumfintley. What is it? Is it the key?" James felt awkward pressing the old man like this, but even back in Martilia, James remembered Mendel saying that MacNulty was hiding something from the group.

"I... I didn't want to use it too soon," muttered MacNulty.

"What is it, Mr. MacNulty? It might help me find my mum," said James, a heavy sensation of dread spreading over his chest.

MacNulty's face softened. "It was under my dad's mattress. I found it about four years ago. I'd dechhided..." MacNulty adjusted his teeth sucking back a length of drool that had dripped from the side of his mouth.

James winced.

"I'd decided," MacNulty continued, "to throw out his bed, but when I lifted the old mattress..." MacNulty reached into his poacher's pocket and produced a brown paper bag. "I found this."

James screwed up his eyes.

MacNulty held the top of the bag shut. Something was moving inside. He shielded it from the others with his big, gnarly hand.

"What the heck...?" James moved closer. "Mendel?"

"I must see what's there," whispered Mendel, his voice full of trepidation.

MacNulty opened the top of the bag and lowered it, as if he was offering James a sweet.

James peered inside and saw a small golden object. It moved again. Gingerly, James placed his fingers round the object and pulled it free of the bag. It was shaped like a key, alright, but the teeth of the key shifted continually, whirring in a blur of gold until they settled on a shape. The key looked different every time it stopped. There were three small gems; one red, one blue, and one yellow set in the metal and, on the thickest part, James saw the shape of a pyramid. He flinched as the teeth of key shifted again.

"It does that all the time," whispered MacNulty, in wonder.

"What's dat?"

James almost dropped the key.

It was Wee Joe, pulling on his shirt.

"Is it a sweet; we're starving," said Helen.

MacNulty stuffed the key back into the paper bag and whisked it back into his pocket. But it was too late. Everyone had rounded on them. Father Michael spoke first. "Archie, what...?"

"The lost Key of Artilis," said Mendel, his voice now clear in everybody's mind. "Unless James's eyes are deceiving me. This could..."

"This could what?" pressed James.

"This is fascinating. Can I see it again, Mr. MacNulty?" said Mendel.

Sheepishly, MacNulty produced the paper bag from his coat once more and handed it to James.

David Peck leaned over his son. "It's beautiful."

Ephie looked first at the key and then at the charred door. "It might be able to open the door," she broached.

"It can do far more than that," said Mendel, his tone suddenly ominous. "It can unlock any door, and..." He splashed over to his plastic window and peered up at the key. "It can be used as a catalyst for time shifting."

"What do you mean?" asked James.

"It can fold space and time, if used in the right way. This is very bad."

"How's that bad?" said James.

"It would be very bad indeed if Dendralon got possession of this key. It was thought that the Key of Artilis was lost forever. When the meteor smashed into this world, it was thrown out into deepest space, along with cities and many poor souls. The people of Artilis tried to find it, hoping beyond hope that they could use it to change the fate of their planet."

"Could they use it now?" said James.

"No, alas the key can only fold space a little. It would be possible to go back in time for perhaps a year or two, no more." Mendel seemed to drift off in thought at this point.

James felt his dad's hand on his shoulder. "Son, can you ask Mendel if the key can help us find your mum?"

"It can," interrupted Mendel. "But just now we need to use the key to pass through this maze as quickly as we can."

"Mr. MacNulty's dad said that the third crystal is in the centre of the maze. But we don't have to go in now that we have the key. We don't need the other crystal," said James.

"I'm afraid we do," said Mendel.

A deep rumbling sound echoed down the tunnel towards them.

"We have to get in to get out. Quick James, try the key in the charred door."

James placed the key in the keyhole and watched as it jiggled by itself and turned. The door swung inward to reveal a very strange sight. Even more doors swept to their right and left. As they stepped inside the huge hall the charred door slammed shut behind them.

"There are one hundred doors in this part of the maze," said Mendel. "And behind all but one, there is certain death."

"Marvellous," said Michael, pulling his white dog collar away from his neck nervously.

Everyone looked at him.

"How's that marvellous, Mum?" asked Helen.

"He's just being sarcastic," explained Jean. She gave Father Michael a withering stare.

James shushed them. "Wait. What's that?"

They heard a rumbling sound that intensified before something very big crashed against the charred door they'd just come through.

A thin wisp of smoke curled round Sergeant Carr's neck. He screamed and ran left, along the row of doors and then stopped dead, in front of a door with a reddish tinge.

Mendel's voice rang in their ears, "Sergeant Carr, don't touch it!"

Chapter Thirteen

The Battle for Artilia Begins

Cathy Peck opened her eyes and instantly felt sick. Her head was throbbing and she found that she couldn't move her arms or legs. White, silken ropes had been laced around her limbs. She was held fast, in a standing position, against a large, cold pillar. The room she found herself in was enormous. Six St. Donan's churches would have fit into the space without too much trouble and the ceiling was barely discernible. It had an Egyptian feel, she decided; and there was a sickly sweet smell in the air that caught her throat and made her want to cough.

"You are awake, at last, my queen," said a deep, steady voice.

It was the kind of voice normally offered up by an actor or perhaps some pompous politician, she thought. Cathy turned her head to see, but her long, black hair swished over her face and covered her eyes. She tried to stick her bottom lip out as far as she could, blowing upward in an effort to get a better look at her captor. "I am not your queen; whoever you are, so let me go." Cathy caught a glimpse of a hideous face. She screamed out: "You're..."

"Dead?" replied the creature.

"I saw you fall. I..."

"You did indeed. But you did not see me die. In fact, *being dead* has given me some time to rethink my strategy."

"What have you done with Craig?" snapped Cathy, straining against the rope and shaking the last strands of black hair free of her face.

"The boy? Well, he was supposed to have been fed to the sand-worms by now, but my staff let me down." Dendralon's voice had assumed a petulant tone.

"What have you done with him?" Cathy's voice echoed off the hard marble pillars and drifted up into the high vaulted ceiling.

"You know, I never really got the time to appreciate you last time, did I? You are so like her. Even your spirit is the same," said Dendralon. He tilted his reptilian head, moved very close and then whispered, "Untamed." She watched him move away. He flicked his scaled hand. "For all I know, the boy is dead," he continued. "He escaped with a known political enemy of the state, but things are too far advanced now for that to matter." He turned back to look at Cathy, his horizontally closing eyelids snapping shut as he sniffed in her flowery scent. "Beldam," he whispered.

"Who?" sneered Cathy.

Dendralon hissed, his long, grey tongue flicking between his teeth. "I knew you would return to be my queen."

"Look, you disgusting... I'm not your queen and my name isn't Beldam."

"Fate has brought us together, though I did not recognize you the first time. I see now that you can be no other."

"Fate? I don't believe in fate." Cathy Peck was beginning to tire of this monster. "Untie me!"

"I'm sorry, my queen; but I have to cause you a little pain before the pleasures of ruling at my side can be allowed to unfold."

Cathy braced. "Why would I want to have anything to do with a psychopathic snake who's tied me up and couldn't care less about anyone but himself?"

Dendralon looked slightly perplexed for a moment, but then resumed his mutterings and reached into a small sarcophagus. He produced a golden object shaped like a large pen and proceeded to slash invisible signs in the air around Cathy's face. "This..." He brought the tip closer to Cathy's white neck. "...is the *stylus*. I used it to kill you the first time. An act for which I can only humbly apologize."

Cathy pulled away from the tip of the golden stylus. "Where is my son?" She spat the words out in defiance, but fear was beginning to grip her and she wondered if she would ever see James again.

Cathy screamed when the needle-sharp tip pierced her skin.

* * *

Craig and Elandria ran forward, through the gates of Artilia, into the maze of streets and alleys that surrounded the base of the giant pyramid. Bare-chested soldiers poured out of a thousand hidden doors, their shields clattering against their spears as they ran up the steps to man the battlements.

Junera yelled out her commands and soon cleared the walls of the young and old while her archers notched their arrows and ballistae were wound tight. The creak of straining ropes soon replaced the chattering of children.

Craig staggered through the mêlée in an effort to reach the top of the gate tower where Junera barked her commands.

Elandria scampered up the sheer wall of the battlements to join Craig and Junera. "You must be prepared for more than this." She pointed a cupped hand at the advancing Inubians"

"What do you mean?" said Junera.

"I can hear them."

"Hear what?" said Junera. "How can you possibly hear anything over this racket?"

"My Lady, I can hear in registers you can't imagine. I can hear my kin; and I don't mean the Ibissynian steeds."

Craig watched as Elandria's fine, green-tipped down rippled in the breeze to reveal the darker mauve underneath. Her wrinkled, bulbous eyes widened.

"There are thousands of them. I can hear them; smell them. Females." Nervously, Elandria scampered up the tower and looked down at the sand beneath the walls. Craig followed her gaze, firstly out across the desert and then, alarmingly, inside the city itself. "They are under our very feet. There are in the tunnels!"

Junera looked shaken. "May the gods preserve us. Blue division! Back down off the walls. Get inside the pyramid and defend the old openings."

Just as she spoke there was a massive shift of sand outside the walls. Thousands of Racnids pushed their way up through the ground, their hairy legs pulling them free of the sand as they spilled over each other in one tangled mass.

On seeing this, the Inubians howled with delight and began their charge. Like a sea of black, they poured down the large dune where the herdsman had appeared earlier, their long ears flattened, their swords raised high.

Craig, mesmerized by the onslaught, almost forgot to say his magic word. "Greenworm," he spluttered. In the heat of the moment he wondered what he was doing here, on this violent alien world, so far away from his family and friends. *Where are James and Mendel now?* he wondered.

"Craig, look out!" Elandria thrust her abdomen forward and plunged her stinger into a large Racnid female who was about to tackle Craig. The attacker twitched and convulsed on the edge of the battlement before dropping down onto her kin.

Shaken from his thoughts, Craig slashed out with his spear, cutting a further two Racnids in half as they clambered over the parapets. He put his back against Junera's and fought as hard as he could against the tide of spider-like assailants. Both of them turned and stabbed out, in unison, as one, fighting their way through the scrimmage. Elandria issued a high-pitched whine as she stung and clambered amongst her own. She was bigger and faster than the other, black-haired Racnids making easy work of the creatures on her side of the battlement. An arrow arced down from the purple sky towards Craig but Greenworm spun from his hand and flicked the arrowhead to his left, its razor tip grazing his cheek. "Argh!"

Junera ducked lower. "That was an Ibissynian arrow. Your bird-faced assassin must have recovered."

"Fantastic!" panted Craig. Blood ran down his face and dripped onto his shirt.

"It's not the same one!" shouted Elandria. "I can sense it."

The Jackal-headed Inubians had reached the city walls and were clambering up a living wall of Racnids.

"That's why the Racnids didn't all come into the city from the tunnels," shouted Junera. "They've formed a living siege tower. Dendralon is behind this evil."

"You're not wrong!" shouted Craig, thrusting up at a huge Inubian. The creature slashed down with his curved sword but Junera jerked round to parry the blow while Craig's spear plunged deep into its chest. The Inubian howled and fell dead at their feet.

"We have to retreat," said Junera. "We have to get inside the pyramid. Come!" She grabbed Craig's collar and pulled him down a set of steps just as twenty or so Inubians, interspersed with Racnids, leapt over the battlements behind them.

Craig was out of breath. "I thought you said the Racnids were breaking into the pyramid from the tunnels. What's the point of going in there? We'll be trapped."

"We'll be killed out here for certain. Trust me!" urged Junera.

The cries of battle subsided as Craig, Elandria, and Junera made their way back towards the pyramid. As the main fight raged behind them, Craig heard the ballistae fire their red sandstone boulders into the desert but knew, as he ran, that the battle was beyond them now. With the Inubians already overrunning the ramparts and the black-furred Racnids stinging their way towards them, they had to retreat. They ran through a huge stone doorway into the gloom beyond.

Junera brought them to a halt. "In here. Quick, before they see us."

"But what about your soldiers?" cried Craig.

"They will be remembered." Junera tugged them into a side tunnel and pulled a lever, which caused a heavy stone slab to slide down and seal them off.

"They'll be remembered? Nice," said Craig, sarcastically. The cut on his cheek was beginning to nip.

"Are you okay?" said Elandria. She reached into her side for one of her water pouches. "The cut is deeper than you think." The green downed Racnid said a small charm and a red light spilled over her cup-like hand. She flicked the liquid onto Craig's cheek. He felt it sizzle on his skin. "Hey! That hurts!" Craig touched his cheek, but the cut had disappeared.

They continued through a small opening and stepped into a larger chamber. "The pain's gone."

Elandria revealed her teeth and nodded. Craig assumed it was an attempt at a smile. "Thanks," he muttered.

Junera spun round, tapping her long sword on the ground as she advanced. "Alright, you two; never mind the complements. There is one, and only one, spot where the Racnids can break through into the pyramid."

"And that's right there, isn't it?" asked Craig.

"It is," confirmed Elandria.

Ahead, Craig could see a large pit in the ground. Above it, an enormous plug of stone hung, suspended by the thickest rope he had ever seen.

"The rock that hangs above is too heavy for any man, beast or magic," said Junera.

"What about a Kraken?" Craig's cheeky smile quickly changed into an apologetic shrug.

A noise sounded from below them. "Craig?"

He tensed. "Mum?"

Junera climbed up the stone plug and began cutting the rope that held it secure.

"Wait! Just wait a minute, I thought I heard my mum!" Craig peered down into the pit, "Mum!"

"Craig! Craig!"

Craig instantly recognized Helen's and Wee Joe's voices shouting up at him in unison.

Elandria scuttled round the edge of the pit and looked into his eyes. "Craig, the Racnid army is only seconds from the opening."

Junera continued cutting the rope.

"Stop!" screamed Craig; his anger spilling out. He edged back, craning his neck while shouting up at Junera. "I know you don't give a monkey's bum about anyone else, but I do. So stop cutting that rope or I'll use my spear." Craig slammed his green-etched spear against the bedrock. Emerald sparks whizzed round the base of the shaft.

Junera glimpsed down at Craig but resumed cutting. "I have over forty thousand people, still inside this pyramid, to save. Thirteen thousand on the battlements have already given their lives so I'm not about to listen to one boy who has a couple of friends in trouble. Got that?"

"It's not just a couple of friends. It's my family." Greenworm twitched in his hand. But it was too late. The huge plug of rock slipped free of its bindings. Craig threw himself back as it slammed down into the hole. A hundred wriggling Racnid legs were severed in the same moment.

"Mum!" Craig broke down in tears. "Why? Why didn't you give them a few more seconds?" His sobs grew louder.

Elandria put her front arms around Craig and opened her big, turtle-like eyes. "That was not your mother, Craig."

"It was. And my sister. I heard them."

"You wanted to hear them."

Craig wiped his eyes.

"Elandria's right," said Junera. "The Ibissynians have ways of playing with your mind. They were trying to delay us. Stop us from blocking the path of the Racnid army into the pyramid of Ra."

Craig gave himself a shake and bristled. "Rubbish! You... You just want me to believe that 'cause it makes you both feel better about what you've just done. You've killed them!"

"I do not lie," said Elandria. "Besides, you said in your sleep, in Martilia, that Mendel is with your family and friends. If that is so, they will be safe. He knows things that nobody else knows, senses things. He predicted that, one day, I would abandon my kind and that they would hate me. And..."

Craig blazed with fury. "What do you know about Mendel? Nothing, I bet!"

"Mendel is a good man, one of the original race."

"Do you think...?" Craig felt his legs weaken as the green spear disappeared. "Do you think my family is here in Artilis?" He tried to hold back his rage. His energy was ebbing away. He threw the ruthless Junera a withering stare befitting of Cathy Peck then settled on the Racnid. "Elandria?"

"Yes, I think they are here. And if there is one man who can defeat Dendralon, it is Mendel."

"Ah," sniffed Craig. "I forgot to tell you. Mendel is a goldfish these days."

Elandria gave him a perplexed stare.

"He is about three inches long and can't perform magic without the help of my best friend, James. He's not at his best." Craig sniffed back a tear and wiped his nose on his sleeve.

Junera kicked a pile of severed Racnid legs out of the way before placing her sword back in its scabbard. "I lost my family to an Ibissynian. We were condemned for harbouring a fugitive; a Racnid fugitive." She glanced at Elandria.

Craig, far from consoled, resumed his hateful stare in Junera's direction. "What now?"

"Now I take you to the apex of the pyramid, above the surface of the planet, and you wait," said Junera.

"Wait for what?" pressed Craig.

"You wait for Mendel and we'll all pray for a bit of luck," said Junera.

Craig didn't particularly believe in luck. "You make luck. It just doesn't come along, like a bus."

"A what?"

"Never mind." Craig tried to put the voices he'd just heard out of his mind. It had sounded so much like his mother and Helen. "How do we get to the top of the pyramid?"

Junera signalled towards a red wooden door set into the rock. "We can reach the top this way. I will go back down and face the Racnids with the remainder of the Artilian army. We will make one last stand."

"Em," broached Craig, "how is Mendel supposed to get to us at the top of the pyramid?" His question remained unanswered as Elandria and Junera pressed on.

* * *

Below the massive plug of rock a huge line of Racnids backed up for over two miles. Standing tall amongst them, an Ibissynian, his long bill gleaming in the dim purple light closed the lid of a small brown box. The children's voices were snuffed out and the shuffling sound of Racnids on the march took over. The Ibissynian handed the box to a particularly big Racnid with a red spot at the end of her abdomen. "Take it, Elhada. The voices did not delay them sealing the entrance."

"No, but the box of delights may yet serve us well. I will keep it, as Dendralon instructed." Elhada pushed the plain brown box into a slit in her side and scuttled after the Ibissynian. "My kin have told me that we have overrun the battlements of Artilia and that the Inubians are now inside the city."

"Unless we can get inside the pyramid, it is useless. Dendralon will have to bring the Kraken back to Artilis."

"Mmm... I think you are correct," said Elhada. "He will not be pleased." The long hairs on her feet tingled as they brushed over the sticky trails left by her kin. "My sisters have found your twin wrapped in silk at the city gates."

The tall Ibissynian hissed up at the purple ceiling of the tunnel. "He has failed in his duty. He will be punished."

Elhada stopped to lick the red patch of fur at the end of her abdomen. "We shall not need the Kraken. My younglings will fare well here." She lowered her abdomen and deposited two small white larvae on the floor of the tunnel and then stepped back. She moved on, looking back momentarily to see her young wriggle up the side of the tunnel below the huge plug of rock that sealed the entrance into the pyramid. "They will burrow through the rock, moult into spiderlings, and then hunt."

"But it will be days before they reach the inside of the pyramid," said the Ibissynian.

"Yes, but there are another thousand Racnids ready to lay, just like me. I shall call them. This will be our nesting site. Perhaps Dendralon will be pleased with us after all."

The Ibissynian nodded. "Good. As long as the Kraken is on the other planet we cannot be killed."

"Why worry about this at all? It is impossible to kill the Kraken, so therefore impossible to kill you and your twin," said Elhada. "Your heartstrings are linked, are they not?"

The Ibissynian made a small clicking sound with his bill.

CHAPTER FOURTEEN

BELLOC THE TERRIBLE

Bero growled as they all edged further back from the door they'd just come through. Wisps of smoke snaked underneath it, wrapping its tendrils round each of them like the eerie fingers of some lanky ghost.

Crash!

The door shook violently.

"What the hell is that?" shrieked Ephie.

"Ephie, darling," muttered Michael. "There's no need to—"

Bang!

Michael jumped back, gathering the children in closer.

Mendel squished a googly eye against the window of his plastic barrel. "Something wants us to panic and run for the row of doors."

"You mean, like Sergeant Carr's just done?" said James. Carr had halted momentarily but was now stumbling forward once more.

Mendel's scales glimmered as he swam away from the window. "James, we need to stop Sergeant Carr from touching any of those doors." The wizard's voice echoed out towards the row of doors ahead of them. "Sergeant Carr. Do not…"

Sergeant Carr, however, had already touched the handle of the door with the reddish tinge before Mendel's shout registered in his terrified mind. James decided that Carr's mind had been unbalanced by his confession to MacNulty. *Imagine those two being brothers.*

Mendel's voice drifted into James's mind. "Take hold of MacNulty's key and point it at the door in front of Sergeant Carr."

The door with the reddish tinge had, however, already opened.

James's head seared with pain. It was much worse than before.

A huge, green tentacle burst through the door above Sergeant Carr's head.

"Wwwsealwwtightwww!"

A flash of red light screamed out of the key in James's hand and snapped the door shut.

Carr gawped and tripped backwards as a writhing tentacle fell on top of him.

James watched as the severed tentacle squirmed, like a snake halved in two, on Carr's chest. The old man rolled away and screamed.

"Wow!" said Helen. "Cool..."

The whole wall behind them shook this time, as something big continued to try and force itself through. James turned the key on the smaller door and repeated Mendel's spell again: "Wwwselawwtightwww!"

This time the small door they'd just come through disappeared completely and the crashing sound stopped.

Only the sound of Sergeant Carr whimpering as he crawled away from the severed, thrashing tentacle disturbed the eerie silence.

James looked at the bedraggled group from Drumfintley and lowered the Key of Artilis. It moved in his hand, changing shape every few seconds. It tickled. He saw his dad's expression and recognized it as a mixture of exhaustion and pride.

"Well done, Son," he said.

Ephie clung to Father Michael's arm and Jean stroked Wee Joe's light brown hair.

Eethan scuttled, sideways, towards James, followed by Bero. The brandy barrel still hung down from the old dog's furry neck. "Eet was not James," said Eethan, "but Mendel who deed thee mageeec," said Eethan.

"He's right, Dad. It's kind of funny, the way it works."

"Achh. Just ach long as it works; that's fine by me," added MacNulty.

James noticed that the old gardener was smirking as he watched his brother, Sergeant Carr, slipping awkwardly on the green slime that poured out of the severed tentacle.

"I preferred it when he wisch ma enemy. Ich no as much fun now a know he's ma, chh...brother."

"That's what it's been all along, MacNulty," explained Michael. "Sibling rivalry."

"Sccchhibling what?"

Michael wiped the spray from his face with the back of his hand. "Bad blood, Archie. You should take this opportunity to make up."

"Straight after you get those teeth fixed," muttered James.

"Whatcchh!"

"Nothing, Mr. MacNulty," sighed James, retreating to a safe distance.

Carr seemed to be aware of them all again. Sheepishly, he wandered back towards them. His police uniform was covered in green slime and his flushed face looked like a cross between a puffer fish and a ripe pomegranate.

"*Medragra felictious*, I should think," said Mendel, matter-of-factly.

"Eets a kind of cat," explained Eethan.

"A kind of cat!" spluttered Carr. "A kind of bloody cat!"

"Sergeant Carr," snapped Jean. "Please watch your language!"

"Bloody, bloody, bloody," repeated Wee Joe, with glee.

"Well done, Mr. Carr," said Helen, scathingly.

James shook his head and sighed. It wasn't the first time he wished it was just Craig, Bero, Mendel and himself on this adventure.

"James?" It was Mendel. "Keep the key with you at all times. Put it in your rucksack. We will need it again for a much greater purpose."

MacNulty seemed to have heard Mendel's instruction but he simply shrugged and edged away.

Ephie shouted back at them. "Shouldn't we be making a move? Which of the doors is the right one, then?" She'd wandered ahead with David and was looking down, with disgust, at the severed tentacle. "Mendel, you said that only one of the doors was safe."

"Yes, Ephie. But it's a little more complicated than that." Mendel's voice was full of regret.

"What's wrong, Mendel?" James just knew that something bad was about to happen.

The others gathered round James and Bero. Eethan had already begun to play with his nose.

"Well," began Mendel. "We have some fairly big decisions to make."

"Which are?" prompted Jean.

"Here's the dilemma. There are hundreds of doors. Only one can take us wherever we want, and that can be literally anywhere, even back to Drumfintley. Archie's key can see to that."

"Thank God," sighed Ephie, beginning to shake with relief.

"Hold on, Ephie."

Here it comes, thought James.

"Only six souls can go back this way."

"But there's eleven of us, including Bero," James reminded.

"Quite!" blurted Mendel. "Which means that the remaining five souls face…"

"Certeen death?" finished Eethan. Rather too cheerfully, for James's liking.

"Ah. And how certain is 'certain'? I'm not being awkward or anything, I just want to know the odds," James added.

"Not entirely sure on that count. Never been done, as far as I know," said Mendel.

James shuffled nervously. "Not great odds then?"

"Not great," the wizard sighed.

Ephie had found the last piece of Galdinie's tablet. It had wedged itself in the lining of her coat. "Well, it's fairly obvious. Jean and the kids should go back along with…"

"The key has to decide," interrupted Mendel. "It's quite fascinating actually."

"No Mendel, it's quite scary." James watched as Ephie blew bits of fluff and shredded hanky off the wrapper before dishing the tablet out to the kids and Sergeant Carr, who'd just shoved his fat hand under her chin.

James gasped. The key lifted from his hand and now hovered a few inches above his fingers. It nodded in Eethan's direction.

"You see," continued Mendel. "It always seems to know the best people for any given task. Eethan is an ideal choice to go back."

"Why, he doesn't even bewong there?" announced Wee Joe.

"Ee do," protested Eethan. "ee ees Scottish too."

"Yes, well that's a matter of opinion, Sir," said Sergeant Carr.

"Yous a blue goblin," snapped Wee Joe.

Helen gave her brother a brisk tug. Without once taking his eyes off of Eethan, Wee Joe took another mouthful of tablet.

Still inches above James's palm, the golden Key of Artilis spun round and dipped in Carr's direction.

"About time too," he blurted, instantly flushing.

The key lifted higher and nodded at Archie, his dad, Michael and finally at Ephie, who spat her mouthful of tablet out in surprise.

"Wrong," she shouted. "Everyone it's picked is a fully capable adult."

"And I'm not?" interjected Jean.

"No. Yes. I didn't mean…" struggled Ephie. "What about the kids?"

"Son." His dad moved to his side and whispered, "Ephie's right and I can't go and leave mum and you here." He bent down and whispered in his ear. "She'll kill me."

James thought he had a good point. "Mendel, can we check that the key's got it right?"

"We can," said Mendel. "But I can assure you there will be good reasons for it picking the people it has." He swam against the plastic window embossed with the words: *Wundadoz Chemicals*. "Key of Artilis, please show which of the group need to remain behind, this time."

The golden key spun with a renewed burst of speed that caused James's palm to tickle. It rose up a further six inches and floated over to Bero. It nodded firstly at the barrel then at Bero, who snapped at the blur of gold as it flew across to Jean Harrison. It gave a bow in her direction, then towards Wee Joe and Helen. After a few seconds it turned and flew back to James. Instead of nodding at James, however, it seemed to change its mind. It flew up into the ceiling and nodded away from them.

"Martilia," whispered Mendel.

It then flew to the opposite end of the chamber and nodded away from them once more.

"And now, Artilia," whispered the wizard, again.

"Mum and Craig," shouted James excitedly. Hardly noticing the key as it came back to hover in front of his face. It gave a reluctant nod at him and then dropped into his outstretched hand. "Do you think that's what it was telling us?"

"It may have been," said Mendel.

"I'm staying," announced James.

"And so am I," said Jean. "If my boy is here, I'll put my trust in Mendel."

"Splendid. That's settled then," said Mendel.

David grabbed his arm. "But Son…"

James really wondered about his dad sometimes. I mean, why was he more terrified of his mum, for example, than leaving his own son on another world to die? Maybe his mum was right when she called him selfish. Then again, maybe his dad was just shell-shocked by the whole weird escapade. Either way he shook free of his dad's grip.

Something inside his stomach, it felt like one of those horrible sand-worms, squirmed.

"Could the first group please stand beside the door to the left of the one Albert opened?" Mendel's voice bellowed out across the cavern.

They all hesitated for a second until they remembered that Mendel was referring to Sergeant Carr. The group destined to return home moved forward and, after a few tearful goodbyes, made their way across to the door.

His dad took a few paces then skidded to a halt. "I'm staying with James!"

"Dad you're going to have to go. There will be a good reason for it. Trust me."

David Peck, his stubbly face racked with indecision, hesitated for about two seconds and then wandered on after his group.

James felt better, relieved. At least his dad had shown a little re-morse or—

Mendel interrupted his thoughts. "Key of Artilis, please open the door back to Drumfintley!"

The golden key flew from James's hand and hovered beside the group of bemused travellers. Only Eethan smiled, always happy, it seemed, to step into the unknown. He tittered annoyingly, interspers-ing the growing atmosphere of sadness and trepidation with his little high-pitched yelps and 'eees'.

The blue crystal on the key glowed brightly until the light filled the chamber they were standing in. The key moved forward and whirred into the correct shape before clicking home in the keyhole. It turned with a clunk.

The door flew open and a gust of warm air washed over them all. James could smell the moor. A wonderful blend of flowering heather and smoky bracken filled his mouth and nose. He had to stop himself from running forward. Eethan had already jumped through but Father Michael and the rest were hesitant.

"Is it real?" shouted Ephie.

"As real as it ever was in the first place," answered Mendel.

Typical, thought James.

Carr jumped through next, followed by MacNulty and Ephie. Fa-ther Michael paused to give them a blessing and then walked through with David Peck, crossing himself as he did.

"A very pious man," said Mendel, as the door closed.

Soon the memories of the moor turned into a dark sense of fore-boding that bit into James's heart. Mendel's words: "certain death" repeated themselves over and over in his head.

Jean huddled the kids in tightly as they drew closer to Bero. The old dog pushed his wet muzzle against Wee Joe's ear and made him giggle.

"Why don't we go through the same door that Sergeant Carr tried to open? At least we know your magic can defeat the cat thing with the tentacles," reasoned James.

"That sounds like a good idea to me too, Mendel," said Jean.

Bero began to pant.

Helen ran her fingers through her dog's soft, blond fur. "I'm scared, Mum."

"We will pick a new door," said Mendel.

"Why? Do you know something we don't? What is Belloc? Is she a demon?"

Mendel puh puhed against his window. "You sound just like your mother. Four questions all at once. Right, the reason I'm changing doors is because I have a good feeling about one of them in particular. Yes, I know something you don't, and finally, I do not know what Belloc looks like or what her strengths might be. A demon…? I'm not sure what that means. To have survived for so long, however, and to have kept the third crystal safe from the likes of Dendralon is, in my book, no mean feat."

James looked along the long line of identical doors. "Willie MacNulty met Belloc."

"And Belloc killed him. Kept him a slave, even in spirit form," replied Mendel. "Do not forget that we are here to prevent Dendralon sending anything more into Drumfintley. We are here to rescue Craig, and now your mum, James, and…"

Jean straightened. "And let's just get on with it. You're frightening the kids with all that demon and spirit talk."

"Quite," said Mendel. "The fifth door to our left, I think."

Bero plodded over to the flaking door, looking decidedly stiffer than he had back home in Scotland. "Are we ready?" enquired Mendel.

They all nodded. James called on Firetongue and the sword rested in his hand. His head was already knocking as Mendel's magic brewed, again more painfully than he remembered.

Mendel cleared his throat before saying, "Key of Artilis, open the door!"

The golden key flew from James's left hand and found the door. It shimmered in the half-light then clicked home. As the door swung inward, away from them, James felt Helen's small fingers clawing at his shirt. There was only darkness beyond the door. An inky black in which no discernible shape or sound seemed to exist. "What now?" he whispered.

"We wait," Mendel whispered back.

At first he thought it was just the sound of their own, heavy breathing, but then a deeper tone came to the fore. It reminded him of Whindril, the white dragon from Denthan. Her breathing had sounded exactly the same. Whatever it was, dragon or not, it was probably too big to squeeze through the door and threaten them. Just as this thought left his head, however, the door began to widen.

"And now?" urged James.

"Do not move until I say so," said Mendel.

The sword, Firetongue, twitched in his right hand as the golden Key of Artilis came to rest, again, in his left. The ground shook as something very heavy took a step forward. Helen screamed out.

"Wait," snapped Mendel, again.

An earthy growl began to build in Bero's throat. "Grrrr..."

Two more giant steps shook the stone floor beneath their feet and caused Wee Joe to topple over. Jean tugged him to his feet again. Black smoke bellowed out of the door, which was now ten times bigger than it was before.

Something moved above their heads.

"What the...?" James spun round and focused on the ceiling behind them. "Up there!"

They followed his gaze.

"Stay put!" Mendel reminded, sharply.

Out of the black smoke above their heads a hazy figure began to solidify. It moved gracefully, like a hummingbird, darting this way and that, amidst the acrid smoke.

Crash!

The whole enlarged doorframe disintegrated as the bigger creature, which James thought might be a dragon, stepped through. Over forty feet high, eight snake-like necks unravelled to reveal an equal number of hideous heads, each one different from the next. The bulky body of the creature lumbered forward.

"Do not move," reminded Mendel. The wizard's voice crackled in James's head as his temples pulsed with pain.

Bero was the first to break Mendel's command. He dashed forward and bit hard into the large monster's leathery shin. One of the heads shrieked in pain and weaved its way down to face its attacker.

James saw Mendel's barrel loosen and swing precariously from Bero's neck as the Golden Retriever continued to sink his teeth into the creature.

"Bero, fall back!" Mendel's concentration had waned.

The head that came face to face with Bero was that of a giant, black-fanged bat. Its snub nose flared as it opened and closed its jaws.

James leapt forward with the power of the sword coursing through him. He jammed the blade into the bat's open mouth, grabbed Bero's collar, and fell back. His chest tightened. *Quick, dummy, bite down.* Almost as if the bat heard his thoughts, it shook its head and snapped shut its black-fanged jaws. The blade sunk home. Fumbling with Bero's collar James heard the creature's high-pitched scream reverberate around the cavern. Its red eyes closed and its neck flopped to the ground.

One of the other seven heads homed in on Jean and the children. It snaked its way round the huddled Harrisons.

James ran back to join them but his sword was still buried deep in the mouth and brain of the creature with the bat's head. The thing that now loomed down out of the smoke to face the Harrisons had the head of child. Huge and bloated with yellow puss that dripped from its gummy mouth, the green-skinned head grew long red stalks from its bald, rancid skull. They wrapped round James's arms and drew him in. He felt the suckers bite into his skin. It was lifting him off the ground. "Mendel!" he yelled.

Two more heads barked down at Bero and the Harrisons. Like werewolves this time, they howled hideously, a hundred times louder than any mortal dog. As the red tendrils that had sprouted from the baby's skull lifted him off his feet, he watched the Harrisons and Bero fall back. They were blasted with hot, putrid air that caught in James's throat. He was being crushed. Coughing, he tried to concentrate on Firetongue. *The sword. I must get it back.* With immense effort he squeezed out his magic word, his heart racing.

"Argh…Firetongue!"

He felt it. Firetongue's carved hilt had found his hand.

The magic sword soon hacked off the tendrils that gripped him, cutting them into shreds. He jumped free and began hacking off the grotesque baby-like head from the monster's slender neck. Black blood drenched the floor of the cavern. Slipping, he reached the first were-wolf head, as its fangs opened wide to bite down on the Harrisons. It was big enough to swallow all three of them. James leapt up onto its writhing neck and hammered the sword home. He gripped with his knees, as tight as he could, trying to keep balance as second dog-like head glided closer. He had to strike quickly. "Get back!" He almost lost his grip on the convulsing neck as he threw Firetongue. It spun twice before burying itself in the second werewolf's black snout.

The racket was deafening now as the four remaining heads swept down from the ceiling. The first, a bizarre blend of petulant girl and blue boar, knocked Bero over with its tusks. James watched in horror as Mendel's barrel rolled free. Bero lay still.

Helen jerked hard on her mum's sleeve. "Mum, watch out!"

Helen pulled her mum and Wee Joe back against the wall as the three other heads bundled into each other in a clumsy attempt to attack them all at once.

James scanned the cavern floor for Mendel; he could feel the wizard's magic brewing. *At last…*"Wwwstonewwrightwww!"

Dizzy with pain, James looked up at the monster in anticipation. He caught a glimpse of the small, faery-like creature through the chaos darting between the bumpy stalactites that littered the ceiling of the cave but then watched, with a sigh of relief, as the nearest head became covered in stone.

"Yes!" He punched the air. His celebration, however, was short lived. The stone that had covered the creature's head began to crack and fall off. An avalanche of debris rained down on him.

"Get back, Mrs. Harrison."

The creature shook its boar-like tusks and stared down at him full of loathing. With renewed hatred it lunged, snapping at him with its jaws while he staggered and tripped. He lost his footing.

"James!" It was Helen. "Mendel's dying!"

As a second head bundled into the one bearing down on him, he momentarily saw what Helen was looking at. The barrel had opened when Bero had fallen and the little goldfish was squirming about on the floor of the cavern. He had to duck as a dragon-faced head lurched towards him. He saw Helen crawl, amongst all the carnage, across the blood-soaked floor until she reached Mendel. She picked him up and screamed.

"Argh!"

Helen fell back, letting Mendel slip from her hands.

The little goldfish was beginning to weaken. James couldn't hear the wizard anymore. "Mendel!"

It was Wee Joe who, swiping up at a snapping pair of jaws, kicked the goldfish back into the barrel and scooped it up in his arms. He sprinted to his mum and jumped behind a rose-coloured rock.

Dust began to fill the cavern making it hard to see where the heads would appear from next. James found his sword but his leg had become caught in a pile of rocks. It hurt.

The tusked, blue-faced, pig-girl head appeared out of the gloom, inches from his face. He tried to swipe it with his sword but it simply eased out of his reach.

Ignoring Jean and the children for a moment the three remaining heads of the creature milled around him and the fallen Bero. One, not unlike a snake, sniffed at Bero's fur. "Get away from him!" James shouted. He knew it was going to be useless. He was trapped and as for Mendel...

Whoosh!

Flames licked down towards him from the dragon head.

He winced.

"Wwwstonewwright!"

The flames drew back in on themselves. Instantly, the whole creature froze. Stone snaked all over its mass until the entire animal stood completely still.

He hadn't said the spell. His mind was racing. "Mendel?"

"Yes, James. I'm with the children."

James glanced over at the rocks against the wall. Jean was urging him towards her. "Quick, James, come over here."

Bero whined and opened his eyes. He turned his head round and licked his flank.

"Bero, you're okay."

Bero's tail bounced off the floor at the sound of James's voice.

"Quite impressive!" shrieked another voice.

James looked up. The voice had come from the roof of the cavern. There were still tell-tale wisps of black smoke hanging in the dank air. He wriggled his foot free of the rocks that had held him and peered up at the bumpy roof of the cave. "Who's there?"

"Perhaps you can be my new ghostly guardian, young James," said the voice.

"Ghostly...? Who is it?" James didn't like the fact that the voice knew his name.

"Belloc, I presume?" Mendel's familiar voice echoed round the cavern.

A shadow, something close to the shape of a faery, moved across the ceiling and then flew down through the thinning smoke. A beautiful winged girl, with elfish ears and gossamer wings that beat faster than the eye could see danced to a halt in mid-air. The creature's hair was as gold as Mendel's scales and she wore a silky, green shawl patterned with Celtic symbols; beautiful animals and twisting trees.

"I thought we'd just killed Belloc?" said James, wondering how Mendel had recovered from his near suffocation so quickly.

"No," said the sweet voice. "No, no..." The delicate creature floated down a little closer. "That pet, my darling boy, was created by me, and you." She tittered, in a way that reminded him of Eethan, and then rose higher again.

James flushed.

"And who is the wizard among you who has turned my pet to stone?" She hovered over the rock where the Harrisons lay hidden.

"Everyone, stay put," warned Mendel.

"Ah... So your wizard is not a human, not a man. But he sounds like a man." She lighted on the floor and walked so gracefully that James stood up in awe to watch. Her feet made the sound of tinsel brushing against Christmas baubles. Gold and silver sparks flew up from her heels and danced around her wings.

"My name is Mendel."

James saw the faery stop abruptly. The animals that covered her clothes were moving, swirling through the cloth. "I have heard of you, wizard. Dead, I thought."

"I came very close to death tonight, Belloc."

"That's not Belloc. You said Belloc was a demon," whispered Helen.

"Ah, the little girl is right, Mendel. How could such a terrible creature as Belloc, never seen by living eyes, be so..." She turned to face James and smiled directly at him.

He blushed. "So beautiful?"

"Why..." she tittered and giggled like a young girl before her head elongated and took on the shape of a terrifying Mantis. "Thank you!" she roared. Her voice caused the whole cavern to quake. Then, just as quickly, she changed back into the beautiful faery.

James's pulse was racing. "Mendel, be careful, she..."

"Took on the form of the worst thing you could imagine at that moment," Mendel finished.

"Yeah," said James, meekly. He could still see the horrible Mantis face in his mind.

"And what is your greatest fear, oh Mendel, wizard trapped in the body of a tiny fish?"

"Now that would be telling, Belloc. You seem to have guessed well so far."

"They are not guesses, Mendel." She performed a delicate twirl before turning into a lithe, spotted Lynx.

"Ah, *Lynx pardina*. How very appropriate," mused Mendel. "Almost killed by one on the planet of Tendra. But as we live to see you, I think you may owe us our freedom."

The huge Lynx snarled and bounded across to the rock where Helen held Mendel's barrel. "I owe you nothing!" it snarled.

"You owe us the crystal you have guarded for so long," said Mendel.

The Lynx stretched upward and assumed the form of a faery again. "How dare you tell me what I should and shouldn't do?"

"It is not I, Belloc. But the book of Ra that states the forfeit," reminded Mendel.

James could tell that Mendel was gaining the initiative because Belloc froze at the mention of Ra. Her wings stopped fluttering. "What do you know of the book of Ra? I was there when he wrote it!"

"And I was not. But I have seen it, and remember your curse."

"Wrong!" Belloc now sounded completely manic. "Wrong!" She shook her head and blasted the rock with a beam of red light. James winced as it evaporated to reveal the cowering Harrisons.

Wee Joe pulled free and kicked a pile of debris towards the faery. "I'll snap yous wingsies off!"

Belloc raised her hand but Bero barked and moved forward. She hesitated then seemed to gather her thoughts. "What the book actually says is: *'they who see Belloc may command her in the confines of her lair.'*"

Mendel asked Helen to walk forward. James saw her move out from the shadows. Her hand was red and sore looking.

"Wait, Helen." Jean Harrison gathered her children together and led them round the creature until they reached James and Bero.

Belloc fluttered up into the air. "It does not say that you can take my crystal away for good."

"No, you're correct. It finishes by saying: *They who see Belloc may command her in the confines of her lair…and if they ask to take, they must a bargain make.*' I will make you a bargain, Belloc. Yes, we will have the crystal, because we have lived to see you, but, as the crystal is of no use to us after we have used it, you may have it back in return for an answer to a question and, of course, our safe passage."

"What?" The petulant faery demon landed back on the ground and faced them, her arms folded tightly. "What question do you have for me that you, the great wizard-goldfish, Mendel, could not possibly know the answer to?"

"How do I kill the Kraken?"

"Ha! This is good. Ha! You fool. Even if I tell you, it will do you no good. It is virtually impossible."

"I want to explore the word - 'virtually'," pressed Mendel.

"Ha!" Belloc rounded on Wee Joe. "Not even this brave soul could do it."

"Do what?" Jean prompted.

"To kill the Kraken and, in so doing, the Ibissynians, who are linked by an invisible heart string, you must pierce both of its giant hearts at the same time."

The silence was only interspersed by the dripping of water from the roof of the cavern.

Belloc knelt down and smiled sweetly at Helen before catching Mendel's eye. "The Kraken is forty five million miles away in a dark lake."

"I know," replied Mendel.

"And it's not a lake, it's a loch." James spelled it out. "L – O – C – H. Loch."

Belloc's features tightened, partially forming the Mantis head before snapping back into the soft skinned face of sheer beauty that so mesmerized him. Her eyes still blazed as she turned away to face Bero. "Your kin, Dendralon, still thinks you are this dog, Mendel Pendragon."

"Enough!" snapped Mendel. "I'll have the crystal now."

James wasn't sure he'd heard Belloc properly.

There was a flash of red. Something lay at James's feet. It was covered in sand.

"Find it, James. Quick as you can," said Mendel.

James poked about in the gritty sand until his fingers touched its smooth surface. He pulled free a dazzling red crystal; more beautiful than any he'd ever seen before.

"Place it in your rucksack and come," ordered Mendel.

Belloc stepped back. "Remember, I will claim it back when the red-eyed giant is in line with the pinnacle of Ra." With these words, Belloc flew up into the roof of the cavern and disappeared in a thick swathe of black smoke."

"Red-eyed giant?" enquired James.

"Jupiter," replied Mendel, matter-of-factly.

"And the Ra, pinnacle bit?" asked Jean.

"We're going there right now." A door had appeared in the wall of the cavern.

"Mendel?" broached Helen, still looking around nervously. "Where are we, exactly?"

CHAPTER FIFTEEN

THE DARK QUEEN

The rosy glow had intensified and shafts of purple light streamed in through the high arched windows. Limpid pools of azure water sparkled as the droplets from a thousand glass fountains peppered their surfaces. Olive green trees bowed down to form a pathway through, what she could only imagine was, a garden or perhaps some kind of arboretum. Her hands had been untied.

Cathy Peck looked down to discover that she'd been dressed in white silk. The material felt cool against her skin as it moved. She stood up and instantly felt dizzy. She'd been drugged, and now she was starving. She looked around for any sign of food and saw that the trees bore fruit. Low hanging orbs of yellow that resembled pears covered in fine orange hairs weighed down the branches of the tree nearest to her. She walked across the marble floor until her toes touched the red earth. She reached up and felt the weight of the fruit before twisting it free of its stem.

"Just like Eve."

She gasped and turned round.

Dendralon stood behind her dressed in full armour. Highlights of red and purple danced across the sheen of its polished surface.

"A woman's curiosity. I remember it well."

His tongue forked out between his thin, scaled lips. Dendralon's face was flattened for the most part with only two slits for a nose and two holes for ears. His yellow eyes had vertical cat-like slits. They widened as he approached her.

"Beldam. There is no doubt, now that I see you dressed in your own clothes amidst your special garden."

"I am not Beldam." Cathy felt her throat tighten as she said the words. It was as if something inside her was trying to stop her saying them. She coughed.

"You know you are. Deep inside, you know you are. Your soul cannot be lied to."

She shivered as he spoke but tried to maintain an air of calm. "I need to get to my son and get home."

"Precisely," whispered Dendralon. "I would like to get home too. You see our paths are going to be as one from now on. I will train you, or should I say, remind you of what you have forgotten. How to fight, how to hold council, how to love…"

"What!" She drew back. "I'm a happily married woman." She felt awkward.

"Ha!" Dendralon pointed at the fruit in her hand. "Taste it."

Cathy hesitated. "Why did you drug me?"

"The stylus contained no drugs or potions, only memories. Taste the fruit of the young Eden trees and see if you remember being Beldam."

"I remember nothing apart from my own life in Drumfintley with James and David."

Dendralon hissed. "You will have had many lives since Beldam. Take it to your mouth and feast on your past."

Cathy felt her hunger rage inside her. "What are you talking about?"

Dendralon closed his yellow eyes. "I have had to live with the regrets and the pains and the losses. Watch while others slipped away to be reborn. I have changed my form but I have never doused the continuity of memory."

"Sorry, but you are talking piffle." She bit into the fruit and felt a rush of power surge through her bones. "Argh!" Her mind filled with images of faces, houses, trees, oceans, towers, animals, monsters and… "Stop it!"

"Take your time. You're trying to see too much too soon."

Cathy fell back into his arms and instantly shook herself free. "Leave me alone." She was too frightened to shut her eyes, or even blink. "What have you given me?"

"I gave you nothing. You picked the fruit."

"But I know all these people and all those places. I…" Tears flowed down her cheeks as she fought the temptation to close her eyes. "I don't want to…"

"Dilute the love you have for your son?"

"How did you know what I was thinking? Stop it!" She pulled free of Dendralon and ran down the alley of trees. Shafts of lilac light cut across her path until she stopped beside the biggest fountain of all. It lay at the end of the arboretum. A fine mist landed on her face and seemed to calm her. She had to stay in control.

Dendralon's deep menacing voice bellowed out down the avenue of trees as he marched after her. "Beldam!"

She closed her eyes and saw Dendralon, not the way he appeared now, in his Hedra form, but as a tall, dark youth with laughing eyes and a wicked smile. "I…"

He continued to walk towards her. "You remember me now, don't you Beldam?"

"I'm just hallucinating, dreaming or something. I'm not her. I'm not Beldam." Cathy knew she would have to fight him or pretend.

"We were once in love. In ten thousand years I have never forgotten you."

"You killed me!" Cathy gasped. *What did I say?*

"I was wrong." Dendralon took her hand. His grey scales were cold and smooth. "Rule with me now and we can start again."

Cathy tried to lock her thoughts away from him. She had to play along with this monster until she could be free of him and find her son. "I will try…" She wept as the visions cluttered her head then, thankfully, subsided.

"We have a battle to win but you are still too weak to fight. It will take time to remember all your skills and powers. Follow carefully for now."

"Dendralon!"

She gawped at the tall, jackal-headed man standing at the far end of the arboretum.

"This is Orsa, my Inubian captain," Dendralon explained. "What news?"

Orsa bowed. "Elhada, the Racnid queen, has reached the base of the pyramid of Ra. She makes her nest there so that her spiderling larva may eat through a great plug of rock that blocks our entrance."

Dendralon walked down the avenue of trees towards the Inubian. "There is more?"

"Yes, my Lord."

Cathy could see that the Inubian was eying her suspiciously, unsure whether to tell Dendralon the news in her presence.

"Tell it!" he barked.

"The Racnid Queen has also found the lair of Belloc the demon."

"Where?"

"Under the Stygian Desert, as you predicted, my Lord. It was in a place they have searched a thousand times already."

"Something has happened." Dendralon reached for his staff and fastened his green tunic. "Mendel." He turned to Cathy.

"You followed Mendel here."

Cathy hesitated. "I…"

"I read it all in your thoughts when you were sleeping. It seems that, after saving your people from the Dust Goblins, Mendel has gone on to find Belloc's lair. Excellent!"

"What now, my Lord?" said Orsa.

"We will pay a visit on this demon." He twisted round to face Cathy. "Orsa will escort you until you are more at ease with your past."

She left the great Artilian arboretum and entered a long, high-ceilinged corridor. She seemed to recognize the glyphs and cartouches that adorned the walls. Painted in gold, yellow and red ochre they told stories she knew. It had to be the drugs Dendralon had given her, or the poison from the fruit. It was playing with her mind. She had to stop it from driving her mad.

They walked for over an hour until she heard the chattering of high-pitched voices. It grew louder and louder. As they turned the next bend the whole tunnel lit up. Ahead, huge crowds of spider-like creatures swarmed round a large black queen with a single red spot on her abdomen. Their heads were more reptilian, like a turtle or a beaked dinosaur.

"Elhada, you have done well," said Dendralon. All the creatures in the tunnel parted to make way for him.

She looked behind the swarming creatures to see a huge palisade stretching for miles. Long spikes jutted out from the walls, each sporting a bleached skull.

"How have we never seen this before?" hissed Elhada.

"Belloc has been weakened. Now, let me see." Dendralon paced up and down for a moment before pointing his staff at a solitary archway. "Gelsandia!" A bolt of black fire scorched forward and hammered into the arch. The Racnids screamed in unison as the structure crumbled and fell. Cracks appeared in the walls of the palisade, and soon the noise of crashing rocks filled the tunnels. A gaping hole appeared where the arch had stood. The Racnids poured through into the cavern beyond. Inside, Cathy saw a huge line of grayish, weathered-looking doors stretching left and right. One was lying open.

"This is all too inviting," whispered Dendralon. He walked to the fore and again raised his staff. "Gelsandia!" This time, however, as the bolt of black fire left his staff, another shot out from the open door to meet it. Black smoke began to blow out from the open door and it widened, all by itself, until it was as big as the giant gates of Gwendral.

The ground shook and the Racnids swarmed forward.

Another belt of black fire issued from the great opening and a hundred Racnids burst into flames.

"Wait!" Dendralon's expression had changed to one of fear as the noise of the dying Racnids resounded off the bare rock.

Cathy saw a small, beautiful girl step out of the huge doorway. Dwarfed by her surroundings, she looked lost.

"Belloc!" shouted Dendralon.

The faery creature took to its wings and circled the burning Racnids. She seemed to be singing.

Dendralon aimed his staff at the faery and muttered some chant under his breath.

A curtain of red fire tore across the open space engulfing the Racnids and faery alike.

Unaffected, the faery creature fluttered through the chaos and lighted on the ground in front of Dendralon, the Racnid Queen, and Cathy.

Cathy shrunk back, all the time scanning for any sign of James or Bero. She hoped, somehow, that they were watching from the shadows.

"Dendralon Pendragon, I presume." The faery performed an intricate bow.

"Belloc, I have come for the crystal, but I fear I may be too late."

"Too late to save your life or too late to take my crystal?"

Dendralon did not answer.

Cathy made to open her mouth but stopped when the girl pointed at her. "This must be the Great Queen of legend."

Cathy flushed.

"Your son has taken my gem. Borrowed it, to be precise."

"James, you've seen James?" Inubian soldiers were streaming into the cavern behind even more Racnids. They began to encircle Belloc.

"Yes. I believe so, great Queen. I would have killed him and his pet had it not been for his magic."

"But it wasn't *his* magic, was it Belloc?" pressed Dendralon.

"Not really," she admitted. "Your brother helped him."

Now Cathy was completely confused.

Dendralon hissed.

"But you have his bride, I see." Belloc smirked before vanishing in a cloud of black fog. She reappeared behind Orsa, having changed into a large, matted creature with a single horn and a single eye.

Orsa screamed in agony as the horn burst through his chest. She rose up, dragging the flaying figure of Orsa with her.

"For God's sake!" Cathy yelled.

Dendralon pointed up at the faery in the vaulted roof of the cave and a hundred arrows whistled upward. Belloc twisted merrily between the swarm of steel-tipped points but then jerked in pain. Dendralon had thrown his staff into the mêlée and it had found its mark. Amidst a shower of golden dust, she spiralled down to the floor of the cavern, several arrows piercing her delicate frame as she fell. She landed lightly at their feet. No-one moved.

Cathy watched as the Racnids scrambled over the burnt corpses of their kin towards her.

As Dendralon retrieved his staff from Belloc's belly, the faery stretched out and gained so much bulk that they had to jump back. Lying before them now was the huge carcass of a winged demon. Green slime covered its rotting skin and puss oozed from its wounds. It was still alive. "You are too weak to test me now, Belloc."

"Where is my son?" said Cathy.

Belloc's long, black tongue slipped free of her hideous jaws. Her voice was the strangest sound Cathy had ever heard. It was like steel knocking against steel overlapped with the growl of a bear. "They have gone to Ra. There is another way insi…"

Her huge jaws fell open and her chest stopped moving up and down.

Cathy felt a pang of sadness when the monster turned back into the beautiful faery. Her gossamer wings were crumpled and her snow-white skin was covered in blood the colour of pitch.

"There must be another way into the pyramid of Ra, Elhada." snapped Dendralon.

"There is none that I know of," Elhada replied. "My children…"

"Your children will take too long to eat their way through the plug of stone. Fetch me the Ibissynians. They will track your son, my Queen." Dendralon wiped his staff on the fallen demon, Belloc, and ordered the Racnids to take her body with them.

* * *

Craig had tried to put the pleas of his family as far out of his mind as he could. He'd decided that Elandria was most probably right. Some trick had been played on him to stop him lowering the great plug of stone and sealing the Racnids off below. Something, however, made him feel uneasy. He just knew that his family was somewhere close by. "Elandria?"

"Yes Craig, are you thirsty again?" She began to push a cupped hand into a slit in the slide of her downy abdomen.

"No, no. And even if I was, I would rather…"

"Die?" Elandria shuffled round to walk by his side up the wide stairwell. "That's my boy. You're beginning to long for an honourable death, aren't you?"

"I am not!" Craig was becoming exasperated by the spider-like creature's morose desire for death. "How old are you, Elandria?"

"Oh, about nine-thousand-six-hundred and seventy, or so."

"There you go then. You see, I'm not bored with my life yet. In another nine-thousand–six-hundred and fifty nine years I might be completely fed up with the whole thing, but at the moment…"

"At the moment you want to get back home to Earth with your whole family and live a full life," finished Elandria.

This last comment made Craig think about his dad, for some reason or other. It was the part about the 'whole family' that threw him. There was James, with his mental mum and his laid back dad, actually going on holidays together and interacting when it was him who'd lost his dad all those years ago. In fact, he'd never really had his dad about that much at all. The Navy had seen to that. Three weeks here, four months away. James's dad, on the other hand, went on jollies with his work, brought James back shortbread from hotels and even took him with him sometimes. And now… Now his mild-mannered mum had decided enough was enough. They were going to get divorced. He'd mistakenly opened the letter from the solicitor five days before.

"You've gone very quiet, Craig," said Elandria. But then, without waiting for a reply, she scampered forward to see what was causing Junera to pause beside a tapestry on the wall.

"I'm just tired," Craig lied. But no-one was listening. Elandria was already chattering to Junera. Craig sauntered on. "What's wrong?"

Junera spoke conspiratorially, "There is another way into the pyramid of Ra, and it's worrying me."

"What, is there a hidden passage behind the tapestry?" The heavy material depicted a great fleet of ships sailing away from a strange city sinking into an angry sea.

"The passage is too narrow for Inubians or even a large Racnid but who knows what Dendralon could send next time?" said Junera. She flicked back the tapestry to reveal a narrow, wooden door. "It leads all the way back to the Stygian Desert. I don't know whether to seal it over or not."

"Well, if nothing too scary can get through, why don't you leave it open, just in case?" reasoned Craig.

"I think it's time we had a look at what's actually happening outside the pyramid," said Elandria. She scuttled over to a recess in the wall that contained a small sink well full of water. "Drinking water for the weary, if you'd prefer to refresh yourself here, young Craig."

Craig took several mouthfuls of the cool water before turning to face Elandria's turtle-like face. "I don't want to be rude; it's just the thought of the liquid coming from inside you. It's kind of gross."

"Ha! It saved your life in that roasting cell of Dendralon's. Anyway, to more important matters. Gather round." Elandria's eyes widened as she mumbled some strange words. With a flash of crimson, the font in the wall misted over then cleared to reveal a pin sharp image.

"A vision pool," declared Craig. "I've seen Mendel do this."

"It was he who taught me how to perform this magic. Craig, put your thoughts into the mix."

"Oh, but I've never been asked to do that before."

"Put your finger into the water and think on the ones you would like to see," Elandria explained.

Craig felt a tingling sensation as his fingers broke the surface of the cool water. Still worried about what he'd heard below the plug of stone before it fell, he tried to imagine his mum and the kids.

"There they are," said Junera.

Craig saw his mum first. Looking completely bedraggled, she teetered up a narrow passage lined with black soot. Bero clambered up behind her but the barrel was missing from his neck.

"Don't tell me Mendel's not with her," Craig moaned.

But then he saw Helen and Wee Joe. Helen was cradling the barrel in her arms. James appeared last of all. He limped quite badly and had a nasty looking wound on his bare leg.

"That's a sandworm bite," explained Junera. "It will need treating. It's poisonous."

"Junera, they're in the passageway that leads to this door," said Elandria.

"Yes. Which means that..."

"They have the third crystal," finished Elandria. "They have faced Belloc and survived."

"Who is Belloc?" asked Craig.

Junera whisked away some red mist from the surface of the vision pool. "Belloc is the demon who guards the third crystal of Artilis. A legend, to most, she is real enough to my family."

"I don't understand," said Craig.

"The Artilian royal family put her in place, in a hidden dimension, to keep the third crystal safe."

"Safe from what?" pressed Craig.

"With all three crystals, there is the possibility of moving the entire pyramid of Ra, and all inside it, to another world."

"That's what happened on Denthan," said Craig. "Only it was a whole city."

"Well, it's the same principle. Many years ago we moved a great number of people to Earth, in the hope of starting again after the destruction here on Artilis, but evil forces led, in the main, by Dendralon, were threatening to take power. We decided to place the third crystal out of harm's way."

"A selfless act," added Elandria.

"Look! In the vision pool," exclaimed Craig. "They're coming up to a door. It's the door we've just seen." Craig rushed back to the tapestry and flicked it back. Someone was pounding on the closed door. "Mum?"

Elandria and Junera followed on. Junera produced a silver key from her pocket. "This is the only key that will open the door."

The words had no more left her lips, however, than the door clicked open from the other side.

Everyone drew their weapons and braced.

CHAPTER SIXTEEN

THE GAS LEAK

Archie MacNulty fell onto the thick heather and rolled against a warm stone covered in orange lichen. He was the last to pass through the doorway from the great hall in Artilis, and now he joined Ephie, Father Michael, David Peck, Sergeant Carr, and Eethan amongst the weathered stones on Bruce Moor known as the Jesus Rocks.

"Everyone okay?" enquired Ephie.

"Yeschh!" answered Archie, rubbing his arm.

"What should we do now?" asked David.

Ephie watched as Michael leaned over a toppled stone and looked down at the dark waters of Loch Echty below. Clouds were rolling in over Ben Larvach and there was a hint of rain in the air. "I think we should get off the moor and make sure that the Rectory is water tight," said Michael.

"I'll get my shotgun," said MacNulty. "Just in case anything comes through."

Sergeant Carr dusted himself down. "Have you got a licence for that thing, MacNulty? I mean, there are certain rules and regulations..."

"Which you probably need to forget for the moment," interrupted David Peck.

"Ee theenks ee all need to be ready to fight," said Eethan. He sat, gnome-like, on one of the smaller stones. "Mendel knows that wee were all sent here for ee reason. Nastee thingees weel come here soon."

"I hate to say it," remarked Michael. "But I think Eethan's right. It's not in my nature to fight, but this village just isn't safe."

Carr looked confused.

"We saw something in the Loch before we left," said Ephie.

"That thing was too big to be frightened off by a shotgun, MacNulty," added Michael.

"Aye. I schhupose so. We needch something bigger."

They all turned to face Sergeant Carr.

"Albert," said Ephie. "We need your full resources."

Sergeant Carr began to move out of the stone circle. "I suppose I could ask young Watt to call for the armed unit from Stendleburgh. Say there's a madman roaming the shore of the Loch."

David Peck pulled up his collar. A light smir of rain had begun to drift down from the darkening sky. "Is that not going to exasperate the whole situation? Do we really want the whole world to know about this? I mean, what would you say: 'I need the hit squad because there's a monster in the Loch'?"

"Right enough," agreed Carr. "When you put it like that…"

A clap of thunder rumbled over the Loch below.

"I don't like the look of that." Michael pointed down at St. Donan's spire. Dark shadows circled the church.

"It's just a few birds," added Carr.

Eethan shook his head and tittered, his shock of white hair flopping down over one eye. "Ees not birdees."

"They're not like any kinda birdch ave ever had in ma sights before," said MacNulty.

Carr bristled. "And you've had plenty in your sights, haven't you MacNulty? Blasted, trapped, netted… Even though you deny it."

"If you're daft enoughch to michh everything under your nose, that's no my fault."

Carr grabbed onto MacNulty's old coat. "Empty your pockets!"

Ephie, in turn, hauled at Carr's police jacket. The arm ripped off with a tearing sound. "You two are supposed to be brothers. Why can't you start behaving yourselves?"

Carr stared at Ephie incredulously. "Look what you've done to my jacket. That's police property you know," he protested.

An eerie cry echoed up from the village below.

"Am telling ye, ch… Thachs no birdch making that sound."

Eethan gave a tight-lipped nod of agreement. "Leet's go see!"

They'd just rounded the reservoir when David Peck pulled them to a stop. "Get down."

They all hunkered down behind the rusting green fence that was supposed to keep kids from fishing for sticklebacks or collecting frog-spawn. "Archie's right," said David. "They're not birds. Look at St. Donan's spire now."

Ephie peered down and saw that things were moving up and down the spire. Defying gravity, they crawled like giant bats, across the stone.

"The gargoyles have come alive," said Michael, loosening his dog-collar. "There are three of them."

"One went missing last year, didn't it Reverend?" said Carr.

"Yes…" Michael answered in a dreamy voice. "Holy-moly. What am I going to tell the bishop?"

"I should think the bishop is the least of our worries," said David. "We have to warn people, get them out of the village on some pre-tence. C'mon Sergeant, surely you can think of something."

"A gach leak!" exclaimed Archie.

"Good one," agreed David.

Eethan looked confused.

Carr was obviously annoyed that it had been MacNulty's sugges-tion. "I suppose that would work," he said reluctantly. Carr tested his intercom and, to his surprise, found that it worked. "Carr to the sta-tion, can you read me?"

"This is Constable Watt," announced the crackly voice.

"It's me; Sergeant Carr. There's been a gas leak at…" he paused and looked at the others.

"The road-works," suggested Ephie, in a whisper.

"The road-works, on Main Street," he finished. "Get everyone onto the school bus and get them out of the village. I'll meet you at the po-lice station. It's a code red!"

"A code red, Sarge?"

"Just do it! Knock on every door. I don't want anybody left in harm's way," snapped Carr.

There was another terrifying cry from one of the gargoyles. It sounded like a mixture between a movie dinosaur and a klaxon.

"There's no way people aren't going to hear those things. I mean, just listen to them," moaned Carr.

"I'll see to that," said David. "The scouts have just finished a pro-ject on World War Two. I've got the original Drumfintley air raid siren in the garage. It's absolutely deafening. Drown out anything."

"Excellent!" exclaimed Michael. "Let's get it going then."

Making their way along Willow Terrace, it was suggested that Eethan remain with David to work on the siren, while the rest of them went to the police station.

Watt pulled up in the school bus just as the siren blasted into action.

"What on Earth?" shouted Watt, covering his ears.

Breathless, Carr paused at the station door. "Just get everyone on that bus. Can't you smell the gas?"

"Eh..." Watt took a few deep sniffs. "No."

Ephie bristled. "It's natural gas. Odour-free. Ah! Here's David. He's got the whole of Willow Terrace with him." Ephie could see her brother Kwedgin, The Fyffes and Mrs. Galdinie all trundling down the hill towards the bus.

"We'll check out the Beeches Housing Estate," said Ephie, tugging on Michael's arm.

"And I'll look in chhe Park," said Archie.

Within about fifteen minutes Ephie and Michael were leading another twenty people up from the Beeches Housing Estate.

"A canny smell no gas, eh?" sounded Mrs. Galdinie. "An am in di middle o' baking."

Archie had found the village drunk, Gauser, dossing on a park bench.

Carr and Watt ushered them all onto the bus and shut the hydraulic doors. Ephie stood beside Carr as he spun the tale. "It's a gas leak!"

There was a disgruntled murmur from the villagers.

"Best thing to do is to have Watt here take you to Stendleburgh. I've been told that the whole village could blow."

"For goodness sake," yelled Kwedgin. Ephie tried to avoid eye contact. He always could tell when she was lying.

"I'll remain here until the gas people turn up. Protect your property," said Carr, in a heroic tone. "I need a few volunteers."

The bus fell silent.

"We'll stay behind," said Michael.

Carr nodded. "Thank you Father. And I know MacNulty and David Peck are checking out a few more places. That will be enough."

Various protests followed them off the bus, but Carr turned round to Watt, who was driving and told him to get going.

In a matter of twenty or thirty minutes they'd managed to clear the whole village of any potential witnesses.

Archie and David shuffled in beside Ephie as the bus turned the corner.

"I think we can turn off that racket now, David," said Ephie, her ears ringing.

"No probs. I'll nip up and..."

"Ees no need!" Eethan clicked his fingers and the siren stopped screaming.

"Where did you come from?" snapped Carr.

Eethan gave him an impish wink.

"What are the gargoyles up to, Archie?" asked Ephie.

"They're just sitting on the church tower. It'chs as if they're waiting for something."

"Theys ees waiting for Dendralon," hissed Eethan. He gave a little shiver at the mention of the Hedra wizard's name.

"C'mon," said David. "Let's get organized then."

After about another half-hour of running about, they all met up with David Peck at the village hall. MacNulty had his shotgun, Carr had acquired a rifle from the station, and the rest of them had rummaged about behind the tables and chairs, piled high at the back of the hall, until they found a metal box full of old swords.

"What the heck are these doing here?" asked Carr.

"The highland dancers use them," explained David. "I knew they'd be here, somewhere. This one's actually a genuine cavalry sword from the Crimean war. It just needs sharpening up." He brandished the weapon, holding it up to the light that streamed in through the leaded windows.

"It looks bloomin' lethal," barked Carr.

Archie shook his head and sneered. "Choo can arrescht the dancers when they come back from Stendleburgh, Carr."

"Shut up, MacNulty. You're first in line, ruddy brother or not."

"Ha. Brother, indeed. I schtill don't believe that nonsense. We look nochhing like each other."

"I hate to disappoint you but you have more than a passing resemblance," interjected Ephie.

The older men gave her a withering stare.

David tried to break the ice. "Well, we can't just sit here in the village hall and wait. We need a plan."

"How can we have a plan? We've got a couple of old guns and a few rusty swords against God knows what," moaned Carr. "You said that thing in the Loch is huge."

"We've got Eethan," said David.

Carr played with the stubble on his big round face. "Yes…"

"Ephie's right," said Eethan. "Remembeer! Mendel said that wee would all play our part. Leet's get as close to Loch Eechty and the church spire as wee can. For all wee know thee rest of them could appear at any moment. James, Craig and… If theee do, theee might need our help."

"And I've just remembered," announced David. "The Scouts' archery equipment is in the basement. I'll go and get it."

Cursing at each other every few moments, Archie and Sergeant Carr made themselves busy rigging up some traps for anything that might come out of the Loch while Ephie and the rest of them stacked arrows and sharpened the old dancing swords.

"What on Earth are we doing?" moaned Michael. "I hope Mendel comes back soon."

* * *

Bounding past everyone, Bero knocked Craig onto his back and covered his face in a generous dollop of drool. "Oh, get off me ye big galoot. Get…" Embarrassed, he pulled himself out from under Bero and stood up. "Mum?"

Jean Harrison beamed. "And Wee Joe, and your sister, Helen. We're all here, Son."

James ducked through the opening and immediately backed away from the large green-downed Racnid. He drew his crimson sword.

"Don't worry about Elandria," explained Craig. "She's okay. Saved my life and stuff." Craig cupped his hand and whispered, "She's a bit weird though. Keeps ranting on about the glories of getting herself killed. Got a bit of a death wish."

"Did I hear someone say, Elandria?" said Mendel.

Junera ducked down and braced, unsure where the disembodied voice had come from.

"Mendel's here," said Helen, holding up the barrel. A blur of gold wavered behind the plastic window.

Craig patted his sister on the back. "Helen, let me fix that back round Bero's neck."

Mendel's voice sat clearly in all their heads: "Craig, some introductions, perhaps?"

"Ah, okay." Craig rubbed Bero's ears and continued. "Mum, this is Elandria."

Elandria performed a strange kind of bow.

"And this is Junera. She's an Artilian." Craig pointed to the Drumfintley group and rhymed them off.

James felt a twinge in his leg where the sandworm had caught him.

"You've been hurt," said Craig.

"I thought Eethan had fixed it up. It's just flared up again." He licked his fingers and rubbed his spit on the red wound. "I don't suppose you've seen my mum?"

"No, thank goodness!" Craig beamed, his freckles merging into one big, brown blob.

James felt his face flush with anger.

Craig shifted. "No offence, pal."

"Sorry, but lots taken, pal." James had been in Craig's company for less than a minute and he already wanted to pummel him. "Mum was with Jean and the kids and she got lost," he snapped.

"Craig, half of Drumfintley's been here looking for you, you selfish git," added Helen.

"Nice to see you too, Sis." Craig shook his head. "I didn't exactly volunteer for the trip."

"Wees nearly got eaten by goblins and monsters and..." But Wee Joe had stopped talking. He looked back down the stairwell. There was a deep rumbling sound echoing up from below.

"The plug's beginning to move. It won't be long until they've broken through," shouted Junera.

"You have Belloc's crystal, don't you?" said Elandria.

"I thought it better to have it in my possession," said Mendel.

"Technically, it's in mine," reminded James. He slipped the green rucksack from his shoulders.

"I've a feeling that Dendralon has planned this whole thing." Elandria sighed. "You see, he has the Racnid crystal already. Elhada gave it to him. He obviously knows that the crystal in the pyramid of Ra is fixed in place, so all he needed was you to seek out Belloc."

Junera looked agitated. "That's why he took the boy from your world. He knew you would come after him. Find the crystal for him."

"Get him the last piece in the jigsaw he needed to take his cur back to Earth," finished Elandria.

James saw Mendel flick his fins against the window of the barrel then move back. "I knew all this, Elandria. But you see, now that we have won the third crystal from Belloc there is a final curse on the stone. It will be banished to another universe as Jupiter lines up with the pinnacle of Ra. It will be lost forever." Mendel sat under Bero's chin once more.

"But there are other ways to move cities or armies from one world to another," said Elandria. Her voice was guarded. "The fact that you are talking to me now means that you know how, Mendel."

She can't know how we all escaped from Denthan, thought James.

Junera looked puzzled. "I need to get back down to the first level. Perhaps Elandria can guard the crystal of Ra. Give my people a better chance."

"It will be another full day before the red-eyed giant looks down on the crystal of Ra," added Elandria.

Junera nodded.

"And what of your own kin, Elandria?" Mendel pressed.

"Mendel, my kin have shunned me and I them. They live only to kill and, worst of all, they obey Dendralon now. If they get through to these people's world," Elandria pointed to Jean and the children, who were busy drinking from the well set into the wall, "there will be carnage."

"Sorry to interrupt," said James. "But I've always wondered what good Dendralon and these spiders…" He nodded towards Elandria. "No offence—would be against the Royal Navy or a squadron of fighter jets."

Mendel appeared back at the window. "Dendralon has the power to nullify all modern energy if he uses the crystals properly, or should I say improperly, my boy."

"Oh," said James, suddenly feeling foolish.

"He's already sent some of his beasts through to Drumfintley," Mendel explained. "There is one beast he cannot send against you here because it is already on the other world."

"I sensed its loss here on Artilis," said Elandria. "To place the Kraken in their world is truly an evil act. I wanted to die an honourable death when I found out. Purge myself of the guilt."

"Not that old chestnut again," mumbled Craig, who'd nestled in beside James.

"But, Craig, you gave me the incentive I needed to fight on." Elandria scuttled round behind the boys. "You know, you could help us, boys. I have seen what Craig can do with his magic spear, Greenworm." She touched James's arm with her pouched hand. "You too have the mark from Denthan." She examined James's hand and saw the mark of Firetongue. "If you could go down into the tunnels again with your weapons from Denthan and delay things a little... If Mendel were to go with you..."

Junera's face lit up. "We need a day."

"But you said you had over forty thousand Artilians. Where are they?" pressed Craig. "Doing a bunk?"

James cringed.

Junera looked perplexed. "Sorry, I don't understand."

Elandria circled Craig, her wrinkled eyes bulging out from the sides of her head. "Mendel, could you explain to the boys?"

Mendel began. "This pyramid is over ten times the size of any on Earth. It is basically an entire city, with hundreds of levels and sectors. The city you saw outside, Craig, was merely the scattering of houses round the city wall. Whole factions, tribes, clans... Whatever you wish to call them will be assembling on the first floor.

"That floor is endless," said Craig, nodding at James. "It's about the size of twenty football pitches."

"Wow! I think we're all forgetting something," said James. "You see, my mum is somewhere down there." He pointed at the wall of the stairwell. "And my dad is probably back in Drumfintley wondering how to tackle a fully grown, immortal Kraken without disturbing the neighbours."

"The Kraken sounds awesome," mused Craig.

"It's bigger, nastier and more deadly than anything we saw in Denthan—big pincers and stuff," James assured.

"Yeah, right!" Craig sneered.

"Trust me."

Mendel's tail swished past the window of the barrel. "I will go with the boys. Besides, I can sense the presence of someone from Drumfintley in the tunnels below."

"Mum?" asked James.

"You're just saying that to get us to go," said Craig, dryly. "And..."

"I most certainly am not!" snapped Mendel. The indignant tone of his voice shocked Craig into silence.

"Firetongue," said James, the crimson sword already twitching in his hand.

"I'll take Belloc's crystal," said Elandria. She stretched out a pouched hand.

James looked down at the barrel for some reassurance.

"It's fine, James. Give her it," said the wizard, still sounding crest-fallen.

"Greenworm," said Craig. "C'mon ye old fur ball."

James had noticed that Bero looked almost as old as he'd done at the end of their adventure in Denthan. The Golden Retriever's eyes were cloudy again and his fur was lank and listless. He reached into his rucksack and gave the crystal to Elandria. Then, taking a quick puff of his inhaler, he made to follow Craig and Bero through the door in the wall they'd come through moments before.

"Elandria?" said Mendel. "Before we go, could you bathe James's wound? He was bitten by a sandworm."

"It's okay," mumbled James.

"Looks bloody sore to me," said Craig.

Elandria plunged a pouched hand into a slit in her abdomen and withdrew a portion of liquid. She scuttled over to James and dribbled it over the red lesion.

"Owch!" exclaimed James. "That's made it worse."

Mendel splashed loudly. "Jean?"

Jean Harrison knelt down in front of Bero. "Yes, Mendel?"

"Would you mind if Helen comes with us?"

"Your havin' a laugh, right?" moaned Craig. "She'll only slow us down."

James felt a twinge of jealousy niggle at him. He tried to shake it off.

"It might get a bit hairy down there, Mendel. Perhaps I…"

"But James, you couldn't perform the last spell I tried to direct through you," reasoned Mendel.

"Yeah, but… You mean that was Helen? She did the last spell?"

"Jean?" Mendel pressed.

Helen looked excited. "Can I, Mum?"

Jean Harrison sighed heavily. "Promise to look after her, Mendel."

"I will do my best."

"But…" protested Craig, "she's only eight."

"Onward!" blasted Mendel. "We will try to get right under the plug of stone. A larvacidal spell should do the trick."

"A bloomin' what?" mocked Craig. "You up to that one, Sis? Looks like James here's, been made redundant." Craig began to put on his fake Scottish accent. "It micht git a bit hairy doon there, lassie and numpty boy, here…"

"Shut up, Craig, or I'll stick this thing where the sun don't shine," muttered James. He waved Firetongue menacingly.

"That's enough, boys," Mendel scolded. "Always better to have a bit of insurance, that's all. James's sandworm bite may have interfered with our connection. A temporary effect, I'm sure."

"Don't tell me," said Craig. "I'll work it out. Sandius wormius."

"*Strongalus arenus*, actually," said Mendel. "A sub species of..."

"Alright, alright," moaned Craig. "Wish I'd never started."

"Yeah, well so do we," snapped James. He'd forgotten how irritating Craig could be.

As they circled back down the narrow stairwell toward the tunnels below, James thought he could hear his mum's voice in the distance. It was probably just his imagination and he wasn't going to say anything with Craig in the annoying mood he was in. Bero growled as they moved down the stairs.

CHAPTER SEVENTEEN

THE CROSSING OF WAYS

"If you think I'm going to help you find and kill my son, you're off your head!" Cathy's face flushed with uncontrollable rage as the strange looking creature leered down at her.

"All I need is a piece of her hair and I will be able to find the boy." The Ibissynian sneered, his long, curved bill wavering inches from her face as he addressed Dendralon.

Cathy reached out and grabbed onto the end of the bill. "Tell him, Dendralon!"

The Ibissynian tensed and reached for his sword.

Dendralon, still preoccupied by the sight of the Racnid grubs slithering around on the underside of the giant plug of granite that blocked their path, raised his staff until it rested a few inches from the Ibissynian's throat. "Never threaten my Queen, Ibissynian."

"I'm not your ruddy Queen!" Cathy yelled.

The Racnid females began to click and utter high-pitched shrieks.

Elhada clambered in beside the Ibissynian. "We do not need you, or your useless twin. I already have the scent of the boy." She eyed Cathy suspiciously.

The Ibissynian pulled away from Cathy and rounded on Elhada. "You will die for that comment, spider queen."

"Enough!" Dendralon pushed past the squabbling Artilians and stood directly under the squirming mass of Racnid young. "Mendel has the third crystal. I know it." He smiled at Elhada. "Your young have done enough for now, Elhada."

"But sire, they will need another seven hours to break through. If you look closely you will see Artilian wasp larvae and winged Centide larvae also. Even with the digestive acids of all three species in full flow they will need more—"

"Silence!"

Elhada bowed and backed off.

"Clear the surface of the plug of stone, unless you value not your young."

Elhada produced an ear-splitting wail that caused the glistening white grubs to shudder then drop to the ground. Heaps of writhing maggots poured along the tunnels and instantly began burrowing through the rose-coloured walls.

Cathy could see that the grubs had eaten away about half the plug of stone, the piece that remained, however, was still about the size of St. Paul's Cathedral.

Dendralon flicked the long black hair from his eyes and, to her surprise, produced a pair of plastic sunglasses. He donned the ridiculous looking things and pointed his staff at the base of the granite block. "I suggest you all stand well back."

Cathy ran with the rest of the creatures to the edge of the cavern and hid behind a cluster of stalagmites.

Just as Dendralon began muttering his strange incantation, however, a blast of blue fire cut across the chamber floor and smashed into Dendralon's staff. It flew from his hand as he reeled back. Tripping backwards he hit the hard stone floor. "Argh!"

Cathy bit her lip in excitement as his dark glasses slipped from his face and shattered. She scanned the chamber for the source of the attack. *Is James here?*

Instantly, a phalanx of Inubians surrounded her and blocked her view. "Get out of my way you bunch of rabid..."

"Mendel!" Dendralon's deep voice echoed out over the cavern. "Where are you, my old friend?"

Through the odd bend in an arm and kink in a leg, Cathy anxiously searched the chamber for any sign of her son. She made to cry out, but a leathery, Ibissynian hand covered her mouth and yanked her to the floor by the hair.

"If your son is here, you will watch him die at my hands, my Queen." The Ibissynian she'd gripped onto earlier had obviously taken umbrage at her attack on him. "No-one may ever touch an Ibissynian's flesh and live."

She pulled away. "Is that a threat?" She tried to shout out for Dendralon but the Ibissynian covered her mouth once more and increased the pressure on her lips. The dark wizard's voice boomed out again.

"Only Mendel has the power to relieve me of my staff with a blast of Denthan blue fire. Show yourself old friend. Let us make a deal!"

Wide eyed, Cathy strained to hear some kind of answer, but there was none. *Why would there be?* She thought. *I hope he strikes again.*

"I have to apologize to young James Peck for killing his mother. It's the least I can do."

What? Cathy struggled to break free of the Ibissynian. Tears poured down her face and ran over his hand. "I'm alive, Jam…" The Ibissynian dragged her further back from the fray.

Dendralon continued. "I know you have the third crystal, Mendel. Well done, and thank you for doing my work for me."

Cathy wondered how long it would be until James or Mendel responded to Dendralon's taunts. She bit down on the Ibissynian's fingers until her teeth grated his bones. The taste was repulsive, like meat gone off. Undaunted, the bird-faced abomination maintained his grip on her mouth.

* * *

James stiffened. "Mendel, is…?"

"He is lying, James."

Helen smiled and shook her head. "I knew your mum wasn't dead. I just knew it."

It was Helen who'd said the spell that had thrown Dendralon's staff into the air. James dug his thumbnail into the tip of his forefinger in an effort to stifle his jealousy. She hadn't even flinched. She'd made the initial painful connection with Mendel when she had picked him off the ground in Belloc's lair but now… Now she spoke Mendel's spells effortlessly. No searing headaches, nothing.

"She did a pretty good job of that, didn't she, James?" whispered Craig.

"Why don't you go raffle yourself, you…" James could feel himself shaking.

"I thought you were supposed to be his friend?" said Helen. "Wait. Mendel's trying his best to concentrate."

James pushed his nail in further. Now that his eyes had adjusted to the purple light, he could see the huge mass of Racnids and Inubians gathered round the edge of the cavern.

"Boys, Helen," whispered Mendel. "Join hands and do not let go. Helen, hold Bero's tail."

Helen closed her eyes and smiled. "Wwwwinvisiwwwbilitwwy!"

Everything went fuzzy. It was just like trying to see out through a bathroom window with extra thick, bumpy glass. The cavern transformed into a blur of black and purple. James felt Helen's hand, small and damp with sweat, grip him tightly. *She is only eight*, he thought. She must be terrified, and there he was, being envious of her. It wasn't her fault that a bloomin' sandworm had bitten him. He wondered why she didn't feel the same knock, knock, knocking sensation that had pestered him whenever Mendel had performed his spells. *Was she better at it? More suited?*

James felt the jerk forward and followed on. Craig was behind with Helen to the fore. "What are you going to do, Mendel?" James whispered.

"Think the words, James. Do not speak out loud again," urged Mendel.

"Can anyone hear me? I'm thinking out loud too," sounded Helen.

"Yes, Sis. Stop showing off." Craig's voice was fainter, more ethereal than Helen's, like a whisper trapped in a biscuit tin.

"She's pretty good at the thinking words thing, too. Eh Craig? Better than you." James mocked.

Craig gripped his hand tighter.

James could just make out the shape of Dendralon ahead. Although the picture was wobbly and blurred, the giant, fearsome frame of the Hedra wizard was all too familiar.

"I am going to walk round him. Nobody say or think any words. He'll hear you."

"Grrrr…!"

Great, thought James. *An invisible Bero had just growled at Dendralon.*

"Ibissynians!" shouted Dendralon. "Find them." He scanned the cavern for any sign of them, poking into the dank air with his gnarled staff.

Two of the ibis-billed assassins broke free of the ranks and marched into the centre of the cave. The one nearest to James crouched and examined the dusty floor of the cavern.

"Wwwflightwwwfootwww!" thought Helen. The word was barely discernible above the murmurings of the gathered hordes.

Immediately, James's feet left the ground. He began to hover about three inches above the floor of the chamber.

The Ibissynian who'd crouched down to look at the dust on the cave floor stood up and scanned the cave.

"Where are they?" hissed Dendralon.

The Ibissynian fell to his knees and flicked his curved beak towards his twin. "I saw their footprints but now..."

"Now they are in mid air," finished Dendralon. "Very good, old friend. I almost had you when you growled at me. What's it like being a dog? Now that Denthan has been destroyed, there is not hope for you. No way to transform back into your old decrepit self."

They were almost amongst the Racnids when Craig lost his balance and crashed into James. His foot touched the ground.

"There!" One of the Ibissynians ran towards them, his curved sword drawn.

James felt a tingling sensation on his palm as he thought his magic word. Firetongue.

Striking out blindly, the Ibissynian's blade slashed through the air above their heads.

Still they floated further towards the Racnids.

The grey-skinned creature lunged this time, emitting a high-pitched scream as he did.

James's sword shot up to parry the blow then sliced downwards.

The creature yelled out as his muscled arm clumped onto the floor of the cave, still clutching his sword.

"Use your silken thread my children," screamed Dendralon. He sounded excited.

In their heads Mendel's voice spoke quietly. "I can sense your mother, James. We are close. She is alive."

James's heart raced. His chest tightened.

The Racnids fired out their sticky ropes as, still holding each other's hands, James, Craig and Helen eased between the gangly creatures. The thick threads shot over their heads and ensnared the Ibissynians behind.

"No!" bellowed Dendralon. He pointed his staff at the Ibissynians and muttered a charm.

James glanced behind him as Bero veered sharply to his left, pulling them deeper into a mass of dry, stick-like legs. Dendralon's spell dissolved the spiders' thread and the Ibissynians followed Dendralon through the host of bewildered Racnids.

The Racnids hissed and withdrew in fright as James brushed, invisibly, against them.

James thought he saw a white robe through the mishmash of legs and downy bodies. "Mum?"

"Quiet!" Mendel's voice jumped into his head.

In the same instant, a set of blackened Racnid teeth snapped at his face. He pulled back. Another jabbed its stinger at his chest but this time Greenworm jerked upwards and caught the creature in the eye.

"Arghhhhh! Ssiissssssss!"

Black blood spattered over their clothes and faces, temporarily revealing their position.

The Racnids clambered over each other in an attempt to attack but simply pushed the few who had actually seen them out of the way.

James saw another flash of white linen. Further away this time, but he didn't dare to shout out. *What was Mendel playing at?*

"We are almost through," said Mendel. "When we reach the back wall I will cast a fire spell that will spread over them all. It will create a barrier between us and Dendralon."

"It will kill my mum," James protested. "I'm sure I saw..."

"She is amongst the Inubians now, James. I'm sure I saw her too."

"It's too risky," said Helen, her voice as clear as Mendel's in James's head. "You might hurt Mrs. Peck by mistake."

"I can assure you that..."

"Clang!"

The two Ibissynians stood in their path, their huge swords crossed to form a blockade.

They piled into each other and pushed Bero forward until he was within biting range. Rather than nuzzle-in with his invisible wet nose, Bero bit down hard on the nearest Ibissynian sword hand while Craig threw Greenworm and James slashed upwards with Firetongue.

The one already missing an arm looked down to see a green-bladed spear in his chest but the other somehow managed to block James's blow and fling Bero away.

The Racnids, still confused, scuttled away from the fight.

As soon as Bero hit the ground they all became completely visible.

"Ahh!" The remaining Ibissynian brought his sword down on Bero but Helen said, "Wwstonewrightww!" and the creature froze.

Their backs against the wall, Helen, Craig and James looked out as Bero snarled at the encircling Racnids. The barrel swung recklessly from his furry neck and James saw Mendel flash past the plastic window.

"Wwwwhindrilwwfireww!"

A jet of blue flame shot out from the barrel and expanded over the screaming Racnids before bursting into a cascade of burning droplets.

Over one thousand Racnids raced about in terror as their downy carapaces ignited.

"I don't see Dendralon," Mendel warned. "Be careful."

The wounded Ibissynian had already grown another arm. He yanked the green spear from his chest. The other had simply shaken himself free of the stone that had held him fast.

"There!" Craig pointed over the writhing mass of burning Racnids at the gathering jackal-faced Inubians. Thousands upon thousands streamed in behind the figure of Dendralon, his staff held high.

Again, James saw the white robe swish in the gloom but he never caught sight of his mum or heard her voice. Perhaps she was dead after all and this was just another cruel trick.

"Quick, before those duck-billed dorks get going again," shouted Craig. He called on his spear and it returned back to his hand.

They all raced away from the burning Racnids and down the open tunnel until they curved round a sharp bend. There, ahead of them, the whole tunnel heaved with what must have been another ten thousand Racnids.

They skidded to a halt.

Bero growled.

They turned to run back into the main cavern but stopped again as the Hedra wizard came into view. He wandered, steadily, towards them, his arms folded, the Ibissynians flanking him.

"Mendel!" Helen whispered out of the side of her mouth. "Make us invisible again."

"Bit low on the old batteries, my dear. Sorry."

"Sorry!" stammered Craig. "Bloomin' sorry? What kind of mad stunt was that?"

"Oh, I'm sure my old doggy friend had a good reason for racing headlong into our midst. And it wasn't just to fry a few thousand Racnids. He knows that they're easily replaced."

The giant female Racnid behind him hissed. "Let me sting them. Let me tear off their arms and…"

"Enough, Elhada." Dendralon walked forward a few paces then stopped. "If there's any tearing off of limbs to be done, I'll let you know." He waved her way with a flick of his long fingers.

"What have you done with my mum?" shouted James.

"First you lose your pathetic father, and now can't find your mother. She is no more!" Dendralon thumped his staff on the hard floor of the tunnel.

James raised his crimson sword and advanced. "You're a liar! What have you done to her?"

Gingerly, the two Ibissynians moved forward to meet him.

"I see your Denthan sword has left its mark on my Ibissynian pets. They hesitate."

The Ibissynians straightened and moved forward. "Halt!" Dendralon pointed at Helen with his gnarled staff.

The staff looks blacker than before, thought James; *singed and cracked.*

"I will kill her now if you do not give me the third crystal. I know you took it from Belloc."

"You know no such thing, Dendralon," said Mendel.

"Oh but I do," the wizard jeered. "Give me the remaining red crystal and I will spare the child's life."

James saw Helen tense.

"We don't have it!" bellowed Helen.

Dendralon's long grey tongue flickered free of his heavy jaw.

"Then, who does?" he pressed.

James felt a jolt of pain in his head. The knocking sensation had begun to build. Mendel was going to try his magic through him again. The thudding in his head was swept away by a mixture of exhilaration and relief. He waited for some indiscernible fishy word to spill from his lips but...

"Wwwwinvisiwwwbilitwwy!"

His heart sank at the sound of Helen's small voice.

Everything went fuzzy again.

"Attack!" bellowed Dendralon.

But the Racnids and Inubians couldn't see them. They jabbed their stings and snapped their jaws in vain as they slipped through the midst of them, back into the main cavern. James heard Dendralon shout out at the bird-faced Ibissynians. They were probably trying to get their scent.

"It will be difficult for them," said Mendel, his voice detached and thin. "The stench of Inubians and Racnids will thwart them."

"Thwart?" said Craig, arching back as a jackal-faced Inubian homed in on his voice. A sword swished past his face.

"Shhhh!" James had thought the rebuke as hard as he could, knowing it was important not to speak out loud, but they were soon clear of the huge army that gathered below the plug of stone. A deafening crack sounded above their heads. James looked up, but it was difficult to see clearly when you were invisible.

"The granite plug is beginning to move," explained Mendel. The spiderlings have weakened the structure beyond any repair spell I could muster. We will have to get back up to the first level."

"Won't Dendralon follow us?" whispered Helen.

"I will seal the stairwell. I only hope the Artilian forces have gathered above us. We've only delayed things a few hours. Elandria needs more time to perform the spell that will kill off the Racnids."

"I know the Racnids are horrible and stuff, but I don't understand how she could kill off her own kind," said Helen.

"Jal did a similar thing back on Denthan," said James, inadvertently coughing as he ran the last few yards to the hidden stairwell. "He helped lock his people out of Gwendral. Shut the gates on them."

"The Hedra weren't exactly friendly," said Craig, in a whisper this time.

"Still," said Helen. "It wasn't very nice."

Craig reappeared beside James. "Look if something is bad, it's better to just leave it behind and move on."

James felt his temper build. "You'd better not be referring to my…"

"Children!" Mendel sounded angry. "The immorality of war is a big topic to discuss when we are running for our lives. Stand back."

Helen opened her mouth to say something but to her surprise uttered the word, "Wwwblendwwstoneww". The small doorway they'd just hared through merged into the surrounding rock.

"What about my mum?" snapped James, anxiously trying to find a crack in the stone or at least some hint of a door. "You've locked her out." He traced the contours of the warm rock with his fingers.

Bang!

James jumped back.

"No James, we've locked *them* out," corrected Craig. He jerked Greenworm towards the door and wiggled his fingers in front of his face like dangly spider legs.

"You are so close to getting a real good smack," spat James.

"Shut up! I thought you two were supposed to be friends," said Helen, pulling Bero up the steep steps.

"If your mother is still back there," added Mendel. "She will follow the horde up through the hole in the floor when the plug fails. I was sure I could feel her presence."

"Well I'm sure I saw her," said James, trying to hold back the urge to dig Craig in the chops.

As they began climbing the narrow stairs back up to the first floor it was pretty evident that Bero was struggling.

"He's getting old again," said Craig. He tried to lift Bero up but soon gave up.

Helen stopped and closed her eyes. "Wwwliftwwwfreeewww!"

Bero's paws lifted from the stairs. He hovered about two inches above the rugged stone.

"Wow, Sis. Your getting good at this, aren't you?"

James ignored the taunt.

"It's not me," she reminded.

Bero looked totally confused. He pawed the air and growled until he finally regained his balance and accepted his new predicament. His tail resumed its steady wag, and he floated up in front of them. A faint blue glow emanated from the window of the barrel.

"Helen?" enquired James. "When you do the magic, does it hurt? I mean does your head hurt?"

Helen looked surprised by the question. "No. I don't even know it's happening until I say the funny words."

"You don't feel anything? Not a slight ache or…"

"No," said Helen. "Should I?"

"No. It doesn't matter."

CHAPTER EIGHTEEN

THE KRAKEN

Father Michael Parr stood beside the altar in the side aisle of St. Donan's Episcopal Church. A single red light hung down from the ceiling, throwing crimson highlights over his vestments, which were green and gold for advent. The robes weighed heavily on his shoulders as he crossed himself and wondered where he'd put the jar of incense. Inexplicably, he had a strong desire to fill the church with a ripe, sickly scent. He had the notion that the substance might protect St. Donan's in some way from the terrors to come.

He administered communion to David Peck, Archie MacNulty, and Ephie before finishing the remaining four wafers and draining the chalice. He cleaned the inside of the silver cup with the starched linen cloth and placed everything, as it should be, back on the altar. He bowed and then turned to give the final thanks and blessing. He said a small prayer to himself but then opened his eyes to see that Sergeant Carr and, more alarmingly, Eethan, were both sitting in the shadows. Carr clutched onto an array of rusting weapons and Eethan, still kneeling with his hands clasped together, cast a nervous eye on the main door. Michael was giving the holy sacrament in a church that had live gargoyles crawling all over the tower and a little blue goblin with a shock of white hair sitting in the back pew. *What would the bishop say?*

"Psst!"

Michael, just about to disrobe in the vestry, paused in the dark doorway. "Yes, Eethan. What is it?"

"Ee feels something bad is happening een dee Loch."

"No doubt," Michael whispered to himself, resigned to the fact that anything could, and probably would happen.

David, Archie, and Ephie all made their way to the back of the church, past the wilting hydrangeas, and round the sandstone font until they reached the shelves of burgundy prayer books.

Michael, back in his familiar black suit and dog-collar, arranged his few strands of auburn hair and strolled towards them. He stopped beside the black-painted, ancient fuse boxes to fix a poster on the wall, which read: *Summer Fete in the church grounds. Free tablet and cakes on admission. All proceeds will go towards the 'missing gargoyle' fund.*

"He's back," said Carr, pointing at the poster.

Miles away in some other train of thought, Michael hesitated. "Pardon?"

"Your missing gargoyle is back."

"Ah, so it would seem. But then again, I'm none too sure that he is. I mean, how many have you seen?"

"There are four now. Here, Father take this." Sergeant Carr handed him a longbow and a quiver of aluminum arrows, fletched with the blue and white colours of the fifth Drumfintley scout group.

"Ee must come now!" pleaded Eethan. He scampered part way up the wall before dropping down onto the ground outside.

They all crept out from the green door of St. Donan's, glancing up at the shadows on the parapets of the church tower. Large, leathery wings flapped impatiently as the gargoyles shifted.

"They're becoming more agitated," said Ephie.

"I could probably take chh…one down right now," said MacNulty, raising his aim.

"No, no… Not a good idea," protested David. "We might get them riled."

"Well, if you schhay schho, Mr. Peck." Archie lowered the barrel of his shotgun.

"Green," whispered Sergeant Carr.

"What?" said Ephie, still moving further away from the church tower.

"MacNulty's cartridges are green. I knew it."

"Achh away an bile yer heed!" snapped Archie.

Carr placed his hand on Archie's chest, halting his progress. "Ye can't see the bloody heather for his green, spent cartridges. They're all over the ruddy place."

"We…" Michael paused to take a deep breath, "have more pressing matters, Sergeant."

"Aye, for the time being. Just for the time being." He eyed his brother with contempt.

Michael stiffened. "Where's Eethan got to?"

David Peck slipped his cavalry sword from its scabbard and handed another quiver of arrows to Ephie. "He's over there."

They all followed David Peck's gaze until they picked out Eethan on the shore of Loch Echty.

"Woof! Woof! Woof!"

Michael frowned. "It's Patch. Ephie, I forgot he was in the Rectory. He must have got out somehow."

Ephie bent down to pick him up. "He seems okay. I mean, he probably realised everyone had gone. Imagine forgetting Patch." She snuggled into the little Jack Russell Terrier, giggling as it nipped and licked her chin and nose.

David paused before opening the metal gate that separated the Rectory garden from the shore. "He doesn't like Eethan much, does he?"

"Ah, no," Michael replied. "Not since they met in the tunnel last year."

"I'll put him back in the Rectory," said Ephie. She turned and cooed Patch all the way to the door.

"Ich getting dark," said Archie.

David Peck opened the gate that led to the pebble-strewn shore of Loch Echty. "It's too early to get dark. What time do you make it, Sergeant?"

"Three thirty-two, according to the church tower. There must be a storm brewing. Look at those gargoyles."

The gargoyles were howling up at the sky over the Loch. They all hung over the eastern parapet, testing their wings as the breeze strengthened.

"I can only see three of them," mused Michael.

"There was definitely four the last time I looked," said Carr, bracing himself against the strengthening breeze. "Something bad is happening. I can feel it."

David Peck shivered as another blast of cold air wafted over the dark water and ruffled his hair. "C'mon Sergeant, let's see what Eethan's up to."

They made their way down to the shore just as Ephie returned with her bow tightly fixed over her back. The string cut into her sweatshirt across her chest.

"You'll never get chat schhing off in time if anything comes at us quick," advised Archie.

"What do you mean?" protested Ephie.

"Your gut ich, too…"

"My what?" she snapped.

"Your gut. The schtring of the bow. It's too tight over you." Archie's face turned a deep shade of puce.

"What are you insinuating?"

Michael tried to intervene. "Look, Ephie; all Archie means is that you've got it on in such a way that it might… Well it wouldn't be easy to… And…"

David cleared his throat. "Take it off, Ephie, and hold it in your hand. So you can be ready to fire at a moment's notice."

"Shhhhh!" Eethan turned to face them. His white hair blew down over his face. Michael saw the concern in his beady black eyes. He still wore the remnants of a piece of pink cloth, which was more of a dirty grey now. He looked so scrawny, standing at the water's edge. "Shh!" he repeated.

Waves had formed on the surface of the Loch, and the sky had darkened even more. They could hardly make each other out. Archie aimed his gun out over the Loch as dirty brown foam blew into his hair and over his clothes from the water. "All thosech bloody detergents from Glen Farm." He spat on the shore behind Eethan.

Everyone gave him a puzzled look then gasped. Behind him, about one hundred yards from the shore, something glinted silver through the waves.

"Down!" Eethan motioned them all to keep low.

Michael crouched behind Sergeant Carr and caught hold of Ephie's hand.

"A Basking Shark?" Shouted David.

Archie returned his suggestion with a scornful stare.

A massive back slithered free of the waves for a few seconds and then disappeared. They all took a step back.

"What is that thing?" said Ephie.

"That fing," said Archie, "is che same fing that killed the other fing in the Loch. The other day," he added.

"It's huge," yelled Michael. The wind was so strong now that they had to shout to be heard.

Again a huge scaled back arched up over the waves and splashed down again. It was only fifty yards away this time.

David Peck cupped his mouth. "I think we should pull back."

Rain began to patter over the stones around them. Big heavy drops smacked into their faces as the wind strengthened.

"Awch!" screamed Ephie. "The rain is beginning to sting my face."

The rain became incessant.

Retreating back over the now slippery stones, they caught one more glimpse of the thing in the Loch. This time a monstrous head edged upward through the waves. Black and covered in scales, it resembled a single-horned bull with wide nostrils and a thickset neck. An enormous set of spiny pincers edged out of the choppy water. The Fintley Bell below Loch Echty began to chime.

"Every time that bell rings ch... something dies," shouted Archie.

Carr sneered. "Don't talk bilge, you... Only you would you say something as stupid as that at a time like this."

"Itch the truth," said Archie.

A scream bellowed up from the depths of the Loch that stopped them all in their tracks. The trees leaned away from the Loch and the rain became even heavier.

Ephie began to cry.

Michael pulled her in close. "Don't worry, the Lord will protect us, my darling."

"The gargoyles!" yelled David. "They're gone."

Everyone looked up at St. Donan's church tower. It was silhouetted against a near black sky, a single spire pointing up to the heavens. The gargoyles had disappeared.

Archie let off a shot. *Bang!*

His shot had caught a leathery wing. He'd hit a gargoyle, knocked it back into the trees. "They're in there."

Sergeant Carr screamed out. "Help!"

Wrapped round his leg a thick tentacle covered in black hooks jerked him off his feet.

Eethan turned and hit the tentacle with a blast of pure blue light. It unravelled itself and whipped back into the Loch. A second feeler even thicker than the first, however, caught Eethan from behind and pulled him under the water.

"Eethan!" Michael pulled Ephie back up onto the Rectory lawn and nocked an arrow. "Hurry! Archie, Sergeant, get off the shore. David!"

He watched in trepidation as three more tentacles lashed out of the water at the remaining men on the shore. Lightning forked down at them from the sky, the flash illuminating two gargoyles as they moved out of the trees behind them. Howling, they lifted several feet from the ground and began to fly towards him and Ephie. Michael took aim and loosed the arrow, but it thumped into the silvery trunk of a birch and wavered.

Distracted by another scream from the Loch, Michael made out the shape of Eethan wiggling free of a tentacle. He was crawling down the flaying limb towards a monstrous, gaping mouth. Two huge scorpion-like pincers snapped around him. The beast's head burst free of the Loch, and Michael saw its hideous face again, the single horn protruding from the bulky skull. It snapped down at Eethan, so small in comparison to the creature. A flash of blue light shot across the water as Eethan hit the creature again.

Ephie screamed as a gargoyle caught her from behind and lifted her off the lawn.

Michael took aim with his bow but was too frightened to shoot in case he caught Ephie. "Ephie!" He felt so helpless.

A good five feet off the ground Ephie lunged up with an arrow pulled from her quiver and pierced the gargoyle's chest. It howled like a wounded seal and dropped her. A second gargoyle raced down towards her but it jerked as Michael's shot hit it in the neck. It fell dead at Ephie's side, on the Rectory lawn.

"Archie!" Michael just saw Archie spin round in time to loose another shot at a feeler that was about to pull him over. He missed, but David hacked down with his sword and cut through the thick limb. Archie stepped free of the squirming tentacle and caught hold of Sergeant Carr. Michael, picking up Ephie and edging back towards the Rectory, could see Carr being hauled backwards into the Loch. "Ephie, get inside the Rectory. Lock the door!"

"What about you?"

"Just do it!" snapped Michael. He raced to the fence in time to see David hacking at the tentacle gripping Carr but a gargoyle flew down at him and whipped him over with its forked tail. David lay still on the shore. *Oh God, is he dead?*

"David!" Michael rushed forward firing another arrow up at a third gargoyle that had just exploded in a shower of leaves from the birch trees. Carr was in the Loch. Michael slipped over the rocks and slime as he tried to get to him, but before he even got within ten feet, Carr was wrenched under the waves.

Archie gripped his gun tightly and dived into the cold water after him. Michael looked down and saw David, lying unconscious at his feet. He hauled him up and dragged him to the grassy bank near the Rectory gate. There was no sign of Eethan, the monster, Carr, or Archie until there was an almighty splash some fifty yards out. The whole creature lifted itself from the Loch. It had four legs that supported a reptilian body covered in shining black scales. A writhing mane of tentacles snaked out from its throat. Michael saw Eethan fire another blast of blue before disappearing below the water. The giant pincers clipped together on the water where Eethan had just gone under.

Still dragging David further up the bank, Michael saw Carr, slumped and gripped tightly by more than one tentacle, being lowered down into the monster's gaping mouth. Archie, his left hand now gripping a long knife, was hacking at the limb that held him. The old poacher stabbed the knife into the snake-like limb before raising his gun. He fired and caught the beast square in the mouth. Archie used the momentary agony of the beast to retrieve his knife and resume hacking through the limb. The limb entwined him as he lobbed it off, but Archie fell straight into the gaping mouth.

"No!" shouted Michael. He felt sick.

There was another blast from the shotgun inside the creature's mouth. The monster screamed and dropped Sergeant Carr into the waves.

Michael raced back down onto the shore and jumped into the water. He swam as hard as he could until he reached Carr and caught his jacket. Another wiry, blue hand gripped Carr's collar and they swam ashore.

The huge creature slipped beneath the waves in a rush of bubbles and foam. The back draught almost pulled Michael under again, but he kicked hard and regained his momentum. *Thank God for Ephie's swimming lessons.* He soon felt the ground beneath his feet. "Where… Where's Archie?"

Eethan slumped down beside Sergeant Carr. "Ee don't think… Ee don't think ees made eet, Revereend."

"Archie!" Michael shouted as hard as he could before toppling back over the stones. "Ugh! Archie…" Tears welled up in his eyes and he began to sob. "Eethan, you need to go and get… You need to…" He desperately tried to think of what he should do next. "Please, God!"

Beside him, Sergeant Carr moved his head to the side and coughed out a lungful of brown loch water. "I'll get it Archie. I'll…" Still choking, he coughed then closed his eyes again. His big round face was paler than Michael had ever seen it.

Michael strained to see out over the Loch. "Where's the thing? Did Archie kill it?"

"Thee Kraken can't be killed, Michael. At least eet ees almost eempossible."

"But Archie shot it in the mouth. He was inside…" Michael covered his eyes with is left hand and clutched his chest.

"Calm yeerself," whispered Eethan, in a high-pitched whine that cut through the noise of the wind and rain. "Lookee! Thee sun ees coming out again."

Michael shaded his eyes as a shaft of sunlight pierced the clouds and hit the Loch. David groaned beside him.

"Michael, Archie? Awe!" He rubbed his head. His hair was stained red with blood where he'd cracked his head on the rocks.

"Archie's gone, David," said Michael. "God rest his soul."

"He… He can't be."

Michael wiped his tearstained face with the edge of his jacket. "Archie gave up his life to save Sergeant Carr."

David glanced down at the semiconscious policeman. "He did what?"

"Ee saved ees brother," added Eethan.

David stretched and pushed himself up on his elbows. "Oh no. Poor Archie."

Michael stood up and took Eethan's hand. "Will it come back, Eethan?"

"Eet will. But ee hopes that Mendel ees here next time. Ee hopes."

"We all hope that," said David. "I can't believe it. And what about the gargoyles?"

"Well, they seem to be susceptible to steel and bullets. There's one lying over there." Michael pointed to the gargoyle lying dead on the Rectory lawn, its leathery wings contorted awkwardly beneath it.

David wiped some blood from his eyes and felt for his sword. "Are you sure it's dead?"

"Eet was never alive," whispered Eethan. The rain had stopped and the wind had subsided. "Eet was only magic you were fighting. Dark magic."

"I'm not sure you've really answered the question, Eethan," pressed David.

"Michael, David, Eethan…" It was Ephie. Michael could see she was looking for Archie and Sergeant Carr.

"Oh, there he is, but where's Archie?"

"Een thee stomach of thee Kraken," answered Eethan, matter-of-factly.

"Eethan," snapped Michael. "Have a bit of tact."

Ephie screwed up her face. "What did he say, Michael?"

David supported Sergeant Carr, leaving Michael to explain.

Ephie let out a pitiful yell and covered her face.

"What's up Ephie?" said Carr, in a groggy voice.

"It's Archie," said David, quietly. "He saved your life."

"He probably says he did," said Carr, still coming round.

"No, he did. And what's more, he's…"

"He's dead, Sergeant Carr," cried Ephie.

Sergeant Carr sat back on the well-mown lawn and turned himself round until he could kneel. "He might still be in the water."

"Oh, ee ees," said Eethan, dolefully. "Ee ees…"

CHAPTER NINETEEN

THE FIRST LEVEL

Bero alighted on the stairs before they reached the door that led into the first floor. He issued a small whine and sniffed at the base of the rock. A tiny glint of light hinted at the space beyond.

"I hope the Artilians are ready," said Mendel.

"I hope we don't open this to find Dendralon," whispered James. He called on his crimson sword, Firetongue, and braced.

Craig pushed forward, carrying his emerald spear, Greenworm, and put his shoulder against the stone. It edged inward. The brightness of the area beyond caused them all to shield their eyes and duck down.

"Woof!" Bero strolled into the huge chamber, the plastic barrel swinging like a pendulum below his muzzle.

With a swish of steel, a phalanx of fifty Artilians drew their swords and raced towards them.

"Stop!"

James recognized Junera, the Artilian leader he'd met earlier.

Craig lowered his spear on seeing the Artilians slow down.

Junera looked resplendent in her polished silver armour. She beamed at the children and the old dog. "We are ready now, thanks to you giving us a little more time." She pointed out across the expanse of rose-coloured stone and jet that formed the floor of the first level. The granite plug was still in place. "It has moved twice in the last ten minutes, but if it falls now we are ready for them."

James decided that the number of Artilians lined up round the edge of the first floor must have numbered over thirty thousand. There were bronze chariots decked with red plumes, ballistae, strange machines that looked to be able to fire a thousand arrows at once and, in the middle of the floor, suspended above the granite plug, a huge bowl hung precariously between two bronze shafts. Its contents bubbled and spattered as a group of Artilian men and women hooked a long pole onto a slot on the side.

"It's going to get very uncomfortable for anything that wants to come up that way," explained Junera. She drew her sword. "The plug is moving again." Junera ran across to the phalanx gripping the pole that would tip the boiling liquid down on the enemy and took some of the strain. "You can join my infantry on the right flank!"

James looked across at a mass of Artilians, all sporting a similar style of armour to Junera's. Their chest-plates were embossed with a copper-coloured band and a golden plume adorned their shinning silver helmets. Their cloaks seemed to be fashioned from a blend of peacock feathers and pure gold, the iridescent greens and blues shimmering in the bright lights as they moved.

Mendel shifted in the barrel. "You are right to think they are peacock feathers, James. The bird forms the main protein constituent of the Artilian diet."

"No way," protested Craig.

"That's not nice," added Helen. "How did peacocks get here anyway?"

"They come from here, Helen. They were introduced to Earth over fifty thousand years ago by the first scouts from Artilis. They are farmed here, as chickens are in Scotland."

"But..." Helen seemed to lose interest in the conversation as the Artilians quieted. The whole first floor of the giant pyramid of Ra fell quiet. Only the sound of the granite plug grinding against the rock below echoed through the great hall.

High-pitched screams and yelps began to emanate from below their feet.

Crash!

The whole circular structure of the granite plug split and then fell down into the depths below.

James and Craig backed into the second row of Junera's troops and waited. Sweat began to trickle down James's neck. It ran down his spine and cooled as it gathered at the base of his back. He shivered.

Nothing came through.

"They've seen the colander above them," Helen whispered.

Either that or it's all a trick, and they're going to erupt from the walls or something," Craig whispered back.

A red bubble appeared beneath the colander. Slowly, it grew in height until it touched the underside of the boiling vat. Like a pink, festering blister it bounced beneath the Artilians' bowl.

"Wwwboltwwfirewww!"

As soon as the words left Helen's lips a bolt of blue fire shot across the open expanse of floor and smacked into the bubble. With a splutter and a crack, the bubble burst.

"Pull!" shrieked Junera.

Her phalanx heaved on the long pole and the colander tipped. Red-hot lava splattered down into the void and a burst of flame flared up from the hole like an erupting volcano.

The screams from below were sickening.

"I hope that finished the old snake off for good," said Craig.

"I hope my mum wasn't down there," added James.

"No chance. She's either still lost or locked up in some cell like I was, ready to be fed to…"

"Craig!" snapped Helen. "Don't be so nasty."

"I wasn't being nasty, I was just telling James that his mum is probably not being burned alive."

Hisssss! The flames immediately snuffed themselves out.

Junera signalled her troops to fall back behind the machines that held the banks of arrows. As she turned, however, the figure of Dendralon rose up from the void. He pointed his staff at the retreating Artilians and shouted out a curse. A line of ice tracked out from the tip of his staff, dividing and subdividing until, like a mass of living white snakes, they wrapped round the legs of the Artilians.

As they fell, the ice crept over their bodies. At first, perhaps two hundred fell. Then, many more were covered in the white ice-mist, dropping with a clatter onto the hard floor before exploding into a thousand fragments. Junera pressed on through the ranks until she was to the fore. To her left, the Artilians screamed out as the white ice caught them up.

"Mendel, do something," pleaded Helen.

Craig stepped free of the front row and threw Greenworm as hard as he could. It shot from his hand and soared towards Dendralon.

Only two Artilians remained alive to the left of Junera as she dived forward to get behind the nearest ballista.

Greenworm plunged into Dendralon and the stream of ice ceased.

Silence fell over the chamber as everyone stared in disbelief.

"It hasn't worked," said Mendel.

"What do you mean?" asked Craig, his excitement dripping from every word.

Unexpectedly, the figure of Dendralon threw off his cloak and pulled Greenworm free of his chest.

"It went right into his heart," assured Craig.

As the cloak fell away and the staff dropped from his hands, the figure lifted his head to reveal a long curved bill.

"It's not Dendralon, it's an Ibissynian!" said James. He saw the look of disappointment spread over Craig's face as his precious spear was bent in two by the powerful bird-headed creature.

"Argh!" Craig gripped his wrist.

"Wwwreturnwwwtowwyourwwwmasterww!"

Helen covered her mouth quickly as if she'd just burped.

The green spear, still bent in two flew back over the chamber, like a boomerang, to land at Craig's feet.

"Another few moments in the grasp of the Ibissynian and your magic spear would have been destroyed forever," said Mendel.

When they looked up, the Ibissynian had been replaced by a mass of spiderlings and Racnids. The spiderlings seeped out over the floor towards the Artilians, racing between their mothers' legs towards their first kills.

"Fire!"

The great Artilian machines snapped into action, launching a blizzard of black steel into the Racnids' midst.

Many of the older Racnids fell dead, pierced by an incredible amount of arrows but the spiderlings were unharmed. Too fast and too small, they raced ahead until they poured over the Artilian army like a black wave of death. Screams echoed out over the floor as thousands fell to the ground. The spiderlings crawled up and under their armour. The noise was completely terrifying.

"Get back!" yelled Helen. "Get them away from me!" She pushed back in amongst the ranks of Artilians, whisking the strange-looking spiderlings off of her shirt.

James hacked at the tiny creatures crushing as many underfoot as he could.

"Your sword, James. Pierce the stone floor!" shouted Mendel.

James stabbed down through a fast-moving spiderling, and plunged his blade deep into a patch of black jet. Immediately, a ripple effect spread outward round the sword, knocking Racnids and Artilians onto their backs. Large, hairy legs flayed in the air as Racnids hissed and singed. Their downy fur sparked and caught light on the reddening floor. The ripples from the sword spread outward for a good fifty yards then stopped. Every Racnid in the immediate area had toppled and burned.

"Why didn't it burn us?" asked Helen, still tearful. She yelped every now and then, flicking imaginary spiderlings from her legs and arms.

Bero had bitten down on a spiderling and was whining in pain.

"Bero, Bero," whispered Craig. "What's wrong?"

"Octuric Acid," said Mendel. "Take some of the water from my barrel and put it in his mouth."

"Quick, help me James," moaned Craig. He unfastened Mendel's barrel and poured some water out into Bero's mouth. James stood guard.

Bero lapped it down eagerly while Craig tipped the barrel back just in time, before Mendel spilled out onto the floor.

"I have produced some chemicals that will help the stinging and give the dog a bit of an energy boost."

"Thanks, Mendel," said Craig.

A blast of white light shot across the cavern and slammed into the wall behind them. It caught several Artilians who fell dead, their swords still in their hands. On the other side of the first floor the Racnids had completely decimated the Artilian ranks. It was at this point that James saw the Jackal-faced Inubians pour out of the hole left by the shattered granite plug. He was sure he'd seen the real Dendralon amongst them. The whole division headed straight for them. He watched as the remaining Artilians, led by Junera, charged forward to meet them.

"They haven't used their ballistae or even stayed in line. They're a complete mess," wailed James. He pulled his sword from the stone and made ready to meet the Inubians.

"We're not going to stay here," said Mendel. The wizard's voice sounded very ominous.

"We can't just leave them to that lot," protested Craig. He managed to re-summon Greenworm. It looked as good as new.

"And I made a promise to your mother," pressed Mendel. "We cannot win this fight. We have been outmanoeuvred and are now outnumbered."

James thought of the brave Junera racing headlong at the Inubians and felt his heart sink. "But…"

"Now!" said Mendel.

They watched as Bero turned and moved back through the charging Artilians. Walking against the ranks of Junera's silver-armoured clan, they had to duck and step aside to avoid being knocked over.

"Mendel, there must be something we can do." said James, anxiously. For the first time his sword felt heavy. The crimson tip trailed across the stone floor.

"It's too late. I have my limits, and I know they have been reached. I can't magic us out of every situation, you know."

"But Mendel, Dendralon will…"

"Quickly, James. Don't look back. Just keep your eyes on the wall ahead."

James soon saw a set of stairs leading upwards. They were fairly narrow and set into the wall at an angle, only visible within five feet or so. His stomach clenched like a fist as he thought of Junera and her clan being swamped by Inubians and spiderlings. *Mendel could have tried to do something. Is he too frightened of Dendralon now?* He also knew that by leaving the fight he was somehow abandoning his mum. He just felt it.

Helen, Bero, and James had just stepped inside the stairwell when Craig pulled away from them and rushed back towards the fight.

"Craig! I need to seal the door." Mendel yelled out in their heads.

James saw him throw Greenworm towards the fight and then turn and run back towards the stairs. Several black Inubian arrows swished towards them, pinging off the stone round James's head.

"Argh!" Craig toppled forward.

"Helen, help me pull him in," urged James. More arrows arced up from the Inubians just as the Artilians clattered hard against their ranks.

"He's too heavy," shrieked Helen.

"Uh!" James heaved with all his might until Craig's legs were free of the door.

"The metal lever!" shouted Mendel.

Skidding on the gritty stairs, James heaved on the lever and saw the door shudder shut. The sound from outside instantly died away.

"Right," said Mendel, in a rather shaky voice. "We need to climb up these steps until we reach the apex of the pyramid. Can you make it, Craig?"

There was no answer. Craig shivered.

"Inubian poison," sighed Mendel. "This is the last thing we need."

"I should think it's the last thing Craig needs too," snapped Helen.

"I know, I know. I'm not feeling too well myself," Mendel sighed. "I think my water is running short of oxygen."

"So am I…" wheezed Craig. His hair was matted to his head and his clothes were drenched in sweat. His freckled skin glistened as he gasped for breath.

James knelt down beside Craig. A sleek black arrow protruded from Craig's left arm. "Quick, Mendel." He turned to Helen to see if there was any sign of a spell forming on her lips. His own head was thumping; not with the knock, knocking of magic, but with the sound of his own pulse beating in his temples.

Craig's eyes began to flicker shut.

Mendel drifted past the window of his barrel. "It's very quick-acting poison. But I…"

"We need fresh water for Mendel," whispered James. "Where are we going to get fresh water from?"

Helen cupped her big brother's head in her arms. She stared up at James. "Upstairs. There was a well set into the wall. Remember?"

"Mendel, can't you manage something?" James pleaded. He ran his fingers through Bero's soft fur.

"I can hardly breathe, James. I…" Mendel gasped.

"Right. I'll take Bero and get to the well as fast as I can." James called on his sword and pulled on Bero's collar. "Come on, boy."

But Bero didn't budge. He licked Craig's face and whimpered.

Craig's eyes flickered open. "Bero, go with James…"

The old Retriever issued a plaintive howl before following James up the spiral stairway.

James felt the energy of the crimson sword sear through him as he raced ahead. Bero had fallen behind. James soon reached the dead-end that, he supposed, marked the doorway back into the main tunnel. He had passed several offshoots to his left and right as he ran but they all fell away into the darkness. This had to be the door they'd come through earlier with Mendel; the one behind the tapestry. He turned round to call on Bero, but the old dog was right behind him. "Good boy. How did you manage to keep up? Never mind. Mendel, can you speak?" He peered into the barrel. "How do I open the door?"

"Use the Key of Artilis…"

He'd forgotten all about the key. James had never heard Mendel's voice sound so sick. He fumbled around in his green rucksack until he produced the golden key. It whirred out of his hand and immediately began bobbing towards the sealed door. He held his crimson sword aloft. Its dim light added only slightly to the purple glow of the luminescent bacteria that covered the stones in Artilis. His mouth was dry and his eyes were losing focus. He rubbed them and tried to focus on the key. "Why is it taking so long?"

There was only the swishing sound of Bero's tail on the rough stone floor.

"I…"

The key sunk home with a dull click.

The door swung open.

Whisking the heavy tapestry aside, he spied the small bowl, shaped like a font, set into the opposite wall. This was the place they'd left Wee Joe and Mrs. Harrison. As quickly as he could, he lifted the barrel over Bero's head and unscrewed the lid. Using his fingers as a kind of net, he scooped Mendel out of the barrel and guided him into the bowl. Listless, the goldfish floated for a moment on the top of the water then drifted down to the bottom. James decided this was a good sign as the last dead fish he'd taken from a tank had been floating on the top.

"Mendel?" He couldn't even begin to know what to do if Mendel was dead. He shouted louder. "Mendel!"

There was a feeble flick of a ventral fin.

James thought that Mendel's eyes looked opaque. Dead. *Had he imagined the movement?* He put his finger into the water and let a few drops of sweat drip into the bowl. Salt, he remembered, sometimes revitalized goldfish. The golden key whirred beside the bowl and seemed to nod its approval.

"Mendel?"

"James…"

James stared down into the water. "Oh, thank God. You bloomin' scared the life out of me. Are you okay?"

Mendel flicked his golden tail and opened his gills. "I need to get some more fresh oxygen. I will be fine in a moment or two."

"I hate to rush you but Craig's not looking too good."

"Yes, I remember. Inubian poison from an arrow that he had no need to get on the wrong end of."

"He was only trying to be brave." James looked down at Firetongue. "These weapons you gave us make us feel invincible. They make us want to fight, try out daft stuff."

"Yes, yes. I'm sure." Mendel was swimming round the stone bowl. His eyes had returned to their usual, clear orange and black and his voice had regained its familiar disdainful ring. "That's much better. Let me focus." Mendel circled then came to a sudden stop. "Helen is beside him. She is very upset."

"Do something, Mendel. Please." James felt a huge gulp build in his throat. It was the kind of gulp that would normally precede a flood of tears.

James tensed as the knocking sensation built in his head. The pain was almost too much to bear. "Wwwvisionwwpoolww."

The surface of the bowl shimmered as whisks of blue mist formed then dissipated to reveal Helen kneeling over Craig. His eyes were shut tight.

"Helen!" Mendel sighed.

Strangely, Helen looked up at the sound of his voice.

"Be quick, Mendel. I don't think he's breathing." Tears streamed down Helen's smooth face.

"Helen, hold onto the arrowhead."

Helen rummaged about until she found the arrow protruding through Craig's arm. Tentatively, she placed her fingers round the black tip.

"Now say this after me: bloodfreeze!"

Helen repeated the spell in a bubbly voice and watched for any sign of change.

James stared frantically at the surface of the vision pool. Craig remained completely still. "It's not working, Mendel."

"Patience, James, please."

"What kind of spell is 'bloodfreeze', anyway? It sounds as though the spell itself might kill him. You don't actually want his blood to freeze, do you?"

"I do, as a matter of fact."

Helen seemed to have heard Mendel's words too. "Why?" she protested.

"The Inubian poison can only be isolated from his bloodstream if we freeze it. The poisonous crystals will remain frozen while Craig's blood thaws."

"And could that not kill him?" whispered James, anxiously.

"Yes. The odds on him dying, however, are reduced by trying this out."

"Trying it out?" James squawked. "You mean you've never tried this out before on a human?"

"On anything," replied Mendel, tersely. "A boy of his height and weight should be dead in approximately three minutes from now with the poison already in his system. He has a fifty–fifty chance of regaining consciousness."

James mouthed the words 'fifty–fifty' while staring blankly down at the vision pool.

Helen sat back. Craig's eyes opened and he was beginning to shake again, only this time, much worse than before.

"Arghh!" Craig tried to stand up but crashed down on top of Helen.

"What's wrong with him?" urged James.

"It's a good sign," answered Mendel. "He is enduring a blood thaw. It's very painful."

"So I can see," gasped James.

"It's a bit like pins and needles," said Mendel.

"It... is... bloomin not!" shrieked Craig, who'd obviously heard Mendel's matter-of-fact explanation. "Arghh!" He doubled in pain again while Helen tried to hang onto him.

"Call on your spear, Craig. Call on Greenworm!" James suddenly wondered if the power of the spear might help.

"Greenworm!"

The spear appeared in Craig's right hand. He knelt and gripped it tightly. In a praying position, he eased himself to his feet and braced. He nodded.

"Good thinking, James," said Mendel.

Helen stood back as Craig eased up straight and looked down at his arm. He closed his eyes and snapped both the tip and the end of the arrow off before yanking the shaft free of his flesh. "Argh!"

"Next time," whispered James. "Don't be such a numpty. Running back out like that. You might have got us all killed!" James shook with a mixture of rage and relief.

Craig straightened completely and wiped his brow. "Thanks for your concern, pal. Where are you?"

Mendel's voice cut through James's jumble of emotions. "Craig and Helen, run as fast as you can. Keep going straight, all the way without turning left or right. We have to get up to the apex of the pyramid before Dendralon gets there. He is getting stronger day by day, and I'm not sure Elandria is capable of heading him off by herself."

"But he's down below in the main floor," said James. He watched the vision of Craig and Helen ebb away before pushing the barrel below the surface of the cold water. Mendel swam back inside.

"He has other routes he can take if he chooses to come alone. Though I think he will be preoccupied for a while. There is still another few hours remaining before the red-eyed planet is in position. "

"What about my mum and dad?" asked James.

"Your father may have to face the Kraken alone if we do not get back in time to help him. That would not go well. As far as your mother is concerned, I have to admit I am a little confused."

"Why?"

"I am sure that I sensed her in the cavern below the plug as you did. However, I also sensed Dendralon's concern."

"His concern?"

"That is why I am confused."

"Sorry, but now I'm completely befuddled," snapped James.

"Dendralon has feelings for your mother."

"He what?"

CHAPTER TWENTY

THE CRYSTAL OF RA

The shock of Archie's death had barely sunk in when there was another disturbance in the Loch.

Michael stood up to look out of the Rectory window. "The monster is halfway up the beach. What are we going to do?"

"We are going to run away. That is what we are going to do. That thing…"

"Thee Kraken," reminded Eethan.

"Whatever—is far too dangerous to tackle by ourselves."

Eethan's thumb was firmly planted in his left nostril. "Ee agree!"

Michael edged back from the window. "It's heading straight for St. Donan's."

"Well, I doubt it's going to confession, so let's get some distance between us and it," moaned Carr.

Ephie appeared wearing her wax jacket. "Let's go then," she urged.

They followed Carr and David out of the front door of the Rectory and headed up towards Main Street. They could hear the Kraken gurgling and roaring behind them but not one of them looked back.

"I hope it doesn't smash up the church," said Michael. "I mean, what does it want here anyway?"

They had just reached the village shop, being careful not to fall into the road-works, when they saw it. The Kraken, about the size of six fully-grown elephants, demolished the bus shelter at the end of the street and let out a terrifying scream.

Michael crossed himself. "May the Lord preserve us and keep us." He backed away with the rest of them in the direction of Drumfintley Park. "It's coming for us."

The creature's tentacles wriggled with a life of their own beneath its gruesome head as it placed a scaled claw on a parked Vauxhall Vectra and squashed it flat. Windows shattered each time it issued one of its ear-splitting roars and its huge pincers snapped shut on lampposts and awnings.

"Eet can't move too quicklee on land. Run!" squawked Eethan.

A huge spiked tail scythed through the village shop sending glass, paper and bricks flying in every direction.

"Where the heck is Mendel?" shrieked Ephie.

* * *

Running ahead, with a surprising burst of energy, Bero bounded into the main chamber at the top of the pyramid of Ra before Craig, Helen, and James reached the door.

Craig, still looking a little groggy, ran in next, followed by James and Helen.

James winced as the sunlight caught him full in the face. Shielding his eyes from a light he hadn't experienced in several days he scanned the incredible chamber. He was standing in a huge glass pyramid-shaped chamber, which poked through the surface of the planet. Looking up, an inky black sky was peppered with a million stars that were almost as bright as the distant sun. The rust-coloured landscape that rolled out in all directions from the pyramid was truly stunning. A great red desert strewn with boulders stretched out towards an endless range of towering mountains that were at least ten times higher than any he'd seen round Drumfintley.

"I thought you were never going to come," sighed Jean. She clutched Wee Joe's hand and drew in Helen and Craig.

"Where is this?" asked James. Quietly enjoying Craig's embarrassment as his mum covered him in kisses.

Craig broke away from his mum. His face was bright red.

"We're above the firmament now aren't we?" said James.

"We are," stated Mendel.

"The landscape looks familiar," he continued.

"Yes," added Helen in a dreamy voice.

"It is Artilis," announced Elandria, proudly. She scuttled over to the nearest pane of glass and threw her arms apart. "We lived on the surface many millions of years ago."

Mendel splashed past his plastic window. "Your familiarity with the landscape is understandable. You may have seen it on TV or perhaps in a book."

"We're on Mars, aren't we?" said Helen.

"Don't be so daft!" barked Craig.

"She's right," said Mendel.

"Ha!" blurted Wee Joe, triumphantly.

Craig shook a fist at his wee brother and smiled. "Ye wee numpty."

"The red planet," added James.

"Quite. The colour comes from the high levels of iron oxide, or rust," explained Mendel.

"Where's home?" asked Helen. "Where's Earth?"

"Do you see that small blur of blue?" said Elandria.

They all nodded.

"That is Earth."

"Whoa!" exclaimed Craig.

Bero wagged his tail and woofed.

"There are, however, more pressing matters," said Mendel.

"Where is Dendralon?" hissed Elandria. She grimaced to reveal a nasty row of black, curved teeth and then scampered into the middle of the ring of stones.

"I'm afraid it didn't go too well down on the first level. They broke through the granite plug, despite our best efforts, and unleashed the spiderlings on the Artilian troops."

Elandria bowed her head in shame. "I should have been there to help."

"Don't tell me," interrupted Craig. "You could have died an honourable death." He grinned but soon shrugged and looked round for support.

"Craig!" snapped Helen. "Don't be such a prat."

In the awkward silence that followed, James took the opportunity to edge away and explore the pyramid. In the center of the room, directly beneath the apex of the pyramid of Ra, a rose-coloured plinth held a large, red crystal. It was positioned in the midst of a very Scottish-looking ring of weathered stones.

James entered the stone ring and circled the crystal. "Is this what he's after?"

"This and Belloc's crystal," Mendel explained. "And, even if he does reach this chamber, time is against him. Remember that we have only borrowed the crystal from Belloc to stop Dendralon using it first. In…" Mendel's eye found Elandria. "How long, Elandria?"

"Mmm…" Elandria focused on a large, red star. "About four Artilian minutes."

"That's ten minutes, in Earth time," said Mendel. "Soon the Belloc crystal will be drawn into another universe, far beyond the reach of Dendralon."

"Which means?" pressed Craig, in an impatient tone.

"Which means that he will not have the power he needs to take the whole Racnid and Inubian army back to Earth."

"Can't we just go back now?" asked Helen. "I'd rather not see Dendralon again."

"I'm sorry, Helen, but we must wait until the Belloc crystal is drawn away before we can be sure it is out of his reach but…"

"What's the 'but'?" pressed Craig.

James and Jean drew him a death stare.

"Only asking," Craig moaned.

"We can't risk the Artilian key falling into his hands either. Do you still have it?"

James pulled it free of his rucksack.

Wee Joe stared in amazement. Mendel paused. James could almost hear him thinking. "It might be prudent to send Jean and the children home. The key can, even without a crystal, act as a portal."

"We have two crystals," reminded Helen.

"Yes," explained Mendel. "And we have to wait until the last moment before using them. We do, however, have another option."

"Which is?" pressed Craig.

"We use these two crystals, plus Elandria's magic, to transport us back to Drumfintley, just before the Belloc crystal disappears."

"What about my mum?" asked James.

Jean nodded. "Yes, what about Cathy?"

"The upside," continued Mendel, "is that we get away from here in time to help your father with the Kraken, if that's possible. The downside is that we have to, temporarily, leave your mother behind."

James shook his head in despair. "But if Elandria is still here, won't she be killed?"

"Only if she chooses to be," finished Elandria, her greenish down assuming a crimson hue as she took her position.

"An honourable death," mumbled Craig.

James felt trapped by the dilemma. Was it best to try and help his mum or was it best to go now and help his dad? He supposed that his mum was, somehow, being protected by Dendralon and that his dad was, as they stood there, probably in great danger back in Drumfintley. "So when we go, the crystal disappears. That means Dendralon can't follow but..."

"But we can still return using the Key of Artilis and rescue your mum once we've helped your dad," reasoned Helen.

"Very well done, young Helen," said Mendel.

An irrational dislike of Helen rose in James's chest. He had to stop this petty jealousy.

"Shhh! Dendralon is getting closer," said Elandria.

James saw the trepidation in Jean's face but he'd made up his mind. "He has my mum. I want to stay here and face him. I want to find out what he's done with her." He called on Firetongue.

"I'm with James," said Craig.

Bero barked.

"Helen, you and Wee Joe stand beside the crystal of Ra with your mother. Get ready to return to Drumfintley. I can't risk the Key of Artilis falling into Dendralon's hands. "

Jean Harrison caught hold of her oldest boy's freckled hand. "Craig, no!"

"You heard Mendel. We have to keep him back from the crystals until the evil fairy-thing takes hers back."

"Belloc," reminded James.

"Whatever. You should go, Mum." Craig bent down to talk to Wee Joe, then feigning his infamous Scottish accent he said, "Look efter that funny key, wee man. We'll come back doon te Drumfintley and finish off the beastie in the Loch. Okay, laddie?"

"It's not the Loch Ness Mmwonster, ye big numpty!" Wee Joe gave his big brother a swift kick to the shin.

"Aw! You little..."

"Craig!" Jean warned. "Stop winding him up."

James tightened his lips in an effort to stifle a smile.

The Harrisons wandered into the stone circle and took their place beside the prism-like crystal of Ra.

James would see if his mum was with Dendralon. She wasn't dead. The best result would be to get his mum back and help his dad. Inside, however, he knew this was unrealistic.

Mendel splashed about under Bero's chin until James heard his voice in his head. "I suspect that you've regained your link with me, James. How do you feel?"

James had performed magic for Mendel earlier. Though still painful, he thought he could manage it again if it meant saving his mum. "Should we ask Helen to stay behind, just in case?"

"It's up to you."

James saw the fear in Helen's eyes. "I'll be fine. What do we have to do?"

"Everyone, apart from the three Harrisons, needs to keep more than ten feet away from the plinth."

Elandria shuffled a few feet further away while Craig said his good-byes.

James felt the knocking sensation begin to build in his temples. "Wwwsusejwwwsevaswww!"

As soon as the strange, bubbly words left James's lips, a bright red flash erupted from the crystal of Ra. A circle of sorts formed beneath the Harrisons' feet. Apart from the plinth, the ground lost its firmness and buckled like jelly. Within the ring of stones, the floor shimmered then took on the appearance of smooth glass. Suspended above the void, the Harrisons braced. They knew what would happen next. Bero barked as the spider-web cracks forked out around their feet.

Mrs. Harrison smiled at Craig. "Bye, Son!"

Bang!

The ring of glass shattered around the plinth that held the crystal of Ra and the Harrisons fell down into the dark abyss.

In less than five seconds, however, the floor had reformed and there was nothing to show that the Harrisons had ever been there.

Craig tapped the stone with his foot. "Are they okay?"

Mendel's voice assumed an uppity tone. "Of course they are. You don't think I would let them go through the gateway if I thought there was the slightest risk, do you?"

James and Craig eyed each other doubtfully.

"Hmm." There was another splash as Mendel disappeared from view.

The sound of footsteps filtered into the chamber.

"My kin," hissed Elandria.

James, Craig, and Elandria formed a protective circle round Bero and Mendel.

Shadows crept up the stairwell before the first of the Racnids came into view. Covered in sleek black down, it screamed and raced towards them. Craig drew back his spear.

"Wait, Elhada!"

Hissing disapprovingly, the oversized Racnid skidded to a halt. Behind her, the familiar figure of Dendralon stepped into the room. As soon as he raised his staff, two hooded Ibissynian assassins stepped through the doorway. They walked forward until they flanked him. One of them held a cloth sack; the other gripped a scythe-like sword. Their curved bills pushed the dark, satin-like material of their hoods forward from the inside.

"So, you already have the Racnid crystal, Dendralon?"

Dendralon scanned the room until his reptilian Hedra eyes fell on the Crystal of Ra. "And you, the Artilian stone and the Belloc crystal."

"Keep back," warned James.

Dendralon smiled wryly as the two Ibissynians removed their hoods to reveal their hideously wrinkled Ibis heads. Covered in grey skin that hung in unsightly flaps, their necks pulsed in anticipation. "You really should train this boy a little better, Mendel. He is becoming extremely tiresome."

James knew they had to delay Dendralon as long as possible. He had to keep him talking long enough for Jupiter to line up with the crystal of Ra. Once that happened, Belloc's crystal would return to the faery demon and be safely out of reach. Without all three Artilian crystals: Belloc's, the crystal of Ra and the Racnid crystal, Dendralon would not be able to take his whole army back to Drumfintley.

"Give me Belloc's crystal," urged Dendralon, his yellow slit eyes narrowing.

"Give me my mother first," barked James, trying to stop himself from shaking. He coughed but kept his eyes focused on the giant Hedra lizard form of Dendralon.

"You are in no position to bargain, boy."

Elandria produced a cupped hand from a slit in her side. It shone an iridescent crimson and as she drew it out in a semi circle, a film of red light rose up between Dendralon and them. James's head pounded. "Wwwwallwwfixww!"

The barrier seemed to thicken between them.

Dendralon signalled the Ibissynian with the sack to step forward. The dark wizard was still visible through the red translucent shield. "You need not think that Belloc is going to save you."

James glanced back at the barrel hanging round Bero's neck. *What does he mean*, he thought? Did he know that Belloc had made a bargain with them? James squinted out of the thick glass that formed the apex of the pyramid. The great planet Jupiter was in line. Dendralon had lost his chance. It was over. He expected the heavy crystal in his rucksack to disappear—lighten his load as it magically returned to the demon, but nothing changed. He looked to Craig then Elandria and shook his head.

"Is this what you are waiting for?" asked Dendralon. He signalled the Ibissynian to open the contents of the hemp sack.

With a shake and a heavy thud, the beautiful head of Belloc landed on the red stone floor of the chamber.

"Yuck," spat Craig.

"She won't exactly be coming to your rescue, so drop your pathetic shield and hand over the crystal, now!"

Mendel's thoughts drifted into his head, "James nod if Belloc's crystal is still in your rucksack."

Surreptitiously, James nodded, without once taking his eyes off Dendralon.

"Everyone has to reach the crystal of Ra in the next few seconds!" whispered Mendel, his voice full of urgency.

James and Craig looked at each other.

Dendralon raised his staff. "I have lost patience, my old friend. You will all die here and now." The Ibissynians and Elhada fell back. "Thgrethna—"

"Wwwjesuswwsaves!"

James felt his head split with the force of the spell. He was sure he'd just managed to touch the surface of the red crystal, but had Craig and Elandria?

He fell as complete and utter darkness closed in on him.

CHAPTER TWENTY-ONE

THE UNDERWATER GATEWAY

Drumfintley looked like a war zone. Chunks of the eighteenth century shop facades were missing. Glass lay strewn over the main street and the lampposts were crumpled or snapped in two. The Kraken continued to push forward, but David saw that Eethan had lingered in the middle of the road. "Come on, Eethan! What are you doing?" Still the diminutive figure of Eethan stood his ground.

"What's he doing?" called out Ephie.

"Perhaps he will try and use some magic on the beast," said Michael.

Sergeant Carr, Father Michael, David and Ephie all waited to see what the little, blue man would do against such a massive creature.

Eethan raised his right hand and muttered some indiscernible words that David could hardly pick out. A blue light began to shine from within the skin of his hand. It grew brighter and brighter until the whole street was bathed in the glow.

The Kraken halted and then jabbed at Eethan with one of its scorpion-like pincers.

"Watch out, Eethan!" cried Ephie.

Carr took a pot shot at the creature with his gun, but the shot simply ricocheted off the glistening amber carapace of its claw.

The light suddenly faded, and Eethan fell to the ground.

"What...?" David felt his heart sink as Eethan dropped.

The creature raised itself higher but seemed to stop too. It eased back, away from Eethan.

Carr moved forward. "Let's get the wee man before it changes its mind."

They all ran forward again, confused by the action of the Kraken.

"Maybe his spell worked," said Michael.

David reached Eethan first. He looked to be quite dead. "I don't think it did." The Kraken was now a good fifty yards away. It was heading back in the direction of the Loch.

Just as they gathered round Eethan, however, the ground began to shake.

"Is it an earthquake?" asked Ephie.

David held onto Michael and Sergeant Carr as the earth beneath their feet began to fold up in a series of ripples. In seconds, they were surrounded by a series of concentric ridges that spread out from Eethan some two hundred yards in diameter. Out of these ridges, thousands of small, pink-fingered hands wriggled free of the dirt.

"Ees friendees," gasped Eethan, suddenly coming back to life.

"You're okay. What's going on, Eethan?" David wondered what was going to happen next and if these weird looking creatures had somehow scared off the Kraken.

Eethan knelt in a praying position and emitted a high-pitched sound like nothing David had ever heard before. Soon thousands of the small creatures, covered in dirt and stones, pulled themselves free of the earth and began to circle the Kraken.

"Ees Gringles," explained Eethan. "Ees usually undergrounders. Ees not liking the sunlight so this darkness produced by thee Krakeen is good." He gazed up at the black clouds over the Loch and then began to mutter to the stooped creatures, ushering them forward.

Barely reaching the height of David's knee, they resembled frail, old men with long, pink fingers that trailed behind them. They nattered in unison as they shuffled off in the direction of the Loch after the Kraken.

"They ees the Kraken's guardians back on Artilis."

"What?" exclaimed Michael. "You summoned them here from Artilis?"

"Don't bee silleee!" retorted Eethan. "Most planets have Gringles. They ees always under thee ground. Most places, even Denthan had eem. Thees only real use is to keep the Krakeen away. Thee Krakeen cannot bear their horrible shrieks or theer smell."

"What shrieks?" asked Ephie, a look of bewilderment on her round face.

"Oh," Eethan tittered. "Ees too high pitched to annoy you."

"I can't smell anything. Where did they come from?" asked Carr, anxiously.

"Under thee ground, sillee," sniggered Eethan. He looked at Sergeant Carr as if he was a complete imbecile.

"Well," Carr backtracked. "I…"

"Theese ees Scottish Gringles."

"But what…? Where…?" Michael was just about to ask another question when there was a high-pitched shout. "Father Michael!"

"The Gringles know my name?"

"I doubt it, ye old numpty," said Ephie. "Look!"

Not more than a hundred yards away, Wee Joe, Helen, and Mrs. Harrison were limping down from Willow Terrace.

"They're all back!" shouted Ephie.

"Not all," said David. "Still missing a son and a wife, as far as I can see."

They ran to meet each other. Jean and Helen, however, shuddered to a halt on seeing the utter destruction in front of them. Helen pointed a shaky finger in the direction of the Gringles. "What on Earth are those things?"

"Gringles, apparently," explained David. "They just frightened off a huge sixty foot Kraken. Tentacles, pincers, teeth and…" David's words, however, fell on deaf ears as interest shifted to the sky over Loch Echty. It was brightening and the Gringles were beginning to burrow, with their long, pink fingers, back into any soft piece of ground within their reach.

Helen nudged Wee Joe. "Gringles, eh. You would never think…"

"Nah. Seen 'em before." He sighed, resignedly.

"Don't tell lies, Joe," snapped Jean, "You know that it's naughty to…"

"Have! In our back garden at night," barked Wee Joe, wandering over to Eethan and Michael. "I'm tired."

Everyone looked down blankly at Wee Joe.

"He's just walked down from the Jesus Rocks," explained Jean.

"Mum, what do you mean, walked? You carried him on your shoulders most of the way," said Helen.

"Helen, stop being so…"

Sergeant Carr stepped forward. "Sorry to interrupt, Mrs. Harrison, but could Eethan tell us what's going on and could you tell us how you are here while James, Craig, Bero, and company are not?"

Eethan began first. "I can only call thee Gringleees one time."

"Brilliant," muttered David.

"They ees very moody about coming to the surface. Very moody." Eethan nodded, toying with his shock of white hair.

"Where's Archie?" asked Helen.

No-one said anything.

Carr checked the barrels of his gun and reloaded. "Mrs. Harrison, what happened on Artilis?"

"Well, where do I begin? After you left we found this demon called Belloc."

"James got bitten by a sandworm thingy," interjected Helen.

"We were there when that happened," said David.

"Oh, yeah. So you were."

Jean pressed on. "We had to kill this eight-headed monster, climb up to the top of a pyramid, and we just escaped with the golden key when..." Jean stopped. She seemed to be looking for something.

Wee Joe produced the Artilian key and held it aloft.

"Thank goodness, Joe. Where is Archie, Sergeant?"

Sergeant Carr looked down at his feet and shook his head. "He didn't make it."

"Didn't make what?" enquired Helen.

"The Kraken got him," said David dolefully. "Nothing we could do."

"Oh God," whispered Jean, gathering her kids in closer.

"Eet will be back," said Eethan. "Thee Kraken will be back soon, and thees time there will be no Gringles to help ees. Very moody..." he repeated.

Wee Joe held the Artilian key like a dagger. "I'll kill it," he snapped. "I'll chop its head off and..."

"Joe! Give me that," said Jean, kneeling down to take the key. "We will just have to hope that Craig and James are okay."

"No sign of Cathy, then?" asked David.

"No sign but..."

"Yes?" urged David.

"James said he thought he saw her before the battle, before the Racnids broke through into the pyramid. Jean updated the Drumfintley contingent on Belloc and the pyramid of Ra. "Dendralon needs all three Artilian crystals to move the whole city and his army here but there were only a few more minutes left until Belloc's crystal disappeared. It was only borrowed. The demon will have it back in her possession by now."

* * *

As soon as the cold water hit his lungs, James opened his eyes. He was drowning. He could feel his heart racing as he flailed in the cold depths. His head seared. "Wwwaterwwright!"

Immediately, his breathing eased and the sensation of panic and drowning fell away. His eyes suddenly opened and he looked up at the huge, black obelisk. He was in the underwater graveyard beneath Loch Echty. He was in Fintley. He felt a tap on his shoulder and turned to see Craig and Bero. Both were covered in silver scales and swimming in circles round him, blowing bubbles.

"Would you get me out of my barrel?" asked Mendel. "It's nice to be in my own element for a change."

There was a blue tinge to the water and a bright light circled the obelisk.

"This is the place I went to with Mendel, Craig. The place I met Ethrita…"

"Before she was slaughtered," added Craig, his thoughts quite clear in James's head.

"Where is Elandria?" asked James, swimming alongside Mendel. Their gold and silver scales sparkled in the indigo gloom.

"I'm afraid she didn't touch the crystal of Ra in time," said Mendel.

"Dying an honourable death right now, I bet," mused Craig.

James swam down and hovered over a half toppled gravestone. "Craig, that's horrible and you know it. Why do you always say things for effect? You know you don't mean it. She saved your life!"

"Of course I didn't mean…" Craig sounded dejected.

Mendel's voice filtered into their heads. "Elandria can look after herself."

"What, surrounded by Dendralon and those undead Ibis things?" snapped Craig.

"You'd be surprised at Elandria's ingenuity," added Mendel.

The current shifted. Something moved towards them. A black shape drifted down behind the Fintley obelisk.

"Take cover," snapped Mendel.

They hid in a clump of thick weeds and watched as the monstrous Kraken glided down. Two huge pincers encircled the obelisk.

Bero flipped over and banked down beside them.

A glistening horn protruded from the creature's misshapen head. Underwater, its tentacles hung down like the legs of a giant squid, wavering beneath its awful jaws.

"The Kraken," announced Mendel.

James watched as it flicked its tail and soared up above the old Fintley Bell. The Kraken's tentacles caressed the church bell-tower, its monstrous shape, covered in hardened scales that looked as though they were made of black steel, hovered menacingly.

"I think it senses the Belloc crystal," said Mendel, his voice barely audible in their heads.

Gently, James touched the straps on his shoulder. "It's here in my rucksack."

Bero barked silently at the Kraken, bubbles rising up from their hiding place.

Craig caught hold of his collar and shushed him but the Kraken had risen again. It drifted closer.

"We need to make a break for it," whispered Mendel.

"Can we out-swim it?" asked James.

"We'll soon find out," said Craig, kicking hard with his silver-finned legs. "Come on!"

"Craig, you...!"

The huge creature moved with incredible speed for its size. It knocked the bell tower with one of its pincers, sending debris drifting to the floor of the Loch.

James swam for his life but the rucksack held him back. Mendel, Craig, and even Bero, were well ahead of him.

The Kraken burst up from the depths, pushing a great pulse of water before it. James was knocked off balance. He kicked hard to right himself, pulling through the water with his finned arms.

A giant pincer snapped down at the side of his head and tentacles darted up around him like a shoal of massive snakes. The suckers were rough and they scraped the silver scales off of his left leg. "Argh!" He tried to find Mendel or Craig, to pick their silhouettes out on the dazzling mass of white ahead that he knew must be the surface of the Loch. The rucksack filled with water again, like a balloon, jerking him back and slowing him down even further. He made the decision. He doubled-back on the Kraken, raced straight past its opening mouth, and twisted away from its suckered beard of limbs. He kicked down now into the depths, alone and completely terrified. It had disappeared behind him, its momentum too great to change course so quickly. *He had to hide in the weeds, find a safe place before...*

A bright flash of light burst out from the direction of the obelisk. Then another. Something was happening down there. He swooshed into a thick bed of reeds and wriggled until he was tightly wedged beneath a slimy boulder. He could still see the graveyard. Three bodies drifted up to the surface, bubbles trailing behind them. There was no sign of the Kraken.

* * *

It was Craig who first spotted Wee Joe and Helen in the Rectory garden behind the shale beach and the rickety iron fence. Once safely away from the water, he gathered Mendel back up into his barrel and fastened the trinket round Bero's neck. *Where was James?* He spun round and searched the surface of the Loch for any sign of his best friend. Nothing. Not a splash or... *Wait a minute.* "Mendel, I think I can see Jame..."

"It's not James," said Mendel. "He is safe for the time being. I can still feel my connection with him. Dendralon is here in Drumfintley."

"He can't be," said Craig.

"He is," assured Mendel. "And he has his two undead henchmen with him."

Three figures surfaced out in the Loch followed by a much bigger disturbance that erupted behind them in a torrent of wash and bubbles.

"That's Dendralon and the Ibysynirats?" spat Craig.

"Ibissynians," corrected Mendel, "and the Kraken is with them."

Craig opened the rusting Rectory gate and hugged his mum, who had run over to see him.

"Thank God." She wrapped him in her arms and shook with relief.

"It's not over yet, Mum. He's here."

"Who's here? You mean James, right?"

Craig screwed up his eyes and seesawed his hand, thumb to pinky. "Well... He is...somewhere. I meant Dendralon, Mum. He's out there with his Ibysynirats and the Kraken."

"Oh no, he can't be."

"That's what *I* said, but..." Craig peered over the rusting iron fence. He could see the unmistakable figure of the Hedra wizard followed by the curve-billed assassins that had pursued him in Artilis.

They were marching through the waves toward the shore. The Kraken was close behind. It towered over Dendralon. "Look, Mum, we need to run."

David waved them out of the garden.

"Run where? Mendel keeps saying the Kraken is immortal, and you've said that those Ibissynian things are too." Jean trailed the younger children behind her.

Bero sidled up beside them, Mendel flashing bright yellow in the barrel. "Craig, we need to buy some time until we can join up with James. Has Wee Joe got the Artilian key?"

They skirted the park before heading up the hill toward the village hall.

"I have," panted Jean.

"Good. We will need every kind of help we can muster."

David Peck looked over Craig's shoulder. His eyes were fixed on something. His mouth dropped open.

Craig turned to see.

From the Loch a steady stream of flying insects arose from the waves, directly above the obelisk. Flying Centides, Artilian wasps and some other insects that Craig didn't even recognize.

"He'll keep the Inubians and the Racnids until last," said Mendel. "What ammunition do we have?"

"Naff-bloody-all," retorted Sergeant Carr.

"Keep your language clean, please!" rapped Jean.

"We have a few arrows and bows, a couple of swords and a shot-gun," said Carr, meekly.

"Perfect. That will do nicely."

"Mendel," Craig began, "How is that perfect?"

The wizard splashed loudly. "Where is Helen?"

Craig located his little sister and muttered, dryly: "Time to do your magic stuff."

"Okay," she replied, matter-of-factly.

David raised his binoculars. "I can see Dendralon and about two hundred flying insects veering left along the beach."

"And the Ibissynians?" pressed Mendel.

"Coming straight this way with the Kraken." He blinked and forced the binoculars back against his eyes. "It's bigger. The Kraken looks bigger."

"Oh yes," said Mendel. "That's quite possible."

"Wait," shouted David, his voice lifting. "I can see James! He's edging round towards the reservoir. He's made it to the trees. He'll probably cut down from Willow Terrace."

"Right," said Mendel, "I need you to place all the arrows in a row. Put the gun behind them and... Did you say you had a sword or two?"

"Yes," said David.

"Hold onto them, just in case."

Ephie and Michael pulled Jean and Wee Joe back a little.

"Helen? Until James reaches us, I need you to do my magic."

"Fine," said Helen. She stood behind Bero and waited.

"Wwwmultiwwwplywww!"

A beam of blue light hit the arrows just as Eethan reappeared beside the rest of the group.

Slowly, at first, the arrows collapsed into one big pile then began to rustle and jiggle on the ground. There was a snap and a thousand arrows with sharpened tips spilled over the road in front of the village hall. The bows cracked and lifted, joining together to form a long row of about five hundred, all hinged at the ends.

Helen smiled. "Cool!" As she clapped her hands in excitement, however, a second bubbly word spilled form her lips... "Wwwfirwwweww!"

Instantly, half the arrows nocked themselves in the bows. The strings drew back and the arrows flew as one deadly cloud straight toward the approaching insects.

The Ibissynians knelt and braced.

Dendralon waved his gnarled staff and produced a red shield.

The arrows thudded into the Kraken and dropped more than half of the flying insects. As the insects fell writhing, the Kraken simply continued to move forward, every arrow shattering on its armour-plated hide.

James joined them, wheezing badly.

"Yes!" Craig punched the air. "You okay?"

"Not... Not really," wheezed James.

* * *

Dendralon waved the Ibissynians forward. "Kill them all. Spare no-one!"

The Ibissynians pulled off their clinging wet, silken hoods and began to run forward below the buzzing insects that flew in from the Loch.

A second shower of arrows arced down onto the shore, catching more insects and piercing the Ibissynians' upper bodies.

They stopped briefly, pulling the arrows free, a mere irritation, then continued on.

The Kraken let out an enormous scream that shook the whole village. The church bells vibrated eerily, resonating in sympathy.

Dendralon set his gaze on the church spire. Two gargoyles still clambered over the parapets. "We will clear this small village and set up a base. I want the Belloc crystal that they stole from Artilis. I need this gem to complete the set of three I need to move the pyramid of Ra to Earth."

"Yes, Sire," said the nearest Ibissynian. He pushed over the rusting fence that surrounded the Rectory garden and trampled onward. The ground vibrated as the Kraken moved over the lawn and entered the street.

* * *

James knew that they had to find a way to kill the Kraken. He knelt down, with Helen, before the brandy barrel. "Mendel, what should we do? There must be a way to kill the Kraken. If we do that, it will destroy the Ibissynians too. You said it would."

Mendel seemed to be mulling things over. "Killing the Kraken is not completely impossible," he admitted.

"Belloc told us what to do," reminded Helen.

While the terrifying drone of the insects intensified and the ground shook with the steady advance of the Kraken, Mendel explained. "Helen is correct. To kill the Kraken, you have to pierce both of its hearts at the same time. If you only hit one, the second will continue to beat and soon repair the first. We have to find a way of holding it in place while we do this properly. We also need to distract Dendralon, deal with the Ibissynians and ward off the insects of Artilis."

Craig had been listening in. "Piece of cake, then."

"Not entirely," replied Mendel.

"I have an idea," said James. He looked down the street from the village hall. "Do you think you could lure the Kraken to the corner of Main Street?"

"Who, me?" asked Craig, his face assuming a 'you must be joking' expression.

"Yeah, you, numpty." James looked at Helen and Wee Joe. "Can Helen do your magic here as well as in Artilis, Mendel?"

"She already has." Mendel drifted across the plastic window of the barrel then raced back and pushed a fishy eye against the aperture. "I could get Wee Joe to use the Key of Artilis," he said, excited. "Hold the beast in place."

"But what about the Ibisynirats? What about Dendralon?" pressed Craig.

"That," replied Mendel, "will be a job for the adults. Carr, Archie and…"

Helen shook her head.

"What's wrong Hele… Oh no." Mendel's tone became mournful.

"Oh no what?" asked Craig.

"Archie is dead," said Mendel.

"He died saving his brother," explained Helen.

"How?" asked James, instantly wishing he hadn't.

"The Kraken…"

Craig shook his head, as if trying to put it out of his mind. "Mum, could you bring the adults here a moment? Oh, and Eethan."

"Ees here."

Craig nearly jumped out of his skin. "I wish you wouldn't sneak up on people like that."

James's head was still reeling with a hundred mental pictures of old Archie. He could still hear his silly voice.

Mendel's tone became ominous. "Ephie, Michael, David, and you, Eethan. You have to lead Dendralon away from the Kraken. We need time to at least try and kill the monster."

James continued. "Craig is going to lure the Kraken to a certain spot further down the road while Mendel, Wee Joe, Helen, and I get ready." He was certain that Mendel knew his plan already, but he still had to explain the basics to Helen, Craig, and even Wee Joe. There would only be one chance to get it right.

"What do you want us to do?" asked Michael. There are more arrows now and there seems to be a shotgun each as well." He looked down and kicked a clump of dirt from the street with a polished, black shoe. "I'm not too comfortable using the guns and stuff. Neither is Ephie," he added.

"I'm afraid you'll be a lot less comfortable if you don't," said Mendel, blithely. "Up to you, though."

"We'll use whatever we need to," assured Carr. "You just get that thing." He looked down at the huge beast as it trampled a set of traffic lights.

Mendel's voice assumed a stern tone. "Listen carefully. You, the adults that is, need to get up the path towards Willow Terrace. Eethan needs to use his magic on Dendralon while you pelt the insects and the Ibissynians with everything you have. James, give Craig the Belloc crystal."

Craig gazed down at the gem in a trance-like state.

"Craig, move as close to the Kraken as possible. After the monster has seen the gem edge back towards the road-works at the corner of Main Street. Wee Joe, you wait at the road-works with James, Helen and, of course, Bero, until Craig's got the Kraken in place."

"In place for what?" demanded Craig. "Dinner?"

"Just do what you've been asked for now," ordered Mendel.

CHAPTER TWENTY-TWO

THE LAST STAND

Cathy Peck felt the ground shake as line after line of the jackal-headed Inubians marched on through the cavern and up through the great hole in the roof of the cave. They streamed up a hundred ladders that leaned against the rim of the great hole. Many more ropes and gears heaved all manner of weapons and provisions through to the upper level. Guarded by Erda, another Inubian captain, she held onto one of the bottom rungs. "I suppose you want me to climb this thing?"

"That is my master's bidding," replied Erda.

"And what is going on, exactly?"

Erda avoided the question, instead, he pointed upwards. "We have won the first of our great battles."

Cathy had heard the screaming and clanking of steel on steel from the upper level. She worried about James and wondered about David. She presumed that they'd tried to rescue her before, when she'd caught a glimpse of James amongst the throng of the Racnids. She knew, though, that the odds had been stacked against them succeeding, even with Mendel's magic. She hoped that James had ignored Dendralon's cruel words, his taunts that she was already dead.

"Be quick, my lady," snapped Erda.

Cathy leered at him contemptuously before beginning her climb. She was not prepared for the carnage on the huge floor above. Thousands of people, at least they looked like people, lay dead. She shut her eyes tight as they accidentally drifted close to the remains of a fallen soldier. She felt her stomach clench.

"Come this way, my lady."

"I'm not your ruddy lady," she snarled.

"No, my lady."

Thick as mince, she decided.

Although the huge floor of the pyramid was strewn with the dead and dying she now felt less frightened. She'd really had to concentrate to avoid having a panic attack in some of the tighter tunnels below.

"James's mother..."

Startled, Cathy turned to see where the voice had come from. She noticed that Erda was busy directing a flank of Inubians round a pile of dead Racnids. As he barked his commands, she scanned the blood-strewn floor. There, pinned under an overly big Racnid, she spied a woman. Her armour was bashed and the black Racnid blood that covered her face camouflaged her against the similarly coloured floor.

"You need to get me out of here. I've seen your son."

Cathy fell back from the marching Inubians and ducked down beside her. "Who are you?"

"My name is Junera. I have seen your son, James, and his friend Craig."

"Where?" whispered Cathy. She'd noticed that Erda was looking for her. "I...I can't help you just now. Lie still and I'll try to distract them."

"Be quick my lady!" barked Erda.

"I thought I saw more people over there." Cathy pointed to the wall furthest from her position. "I didn't want to say but Dendralon may be angry if..."

"I will check. Stay there," he commanded.

While Erda gathered a small group to check out the movement at the far wall, Cathy caught hold of the dead Racnid's legs and pulled as hard as she could.

Junera pushed up with her feet at the same time and rolled free. She scampered forward and pushed her back against an empty plinth. "Come with me," she whispered, pointing to what looked like a bare piece of wall several feet away.

"Come where?" asked Cathy. "It's bare rock."

"Trust me," Junera whispered back.

Cathy, still alone and temporarily out of sight, pulled off her white shift and ran after the woman fighter.

They reached the wall, pressing their backs against the rock as Junera fumbled for something. "Got it," she spat.

A narrow door lurched open and they dived inside.

"Oh no," cried Cathy, as it thudded shut behind them. Inside it was completely dark for a second. Then there was a scratching sound and a burst of purple light. Cathy could see that the woman was very beautiful, despite her filthy face. "I can't stand narrow places," said Cathy. *Not this narrow.* Her mouth went dry and her palms moistened.

"It gets bigger up here." Junera pointed to a set of stairs leading upwards.

"What happened?" asked Cathy, trying to keep her mind busy. "Where did you see my son, and was his father with him?"

Junera smiled, pulling Cathy up the last few steps. "Three questions at once, eh? Well, Dendralon aims to take his new army to the Earth world. We were one of the last things in his path, but now…" Junera's voice dropped off, "now we are in a mess." She slipped a bolt and opened another door. "As for your son, I met him further up this passageway. He is in great danger now. I saw no sign of his father."

"I could have guessed that bit," said Cathy, trying to stifle her impatience. "Never where he should be in a crisis."

* * *

David Peck drew back the bow and fired the arrow. It curved upwards before thudding into a flying Centide. The insect fell on one of the Ibissynians.

"Well done," smiled Michael. He smacked David on the back just as Jean fired her arrow. It pinged to the side as the gut whipped back and caught her finger. "Shiii…." She tucked her fingers under her arm as her eyes began to water. David put his arm round her, saw Ephie's expression, and then instantly drew away. "I was only…"

Twenty or so insects buzzed overhead before diving down at them. They all crouched behind an old Second World War air-raid shelter that had been turned into a garden shed.

Eethan lifted his hand and muttered an incantation.

With a flash of blue light, the insects' wings crumpled. They all spiralled down into the garden clicking and whirring. One of the writhing creatures clanked off the green corrugated roof of the shelter next to Ephie.

David caught Ephie's wrist. "Watch out, Ephie!"

A wriggling, hooked insect leg whipped past her face. She ducked and then shook David's hand free. "I'm fine."

"What's up with her?" he whispered to Jean.

"Stressed out, I should think. I hope Craig's okay."

David could hear the screams of the Kraken further down the hill. He peered out from behind his hiding place. There, not far from the village shop, Craig was waving something shiny in front of the lumbering hulk of the Kraken. The monster flicked out its tentacles but Craig sliced them through with his green spear and edged further back.

"Eee…" Eethan let out a cry as a bolt of red fire seared the paint on the top of the shelter. "Ee theenks Dendralon has found ees."

* * *

James and Helen picked their way through the broken tarmac. Bero plodded behind them with Wee Joe holding onto his tail.

This is absolutely crazy, James thought. *I don't even know if Mendel can do this.*

"I can only try," answered Mendel. "Has Wee Joe got the key?"

James glanced behind him, almost toppling into the hole in the road. He steadied himself on a wobbly orange and white traffic cone. "Yes. It's whirring away in his hand.

"Excellent," said Mendel.

There was a loud crack from the direction of Willow Terrace.

James looked behind Wee Joe. Flames poured out of a yellow car he'd never seen before. "That's a write-off," he shouted to Helen.

"Yeah, but what did it?" said Helen. The insects were lighting on all the roofs of the village. The trees were covered in them too. It looked as if a giant plague of locusts had decided to devour the whole village and everything that surrounded it. A great line of wasps headed over the Loch toward the reservoir and the Jesus Rocks. The remaining gargoyles circled the church tower.

Bang!

This time the explosion came from the village shop.

The overhanging wires of an electric pylon had become wrapped round the Kraken's left pincer. It was caught tight. Sparks and bolts of light erupted from the cables and toppled lampposts. Craig had to retreat amidst a storm of whirling embers.

"It's caught tight. Can't you do what you have to do now?" He panted. The Belloc crystal glinted in his hand and caused the Kraken to bellow out in an ear-splitting cry.

James shook his head. "No way. We have to get it over this pit. It has to come another fifty yards further forward."

"What!" Craig slumped down on the pile of earth.

Drumfintley looks like a war zone, thought James.

"Craig, hurry!" yelled Helen. "Before Dendralon comes this way and ruins the whole thing."

"Fine, fine," he muttered as he pulled himself to his feet with the shaft of Greenworm. Tentatively, he walked back toward the Kraken. "Ya! Hey! Come on, ye big numpty!"

* * *

David looked round the other side of the domed shelter. A tall, scaled figure holding a gnarled, black staff hissed at the sky as more winged insects flew over his head. Stranger still, two other figures with long, curved bills bounded ahead of him. He'd never seen anything like them. He turned to look at Michael.

"That's Dendralon," hissed Michael, his face covered in beads of sweat. He crossed himself and pulled Ephie closer.

"Eethan?" barked David. "Where are you?" Eethan was on the roof of the shelter, waving. "What? Get down!"

"Wees here! Dendralon, wees…"

Another blast of red fire torched the roof.

Eethan flicked the hair from his eyes and grinned. "Ees good at aiming, Dendralon ees."

"Yes, well, don't go setting us up as the main target," snapped Sergeant Carr. He cocked his gun, poked it round the corner of the shelter, and fired.

David saw one of the Ibissynians jerk back, his shoulder hit. Within another step, however, the wound had healed and the creature was on the move again. "They're only feet away. Do something, Eethan."

"Please!" begged Jean.

"How did he do that?" exclaimed Carr.

Eethan scuttled out and under a clump of fuchsia. Bouncing crimson and violet flowers marked the little, blue man's progress. David saw Dendralon raise his staff. "Get down!" He motioned the others to lie flat.

Crack!

A flash of blue light hit a flash of red, combining to form a perfect purple arc that lit up the dark sky. The light intensified until the colour changed to pure white.

Zzzzz!

Like the sizzling sound of electricity out of control, the noise rose then faded away to nothing. The air suddenly smelt of rotten eggs.

David edged round for a look but came face to face with an Ibis-headed giant, the tip of a copper-coloured sword cold against his throat.

"Wait!" said Dendralon. "Let us have our first sacrifice to the new god of this world.

"There is only one God and that certainly is not you!" said Michael. He was visibly shaking.

Dendralon flicked his long, black tongue in and out of his reptilian jaws. His yellow eyes ablaze, he asked, "Haven't we met, Reverend?"

The whole group was surrounded. Carr tried to fire his gun, but an Ibissynian flicked it from his chubby fingers with his curved sword.

Michael shook his head. "Not properly."

"You mean, you saw me fall on Denthan too. You saw me burned alive." Dendralon pushed his scarred face right up to Michael's. "You cannot hope for salvation this time, Reverend. You see, I have just killed Mendel's little helper and…" He turned his attention on the rest of the group. "I don't imagine any of these specimens will come to the rescue." He panted excitedly. "This world is a fair price to pay for the destruction of my entire race in Denthan, don't you think?"

Michael closed his eyes. "That was nothing to do with—"

"Nothing to do with Mendel and James Peck?" Dendralon drew back. "Enough of this. Make the sacrifice!"

"Yes, Lord." The nearest Ibissynian bowed. With his gruesome twin, he yanked the group, one by one, onto the Fyffes' front green.

"Your sun exploded. It was nothing to do with us," protested Jean.

David knew she was tying to stall for time. His own mind was churning. *What had Dendralon meant? Where is Eethan? He must be hiding somewhere nearby. Now, Eethan. Come out now!* Then he saw it. Curled in the foetal position, a little, blue man was lying, quite still, in the middle of Willow Terrace. It was Eethan. He looked as though he'd been run over and… *Now there is no hope. I'll never see Cathy again.* The Ibis-faced creatures raised their swords.

* * *

With a roar to split the heavens, the Kraken broke free of the electricity cables. Driven into frenzy by Craig's taunts and by his incessant waving of the crystal, just out of its reach, the Kraken had cracked. The cables, thick as James's wrist, lashed outwards and arced over his head just as he ducked. They crumpled, like lifeless snakes, onto the village hall roof.

Craig was running, full pelt, now. "It's coming! Get ready!"

Mendel's voice cut through the din. "Wee Joe, are you holding the Key?"

Wee Joe nodded and stepped forward like an Olympian, brandishing the Key of Artilis like an ever-burning torch.

James was terrified. His legs were shaking and he knew that in one more step the Kraken would be directly over the road-works. Its tentacles stretched out, searching for him. Its pincers snapped in mid-air.

Helen stood right beside him. Bero just behind.

"Say the words I taught you, Joe!"

Wee Joe moved forward, and with a high-pitched voice, full of determination shouted, "Move no further!"

The Key of Artilis whirred into a blur.

The Kraken stopped, mid-pounce, right over the hole made by the Drumfintley council excavations.

His head pounding, James shuffled to the edge of the pit and looked down. The old tramlines were still visible, unearthed for the first time in fifty years.

He held Helen's cold hand and, together they shouted, "Wwwpiercewwwheartwww!"

The old tram rails snapped and sprung up, plunging deep into the underbelly of the Kraken. Like a pair of parallel spears they thudded to a halt.

"Rrraaaaaarr!"

One of St. Donan's bells shook free and slipped down the face of the tower where it crashed onto the gravestones below. The water on the Loch thrashed about like waves in a force ten storm.

The Kraken's huge tentacles flicked out one last time; its pincers dropped to the ground, crushing a line of parked cars. The huge bulk of the Kraken shook convulsively and then crumpled.

* * *

The Ibissynians dropped their swords just as David braced. The sharp point of one narrowly missed his ear before piercing the lawn. Screaming, the curve-billed monsters arched their backs and flayed at the heavens.

David fell forward and scampered away, hauling Jean with him. The sky turned a deadly shade of purple. Wind gusted down over Bruce Moor and they watched, transfixed, as their hideous executioners dropped to their knees and then toppled forward, dead. The Ibissynian nearest to Jean and David hit the ground with such force that his long mandible broke in two.

"No!" Dendralon's voice was even louder than the roar of the Kraken. He clenched his massive, scaled fists and scanned the skies, as if looking for some greater force. Peering down the hill, he screamed out in a booming voice that cut through the heavy air. "Mendel!" In a blind fit of rage, Dendralon raced out of the garden leaving the Drumfintley group stunned and out of breath, though completely relieved to still be alive.

"Craig's down there!" whispered Jean, her nails digging deep into David's flesh.

Carr cocked his shotgun and blasted it at Dendralon's broad back.

"NO! Don't …" Ephie was still trying to stand.

Dendralon, however, did not even turn round. The shot merely pinged off of his black, Hedra scales.

"We have to go after him!" shouted Jean.

"Jean's right," said David. "Take everything we have. It's not over yet."

Chapter Twenty-Three

The Broken Vow

Cathy never quite got used to the narrow stairwell. All the other tunnels and caverns in Artilis had been fairly huge but now as she climbed, the thought of seeing her son again kept her going, gave her the strength she needed.

"The red planet will have lined-up with the crystal of Ra by now," said Junera. "With luck, your son will have gone back to his home."

"Then I need to go back home too," said Cathy.

"There is a back entrance to the apex of the pyramid. We should check the Dendralon is well away from the chamber."

"Can you take me back to Earth?"

Junera issued a dry laugh. "Absolutely not; Elandria, however..."

"Who?"

"She is a Racnid."

"Why would one of those spider things help us?"

"Shhh! We're level with the apex. There is a hole in the wall." Junera scraped a dirty piece of glass with the edge of her sword and looked through. Cathy edged in beside her. "It's empty."

"What does that mean?" asked Cathy.

"It means that they have gone back and that Dendralon is most probably the angriest person in the universe. Wait!"

"What now?" Cathy was beginning to get irritated.

"There, on the floor," whispered Junera.

Cathy followed her gaze and drew back her head from the aperture. "It's a girl's head. Oh no!" Cathy felt her heart drop to the pit of her stomach.

"It's a demon's head," explained Junera.

Cathy looked again.

"Belloc," said Junera. "Only the crystal of Ra remains. Someone has the Belloc crystal, and it's not Dendralon, otherwise he would have used all three to take his army to Earth. The whole pyramid of Ra would be on Earth by now."

They stepped into the apex of the pyramid, its massive glass walls protecting them from the hostile environment outside. Stars lit the chamber and a red desert stretched out until it met the blackness beyond. "This is Mars," whispered Cathy. "We're on bloody Mars."

There was a low drone. The single red crystal on the plinth began to glow. It pulsed like a heart.

"Something's coming through," said Junera. "Hide!"

* * *

James could not believe it had worked. The gigantic corpse of the Kraken hung, like a grotesque puppet, impaled on the double spikes formed by the old Drumfintley tram tracks. As with all other creatures from Artilis who perished on Earth, the Kraken was beginning to disappear. Its ugly shape wavered like a mirage, tiny bits of it vanishing as they watched. Its open mouth was the most horrible sight of all, especially when James thought of poor Mr. MacNulty. Wee Joe danced in a circle waving the spinning key.

"James?" prompted Mendel.

"I'll get the key from him." James looked beyond the fading body of the Kraken. There were still other creatures from Artilis, thousands of them. They had, however, stopped moving. The gargoyles seemed to have transformed back into stone and the winged insects had all lighted on buildings and trees. None were in the air.

James slipped the Key of Artilis in his rucksack and gave Helen a high five.

"Well done, Sis," barked Craig, his expression morphing from beaming, freckle-faced victor into stern, worried-looking victim. Surreptitiously, Craig moved the Belloc crystal behind his back and stepped down from his vantage point.

James, Wee Joe, and Helen all turned to see what he was looking at, although, by Craig's actions, James had already guessed.

"Dendralon," said Mendel.

Bero's hackles rose and he began to emit a constant growl.

"Where are you Mendel? I will finish you this time," screamed Dendralon. He marched past the village hall, his staff raised.

"Helen, James, you have to act together again."

"So, you have two wizards doing your bidding now, my canine friend?" shouted Dendralon, a blast from his staff pounding into the mound of earth beneath James's feet. The power of the blast threw him backwards.

"Wwwblueewwfirewwww!"

Helen alone cast the spell, which sent a blue burst of flame from the barrel. It ripped into Dendralon's staff, knocking it from his scaled hand. The dark wizard, however, threw a ball of red light from his left hand, which fell over Bero.

James held still, winded in the pit beside Craig and the mangled tram tracks. There was a creaking sound. James looked up. The remains of the Kraken fell forward, still fixed to the tram tracks. As pieces of the creature disappeared, it began to topple.

"The bloomin' thing…could still kill us," wheezed Craig. He was lying on his back too.

"Say your magic word. Summon your spear!" urged James. He felt a burning sensation against his back. The Belloc crystal was red hot. "Awch! Need to get this thing off…"

A heavy pincer fell away from the carcass and smashed onto the pit. Everything went dark.

* * *

David saw the blue fire hit Dendralon and then the ball of red light cover Bero. He ran as fast as he could, not sure what he would do when he reached the dark wizard. Mendel's voice was in his head. "Helen, stay close." David saw Helen gather in Wee Joe. The brandy barrel had fallen from Bero's collar. Wee Joe had it in his hands. He could hear Sergeant Carr behind him, cursing as he tried to aim the shotgun. He lifted the rusting highland dancer sword high above his head, and hoped the threat would be enough. The figure of Dendralon was fading. His arms were glowing with the same light that had covered Bero. Bits of him were disappearing.

"You used the Kraken as your talisman, didn't you Dendralon? Your power is fading and soon you will return to Artilis."

Dendralon eyed the barrel suspiciously. "You are still a goldfish, you… Granthardeth!"

David swung the sword through Dendralon's neck and fell over.

* * *

Junera's face flashed red in the glow from the crystal. Cathy turned towards the great door of the pyramid chamber. She could hear James.

"Mum! It's me. You're in there, aren't you?"

"Yes! Yes," she cried out, pulling away from Junera's grip.

"Mrs. Peck. NO!"

It was James. She ran towards the great door and pushed it open.

Her heart almost stopped. Blinded by the brighter light in the outer hall, a thousand torches burned in a huge row as far back as she could make out. There, a few yards away, was the horrible outline of the Racnid, Elhada. Laughing the giant spider held a small wooden box in her cupped hand.

"Sieze her!"

The tall figure of Erda grabbed hold of her arm and pulled her down onto her knees. "You will never escape me again, my queen."

"No! What...?" Her head was spinning. This had to be some kind of dream. She'd heard James's voice. Desperately, she scanned the great hallway for any sign of her son.

"The box of delights never fails to let you hear what you want to hear," hissed Elhada.

Cathy glanced back into the chamber, but there was no sign of Junera or the Racnid, Elandria.

There was another flash of red light from the pyramid chamber.

* * *

When James's eyes recovered from the blast of light that lit up the pit, he said his word, Firetongue, but nothing happened. His head seared for a moment but the magic sword never appeared. He knew then that something very bad had happened. "Craig? You okay?" He'd begun to wheeze badly.

There was a shuffling noise to his left. *Oh no...* He covered his eyes and looked up at the giant silhouette looming above him. Trapped by the weight of the pincer, he was helpless. He couldn't even swing a punch. His chest tightening, he braced and closed his eyes.

"James?"

Tentatively, James glanced up at the figure. "Dad?"

"Son, I'm coming to get you. Don't move."

"Dad! What's happened?"

"I'm here too," moaned Craig.

"Craig. I don't understand. What's happened? I can't feel Mendel in my head anymore."

James heard Craig moving beside him. There was a faint glow of red and a section of the pincer disappeared. The weight on his leg vanished.

As sunlight filled the pit, a sea of hands caught hold of him and pulled him out. His dad handed him his inhaler, and he took a deep puff. His chest opened. The warm highland air filled his lungs. "Where is Dendralon?"

"We don't know," answered Ephie.

Jean was holding onto Bero, crying.

"What did he do? Where are Wee Joe and Helen?"

Sergeant Carr lowered his gaze, unable; it seemed, to come up with any words to describe what had happened.

"Dad, tell me what happened."

Craig moved over to comfort his mum.

David Peck sniffed and looked at Father Michael.

"Your dad swung his sword at Dendralon but it passed right through him. There was a flash of red light from Dendralon. Helen and Wee Joe moved back but..."

"Wee Joe was holding Mendel's barrel," added Ephie.

"They all vanished," finished Carr.

There was another crumbling noise behind them. The remains of the Kraken disappeared completely. Two twisted tram tracks stood proud of the pit, curved, like a giant cobra poised to strike, in mid air.

"But where have they gone?" James sighed. "What are we going to do?"

Ephie knelt down to comfort Jean.

"We will just have to pray that, somehow, Mendel managed to keep Wee Joe and Helen safe."

James unfastened his rucksack and dropped it to the ground. He rummaged for the Belloc crystal, but it was gone. His rucksack had a singe-mark on it the size of an ostrich egg.

"Ees back on Artilis."

They nearly all jumped out of their skins. James slipped back into the pit.

"Eethan?" James scrambled back up the soft earth.

The diminutive figure of Eethan, looking a little more frail than usual, staggered down the path that led from the village hall. His wisp of hair was lank and dirty. "Dendralon ees been taken back to Artilis. So ees thee Belloc crystal, ee thinks."

"Where are Helen and Wee Joe?" screamed Jean.

"Mum, it's not his fault," whispered Craig.

Eethan shook his head. "What was thee spell?"

"Sorry?" said Michael.

"What deed Dendralon say to Mendel and thee children?"

James thought hard. "It was something like: grand tar..." He couldn't remember. What was it?

"Granthardeth," said David.

"That was it," remembered James. "Dad's right."

Eethan wandered into the bedraggled group and sighed. "Ees a Hedra banishment spell. Dendralon useed these spell to send Mendel to thee Earth before. From Denthan," he added.

"So, where are they?" urged Jean.

"Dependees," answered Eethan. *Rather unhelpfully*, thought James. "Dependees if Dendralon's magic was confudeeled by thee killing of the Kraken, by thee destruction of hees catalyst, hees talisman. You see, heed neever expect thee Kraken to be killed. As soon as both eets hearts were pierced it died. The Inubians, joined to thee Kraken's fate, died too."

James looked around him. The village was totally trashed. Ephie and Father Michael were comforting Jean and Bero. Craig was looking into the distance, his face dirty and tearstained. His dad was listening in on Sergeant Carr's police intercom, which had just sprung to life.

The sound of sirens on the bypass tore across the valley, echoing out over Loch Echty. Carr looked up. "They want to re-open the by-pass even though I've told them that the gas explosion was worse than expected."

"There's about a hundred fire engines up there," said Craig. He stared down at Eethan. "You might be a bit hard to explain," he added.

"Yees, Craig. Ees know." Eethan took Jean's hand and looked into her eyes. "Your children ees safe. Ee sense eet." Then, with a small bow, he vanished.

"And Cathy?" asked David, staring at the spot where Eethan had just stood.

"Eethan's gone, Dad." James felt his heart thumping hard inside his chest. "She must still be…" He looked up at the reddening sky. It would soon be dark.

* * *

James's dreams had been bothering him ever since returning from Artilis. Putting off sleep for as long as possible, he crawled from his single bed and glanced over at the empty tin bath. He'd stood it against the side of his wardrobe, just in case.

After walking over to his window, he peered up at the midnight sky. Every night he tried to pick out the star that glimmered crimson. He tracked it as it traced the heavens. Mars, the red planet; the place where, in his heart, he knew his mum still lived. Trapped beneath the surface and at least forty-five million miles away, he wondered every day whether he'd ever see her again. He sat down to write his diary. The page lay open at Sunday the twenty-seventh of July. James picked up his yellow plastic pen and began to write.

We had a special church service to commemorate the life of Archie MacNulty today. There were at least a hundred people there and, amazingly, Sergeant Carr did the eulogy. I found out that the eulogy is the sad bit, where someone stands up and talks about the dead person's life. It sounded all the sadder, hearing it read out by Sergeant Carr. He began to cry at one point when he told people that they'd had the same dad. I hate seeing old people cry. It sets me off too.

Craig is really beginning to bug me again. I know he always does but he's started saying things like 'we could end up being half brothers' and stuff. Dad and his mum, Jean, get on really well. It's kind of nice to have a mum and dad that don't fight, but it's just not the same. Mum is still alive, somewhere, and dad knows that. He wouldn't marry Craig's mum or anyone else while he still believed that. He's told me so.

I watched Bero and Patch playing together on the Rectory lawn at St. Donan's. Father Michael and Ephie invited all of us over for afternoon tea and cakes. It was kind of boring but Craig says we need to do things like that sometimes to give his mum hope. She's totally broken up about Wee Joe and Helen. I know Mendel will be looking after them, wherever they are. He said he would, and now that Helen can do his magic and stuff…

We haven't heard from Eethan since he disappeared that day, but he's probably back in Gwendral. At least that's what Craig says. Drumfintley is beginning to look like its old self again, but all the villagers still go on about the infamous 'gas leak' that totalled the place. I suppose it did make the national news.

The weirdest thing, and it's just started to happen in the last few days, are my dreams. They're so vivid, so real, in colour and stuff. I've had the same one now every day since Thursday. In it, Mum is walking down a huge aisle lined with white trees. It's in a temple or something and at the altar, waiting on her, is Dendralon. He's wearing, what looks like, gold armour and so is she. Mum bows to him and then takes his big scaly hand. They say some chants and things and then turn to a massive crowd of jackal-faced Inubians and Racnids. When they are pronounced King and Queen, the whole place erupts with howls and cheers and hissing. It really gives me the creeps.

Closing his black diary, James placed his yellow pen back in his pencil-case and sat down on his crumpled duvet. He knew that trying to stop dreams from happening was a bit daft but he was up for anything. So every night, he repeated the words out loud, twice, hoping they'd double-jinx the dream. "I bet I have the really bad dream about Mum getting married to Dendralon. I bet I have a really bad dream about Mum marrying Dendralon." Tucked up in bed, he shut his eyes and wondered about telling his dad. *It might complicate things,* he decided.

I'll tell him when Mum comes back.

Whenever that is.

Poor Mum...

ABOUT THE AUTHOR

BORN IN Helensburgh, Scotland, Sam Wilding grew up beside Loch Lomond on the very edge of the Scottish Highlands. He gained an honours degree in Zoology at Glasgow University and always maintained a strong interest in nature and the outdoors. He also became involved in song writing and through the years played guitar in the UK, Holland and America. He soon moved on from song writing to poetry, short stories and eventually on to his first novel, "The Magic Scales". As he continues to write the Denthan series this, "The Second Gateway", is the second book to feature James Peck, the asthmatic boy-hero from Scotland. Sam still lives and works in the Scottish Highlands.

Visit him on the web at: www.sam-wilding.com
or contact him at samwilding1@gmail.com

Other titles:

The Magic Scales – Book 1 of the Denthan Series

Printed in the United Kingdom by
Lightning Source UK Ltd., Milton Keynes
141355UK00001B/119/P

9 780955 878961